Praise for Christian Jungersen and

YOU DISAPPEAR

"Jungersen's sparse, Danish approach to language is effective . . . leaving us with a humming tension."

—*Minneapolis Star Tribune*

"An argument can probably be made that some of the best recent Nordic writing has been detective fiction. . . . Jungersen stakes out a path all his own."

—*The New Yorker*

"Thought-provoking. . . . An intriguing read."

—*Booklist*

"Jungersen's view of things is enjoyably nasty. . . . A smart variation on the 'neuronovel.'"

—*London Review of Books*

"This fast-paced, well-researched literary suspense novel keeps readers hooked until the final page. . . . Superb."

—*Library Journal*

"Jungersen . . . writes evocatively and perceptively about sensitive topics, and offers provocative theories about what makes each of us who we are. . . . [A] poignant, compassionate, and uncompromising look at how people cope (or fail to cope) when they are in danger of losing everything that they cherish."

—*MostlyFiction.com*

"Brilliant. . . . Mia begins to suspect that many people around her suffer from brain damage, leaving the reader with an exciting sense of unease."

—*Publishers Weekly*

Christian Jungersen

YOU DISAPPEAR

Christian Jungersen's first novel, *Undergrowth*, won the Best First Novel Award in Denmark in 1999 and became a bestseller. His next novel, *The Exception*, won two of Denmark's highest literary awards, remained on the bestseller list there for nearly two years, and has been published in twenty countries. He lives in Malta.

www.christianjungersen.com

YOU DISAPPEAR

YOU DISAPPEAR

a novel

Christian Jungersen

Translated from the Danish by
Misha Hoekstra

ANCHOR BOOKS
A Division of Random House LLC
New York

FIRST ANCHOR BOOKS EDITION, OCTOBER 2014

The Library of Congress has cataloged the Nan A. Talese/Doubleday edition
as follows:
Jungersen, Christian.
[Du forsvinder. English]
You disappear : a novel / Christian Jungersen ; Translated from the Danish by
Misha Hoekstra.
pages cm.
Originally published in Denmark as Du forsvinder by Gyldendal A/S, Copenhagen,
in 2012.
1. Psychological fiction. 2. Medical fiction. I. Hoekstra, Misha, translator.
II. Title.
PTB176.2.U47D813   2014
839.81'38—dc23   2013029148

Anchor Books Trade Paperback ISBN: 978-0-345-80462-4
eBook ISBN: 978-0-385-53726-1

Book design by Michael Collica

www.anchorbooks.com

Printed in the United States of America
10 9 8 7 6 5 4 3 2 1

YOU DISAPPEAR

1

We whoosh down between dark rock-faces, through hairpin turns, down and around past dry scrub, silver-pale trees and back up, then over a ridge where the car nearly leaves ground and Niklas and I whoop as our entrails become weightless.

The hot Mediterranean air buffets our faces, for all four windows are open. Frederik takes a curve so fast that I grab my headrest. The sea beneath us keeps switching left and right.

Normally Frederik's never brave behind the wheel, so I try not to be afraid. And the heat makes the rocks steeper, darker, the lemon groves prickling even more tartly in my nose, the sea shining blue like I've never seen it before.

Around yet another rock outcrop and suddenly we're engulfed by cyclists. I scream. A swamp of neon-pink cycling jerseys. I look out the back window: no one's fallen, but they've dismounted from their bikes; clenched fists, open mouths. We round the next curve.

"Frederik, it's not funny anymore!"

He doesn't answer.

"Frederik!"

He lets out a small sigh and maintains his speed.

I observe his long slender fingers wrapped around the wheel. They don't belong to this way of driving. Once I found them erotic, like miniature versions of his body—tall and thin, a swaying, relaxed body. Not a speed demon's.

And is it the speed that makes his eyes look deeper? Black-violet massifs. He seems strange, though I can't say where the difference lies.

Another hard bump and again all three of us rise into the air.

"Stop, Frederik, stop!" I yell.

Niklas has had his head out the window. Now he pulls it back in. "Mom, just leave off."

"*I'm* supposed to leave off? *I'm* supposed to leave off? Your father's driving like a complete madman! He'll kill us! Is that what you want?"

It's the speed, the colors, the heat, and all the outrageous Majorcan beauty. Niklas sighs with precisely the same sibilance as his father and again leans his head out the window.

"Niklas, keep your head inside. It's dangerous."

He acts as if he doesn't hear me.

"Keep your head in, I say. It's dangerous!"

Still he doesn't. I don't care if he's sixteen now; I turn around and pull him in myself, I use some force, and then he stays in his seat.

The Mediterranean shines so brightly it's impossible to look at it straight on. It floats up through the terrain and calls us. Like the tunnel of light the dying see: *Come, become one with my beauty and eternity.* A nudge to Frederik's hand and we'd swerve over the berm and all become weightless again, and then we'd be lifted out of the landscape too.

I want to say *Stop, stop* again. Instead I look at our son; *he's* having fun. Am I just a killjoy?

An oncoming driver lays on his horn. Frederik keeps his eyes fixed on the road before us.

"They drive like total madmen down here," he says.

"Will you please drive more slowly?" I ask again.

Niklas and Frederik laugh.

The road twists. And then we're back in shadow and close to the rock wall. An oncoming truck suddenly fills the space in front of us. Frederik swings our car up against the rock-face. Granite grates against the panels with a sound like we've been tossed in a metal grinder. And then we are past.

Frederik says, "We took out full coverage. The rental agency'll cover it all." He doesn't slow down.

Now Niklas pulls on the back of Frederik's seat. "Dad, stop! Stop!"

And I join in. "Stop the car *now!*"

But he doesn't lift his gaze from the road. He sighs like before. I pull back on the hand brake as we drive. He laughs and releases it again.

"Frederik, look at me. Won't you at least do that?"

He keeps looking straight ahead as he speaks, and as always, his voice projects reason and calm. "I need to keep my eyes on the road."

...

Five days ago, on the day we were to fly to Majorca, I stopped on my run along the wooded path beside Lake Farum, and I gave myself some time to think about how good my life really is. I walked out on one of the short piers, and the breeze chilled the sweat beneath my top. I thought about what has made these years so different from my life a few years ago.

Out on the lake the water rose in small swells that weren't actual waves, and the woods on the opposite bank looked like they'd gone deeper into autumn than the trees above and behind me. I have a lovely son and good friends, meaningful work, a house we are fond of. But I had all of that three years ago too. The difference—the major, critical difference—is that now I feel loved.

How many people can say that, that they really feel loved? It's something I should relish. Finally, I thought, everything's fallen into place. And then I continued my run, down the path through the woods.

Farum is a peaceful place, a suburb you move to only when you have two kids, or in any case have plans for number two. Between the charming medieval village and the lake lies an older neighborhood with large houses, the neighborhood where we are so lucky as to live. From this original core, Farum grew more than fourfold in the '60s and '70s. In the fields east of the village, miles of new streets were laid out with yellow-brick single-family homes, schools, kindergartens, and then more single-family homes, another school, a few more kindergartens. All connected by a vast network of car-free bike paths surrounded by grass, so that kids can bike from school to the rec center and from soccer to a friend's house without crossing a single street, while their parents take the train or the freeway home from work in Copenhagen.

We were trying to have a second child when we moved here, not yet

3

knowing that it would never happen. And not yet knowing how Frederik would succeed so unbelievably well in his career, for we were mistaken in that too—we thought there'd only be a couple of years when he'd have to spend all his evenings and weekends at work as he glided from one success to the next.

In one of his many speeches to the children, parents, and staff at his school, Frederik said that he became a teacher and later a headmaster "because helping a child through difficulty is the most meaningful thing you can do with your life."

Big words, and sometimes I've wondered if they weren't too big. Yet no one can doubt that Frederik could have earned a lot more money if he'd been the leader of almost anything but a school. As for me, I studied to be an architect for a year before I transferred to a teachers' college. While I was in architecture school, I made a bit of money as a tennis instructor, and the difference I made in the lives of my young tennis students—especially when we talked about something besides tennis—soon came to mean more to me than my studies. Changing schools was an unavoidable outcome of thinking about what mattered in life.

From the lake, I ran a few hundred yards on the path along the railway and soon reached home. On my way up to shower, I knocked on Niklas's door. He was sitting in front of his computer.

"Have you started to pack?" I asked.

He didn't answer.

"Have you started to pack?"

"Yeah yeah, I heard you."

His best friend in gymnasium, Mathias, was going to have his house to himself for the fall vacation, and we'd had a hard time getting Niklas to join us, away from the week's approaching party madness. Mathias composes electronic music, and Niklas spends a lot of energy making music videos for him. They'd planned to stay together at Mathias's the whole week.

"You'll be really happy you came, as soon as we get down there," I said.

My cell phone rang in our bedroom, and I ran in to answer it.

It was Frederik, saying that he would be home later than planned. He apologized profusely, but he had to take care of something with the school's bank.

4

"That's okay, Frederik. Really."

"But it might make it hard for me to get all packed."

"I'll pack for you too. I'm looking forward to seeing you."

It was the sort of thing that would have once made me angry and unhappy. *The day we're going on vacation, and you can't even . . . !* But now it's fine, because our relationship is fundamentally in order—and because Frederik no longer does it every time.

Sometimes it's hard to be married to an idealist. You feel rejected while at the same time feeling like a huge egotist, just because you think that school kids shouldn't rob you of your family life.

Fortunately, that's all behind us. Frederik has made us more of a priority, and the two of us have never had it better.

...

Frederik turns off sharply onto one of the small gravel roads, low drystone walls on either side, and we skid in the gravel and scream, strike a stone wall, are flung to the other side of the road, hit that wall too, skid. Stop.

I turn toward Niklas. I want to be beside him in the backseat, clutch his head to my breast to protect him. But the car's already come to rest. It's too late.

"Are you okay?"

But I know he hasn't been hurt. It was only a couple of minor collisions; we're extremely lucky. I close my eyes for a moment and exhale. My pulse is throbbing in my temples.

"Are you okay?" I repeat.

"Yeah. How about you?"

"I think so."

I look through the windshield. Frederik is already out front. He kicks the car with a resentful expression, squats to examine something by one of the fenders.

I yell, "Aren't you even going to see if we're all right?"

He doesn't answer.

"Don't you even care?"

"Well, I can *see* you're doing fine."

I jump out of the car. And for the first time in our twenty years together, I hit him so hard that it's not just a game. He falls to the gravel and I shout, "What the hell, what the fucking hell? Have you gone stark raving mad?"

Sweat drips off of me and my fists are clenched, my pulse still pounding in my temples. He gets up staggering but unconcerned, as if he hasn't noticed my blow, and takes a few steps.

"I don't think I can get it to run."

"*That's* a stroke of luck, you big idiot. Maybe we won't die today after all."

"Mom!" Niklas's voice calls from inside the car.

I breathe deeply, several times. For my son's sake, I need to be the reasonable one here. And so I manage to pull myself together.

"What should we do?" I ask in a somewhat calm voice.

Frederik doesn't answer. He climbs up on the stone wall and stands there, surveying the landscape.

Niklas gets out of the car too. His hair lights up in the sun. It's lighter than mine, almost white. After cultivating a grunge look all summer, he resembles a sixteen-year-old Kurt Cobain.

"It says in the guide that you should ring 112," he says.

I glance up at Frederik on the wall.

"What's *with* you? Why are you doing this?"

"What's with *me*?" At last he looks me in the eye. "*You're* the one who's been after me without a break on this trip! First I drive too fast, then I talk too loud in the restaurant, then I eat too much. Whatever I do, you say I'm doing it wrong!"

I look up at him and it seems he's swinging his arms too much. The wildness of his gestures feels contrived.

"But I only say those things because you've been acting strange," I say.

"I have *not*! But you're after me all the time. And then you say I'm happy at the wrong time, and then you say I sleep too late."

I can see what he means. It's been a lovely vacation, but I've also been oddly irritated. And we've argued a lot.

"I promise to stop criticizing you," I say. "Okay? Will you come down now?"

"It's that way back home too. And why can't I stand up here, if that's what I want?"

"Look. You've just driven our car into a wall, so maybe I have a right to—"

"Now you're doing it again. I can't stand it! Look at Niklas. *He's* not riding me the whole time. So it *is* possible."

"Do we really have to go through all of this now, Frederik?"

"And I love Niklas too. He and I . . . we're . . . he can really . . ." Frederik begins to cry.

I look over at Niklas, who appears moved. I sense that his sideways glance at me isn't completely friendly.

I step closer to my husband.

"Are you going to weep now about how much you and Niklas like each other? Do you have heatstroke, or what?"

"And now I'm not even allowed to love our son anymore . . ."

"Of course you are. It's just that—"

Frederik starts waving his arms around even more wildly.

"You piece of shit, Mia! You big fat piece of shit!"

And then he falls.

We run over to the wall. See him tumble down the mountainside, strike his head against a tree, and stop, caught lifeless at its foot, five yards away.

"Frederik! Frederik!"

"Dad!"

But he doesn't move.

The mountain drops away just past the tree. We call 112, stare down at him, wait. And worry that he'll start stirring and roll free.

2

I bat my tennis racket against the black chair leg in front of me in the emergency room at the Hospital Universitario in Palma de Mallorca. Eight hours, and Frederik still hasn't regained consciousness. Then I bat it against the other leg. Maybe he'll end up in a wheelchair. Could he continue as headmaster then?

I see before me the last day of school at Saxtorph. The headmaster rolls his wheelchair up a ramp to the podium. He's clad in an elegant suit, the students and teachers prouder of him than ever. A triumphant look lights up his face. I feel proud too; he's a hero. But then other images arise. At home: Do I change his diaper? Do I lift him into bed? Do we . . . sex?

And then maybe not. Early retirement. What if he's not well enough to stay on as headmaster? He sits in his wheelchair while I spoon him soup. I am his nurse and wife three years from now, in ten and twenty, thirty. I am the old woman who drives around the suburban streets of Farum with a paralyzed husband. Thus our marriage; thus our life. I press my face against his loose hanging jowls and we weep, rubbing noses and foreheads and cheeks together. That's what we'll be doing in three years, in ten and twenty, thirty.

There are tennis courts in the mountains of Majorca. An odd notion, bringing my racket in the car. Of course I'd never use it. What was I thinking? I bat the racket against the first chair leg again. Look at the clock. It's now eleven.

The emergency room isn't like Danish emergency rooms. Cheap metal chairs with vinyl seats arranged in long rows. There's room for at least seventy people to wait for their number to appear on the big red LED over the receptionist's glass cage. Like the waiting room in a rundown bus station abroad.

We were supposed to fly home the day after tomorrow. Now I see Frederik's funeral. His parents, his friends, all of us in black. Hundreds of bouquets and wreaths from school parents and teachers. I see how broken up I am. My hero, my beloved, my husband. The casket is lifted into the hearse. Niklas is a pallbearer, dignified and pale.

I'll get on Niklas's nerves soon if I don't stop batting my racket against the chair. Thock, thock, thock. In a minute he'll say, *Stop it! It's driving me crazy.* I know. I hit the chair legs again, harder, harder.

I raise my head and glance at him. Thock, thock, thock. Isn't he going to tell me to stop? No, he's playing some game on his cell phone. He has the earphones in and doesn't hear a thing.

I poke his leg.

"What?" He pauses his game.

"Don't you think it's getting cold?"

It's dark outside. He's in shorts and a T-shirt, while I wear a cream-colored top with lace trim and a pair of army shorts.

"Yeah."

"Should I ask if they have a couple blankets we can borrow?"

He mutters something to express indifference and starts his game again.

"I think I'll ask for some blankets. Or perhaps a couple sweaters from the lost and found," I say. He can't hear me. "Or some pants. If we can fit them."

Thock, thock, thock: the sound drives *me* up the wall. I set down the racket.

"Pants or sweaters," I say. "Maybe both."

The funeral reception, our weeping friends, the neighbors who come to the burial—just like when the woman across the street got breast cancer. Would her husband find a new wife and move on? That's what we all wondered then.

No, he's grown strange. Keeps to himself, acts aggressive. A tragedy. He isn't recovering.

Me. Niklas. I see myself six months from now, making him elderberry cordial and baking him rolls. It's evening, and we're still living in Farum.

We're going to try to get our lives together, I'll say. *You know I'll always be there for you and support you any way I can.* We'll sit on the sofa and talk, cry, sip the hot cordial.

But that's not the way it'll be. Niklas doesn't want to sit on the sofa with me. Other images: I shop alone, let myself into a cold dark house, go up the stairs knowing that Frederik will never go up the stairs with me; I lie on the bedspread of our bed, entertaining a desperate desire to see his ghost.

A bell rings. I look up at the red number: it's ours. My throat is dry.

I want to poke Niklas, but he's already packing up his earphones; he wasn't so lost in his own world after all.

My legs are numb when I stand. From the counter, a nurse brings us to a small room with bare pastel-green walls. A dark young man in a smock is waiting for us. Under his eyes the skin is almost black. I'm freezing, I should have asked for a sweater after all. And something about the fluorescent lights in here hurts my eyes.

We sit down on plastic seats. Dr. González, it says on the man's name tag, and he addresses us in English.

"Frederik has been scanned. I am very sorry to say . . ."

Blood drains from my head. I feel faint and grab my son's hand. "Oh no. A skull fracture?"

"Yes. He has a brain tumor. I am very sorry."

"The fracture, will it paralyze him? Will he be able to talk? Will he die?"

"The fracture?" The doctor looks at me curiously.

"Yes, he fell . . . The fracture."

"There is no fracture."

"You just said . . ."

"He has a brain tumor. It has been exerting pressure, and it triggered an epileptic seizure. Fortunately, there was no serious blow to the head."

"You said there was a fracture!" I find myself shouting. "You said, 'Yes.' I heard you!"

I know my behavior is totally inappropriate. I'm going to stop. I hold my tongue and lean back in the flimsy chair with such force that it almost falls over.

"Sorry," I say. "I'm sorry."

Niklas takes over, with a tone that is the complete opposite of mine. "He's got a tumor?"

"Yes." The doctor adopts a mournful air and nods his head a little too much. "Unfortunately, I cannot say much more. We are transferring him to the neurological ward. The experts there will examine him tomorrow morning."

I grasp my seat with both hands. "Is it cancer?"

"We cannot say. The neurologists will examine him tomorrow morning."

"But then it *isn't* cancer?"

"Unfortunately, we cannot say that yet."

"But it's *probable* that it isn't cancer?"

"The neurologists will be able to say a great deal more tomorrow."

The peculiar light in here is getting to me: cloudy as pus, sharp as the scalpel that cuts an inflamed area away.

"What is it if it isn't cancer? Would it also—"

"It is much too soon to say anything. But the neurologists tomorrow will—"

"Can you do something about this light? It hurts my eyes."

"In the neurological department I am sure they will do everything they can."

Niklas and I hold hands as we walk slowly back to the waiting room. We are quiet. He doesn't play any more games on his cell, and I no longer fumble with my racket.

Just quiet.

I have no idea what time it is when a nurse comes out to us. "You're free to go home now. Nothing else is going to happen tonight. And then you'll be more rested tomorrow when you go to the neurological department."

From the taxi windows we look out on the streets: rose-pink houses with green shutters, palm trees and narrow lanes, small idyllic plazas with ice-cream stands and oversize parasols. Everything is dark and abandoned. And meanwhile I know I need to be the rock that Niklas can lean upon. I can hardly make my voice heard in the taxi. "He's going to make it, Niklas. Dad is so strong."

We drive down an avenue of tall palms, toward the hotel strip along the beach. A little while later Niklas tells me the same thing. And I repeat it back to him.

"He's going to make it. Dad is so strong."

...

I met Frederik twenty years ago, and soon I knew he'd be the love of my life.

I was twenty-two and a student at Blaagaard Teachers' Training College, majoring in math and PE. In my second year, I started my student teaching at Trørød Elementary in Søllerød, where Frederik was a teacher. There were more than sixty teachers at the school, and in the beginning there was no reason for me to speak to him. But I knew who he was because people talked about him.

During a meeting with my supervisor in a corner of the teachers' library, she mentioned that Frederik had no doubt set his sights on becoming a headmaster, just like his father, who led the conservative, well-respected North Coast Private Grammar School. Frederik was only twenty-eight and had already been elected chair of our school's Danish committee. He'd also organized a joint project with three other schools to develop a continuing-ed course for Danish teachers in creative writing for children.

At the time, it didn't occur to me that my supervisor might've easily been annoyed by such an untried teacher trying to outshine her. Instead, she spoke with gentleness and pride, and only later did I learn that that was typical of the way people around Frederik reacted to him.

Then they packed us off to school camp, five classes and twelve teachers for a week together in a small group of log cabins, deep in a Swedish forest.

Our departure was delayed, of course, and the buses had to stop several times en route because of carsick kids. After I'd been on the bus five hours, the stench of puke was stinging my nostrils and I was exhausted from the constant shouting, hooting, laughter, and tears—and by a massive drop in blood sugar from the banana bread we'd shared two hours earlier.

We finally reached the cabins. It was still early afternoon, but the clouds and rain were so heavy and low that, hours before sunset, they lent the day an air of twilight. We got the kids in their rubber boots and rain gear, and the teachers who'd been there before led them down to the ocean. I went last to make sure no one was left behind on the path through the pine forest.

The raindrops weren't falling close together, but each one was large and fat and crashed against the hood of my raincoat. I lagged behind the group more than I needed to, and when I finally made it out of the trees, I found myself alone.

The beach was endless and deserted except for the children, who were already a fair distance away. Not a single plant, not a patch of light in the sky, and the sand beneath my rubber boots was sodden and monochromatic lead-grey, only a shade darker than the sky.

In the distance, the teachers and children in their flame-colored rain suits became a bag of bright candy that someone had dropped in the clumpy sand and kicked open. The cold wet wind tore at my face. Then one colored blob detached itself from the others. A little later he stood before me, raindrops dripping from his nose.

He didn't move, just looked at me inquiringly. And I looked at him.

"Maybe I shouldn't become a teacher at all," I said.

He didn't answer. I looked into his eyes, which were wide open under his rain hood.

We talked, and walked down toward the water's edge, and gradually the monotonous rumbling of the water gave way to the rhythmic boom of each individual wave. No stars, sun, or moon. No ground beneath us. And yet that sound. The world still uncreated. No light or darkness, time or children. Just a roaring snore from the waves, from some creature who rests before the world is to be formed.

I don't know how it happened, but I started telling him about my good friend who'd died two months earlier. Her boyfriend had been unfaithful for months with one of our mutual friends, and finally he moved out from my one friend and in with the other. And Hanne leapt from a high-rise.

"The weird thing is, I have the sense that she's still here," I said. "She floats beneath the ceiling of the rooms I enter. And she's out here in the rain. She's following me."

Frederik stood with his back to the waves, the white edges crashing behind him. "Does she say you'll be glad you became a teacher?"

"Just a moment . . ." I closed my eyes for a few seconds. "Yes. She does."

"Do you think she's right?"

13

I paused again to consider. "Yes."

"And maybe she knows why you started to doubt that?"

"She knows," I said. "It's because I'm so unhappy. Because I miss her."

Already then I felt a desire to push my arm under his, so we could walk linked together back to the other teachers.

As we approached the others, with a suitable gap between us, I said, "I don't really believe in ghosts, of course. You don't know me, but I'm not crazy."

"I didn't think so."

That evening we took a flashlight and snuck back down the forest path to the beach, which was now pitch-dark. It was no longer raining, but there were still no stars or moon.

"What then?" I remember him asking. "Do you think we have a soul that lives on when we die?"

It ended up being a lovely school camp. Frederik had unusually bright pale-brown eyes with a fine dark ring around the outside of each iris and a long thin nose. There was something cultivated, something elegant about him. On two evenings we slipped out into the forest, Hanne's ghost vanished, and I became more convinced than ever that teaching was the right job for me.

When we returned home, we tried to keep our relationship secret at the school. We didn't succeed, of course, and some of our female colleagues became annoyed, with Frederik and especially with me.

Exactly as predicted, Frederik became headmaster of another primary school four years later. He was appointed to a seat on the Ministry of Education's Curriculum Committee, and he threw himself into writing a series of textbooks that sought to introduce philosophy as an independent subject in the higher grades.

When he was thirty-five, he was headhunted to lead Saxtorph—the private elementary school in Copenhagen where he's been ever since, and where in the course of thirteen years, he's almost doubled enrollment.

...

When Niklas and I walk through the enormous hotel lobby with its furnishings from the '80s, three Danish tourists yell after us. We talked with them earlier by the pool, though they're people we'd never have been friends with back home. From a distance, we can tell they're drunk.

"Well, it's been a late evening, eh Mia? Have you guys had fun? Where'd you go?"

Neither Niklas nor I reply. We make a beeline for the long, ugly corridor going to our rooms. I stop in front of his door.

"Come over to my room if you don't want to be alone tonight."

A moment's hesitation, perhaps. Then he looks at me.

"You should knock on mine too, if you . . ."

He's never said anything like that before. Then again, no one knows whether tonight he'll become the only man in the family.

The gilded wall lamps, the landscape windows facing the Mediterranean. A faint breeze through the nearly closed sliding doors to the balcony. Frederik's trousers lie on a chair, and on the floor are three magazines he bought on a sudden whim at the kiosk, as well as his snorkel and belt and a T-shirt too. On the table are his towel and sandals.

He didn't use to be messy. It's one of the things we argued about—also during the last few weeks back home.

I walk out on the balcony in a T-shirt and panties. I feel the wind, listen to the suck of the sea, watch the water the few places it's lit by the hotel lights. I stood here last night with Frederik and we held each other, we kissed, we thought we were healthy. It's as if I feel him now at my side, his armpit against my shoulder, his lips and breath against my cheek. For a second I wonder if this is the instant of his death, at the hospital. Is that what I feel? Is he visiting me?

They said it was safe for us to go home tonight, that nothing would happen.

I have to try not to think too much. Tomorrow's going to be a hard day. I have to empty my head of thoughts and lie down.

I don't manage to stay very long in bed. My gut rumbles, it is tense, churning. I run out to the bathroom at the last moment. There I start feeling nauseous, my body contracts and I lose control at both ends. My skin glistens with sweat.

Shaking, I collapse on the toilet, and there I die of food poisoning from the lunch we had at that small restaurant in the mountains. My soul flies out relieved, suspended beneath the ceiling and watching the next morning when Niklas gets the hotel staff to unlock the door and they find my cold stiff body. The stench of caustic toilet cleaner, of my feces, my death.

Or.

I do survive the food poisoning during the night, but I have a brain tumor. I die quickly all the same; Frederik's infected me, and in half a year, a doctor administers the final morphine in a hospice after weeks of pain, seizures, and nonsensical ranting.

Or.

It's not me who dies, it's Niklas. Tomorrow morning there's no answer to my knock on his door. I run down to reception, and the clerk and I find him dead in the bathroom.

He's lying like I am now: the stench of the cleaning agents and feces, his death and my despair. All families are one body. The tumor has long tentacles, red filaments, it resembles an octopus, a red jellyfish, it spreads from Niklas to me to Frederik. It grows from Frederik and Niklas to me.

I wake up with my head on the toilet seat, thinking I've slept only a few minutes, but the nausea is almost gone. I get up, bent over on wobbly legs. Rinse my mouth, drink water, rinse my face and look in the mirror.

I have to find out how Niklas is doing. Perhaps he has food poisoning too. It must be those little fried fish, I think.

In a white hotel bathrobe I walk out into the hallway. I knock, but he doesn't answer.

I knock again. Harder. Should I go down and get someone?

The door opens. His face isn't swollen in the least, not by sleep or heat or grief. It's untouched, as young people's faces are.

I ask, "Are you sick?"

"No."

"I thought there might have been something you ate."

"I'm not sick."

He looks at me and wakes up a bit.

"What's wrong? Other than, of course . . . Dad."

A few years ago, after a harrowing day like this, it would have been only natural for him to crawl into my bed, or for me to get into his. There wouldn't have been the least thing odd about it: falling asleep as I embraced my son. A few years ago.

16

3

"Mia. We talked to him."

Immediately I'm awake, and I recognize the voice of Thorkild, my father-in-law, on the telephone.

"Talked to him?"

"Yes, on the phone here in Denmark. He seems lively enough. And cheerful! We called the hospital, but now they're going to run some tests."

Half an hour later, Niklas and I are sitting in a taxi on the way to the hospital. Yesterday I called my in-laws from the emergency room. Now I try the hospital one more time, in vain, before calling Thorkild again—just to hear him repeat the last thing he said. "Frederik seems to be in good spirits. He doesn't have any pain or paralysis or speech difficulties, and he feels well. I think we've been lucky—this time around."

The neurology department is in a cubic metal-clad addition to the old hospital. It is more modern and better maintained than many Danish hospital wards, and the contrast with the emergency room in which we spent yesterday is striking.

On the other hand, not everyone here can speak English. We present first Frederik's passport and then our own, and at last a smiling nurse's aide leads us into Frederik's room without us understanding what she's saying.

There's an empty place where Frederik's bed must have stood, and once again, there's nothing for us to do but sit and wait. We try not to stare too much at the patient next to us, but it is hard. He's a thin man in his early thirties with a white bandage wrapped around the upper part

17

of his head. A square rack of steel pipes presses against the bandage from several directions, probably to immobilize his head, yet it looks as if big metal bolts are screwed directly into his skull on every side. He can blink, but his face registers no expression. He stares up at the ceiling while his cheeks hang loose. Doors open and shut, nurses talk in the corridor, two nursing students come in and drag out some large apparatus—he reacts to nothing.

In the distance, a man is shouting unintelligibly in Spanish, his angry voice resounding down the halls.

Niklas and I walk out of the room. And from the farthest end of the corridor we see an orderly approach with Frederik, sitting up in a bed.

"Frederik!"

We run toward him, and he smiles broadly when he discovers us.

"Whew! It's good you came! Such a fright," he booms. "Good thing *that's* over now."

The orderly begins shouting again, just as angry as before. It's clear he wants Frederik to lie down while he wheels the bed along, but Frederik doesn't care.

I don't know if I'm allowed to stop the bed in order to kiss him, or to lean over and embrace him.

"It's all over?"

"Yes, they're going to give me some medicine and discharge me today."

We follow the bed at a half run. "That's fantastic!"

Niklas and I hug each other while we timidly watch Frederik, who's grinning broadly.

"But what about the tumor?" Niklas asks. "Doesn't it have to be removed?"

"Not for the time being."

"Great. But . . . how are you doing?"

"I'm doing super! They say they can discharge me in a little while, and that's good. For if we're going to make it to the dripstone caves, it's going to have to be today."

"Do you really think . . ."

It seems crazy, but Frederik wants to keep to our itinerary. And after the orderly has parked the bed and left, we tentatively let Frederik's optimism rub off on us. I call Thorkild and Vibeke and turn my cell on speakerphone so we can all talk together.

"We have awakened from a nightmare," Thorkild says.

"You're right," I say. "That's *exactly* what we've done."

I hand the telephone to Niklas and lie with my chest against Frederik's, I close my eyes so I can shut out the sight of the man with the bolts coming out of his head.

"I got so scared, Frederik," I whisper. "I got so terribly, terribly scared."

"So did I," he says.

But he doesn't lower his voice, even though I'm lying right next to him. He speaks in the same cheerful, almost shouting voice as when he came riding toward us in the hallway, the same voice as when he stood on the stone wall yesterday.

I know. I know right now that this man is not my real Frederik. But he can become him again, I think. Of course he can.

I nestle against him, pressing my face into his long white hospital gown. I don't want to have diarrhea and nausea again, I don't want to wake weeping in the hotel room tonight, I don't want to be afraid.

He is half shouting. "We'll have to rent a new car straightaway if we're going to make it to the dripstone caves today."

"Yes, Frederik," I say. "We'll have to."

...

Last year we decided to hold a big birthday party for Frederik, even though he wasn't entering a new decade or anything. There were so many other years when we hadn't had time to celebrate, so now it was time.

We invited thirty-eight friends, and almost every one of them could make it, so there was no way we could seat all of them at a table. And we agreed that that would be okay. It would make the party more festive if some folks had to sit on folding chairs spread about the rooms and others had to eat standing, or sitting on a sofa armrest or the stairs or wherever they could find a place.

Several of our friends had known us only at Saxtorph, and I could see that our home took them by surprise. During the long years when Frederik essentially left Niklas and me to our own devices, I became obsessed with buying and selling furniture as a hobby—especially Danish design classics from the '50s and '60s. On numerous weekends, I took my trailer to check out bargains I found in a weekly classified-ad paper, and from scratch I slowly traded my way up to quite an exclusive collection. But while our house and furnishings were beautiful, I also knew that I squeezed too many pieces into a place that was too small.

From the moment the first guests arrived, the mood was exceptional. Niklas had compiled a mix of lounge music he thought we might like, and it worked like a charm. My best friend, Helena, and I had made a bunch of salads that we had put a lot of effort into, and then we had a butcher deliver some grilled free-range chickens and meatballs.

Early in the course of the dinner, Laust Saxtorph, the diminutive chairman of the school board, stood up on a chair to make a speech, and the guests crowded in the doorways to listen.

"Frederik, you have a secret," he began, pausing for effect. "Somehow or other, you get the rest of us to suggest doing what *you* want us to do."

Half of our guests worked at Saxtorph, and they laughed out loud.

"And as headmaster, you use this talent every single day—for both raising children and raising teachers . . . and the chairman of your board!"

The guests laughed again.

Before Laust became chairman, his father had held the post, as had his grandfather and great-grandfather, the school's founder, the renowned educator Gustav Saxtorph. Besides chairing the school board, they'd also been headmasters, and in the old days the headmasters had lived at the school. So that Laust, just like his father and grandfather, had his childhood home in rooms that are now used for after-school activities.

Ever since Laust hired Frederik, the two of them have been on the phone to each other pretty much every day, like a pair of fast-talking teenage boys. Laust lets the school take up a lot more space in his life than he ought to, given his wife and his position as section chief in the Ministry of Education. And it's safe to say that Frederik's boss has also become his best friend.

Laust sketched a series of amusing minor incidents from school life, describing how he and Frederik had responded to them together. But then, late in the speech, he grew serious.

Some years ago, a girl at the school had become quite introverted, and her PE teacher had noticed bruises on her. The girl said she'd gotten them from climbing trees, but Frederik called her mother and stepfather in for a meeting anyway. They said that they would *never* hit her.

But Frederik went with his gut. Though the school had hundreds of students, he kept on the case. He arranged further meetings, and at last the stepfather admitted that he couldn't govern his temper, and the couple elected to go into therapy.

"Frederik," said Laust from up on his chair, "what makes this story so typical is that at no point did the parents become angry with you. Nor did they, once they owned up to their problems, feel too humiliated to let their daughter keep attending our school. On the contrary—they thanked you for your help, and they became even more involved in school activities than before."

Laust must have also known the girl and her parents; he paused to take a sip of his red wine. There was something delicate in his pale skin and thin hair. He caught Frederik's eye and was ready to go on.

"If they hadn't understood before why your abilities as headmaster were so highly respected, they understood now. You made a difference in that girl's life forever, Frederik. And she is only one of many. Very very many! And you've made a difference in parents' lives, and in the lives of the people who work at the school. And you've made an even greater difference in the lives of those of us gathered here—we who are lucky enough to be counted your friends."

He got down and we toasted, shouted *hurrah!* and applauded, and Frederik went over and gave him a hug.

There were other speeches and songs. A friend from when Frederik worked at Trørød Elementary told about when we met. "Frederik got the young, fair-haired tennis girl that every man wanted," he said. Later another old friend said, "And then he snagged the hot babe, Mia," and again people laughed.

Niklas changed the music, a couple of his friends joining him; we pushed the chairs back against the walls and some people danced, we opened the door to the yard even though it was November, and people stood on the back stairs and smoked. Frederik and I danced too, the light uneven on the dance floor, I flung my arms around his waist, more wine, a shelf toppled over and so what, the clock struck two, there was noise and then the music grew more mellow.

Frederik and I were sweaty from dancing. He pulled me out the back door, down the stairs, and out into the yard, so far from the windows that we were standing in darkness. He kissed me under the black branches of the apple tree.

It was much too cold, but we picked our way across the black lawn toward the white steel skeleton of our hanging sofa where it caught the light in the shadows. There were no cushions, and the seat's dark springs shaded into the space and the grass beneath them. We sat down, and with the alcohol and dancing in our blood it was as if we were hovering suspended in the cold night.

Hell, the price Niklas and I paid that Frederik might merit such a collection of speeches. It hadn't been my vision of a marriage, to endure so many years essentially in solitude while my husband lavished his attention upon anyone connected to Saxtorph—and too much attention upon a couple of female teachers and board members in particular.

Ever since, I've tried to forget how lonely I was during all those years. No one except my girlfriends and Niklas to look me in the eye, no one else to hear my trivial asides and understand how I felt just from the tone of my voice. The longing for another kind of marriage and my despairing wonder about why I stayed with Frederik. What had he done to me? Why didn't I go out and seek the marriage I'd always dreamt of?

A few years ago he finally came back to us. It'd been a hard struggle, but I thought I succeeded in swallowing my bitterness. And now it felt as if we'd really only been with each other the last couple of years, as if our relationship were still brand spanking new and full of possibility. A joyful feeling that his betrayal belonged to another world than this.

There was almost nothing in the yard we could see. So it was more a sound, or a sense that something was moving in the apple branches. As if a bird were taking flight, or a dried-up winter apple were letting go of its stem.

"Frederik, the others praise you for so many marvelous things. And I'm so proud of you. So very proud to have a man who's so clever and so good with people."

I pressed myself against him, and there in the hanging sofa, in the night, in the cold, I felt in my trembling body that he and I belonged together.

"But this is what I love you for."

...

Another nurse enters Frederik's hospital room. We can't understand what she's saying, but with gestures she makes us understand that Frederik and I are to follow her to see somebody else—perhaps another doctor.

Frederik gets up from the bed as if it were the most natural thing in the world. Niklas remains behind, and Frederik and I are led into a large corner office where we sit across from an older doctor with an immense mustache. The exaggerated rectitude of his bearing gives me the impression that he's been a military doctor most of his life. He speaks excellent English with great pride, an old-fashioned, British boarding-school English.

"I can say with almost complete certitude that it is not cancer," he says. "That means that my colleagues in Denmark can probably remove the tumor completely. Before the operation, however, no one will be able to say precisely the extent of the procedure they will be required to perform. Perhaps afterwards you will be completely as you were accustomed to being before; perhaps you will find yourself changed."

Frederik doesn't say anything, so I ask for him. "Changed?"

"Yes, for you must have already experienced changes recently. Am I correct?"

I try to think, but my thoughts lead nowhere. I have no idea what the doctor is talking about, and yet I hear myself saying, "Yes."

"What you must be particularly prepared for is for your husband to lose all empathy for you and how you are doing," the doctor says. "He will have a harder time restraining his more primitive impulses. He may have sudden fits of anger and deny every suggestion that he is unwell. Those are the most typical symptoms when there is pressure on the orbitofrontal region of the brain."

I stare at Frederik, still not knowing what the doctor is talking about. The doctor folds his sunburned hands on the desktop and looks into my eyes probingly.

"But to judge by the size of his tumor, you know all about these orbito-frontal symptoms already, do you not?"

In my head I hear myself asking *Do I?* but I answer, "Yes."

"Good. Frederik, we shall give you corticotropin to reduce the swelling in your brain, as well as some anticonvulsants so that you do not risk another epileptic seizure like the one you experienced yesterday . . . Frederik?"

"Yes," he says.

"You may return to your hotel today. And you may fly back to Denmark in a couple days. If everything goes well, they should be able to operate on you in Denmark in one month's time."

Frederik appears to be chiefly interested in some red and yellow files with tables and diagrams that lie on the desk in front of us.

"That long?" I ask. "But what if it's cancer?"

"They must ensure that they remove the entire tumor, but also that they do not remove more than is necessary. They can accomplish that best if they wait until the swelling of the brain itself has disappeared."

"Is it a dangerous operation?" I ask.

He turns calmly to Frederik.

"Will you be so kind as to replace those papers where they were?"

Only now do I see that Frederik has been intently riffling through one of the doctor's files.

"Frederik! I do hope you're not reading the doctor's papers!"

"No, pardon me." He smiles his disarming smile and returns the folder to the desktop.

"You must really excuse him," I say.

"Well, yes." The doctor makes a deprecating wave of his hand. "I know how it is—diminished inhibition of impulses, eh?"

Based on his examination, the doctor evidently thinks I've been living with a series of obvious changes in Frederik's brain for a long time. But have I?

Yes, I suppose he *has* been different in recent weeks. More self-centered, disorganized, hotheaded. But is he any worse than Helena's husband, or my other friends' husbands? I really don't think so.

The doctor gets to his feet and gives me his hand in parting. He squeezes hard.

"You must be prepared for the corticotropin to make his personality changes gradually less pronounced in the coming weeks. On the other hand, the treatment may induce manic tendencies as a side effect. Which make it critical for you to take away his car keys. He must not drive before the operation."

"Yes. Thank you," I say. "I will." And meanwhile I wonder if Frederik is so intelligent that the pressure from the tumor might not have resulted in the usual symptoms, but merely brought him down to the level of other men.

But how can I ask the doctor, without it sounding as if I have an inflated image of my husband?

4

Copenhagen Airport. I love when the doors glide to the side after customs and we push our baggage carts into the big triangle of other passengers' friends and families. Danish faces waving flags, flashbulbing reunions, and hugging kids, spouses, and friends they haven't seen in months.

We look like a normal family too; there's nothing about us that anyone can see is different. The first person I catch sight of is Laust, even though he's so short and pale. He's squeezed in front of the others in the crowd, and his eyes are wide and worried.

His skin seems more transparent than usual, like the rice paper wrapped around a Vietnamese spring roll—poke him with a chopstick and muscle and guts would spill out, blue, red, and grey.

Frederik's parents smile, unhappy and tired, they push their way through behind Laust. Thorkild is dressed as always in a dark blazer and white shirt. Despite his retirement, he still feels most comfortable in the kind of clothes he needed as president of the Association of Danish Private School Headmasters, and as the leader of a school that was much more conservative than Frederik's.

Tears run down Vibeke's cheeks as she clasps me to her and tries to peer deep into my eyes. I quickly rearrange some suitcases on the baggage cart, and while I pretend to be occupied she naturally throws herself upon Niklas.

"It's so great to see you," I say.

And for now there's not much more to be said. In the last two days I've spent a fortune calling them from my cell phone and bringing them up to

26

speed on everything—right until the moment we were going to fasten our seat belts on the plane and turn off our phones, and then here in Copenhagen when we could turn them on again. It's best if we postpone the tête-à-têtes until we're not surrounded by others' embraces.

We hug each other silently, and then Laust leads us out to his car in one of the parking garages. Vibeke holds Niklas's hand and weeps, and with a little burst of speed I pass them and come up beside Laust and Frederik.

Seeing Laust has made Frederik liven up visibly. He tells Laust about the great vacation we've had, and after we've been walking for a while in the long corridors between the basement parking garages, he says, "If Dad'll drive the rest of you home, I can borrow Laust's car and pop by the school to grab some papers I need this weekend."

Despite everything I've told them on the phone, they're not prepared for this. Thorkild had begun to relax during his son's upbeat descriptions of being on holiday; now he replies slowly, deliberately. "But Frederik. You're not supposed to drive."

"Ahh, that's just something the doctor said to avoid risking a lawsuit or problems with insurance. Anyone can see that." He spreads his arms wide. "Look at me! Of course I can drive."

I put my arm around his waist and give him a reassuring squeeze. "Frederik, I can drive you. Then everyone else can go home. Or we could *all* drive past the school."

"You're not really going to listen to what that fellow said? Then I wouldn't be able to drive for a month. That's obviously out of the question."

Laust shifts his weight uncertainly from one foot to the other before breaking in. "Frederik, there's something else we need to talk about."

Frederik is so happy that his smile borders on laughter. Laust continues.

"It may be that it's a good idea to take a break from work until you have a clean bill of health again."

"What?"

"It's just that . . . if there's the least chance of the illness affecting the choices you make, then it would probably be for the best."

"What!"

I release my hold on Frederik's belly and look around. His shout echoes in the concrete garage, but nobody else is down here.

Laust has a muted, solicitous way of focusing on his friend. "I merely

27

think . . . if you end up making a couple of wrong decisions . . . It's a foolish risk to run."

"I'm *not* going to make any wrong decisions!"

"It's just for safety's sake. Until we're one hundred percent certain you're in top form again."

Frederik's voice breaks. "But Laust, you're not really going to shut me out from the school, are you?"

Laust always looks so small standing next to Frederik, who towers above him by more than a head. "Frederik, you would be the one who would regret it most if you were to misjudge—"

"But I *won't* misjudge anything! I won't!"

Thorkild interposes in his husky voice. "Perhaps you should take a little time to consider—"

"You want to shut me out of the school!" Frederik yells.

His fist strikes Laust's face, and then he shoves him down onto the asphalt.

"Frederik! Frederik!" we shout.

Without thinking, I throw myself upon the two of them and try to grab Frederik's arms to pin them behind his back, while he rains blows down upon Laust. I get hold of one arm but he pulls free, I get the same arm again and he bites me on the hand.

I've never done this kind of thing before, but two deep breaths and I can focus. With both hands I grab Frederik's right arm and wrench it behind his back as quick as I can so he can't bite or hit me. I shove him forward facedown against the concrete floor and sit on top of him, holding him in an armlock. He's the one who's sat behind a desk most of his life, while I'm six years his junior and a PE teacher to boot. He screams in pain.

And keeps on yelling. About marital violence, about the school, about how we're all shitheads.

"Shut up!" I shout. "Shut up!"

Laust manages to crawl out from under Frederik. I twist Frederik's arm even harder, up toward his neck. Another scream. His brain, his poor sick brain: all that fat and blood in there, and furrows and fissures and something that's growing—the fetuses I lost, so that we never had any more children.

28

I glance up at Niklas, his long blond hair against the concrete ceiling of the parking garage. He's bowed slightly forward, ready to fight, my pale boy, albeit with eyes confused. Whom should he fight?

"Lie still, damn it," I say.

But Frederik continues to thrash whenever I'm not pressing on his arm and back. Vibeke squats down in front of his face.

"Frederik," she says, in a tone she might use to talk to a puppy that's been mischievous. "Frederik, how *could* you?"

Laust's nose is bleeding and he has abrasions on one cheek. He sees my inquiring look.

"I'll be okay," he says.

The sound of his voice makes Frederik start to struggle again. "You want to shut me out of the school! From *my school*! *My school!*"

I grip the hair on the back of his head and let my weight press his skull down against the concrete, but I let go as quickly as if I'd been shocked—I don't want to press on the tumor.

"Is this what it's like?" asks Laust. "Is he really like this?"

"We haven't had any physical fights before," I say, panting.

The only one who keeps a cool head is my father-in-law. He gently lays a hand on Laust's arm.

"You know it's not Frederik who's doing this," he says. "You know that. It's the tumor."

"Yes."

"There are police everywhere out here, and they may have a hard time understanding that. I trust you won't mention this to them."

"No, of course not." Laust looks almost alarmed by the suggestion.

Thorkild's mild voice and confidential tone are exactly like the voice Frederik uses in crisis situations. It's so familiar. Even Frederik seems to grow less tense beneath me.

"Perhaps you should go," Thorkild says quietly to Laust. "Then I think he'll become himself again more quickly."

Laust nods. He takes leave of us silently, walks over to his car, and drives away. Once he's gone, I want to release my tight grip on Frederik, but I don't know if it's too soon.

"What do we do now?" I ask.

Vibeke speaks from her position by Frederik's face. "Not to tell you what to do, Mia, but aren't you being a little rough in the way you're handling him? I think you're hurting him."

...

Until three years ago, Frederik got up every day at five thirty to answer e-mails in his home office. Then we ate breakfast, he left, and the next time I saw him would be late at night. He would be tired and we seldom had sex. Then a new day would begin. On weekends too, he often spent most of the day in the home office, and all too many Sunday evenings passed with me grousing.

One day when I was complaining to Helena, she said, "A lack of love would drive anyone crazy."

"Crazy?"

"Yes. Not that you're crazy, of course. But it's not strange that you react the way you do."

When we'd been married eight years, I found in his bag a note to a female English teacher. The note looked like all the little love notes he'd left in my mailbox in the teachers' lounge, during the months after we came back from the school camp in Sweden. The note said that he was eager to see her that evening.

I arranged for Niklas to sleep at Thorkild and Vibeke's and took the train into Copenhagen, where I used his spare key to let myself in a back door. Frederik was alone in his office, and he denied everything. But as I was on my way out of the office, the English teacher came walking down the hall.

I was ready to do anything—and not just for my sake, but for Niklas's too. I made a humongous scene, screaming that if she didn't get a job at another school, I'd contact the parents of all her students and bring her affair with Frederik before the school board and make her life miserable any way I could.

She quit, and Frederik promised once again to change. And so began another week when I stayed with him, and when I hoped he would show a little interest in Niklas and me, the following weekend perhaps or the next vacation or the vacation after that.

Three years ago it happened again. This time it was a woman on the board I discovered him with, and this time I threw him out. First he stayed a week in a spare room in Laust and Anja's big apartment in Copenhagen, and then he moved into a one-bedroom sublet fifty yards from the school.

The first week was tough for both Niklas and me. But after that I was ecstatic. I wanted to start to paint, and I wanted to have a *real* husband, one who wanted to share a life with me. For years I'd dreamt about having the courage to make this leap. Now I wouldn't be so damn lonely; now I'd no longer overwhelm Niklas with my attention. And from the moment it got out that I was single, lots of men began to approach me, both married and unmarried, men who'd apparently been holding back only on account of Frederik.

For the first time in many years I was free, I was exultant, and everything was slated to begin, everything was looking up.

I still can't comprehend what happened then: Niklas found me unconscious on the kitchen floor with an empty tequila bottle. What was that about? It was so far from who I was. Where did it come from? I couldn't remember anything, only waking up in the emergency room with Frederik and Niklas looking at me in my hospital bed.

I'll never forgive myself for letting my son see me that way. Did I go insane for one night? Had freedom come to me too suddenly? Was it impossible for me to live without Frederik?

After that he moved back in—maybe to take care of Niklas, maybe to take care of me. And I let him, because I didn't know what was wrong with me.

I distinctly remember one of the first dinners Frederik and I had together when we were both back home. Niklas was at a friend's, and Frederik had brought me a large bouquet of flowers. He set the table with the cloth napkins we never used, and with candles that we did use, but only when I set them out. From the kitchen I could hear him uncork a bottle of red wine, even though his mother thought I should stop drinking.

As soon as we sat down, he said, "Isn't there something we can do to make this romantic?"

"Candles, wine?"

"No, not that."

31

His lips touched the edge of his glass; they were dry despite the fact that he had just drunk. He went on.

"There are two lovers and one almost dies, and so they learn that deserting each other will never be an option. That's how it goes in the best love stories. Aren't we in the middle of a story like that?"

I wanted to shout *It was only* me *who was about to die. You were out screwing! Maybe you know some love stories where the woman would have drunk herself to death if her son hadn't found her on the floor!* But I said nothing.

He was looking at me with unwonted intensity.

"Can't we learn from this how impossible it'd be for either of us to live without the other? That has to be the most romantic thing in the world, Mia! We're meant for each other, with all our failings. That's the essence of love, is it not? You and me."

I deeply admire Frederik's ability to find something positive in even the direst situations. And he was right, of course—though I was furious with disappointment, though he'd kept me out of his life year in and year out, though our relationship had become something radically different from the one I'd first known. Despite all that, he was right. The two of us were meant to be. We were meant to be, from the moment we first met on that beach in Sweden—to when I forced his first lover to quit her job, to when I nearly drank myself to death, to this dinner and on till we die.

And then he finally settled down.

He no longer stayed at school every evening. He finally began to relax, and I felt I could engage him. He ate at home and we watched TV together, visited friends together. He spent time with Niklas, and the two of us talked about our son, our house and yard. All the things that other couples enjoy doing together.

Again and again, my friends had told me that you cannot change a man. They advised me to get a divorce. But I fought and persevered.

And it turned out they were wrong.

...

Twenty minutes later, we're on our way home in my in-laws' car. Thorkild handled the conversation with the two airport cops who showed up, and he's also the one who's driving now, with Vibeke seated beside him and the other three of us in back.

I said a lot of sweet things to Frederik, and I have to say that they worked. He's asleep now, with his head up against the window.

On my other side, Niklas sits erect. He looks so lovely and fragile. In the dim light through the thin clouds and the light rain he looks almost like a girl, a wistful model, and I cannot stop thinking that it would have been easier on him if it were me who was ill, instead of his father.

For our son's sake, Frederik would have sometimes been able to transform the depressing daily round with a sick mother into a Help Our Crazy Mother game. Of course they would still feel sad, but they'd also have fun—and Niklas can't live without humor. It's not the same with me; when I'm unhappy, my sorrow eclipses everything. And he knows that.

Niklas gazes insistently out the window. I take my eyes from his neck and look out the other window, through the small vibrating drops that the wind presses across the glass.

And I resolve with myself that I don't owe Frederik anything. On the contrary, he owes me, for all the years when I trusted him and suffered so terribly from him never being home. I thought I was sacrificing myself for the students of Saxtorph, while in reality he had something going on with other women in Copenhagen. Year after year. The years of my youth.

If I became seriously ill, he ought to care for me for a long, long time to answer for that.

And I decide, as I've already done several times in the last few days, that if the operation doesn't cure Frederik, I'll stick with him for a year and a half, maximum. Only until he's gotten as far as he can with rehab; after that it's over. It feels good for me to think that. It's necessary to have an emergency exit.

Frederik's head shifts over, so it no longer rests against the window but on my shoulder instead. Warmth, the soft press of his ear, the little sounds of his halting snore.

I start to cry, muted and still. For that's not the way it'll be; I know that. In the end I won't leave him. Not after a year and a half. It'll be Frederik and me forever.

Will he keep hitting people after the operation? Will I have to quit my job? Will we have to move? I throw him to the concrete floor of the parking garage and pin his arm behind his back, I strike him in the supermarket when he attacks me for not letting him decide what to buy, I hold him down while he struggles on the patio of Thorkild and Vibeke's summer cottage.

"Thorkild, could you please pull over? I'm not feeling well."

My father-in-law stops on the freeway shoulder, and I tumble out onto the strip of overgrown grass along the roadside. I sink to my knees and raise my hands to my forehead.

I want to throw up, but nothing will come. Sweat trickles down my back. I try to hawk something up. Again. And again. Then I feel a warm hand upon my brow. It's Niklas. He learned it from me, that's the way I always placed my hand against his forehead when he threw up as a little boy.

It should be me who's taking care of him. I want to get up and press my hand against his brow. It should be him who's throwing up. When I finally do rise, he embraces me; he's taller than me, his arms are strong, he pats me on the head.

Orbitofrontal Injuries

The orbitofrontal cortex coordinates emotions from our limbic system with our overarching control systems.

The limbic system sends strong signals to the rest of the brain with messages to flee, fight, mate, feel sadness/pain, or grow angry—survival signals that we share with other animals. The orbitofrontal cortex is the region that modulates these all-or-nothing signals and gives them a more nuanced, human expression.

Orbitofrontal damage results in the injured person losing the unique, personal way he modulates his emotions. He possesses only two levels of emotion: quiescence and maximum strength. There is no middle ground.

The injured person will often experience pathologically high spirits and feel strikingly uninvolved with and indifferent to what happens around him. The personality and subtlety in how he reacts to his surroundings have disappeared. Instead, when he cries or is angry, he cannot govern the strength of his emotions—just like an infant.

Frequently, an isolated orbitofrontal injury will not affect intelligence, memory, or language. Yet it will lead to a fundamental personality change, in which the injured person's sense of what constitutes a good or bad choice is nullified. He becomes a more fearless, "simple" person, who has a hard time controlling his immediate impulses and making long-term plans.

It is characteristic of frontal-lobe syndrome that the person who suffers from it mistakenly believes he is healthy and completely unaffected. No test or argument can convince him otherwise. The absence of empathy for others, and of a sense for when he is about to make a poor choice, often leads to a radically altered way of life for a person with orbitofrontal damage—even one whose injuries are so minor as to be undetectable by conventional psychological tests.

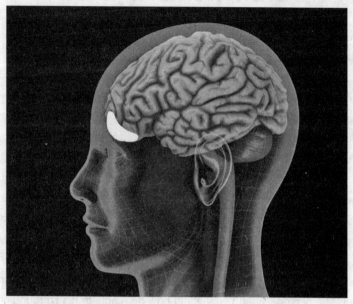

The orbitofrontal cortex sits in the very front of the brain, just over the eyes.

Some people with orbitofrontal injuries may exhibit only a few of the following characteristics, while others develop most of them:

- lack of empathy for and interest in other people
- recklessness, tactless behavior, unacceptable sexual advances
- unnatural jocularity involving trite, childish jokes
- fearlessness and emotional callousness, with minimal capacity for self-criticism
- distractibility and a tendency to give up when confronted with any difficulty

These symptoms can manifest themselves without any evident sign of neurological illness, such as paralysis. Moreover, the injured person experiences virtually no sense of being ill. As a consequence, he is completely uninterested in consulting a physician or psychologist.

5

"Of course you're going to stay with him," Helena says on the telephone when I call her at three in the morning because I can't sleep. "You'll stay. Because that's the way you are."

An eternity ago, we were three girls from the same dorm studying architecture together: Hanne, who died shortly before I met Frederik; Helena, who with her iron will was the only one to finish the degree; and myself. Helena and I also played tennis together, which we've done ever since. Perhaps she doesn't have quite the finesse in her game that I do, but she's a tall woman with slightly masculine features and well-defined muscles, so we're an even match. After five years as a more-or-less unemployed architect, she took up my suggestion to get a second degree in primary education. And then she got a job at my school, so now we're colleagues as well as tennis partners.

Helena says, "I've thought about this. If I were attacked some night by a man who knocked me over so I couldn't run away, you're the woman I'd most want with me when it happened. Because you'd go after him, you wouldn't bolt. And together we could handle him."

I'm so tired, so very tired. Lying on my back in the bed, knowing that I can talk as loudly as I want and Frederik won't wake up. As soon as he falls asleep, he's out cold.

"Does the man have a gun?" I ask.

"You know, if he's holding me down on the ground, it really doesn't matter."

"If he has a gun, I'd be an idiot not to run away."

37

"Sure, there'd be a thousand things racing through your head: should you risk your life by staying and fighting these men? But even while you're thinking these things you'd stay put. For it isn't your thoughts that decide what you do. It's your instinct."

"Oh, so now there's more than just one guy?"

"There are three, and they don't have a gun, and we take them down."

"As long as it ends well."

I don't know where she got the idea of us being attacked some night by three men. Yet she's right about how in the space of a single moment, everything in your life can turn upside down. You're sitting in an endless teacher's meeting yearning for it to end, or finding a blouse to pack in your tennis bag, or hurrying out to the kitchen for some chocolate ice cream while a British detective show is on the tube. The sort of moment that feels utterly dependable—a moment everything can be snatched away. If, say, a blood vessel bursts in your brain.

I was twelve the first time my world exploded. My parents had taken pains to make their everyday lives indistinguishable from thousands of other young couples'. I was happy enough in the newly built suburb where we lived, outside Fredericia, and they managed to get everyone to think they were happy too—my father with his job as a bank clerk, my mother with her housework and her shifting part-time jobs in company canteens.

For my father, the high point of each week was Thursday evening, when he played soccer with his friends on a field behind the school. Through his soccer friends he met a bunch of Copenhagen "freaks" who'd just started a commune in a run-down building on Prince Street. And then without warning, one Saturday morning he moved out of our house and into theirs. I couldn't comprehend what had happened, and neither could my mother.

Whenever I ran into my father around town, he seemed happy to see me—though not enough to make me think he missed me. He talked about the revolution they all were convinced was about to break out. He talked about oppressed peoples and about traveling to see the world, especially the Third World. One day when I happened to mention to my mother what he'd been saying, she screamed, "Don't believe him, he's lying! The only reason he moved in there is to ball hippie chicks!"

She tried to find a new boyfriend, but they all left her, and I learned to block out her stifling bitterness toward my father, toward the latest man of

38

the month, toward everyone else she knew. Today you'd say she suffered from depression, but nobody said that back then.

Meanwhile, my father became more fun to talk to. I secretly visited him at the commune, until one day when I showed up unannounced and they told me he'd been arrested in Thailand for smuggling hash.

Then my mother became obsessed with writing long letters to him in prison, and a year later she traveled over to visit him. When she got back home, she showed me photos of how thin he'd grown and said he shared a cell with two murderers. I wrote to him, and to Danish politicians and journalists too, so that they'd do something to bring him back to Denmark.

When he finally returned, five years later, he looked like a concentration camp inmate. He received a disability pension on psychological grounds, and when I went by his small cluttered apartment, he often said strange things, especially about the neighbors being after him and wanting to kill him. During my visits he remained stretched out on the couch with the TV on and a foul blanket over his legs. He died before I turned thirty.

Even though he abandoned our family for the sake of long-haired girls from Copenhagen, I never felt anger toward him—only toward my mother. She's the one who dumped me into a sobbing swamp of adult problems, a swamp that reeked of biscuits and tea. She still lives in the same small house in Fredericia. We don't talk on the phone or see each other very much, and I don't miss her.

...

Three weeks after Frederik's fall, and he still hasn't been operated on. Thorkild and Vibeke have to be at the house while I'm at work because he ends up doing the queerest things.

In the first days, it seemed natural that he talked only about himself. Who wouldn't, after such a grave diagnosis? But then he didn't stop. It was unending, and always with the same energetic, cheerful voice. No modulation in his tone, no resonance in his thoughts or feelings.

During dinner, I'd have lunged across the table and strangled him if it would have killed just the voice. That voice gave me nightmares. I dreamt that it possessed him, that it resided in the tumor like a little spiny monster that talked and talked. The voice decided everything, and in my dream it got tangled up with a gross tennis coach in too-tight shorts whom I had when I was sixteen, and whom all the girls in the club hated.

I go on the web every day and every night now to read about the disease, and I've been inhaling books on neuropsychology. I have to know everything I can about the situation I find myself in. Do the books say Frederik will survive? Will he become himself again?

Several doctors who've had kids at Saxtorph call to see if they can be of assistance. I ask for their prognoses, but nobody can say. So I listen to their tone when they speak. How long do they pause before answering? How often do they clear their throats? I read everything as an omen.

A lot of other people call too, offering help and support. They say, *Normally, I wouldn't ring up the headmaster of my child's school, but it's different with Frederik.* In the end, Laust has to send an e-mail to "Friends of Saxtorph": please do not call or bring any more gifts.

In the evenings it's me who talks and talks, and just like Frederik it's always about the same thing, only my audience isn't him. I call my friends and describe the mountains in Majorca and how dangerously he drove; the three lovely years we had; what the doctors said today. And Niklas, who's out with his friends every night. My rasping monotone lament becomes an evil twin of the voice that's laid siege to our house.

Laust doesn't visit us anymore, since Frederik is still furious with him. But he listens to me over the phone, asking how he can best support us, and he never whines about how the rest of the administration has to work overtime. And he often calls with questions about the school, just like before Frederik got sick, only now it's me he rings up. In the beginning, we worked out complicated strategies to worm the answers out of Frederik, but we quickly discovered that it wasn't necessary.

I can just ask, without prelude, "Frederik, the last letters from the lessee of the school cafeteria are missing from the file with the other letters. Where might they be?"

He's unable to imagine that other people's words are the calculated product of thoughts and feelings, so he doesn't worry about motives, he just answers. "They're in a folder beneath the file with our cleaning agreements. I'm planning to use them when I draw up a new contract with the cleaning firm."

"Aha, so that's where they are. And something else I was wondering: What did you decide at the meeting you had in September with Fatima from the after-school club?"

On top of everything else, there are all the public offices to get through to on the telephone, the government forms and insurance forms to fill out, and the confusing bills that Frederik used to pay. By the time I lie down it's late. Now I have to try to relax and go to sleep with a man who snores differently, smells different, and twitches in his sleep in an unfamiliar fashion. I may as well be sharing our queen-size bed with some burglar.

Will we ever be able to make love again? When he lies there pestering me for sex, I turn my back on him, squeeze my thick pillow between my breasts, and use my legs to push him away.

And then one night I decide he's got a point. We're still man and wife, after all. Why keep insisting that he stay on his half of the bed? We both want the same thing, and he's been a stranger now for five weeks.

Besides, night after night when I'm half asleep under the comforter, I've been entertaining a fantasy about making him well again. I know it'll never happen, but I'm seized by the notion of it all being some misunderstanding. Something in me says that there's no tumor, that he'll return to normal if I just let him have sex with me. That the last five weeks have been nothing more than a test of my love for him, and in a short while he'll become himself again if I only let him.

So one night I consent, and seconds later he's on top of me, frenetically trying to grind away. There's nothing erotic or loving about it; for him I'm not really a person, that's abominably clear. Some creature is pawing at me and attempting to mount me, some creature without age or face, eyes or voice.

I try to instruct him in what I like, in what we used to do. He hears me but keeps going, heedless. His rough snorting in my ear, his clumsy hands; a dog that only wants to hump. His cock bangs against me without him seeming to realize that I'm straining now to keep him out. The unfamiliar sheen of sweat on his face.

I writhe, trying to shove him away, but his response is to pin me to the mattress. Even the smile on his face is someone else's.

"Stop it! Stop!"

But he won't.

"Stop, Frederik! God damn it, Frederik, stop!"

He just keeps at it, and in the end I have no choice. I butt him with my head.

"Ow! You fucking sow!" He grabs his nose and raises himself up a little. He howls as I heave him off of me and run out to our bathroom, where I lock the door and lift the door handle, since the lock alone probably won't hold.

Two seconds later, he's rattling the door in the jamb, hammering away on it, and shouting, "Come out, you whore! Come on, you know you want it. I'm going to fucking pound you!"

I whisper through the door that he mustn't wake Niklas. But he doesn't care.

"You bitch, time for some prick!"

There's a knock on the bedroom door.

"What's happening in there? What's going on?" Niklas's voice is high and shrill, like it used to be a few years ago.

"Mind your own business!" Frederik yells. "Go to your room! I order you, go to your room!"

I shout through the bathroom door and the bedroom door to where he's standing in the hallway. "It's okay, Niklas, it's no big deal."

He doesn't hear me. "Where's Mom?"

"I'm in here, Niklas! Can you hear me? I'm in our bathroom!"

"Stick it up your ass, you little shit!"

Niklas's voice sounds panicked now. "Where's Mom, I want to see her!"

I unlock the door and rush into the bedroom. Frederik is naked, standing with his back propped against the door to the hallway. The door booms and shudders each time Niklas throws himself against it. Frederik's erection hasn't subsided. In the dark it looks bigger than when he was healthy.

I come closer.

"Niklas, it's okay. I'm here. There's nothing the matter."

The booming ceases. He must be standing still on the other side of the door. His voice becomes gentle. "I want to see that you're there."

"Let me come out to you," I say, looking for something to throw over myself.

Frederik's no longer leaning against the door. The tension eases for a moment, then the door flies open with a bang and Niklas tumbles past us.

The light from the doorway falls on me standing there, just as naked as Frederik. Niklas has a wild look in his eyes and his hair is all mussed. He's ready to fight. And then he crumples to the floor.

"I'm sorry."

"No need to apologize." I glance over at Frederik's cock sticking up, as undaunted and brown-violet as ever. I don't understand why it doesn't droop. He doesn't seem self-conscious in the least, though Niklas tries to look away. I hurry to the bed for a comforter to cover myself with.

Niklas is crying with the same irregular rhythm as when he was five years old, the same deep wail broken by a sobbing whimper. "Sorry . . . sorry . . . sorry."

I throw another comforter over to Frederik to wrap himself in. "No need to be sorry about anything, Niklas. It was sweet of you to want to make sure I was okay."

I crouch down on the floor next to my son and feel a desire to hold him, to hug him, but he pushes me away.

I get up.

"Go back to your room," I say. "I'll come in to you in a little bit."

I gather some clothes together, give Frederik one of the motor-sport magazines Thorkild bought for him, and hurry to the bathroom to get dressed. When I come back out, Niklas is gone, and Frederik's immersed in the magazine.

I disappear into Niklas's room. He's sitting up in his bed, wrapped in his comforter. I slide his desk chair over to the side of the bed and sit down. I know I should remain calm—inhumanly calm, given the situation. His face is stiff, as if all the tiny muscles under his skin are paralyzed, and when he brushes a lock of hair off his forehead, he does so slowly and with physical effort, as if he suffers from some neurological disorder that makes him incapable of normal movement.

I assure him that nothing's happened to me, and that his father didn't hit me. Then I repeat it. And repeat it again. The whole time in an artificially calm voice.

And at some point, I feel my false calm start to seep in and become genuine. There's also something about talking to a healthy human being. The difference is so vast.

"Did Dad hit you that other time too?" he asks at last, and I know he means the time I kicked Frederik out.

"Your father's never hit me," I say.

It's warm in his room. Black-and-white posters printed from his own photos hang on the walls, along with a single colored poster from a techno party in Copenhagen. The room smells of teenage boy, and his clothes lie on the floor in a heap that resembles a fat little troll.

"It'll be over soon," he says.

"Yes, after the operation he'll become normal again."

"Three weeks max."

"Three weeks max."

We both stare into space, saying nothing. A weak light from a streetlamp outside casts a pattern on his cheek and a car drives past; we listen to the sound slowly die away.

It's become necessary for us to keep an eye on Frederik's whereabouts at night. Three days ago, I discovered him in our living room at four thirty in the morning, just a few clicks away from e-mailing an apoplectic op-ed to our daily paper, *Politiken*, about a bunch of headmasters from other private schools who he said were incompetent and should be fired. There's so much he could destroy—for himself, for us all. Someone has to sleep beside him, ready to wake up if he does.

"I can't sleep in there tonight," I say.

Niklas begins to tremble almost imperceptibly. "I can't either."

"No, no! Of course not, you're not going to!"

His shaking becomes more pronounced. "But I want to. You should sleep in here. In here. It should be me who . . ."

He buries his head in the comforter over his knees. He's still shaking.

"No, Niklas. You're definitely not sleeping in there. I will. No. No. I'll put the air mattress outside the door to the room."

Now we can hear Frederik through the wall, weeping loudly. Someone ought to be there with him. Someone ought to comfort him.

"Niklas, you have to sleep in here, like you always do. Then I'll lie down on the sofa in the living room . . . No, I'll sleep outside his door . . . No."

In the end, Niklas says it's okay if I sleep on the air mattress on his floor.

I have to work tomorrow, and I know I won't get a wink of sleep if I have to lie down alone somewhere in the house.

Although the air mattress is on Niklas's shelf, all the comforters and linen are in our bedroom closet. But I don't want to go in there, so I fetch a blanket from down in the living room.

As I make up the mattress on the floor beside Niklas's bed, I can't help but wonder who I'm doing all this for. It's obvious that Frederik doesn't care about me now—despite being completely dependent on his parents and me around the clock, to protect him from himself. But his callousness since the seizure is due to the disease. What about back when he was himself?

And then I let myself be tormented again by a memory that's been plaguing me the last five weeks. In Majorca, just before Frederik fell, he was standing atop the stone wall, swinging his arms, he was shouting, and then he started to cry at the mere thought of Niklas—his paternal love so great that his weak brain could no longer hold it in.

But toward me, it wasn't love that burst forth.

The black mountainsides, the brush we'd driven past, the scent of lemon. "You piece of shit, Mia! You big fat piece of shit!"

He began thrashing about with his arms even more wildly. And then he fell.

"Frederik! Frederik!"

"Dad!"

A piece of shit. Just like his love for Niklas, was that something he'd felt for a long time—but had had enough brainpower to hide till then?

The slope where he fell. The tree that saved his life.

...

At last. A month and a half after Frederik's seizure, the doctors finally gauge that it's time to operate, and then it goes quickly. They schedule the surgery for two days later.

The evening before the operation, I go to the kitchen. Niklas has been out with friends all day, as usual, and I pour myself a generous tumbler of whiskey.

I haven't raised the glass yet when I hear his voice behind me. "Please don't."

I turn around. Niklas is standing in front of the broom closet.

"Where'd *you* come from?"

He stares at me, a disagreeable tightness around his eyes, and I don't know where to look.

"It's just one glass. It's not—"

He doesn't budge. "Then I'm moving over to Mathias's."

I don't know where to go. I can't stand to be in the kitchen anymore, or in the front hall either. I rush into the living room, where Frederik is stretched out on the sofa, watching TV, and I throw myself into his arms, just as if he were well. Lie there and press myself to him. He doesn't take his gaze from the screen. There's auto racing on Eurosport.

We're quiet for a little while, and then I say, "I'm so unhappy."

He doesn't answer.

"Frederik! Can't you say anything? Can't you ask me why I'm unhappy?"

He looks at me with a big grin. "Yes, I will. I'll ask you. Why are you unhappy, dear?"

"It's because I'm so scared of your operation tomorrow." The words come out in a rush. "It's because you mustn't die or get any sicker."

"Well, is that all. It'll be fine. Don't you worry about it."

He turns back to the cars whizzing around and around. And I just lie there with him. I could probably squeeze more of a response out of him, say that I'm also unhappy about my conversation with Niklas, but instead I get up and go over to the other end of the room and call Helena through the engine noise from the TV.

She only has to hear the sound of my voice before she's offering to spend the night at our place. And she can hear how relieved I become once I say yes.

Standing in the kitchen, I swallow three scoops of chocolate ice cream so quickly that they burn against my palate, and then I go upstairs and knock on Niklas's door. He opens it halfway and stands there blocking the opening.

"Helena's coming over," I say.

He makes a sort of humming noise in response.

"Is there anything I can do for you?" I ask.

"No thanks."

"What are you doing?"

"Just sitting and watching some videos."

I don't have anything to base it on, but I get the feeling he hasn't heard me. I find myself repeating my words. "Helena's coming over, to sleep. I'm really glad she's going to."

"Okay," he says.

"I'm really glad that you're so . . . *manly*," I find myself saying. And then I repeat myself. "Do let me know if there's anything you'd like to talk about, anything I can do for you."

But apparently there isn't. I'm stranded on the Swedish beach where I met Frederik twenty years ago. Everybody else has gone home, they've gone on with their lives and I'm still here, half buried in the sand, the waves washing over me, cold as a corpse.

I return to the kitchen and put some water on for tea, for Helena. Maybe I really died then on the beach, I don't know. I go to set out a couple of tumblers and the fifth of Scotch too—maybe she could use a little whiskey.

But the bottle's gone. I look in all the cupboards. It and the cognac bottle have both disappeared.

6

Frederik *doesn't* have cancer. He *won't* die from his disease.

But the meningioma sits directly in his brain's median plane, which makes it much more difficult to remove. As a result, I spend so much time in the short week after the operation at the National Hospital's neurointensive clinic that I practically live there, and after that three weeks in the neurology department of Hillerød Hospital, where Frederik totters around, taking small steps like a dying dog.

And then he comes home to our house. He slowly fights his way back to being able to remember and speak and walk. Each week he improves, but after four months, he seems just as alien as he was in the month before the surgery. Perhaps his progress will stop here, perhaps he'll continue to get better for a few more months. Nobody can say. But he'll never completely be himself again.

When fury overcomes him, it distorts his face exactly like Niklas's when Niklas was three: the same knitted eyebrows, the same hollow in his cheeks; the same quiver in the skin and arch to the lower lip. And now Frederik's fits of rage are rubbing off on Niklas. The pettiest things set them off. They yell at each other and slam doors throughout the house, two spitting images divided by thirty-two years and an unforeseeably complex brain operation, while I run around after them trying to calm Niklas down. The only one who mustn't get angry is me. If I succumb, everything will fall apart.

...

My first meeting with the support group for spouses of people with brain injuries was supposed to take place at the house of someone called Kirsten. But her husband was rehospitalized this morning, so at the last minute the meeting was moved.

At Gerda's apartment, the scent of sugar and vanilla hangs in the air; she's baked cookies. We squeeze in around her dining room table. Six women, five of them looking at least twenty years older than me, and a single lean, grey-haired man.

The thermostat has been turned up for old ladies' bones. The furniture consists of antique reproductions in dark wood, and atop a high vitrine there perches a stuffed condor with outspread wings. Gerda warned me about the condor on the phone earlier today. "Don't be alarmed. When new guests come for the first time, they often find it unsettling, but my husband purchased it from a good friend before we got married."

Gerda is retired, and she had plenty of time to talk on the phone. "We argued about that foul monstrosity for almost fifty years. Now he doesn't give a fig about it! I could throw the bird away, or our vacation slides, or whatever. He just isn't attached to anything anymore."

Beneath a row of commemorative Christmas plates and the condor's shabby, dust-colored feathers, we wait for the last participant to show. The meeting hasn't started yet and the rest of the people laugh and chatter, exclaiming about how glad they are to see each other. They ask me about Frederik, and already we're talking in a way that's markedly different from the way I speak with my friends. This is what I've been yearning for. But I begin to shiver, even in this overheated apartment. Suddenly I feel this is my last chance to escape.

The woman to one side of me is a stout lady in her mid-sixties. If she's wearing a bra under her loose rust-colored blouse, it's not providing her with much support.

"You can say anything you want here!" she says, her voice rising with excitement. "Everything is permitted. There are so many emotions that can be understood only by someone who lives with a victim of brain damage. Your intense anger—which you might direct at the wrong person completely. Your grief—which you have to learn to live with. Your—"

"Ulla!" says the woman on my other side, interrupting her. "Do give Mia a chance to experience it herself."

"All right, all right, I will. You should just know that here, you can be utterly frank. Utterly! That's the way we are."

When I talked on the phone last week to Kirsten, she took her time too, relating the medical history of every group member's partner. Yet their tragedies all ran together in my mind. There are just two people I recognize from her descriptions. One is the only woman younger than me, Andrea, who's in her mid-thirties and skinny, with a blond pageboy. I know she has a PhD in marine biology and two small children, and her husband fell down a mountainside while climbing in Norway a year and a half ago. Now he speaks with difficulty, has disturbing nightmares every night, and is paralyzed from the waist down.

The other one I remember is the grey-haired man, who's one of two men in the group. I don't understand why he looks so old, because he should be my age. He's French, his name is Bernard, and he was in a car accident with his Danish wife eight years ago. Now she's in a wheelchair and goes to a day-care center for handicapped people while he's at work. They have twin boys Niklas's age, so Kirsten thought we might have a lot to compare notes about.

Why this strong impulse to run away, flee?

The last woman arrives. Everybody's been asking about the hospitalization of Kirsten's husband, and complimenting Gerda on her cookies. Now we can begin. Soon I'm telling about my life in the four months since Frederik's operation.

I feel so cheated when I tell about it. Cheated of a life. My coworkers and friends have lives; everyone has a life.

The others in the group can see that I'm not able to say anything more, and the woman at one end of the table takes over. Her husband suffers from what I've learned is called *neglect*. He doesn't see the left half of anything. And it's not that there's anything wrong with his vision. In the first weeks after his stroke, he only ate the food on the right side of his plate and was constantly crashing into furniture and other things on his left side. It's still impossible for her to watch TV with him, because he doesn't grasp everything that happens on the left side of the screen.

Late one night when I was a little girl in Fredericia, I saw a film for grown-ups on our black-and-white TV. Dark grainy images set in colonial

India. Some eminent man had died, and everyone expected his wife to accompany the corpse onto the pyre and be burned alive, in accordance with local custom. Her friends, her immediate family, everyone gathered around the pyre, staring at her in the night. Often now I see images from that night in my mind: I'm sitting on the sofa, my parents elsewhere. The faces, the darkness, the flames in black and white, and the snowy static on the old screen; the row of large dark Indian eyes. She climbs up on the pyre. Her husband's family sets fire to it. She screams for a long time. And she dies.

I have a desire to hit someone. I want to hit the woman who came to our meeting late, I want to hit another woman for the way she spreads her lips and takes tiny bites from her cookies, so that everyone hears each crunch. I want to hit Bernard because he sits in his chair so unperturbed, with such masculine self-assurance. I want to smash the nasty condor.

Now another group member is talking, about her husband's problems with food falling from his mouth when he eats.

This cannot be happening to me. I am young and play tennis and have a house in Farum. The others here must be full of fury too, but I just don't see it. How do they do it? How do they excise the rage from their lives?

One by one I examine them. The weathered faces, the paintings on the wall, the vitrine and more faces, the mildness there; Gerda taking one of her cookies and quietly biting into it, holding the dry unbroken half before her where her eyes can bring it into focus and inspect it, then smiling softly and eating the rest; Andrea's little pursed-up mouth, her tired eyes.

And then I see it. I see what distinguishes these women from the others I know.

They've effaced their sexuality. They've climbed onto the pyre, they've burned away their flesh. And Andrea's the scariest of them all—so much younger than I but with those thin lips, the way she cowers, the way she looks as if no one loves her. As if she's resigned herself to never being loved again.

And I look at Bernard. Eight years with a woman who goes to a handicapped center? Can a man stand it? Men aren't the same as we are when it comes to sex.

Does it really suit him? His firm flesh, his short grey hair. Does he get a kick from having complete control over her? Sexually? Is he some sort of sick bastard?

His muscles are working beneath the skin of his jaw. A handsome man yet with something wolfish about him—and it isn't just the well-trained body and the grey hair on such a young man. He hasn't climbed onto any pyre, that's for sure.

A woman at the other end of the table is saying, "Could we go around and each say something about guilt feelings? For instance, I know there's no way I could have prevented Steffen from having a stroke, but it doesn't feel that way. Especially when I think about our kids; I ought to have made sure it didn't happen."

Ulla leans over so that her hanging breasts brush against the tabletop. "I feel that way a lot! I ought to have kept their father healthy. It doesn't make sense." She glances at Bernard. "And my kids are thirty-eight and thirty-six. What if they still lived at home?"

Against my will, I find myself getting to my feet.

"I can't imagine how you manage it," I say. "It's truly impressive. And year after year."

I don't give them time to reply, and I can hear I'm talking too fast. "What all of you put up with is much harder than what I have to. I'm not as strong as you . . . so maybe it's me who . . . I don't know if I ought to be here, I think I need to leave."

I bend down to the table and slide my cup over so that it stands in front of my chair, precisely in the middle, as if I'm tidying up on my way out. Andrea looks up at me with her small pale eyes and says, "But my husband is still himself, Mia. That's the difference. That's the huge difference."

I manage neither to sit down nor to leave the table.

She continues, "My husband is still the man I've always loved, the same laughter and interests. He just has some problems now. Your situation is much more difficult. It's totally natural that you think it's hard!"

"More difficult? Yes, but when I hear about you . . . the wheelchair, the two small children!"

"*Your* husband's injury makes it so you no longer know who you're sacrificing yourself for. *That's* hard!"

My body got up without my deciding to, and now it's on its way to the door, about to burst into tears without me having control over anything at all.

"I think you're right, Mia," I hear Bernard say behind me. "You *aren't* like us. It's obvious that your husband isn't nearly as sick as our spouses."

Such a weird thing to say. *You aren't like us.* No one's told me anything like that since I was a schoolgirl. But now I suppose I should understand the words as something positive. I turn toward him.

"No I'm not. He's not so very sick."

He gives me a reassuring smile, almost like Frederik or my father-in-law. "But that's why you might find it interesting to hear about our very different experiences."

"Yes," I say, "I might. And Frederik's going to get better, of course."

"Exactly. He might make a lot of progress in the coming months."

I'm trembling, yet when I look at my hand, it isn't shaking. And I feel something gnaw at me deep inside, far down in my abdomen, just like the cramps that used to plague me as a teenager. I never figured out if it was due to the mechanics of puberty, or to everything from my mother that I had to put up with—or being terribly infatuated with a boy two grades above me.

At last my body begins to return to my chair. The group waits, considerate and curious, while I seat myself.

"The first meeting can sometimes be a little overwhelming," says a woman whose husband used to be a department head in the Ministry of Justice. Earlier she was explaining how he's been stealing trash and odd items from the neighborhood and putting them into big piles in their yard.

And several members repeat what Bernard said, which they now understand is what I really want to hear. *Your husband isn't like our husbands.*

"Thank you. I'd really like to stay. You have a fantastic group here. I don't know what happened . . ."

We grow quiet. We drink from our coffee cups and look at one another.

"Thanks for urging me to stay," I say—not to Bernard, but to Gerda. "You should just keep going."

A short while later, Gerda receives a call from Kirsten in the hospital. We try to listen in, and soon we understand that something's gone well.

Gerda takes the handset from her ear and tells us that Kirsten's husband is now in stable condition; it was a much smaller stroke than the last one. It's a terrible setback for his rehabilitation, but he survived.

"Congratulations!" we all shout in chorus to Kirsten on the phone.

After Gerda's hung up, she slumps in her chair. "Kirsten's greatly relieved," she says. "Both of them are." She tells us in detail what Kirsten said, and then she goes out to the kitchen to put on some more coffee.

We talk among ourselves. Through the even murmur of voices, I distinctly hear Ulla say, in a subdued voice to the woman who feels guilty toward her adult children, "It would have been better if Kirsten's husband had died this time."

Can you say that? Am I the only one who heard it?

A quick ripple of unease passes around the table. Andrea raises her voice, so that even Gerda out in the kitchen will be able to hear her. "Ulla, how'd you feel if someone said that about *your* husband?"

Ulla gazes at her with vague, tranquil eyes. She shrugs her shoulders and says nothing.

Glancing back and forth, everyone's eyes meet, and now I see a warmth in their faces that I've had a hard time seeing in anyone's for a long time. There it is: warmth. I can feel it. We smile controlled, crooked smiles that are anything but merry.

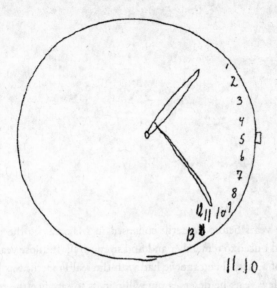

Figure 8.3. A common test for neglect, in which the subject is asked to place numerals and hands on a clockface. The test shown here reveals pronounced neglect.

7

The three years before Frederik collapsed in Majorca are the ones that Niklas and I need to remember and find strength in. In those years he was a dream of a man. The time we had with the real Frederik was brief, but for those few years he deserves my willingness to sacrifice the rest of my life in caring for him.

We spent extended weekends in Budapest, Prague, and Vienna, sometimes with Niklas, other times just the two of us. We repaired the roof on the house by ourselves, sitting up there with our safety lines tied to the chimney, him so funny and happy while the house and the yard and the other fine homes of Farum lay spread out beneath us. Together we chose new plants for the yard, so that the blooms would be better distributed over the course of the summer. And we redecorated the bathroom, building a large shower stall that we inaugurated twice in one evening while Niklas was sleeping at a friend's. It felt strange to fall so wildly in love with my husband again, after so many years of feeling cheated.

Even after spending one entire summer Saturday alone together, we found ourselves slipping away from a garden party at a neighbor's because the other guests bored us and we would rather spend a few more hours by ourselves. We ran back to our yard and sat in the hanging sofa that had become our special place. We opened our own bottle of wine, and there we sat and watched the pale blue summer sky turn slowly to night. Beneath us, the gentle swing of the sofa. I took off my shoes and sat with my legs tucked up. We looked up at the outermost twigs of the apple tree. Gazed at each other and our small yard.

We had created everything here. It was good. Niklas and the house and yard and each other, our whole life together. Because we had stuck it out, because our love was strong enough.

And when it became full dark that night, we went up to our room and made love, still taken with each other and how lovely life could be.

Yet even more important than the marvelous days I enjoyed with Frederik, again and again, was the fact that Frederik began to cultivate a relationship with Niklas. During the bad years, we'd had a recurring quarrel about him not spending enough time with our son. It was one thing that he'd quit being with me, but he'd damn well better not quit on Niklas.

That all stopped. Occasionally the two of them would sit in the living room until late at night, listening to Frederik's large collection of old classical LPs. Perhaps they had deep discussions those nights, though probably not—that's no doubt just my own fantasy of how it must be to hang out with a dad you've seen all too little of. For them I suppose it sufficed merely to be in the living room together, listening to music.

At times I even felt that Frederik went over the top in his enthusiasm for Niklas—like the time a consultant from the Ministry of Education visited Saxtorph and happened to mention that down in his car he had a professional-quality camera with extra lenses, and that he was going to sell it all on the web.

The present that Frederik brought ecstatically home for Niklas was worth more than several years of Christmas and birthday gifts put together. We argued about it. Yet now I can see that, as usual, Frederik was right. Niklas had started to become interested in photography, it was a gift that might change his life, and it was a good deal from a seller whom Frederik could trust.

...

It's after eleven, and I'm beat after the long evening with the support group and, before that, a long day at my school. But I'm glad to have met these people, for now I feel there's someone I can talk to who understands. And that changes everything.

I park in front of our house, and even before I've turned off the ignition,

I notice an orange glare from the lawn. I rush over and find the remains of a campfire still glowing a few yards from the house. I stamp out the largest of the embers close to the house, then storm in the front door.

"Niklas!"

He comes out of the living room, a confused look on his face. "Yes?"

"Who lit the fire on our lawn?"

"Mathias and I found some branches on the sidewalk. I asked Dad, and he said we could."

"But you can't just light a fire in the yard! What were you thinking? The entire house could have gone up in flames, and now the lawn is ruined!"

My hand passes close to his face as I hang my coat on the hook behind him.

"And you know very well that it doesn't matter what Dad says you can do!"

"Yes, but I wanted to take some pictures, and he said as long as we were careful."

I proceed to the living room. "Why did you say Niklas could burn up the yard?"

There's an auto race on TV. Frederik lies on the sofa watching it with the sound cranked up way too high. On the rug there is a clump of pillows where Niklas must have been lying and watching with him.

Frederik knits his brows, trying to think of what to tell me. But I only ask him from force of habit. It means absolutely nothing anymore.

Rather than wait for an answer, I turn back to the narrow entry to change into my slippers, squeezing past Niklas on the way.

"You *knew* that wasn't okay," I say.

No response. I take a few deep breaths, and I consider that it ended all right after all. The house hasn't burned down, and in a little while I'll go out and extinguish the last embers. But now I see that my boots have toppled over, and when I pick them up, one seems oddly heavy. I turn it upside down, and a large salad onion tumbles out.

Back to the living room. "Why's there an onion in my boot?"

Niklas is lying back down on the rug, his eyes glued to the set as he answers. "We had an onion fight."

"An onion fight? You mean that you and Dad ran around after each other throwing onions?"

"Yeah."

"But you can't just do that!" I shout, though in reality I'm relieved they've found a way to have fun together. A day of onion fights and fires in the yard is a hundred times better than the life I feared of having to be his nursemaid.

I have to force myself not to laugh. "Did you break anything?"

"Just a vase."

"Just a vase! There's no such thing as 'just a vase'!"

"It was Dad who started it," he says, still following the race.

"No, it was him!" Frederik shouts, and at last they both look at me.

I can't hold it in anymore. I splutter with laughter, and they start laughing too. I go over to Frederik and try to kiss him on the forehead, but he turns his face away. It's like trying to kiss a ten-year-old boy—he doesn't like it or see any point in it.

"I swept up the pieces," Niklas says. "And besides, it *was* him."

"Good. It's good that it's only one vase that broke. Which one was it?"

"The little green one."

"That's okay. You got all the shards, right?"

"Yeah."

Against the noise from the cars on TV, I go out and mix myself a big glass of black-currant juice, the way Niklas likes it. Glass in hand, I stand by the end of the sofa where Frederik's legs are and prepare to sit down. But he doesn't move them, and several seconds pass before I remember that I have to ask. "Frederik. Would you kindly move your feet, so I can sit down too?"

"Oh yes, of course."

Then I sit down and watch the race. In the old days I would have thought *with my two men*, but tonight I think *with my two boys*.

I listen to how they sigh with irritation or satisfaction, and after a bit I ask, "Are we rooting for the yellow?"

"Yes," they both say.

I swing my feet up on our small Ole Wanscher coffee table, not caring whether I make any scratches. I sip my juice and cheer the yellow car on. We're almost a real family again—except that a sex life is out of the question, and my husband doesn't care what I think or feel. I say to myself,

Just like lots of other families. Again I chuckle to myself, thinking I should remember to pass the joke on to Helena.

And I can be happy, I think. I'm happy now. And if I can be happy now, then anything's possible—for then I can be happy other times too.

I slip off to our bedroom, to call Helena and thank her for pushing me to go to the support group. It's changed everything. I know it's okay to call, even though it's almost midnight.

I lift the receiver, but there's no dial tone. I see at once that someone's pulled the cord from the jack. With vague unease I decide to wait with the call and go instead back to the living room.

"What happened to the phone?"

Neither of them replies, and now I see that the cords have been taken out of both the answering machine and the living room phone. I stand there waving the two phone lines.

"Frederik, what's this all about?"

He keeps looking at the TV.

"Frederik!"

He looks up for a moment. "Well, Laust kept on calling, and I didn't want to talk to him."

I know right away that something is very wrong, and hurry out to my bag where my cell phone is. I set it on mute during support group. There are five messages from Laust.

"Mia, will you call me?"

"Mia, it's urgent that you call me!"

"Mia, pick up the phone, damn it! What's wrong with you all?"

"What the hell's going on? Are you mixed up in this too, Mia?"

"You've ruined us, haven't you. And Mia, don't try to tell me you aren't involved!"

I run upstairs, shut the door, and call him.

He's furious and won't talk to me.

"But why were you calling us then?"

"I couldn't get myself to believe it about you. But then Benny showed me the documents. There's no other way to understand it."

"No other way to understand *what*?"

"You *know* what!"

"No."

"Frederik didn't bring home an extra twelve million crowns without you noticing and buying a few pieces of designer furniture or whatever it was?"

"Twelve *million*?" I let myself fall on the bed. "I'm coming over to your house now."

"No. Anja's sleeping, and she doesn't know anything."

"Where are you?"

"Where Frederik keeps the ledgers."

"Then I'm driving over to the school!"

I hang up.

In the living room I pull Frederik away from the TV so that Niklas can't hear us. Niklas doesn't even look up, he's so used to me dragging his father off.

Up in the bedroom, Frederik denies everything. He insists that he knows nothing. I grasp him by the shoulders and look into his eyes, probingly.

"Can I trust you?"

"Yes." He looks back at me with large wide eyes that show not a trace of bad conscience.

"One hundred percent? Can I trust you one hundred percent?"

"Yes."

But I know that I can't. He's discovered how ridiculously good he is at lying now and he does it constantly, completely unfazed by the fact that I usually find him out a short time later.

...

I taught six classes today, went to school meetings all afternoon while Niklas promised to keep an eye on Frederik, had an intense but good session with my new support group, and came home to the remains of a fire still burning in my yard. Now it's quarter to one, and I have no clue when my day will end.

At Saxtorph I enter the alarm code and unlock the front door. On countless late evenings, I've walked down these long corridors in half

61

darkness. When I was in Copenhagen anyway and wanted a bit of extra time with Frederik, I'd stop by so we could follow each other home. Often I ran into Laust, and sometimes Morten, the deputy headmaster, and once in a while we sat with Frederik at the conference table in his office and ate leftovers from the cafeteria, drinking red wine and kicking back after one of their fourteen-hour workdays.

Now I open the dark mahogany door to his office and see Laust, Morten, and the school's accountant, Benny, standing around stacks of papers spread out across the big conference table. On the walls hang the usual gloomy portraits in oil, some of them Laust's forebears.

Laust catches sight of me. He shouts at me in a strange, shrill voice, "The school's bankrupt! The teachers have to be fired, we have to sell the buildings, we're *finished*! Happy now?"

"What?"

"You helped him! There's no way he could have done it alone!"

"What?"

"There had to be more than one person down at the bank."

"I have no idea what you're talking about."

He keeps shouting, and I don't know how to get through to him.

"I have no idea what you're talking about! I have no idea what you're talking about! I have no idea what you're talking about!"

But nothing can penetrate Laust's hysteria, and at last I raise the bust of Gustav Saxtorph from the sideboard to smash it down on the table.

"Don't you touch that bust!" Laust screams. He flings himself at me, trying to tear it away. I drop it and parry his attack so that he lands on the floor. It isn't a hard fall, and he should be able to get right up. But he keeps lying there, fingers scrabbling against the smooth floorboards.

Morten squats by his side. I'd like to help too, but first I turn to the accountant. "Benny, just tell me what's going on. I don't have a clue."

"Frederik has had the school stand surety for loans worth twelve million crowns."

"But he can't have!"

"If there's anyone who can, it's him."

"But there must be some sort of misunderstanding. You know that Frederik could have never done such a thing. It's somebody else, or a misunderstanding. It's a misunderstanding, right?"

"Mia, there's definitely no misunderstanding. And you know that all too well."

My thoughts are racing. *Could* he have done it? I no longer know who he is. But that much money?

Yet right away I know how it could have all vanished. On a vacation in Portugal once, we went into a casino. Frederik just wanted to try. I got him out again, but not before the fierce concentration in his face had made me afraid.

"I don't believe it," I say. "I've installed passwords on the phones and the computer. And how could he have gotten to the bank by himself? It doesn't make sense."

I crouch down next to Laust, who's still on the floor.

"Laust," I say. "I'm sorry about the bust, Laust. It wasn't on purpose." I try to shoot Morten a worried look, but he won't meet my eyes.

Above my head I hear Benny's voice. "But he did this all *before* he became ill. It began more than a year ago."

I get up so quickly that I momentarily lose my balance. "A year ago?"

"Yes."

"Not a year ago."

"I said 'a year ago.'"

"Yes, but you all know that he . . . But back then he was himself!"

Morten gets up too, and he places himself next to the accountant.

"The papers are all here. Benny's uncovered everything."

I have the odd sensation that it's me who's lying on the floor grasping after something, while Laust is standing up with the other men.

"Yes, but you know Frederik. He wouldn't do something like that. Not the real Frederik."

"We *thought* we knew Frederik. And we thought we knew *you*."

I feel as if whatever's pressing me against the floor has grown heavier now. As if I'm scrabbling even more frantically on the floorboards.

"God damn it, I'm disappointed in you!" I yell. "Right now, when Frederik needs you more than ever, you make up a story like this! How the hell do you know it's Frederik if the signatures have been forged anyway?"

"It required a special kind of genius for accounting, what he did," says Benny. "I don't know anyone besides Frederik who . . ."

Laust starts to get up. It feels strange, because in some way it really felt

63

like it was me who was lying down there. I have an urge to kick him so that he falls back down.

I say, "If there's one person you can trust, it's Frederik. Everybody knows that! You know it too."

One corner of Morten's mouth begins to twitch. "Is that what you said when he was with Gitte and Dorte?"

I slam the door behind me, and after a couple of steps down the hallway I break into a run.

...

The lights are off in the house, so Niklas and Frederik must have gone to bed. The fire on the lawn has burned out, leaving only a black circle behind.

I let myself in and sit down on the bed next to Frederik, who's sleeping heavily. When he's lying like this, I can see bits of the long narrow scar that runs beneath his hair in a half-moon. My index finger gently traces its course. The real Frederik would have been so disappointed in Laust. We would have held each other, figured out a plan, come up with an explanation. We would have done it together. But the real Frederik isn't here now, no matter how long I talk to the body in this bed, no matter how long I try to hold it or to rest my head on its shoulder.

Driving home on the freeway, I hit on the only possible explanation: that it's all something to do with his employment contract. They want to fire him, and they can't while he's on sick leave. So they came up with this. On the other hand, Laust wasn't acting, and could Morten and Benny really have staged the whole thing behind his back? I run through all the possibilities, then I discard them. There must be something I don't know.

"*Frederik,*" I say, very loud.

I am almost shouting.

"Frederik, something's happened. Frederik! *Frederik!*"

He doesn't wake up.

I shake him by the shoulder; no reaction. I don't want to risk jarring his head, so I go down to the foot of the bed and start shaking one of his legs hard.

Slowly he comes to life.

"Whaaat?" he says with a plaintive moan. It's the way he sounded at the neurointensive clinic; our week there, the despair we felt, Niklas locking himself in the handicapped toilet, and back home Vibeke taking to her bed. It's terrible, every time he wakes up with that voice. The limp crackers in the visitors' kitchen; the distant round eyes of the other patients' relatives.

I try to make him understand what Laust, Morten, and Benny said.

"It wasn't me." He sighs.

"No, I know that." I sit down again on the edge of the bed next to his head; his eyes are still closed.

"It's all your doing." He groans.

"What?"

"The two of you."

"Who?"

"You and Niklas."

"How could we have done anything?"

"You said I couldn't use the computers. So the school lost the money."

"What the hell are you talking about?"

"You installed passwords on the computers."

I thought that our drive through the Majorcan mountains had been the major turning point in my life. The day everything disappeared. But I was wrong.

I don't yet know what happened, but I have a premonition that today'll be the day Frederik's exposed as the headmaster who destroyed Saxtorph Private School. The day we lose the friends who've supported us. The day we lose our house and jobs. Everything. Today.

He wakes up enough that I can get him to sit up in bed. And slowly he tells me what I tentatively have to accept as true.

Frederik secretly borrowed money from the school's accounts to gamble on international commodity indexes. Of course he was going to repay it, but then he lost a few hundred thousand crowns when copper slumped and coffee spiked. He took more money so that he could recoup the school's losses. He set up three private firms to siphon the money away from the school in a series of obscure transactions, falsifying documents and sureties and signatures. He lost even more money. And it just grew worse.

65

"I would have gotten everything back again and earned millions, both for us and the school. There's no question. It's only because Laust shut me out. It's only because you installed passwords on the computers. It's your fault."

There's no way the real Frederik could have embezzled from Saxtorph; it goes against everything he stands for. The tumor had been growing slowly, which the doctors say is normal. Already a year ago it must've been changing his personality. Before it occurred to anyone that he'd become somebody else—and that's normal too, the doctors say.

Laust is still awake when I call.

I apologize, as emphatically as I apologized to Niklas when my stomach was pumped out. More than I apologized any other time ever. I start crying for the school and hope he will cry with me. But he's silent.

"I'm your friend, Laust! I knew nothing! Nothing! We must be able to find some of the money in his accounts, maybe coffee prices have fallen since then—or copper gone up—whatever it needs to be. There has to be something! Some way or another. I'll do *anything* I can to help you."

Laust continues to say nothing.

"I really understand if you're angry with him," I say. "I get angry with him a lot too. And then I forget that it's the illness. That's what it must've been back then too. It's the illness and not Frederik himself that dictates how he acts."

Still saying nothing, Laust hangs up the phone.

8

I'm lying on the air mattress at the foot of our bed. The streetlight through the trees casts a glowing pattern on the bedroom ceiling. The tree branches vibrate and the pattern comes to life: the sign's the same as the one in the embers on the front lawn.

Thus are we branded everywhere; thus will healthy people walking down the street know not to stop. Here live the sick people. Enter a house marked with this sign, and you renounce all claim to protection and safety. Expect no help if the poor devils savage you and tear you to pieces.

Before I lay down, I decided I wouldn't wake Niklas, but after I stare at the sign on the ceiling for a couple of hours, I realize I was wrong: his future's at stake. Will his father go to jail? Will we have to sell the only house he's known? Will the papers call his father a swindler?

I pull on a pair of sweatpants. I knock on his door but he doesn't wake up. I go in and sit on the edge of the bed, whisper his name.

"Niklas. *Niklas.*"

He sits up with a start, and I touch his arm.

"Nothing's happened, Niklas. Easy now, quiet; nothing's happened."

This is the worst part: telling Niklas. Because now I have to say it.

"Or actually something has, Niklas. Something *has* happened."

His pale face; the streetlight's glowing sign on his cheek.

"It's Dad," I say.

"What? Is he dead?"

"No, he's . . . they say at the school that he . . ." And I tell him what I know.

"I don't believe it!" he exclaims, with the same conviction I had. He lets himself fall back on the bed.

"I didn't believe it either," I say.

It takes but an instant for all the thoughts I have when I talk with him to run through my head: Niklas as an old man, grey-haired and distinguished, perhaps a headmaster, perhaps minister of education, in a suit; Niklas as a baby on the changing table, peeing up in the air with his tiny penis, so I have to dry him and table both; Niklas running around in the yard playing with a wheelbarrow; Niklas's photos on exhibit in the gymnasium library and us so proud.

"But Dad's confessed," I continue. "And they think I'm involved too."

"Confessed? You?" He sits up again.

They aren't so much thoughts as glimpses, and not individual glimpses so much as a state of mind: he falls on his bike, scrapes his smooth little knees; he plays in the sand on the beach.

"Yes. So the police will probably question us tomorrow," I say.

"Yeah but of course you guys haven't . . . of course *you* haven't—"

"*I* haven't done anything. And Dad only did it because he was sick. The police will understand that, and so will Laust, when he's no longer so angry."

The air in here is warm and pungent—and the room's a terrible mess, something I've stopped commenting on. In the darkness, I see something catch the light in his pile of dirty clothes; from here it looks like a bra. A white, almost luminous bra among the worn jeans and shirts. I can't go any closer to be sure.

"You have to stop now, damn it!" he shouts. "Don't you two ever think of me? You keep doing one crazy thing after the other!"

I must accept his anger, I tell myself. I have to give his emotions room.

"Of course I think of you. All the time. And I'll do anything. You just have to—"

"You don't think of me at all, and that's the truth! Both of you have gone totally whack!"

Room for his anger. It's a state of mind: he's overnighting at a friend's for the first time, but at midnight the parents call, they say he's crying, and I drive over to get him. His first year of gymnasium, and two girls and a boy from his new homeroom wait for him out on the street, they're going to the beach with mats and a cooler bag.

"Niklas, you know it isn't me who embezzled from anyone. I haven't done anything."

"But you're the one I can never trust!"

I tell myself that it's important not to yell. I answer him calmly.

"You can trust me now, Niklas. Now."

"The hell I could! You're the one who should have been watching out! You! That's what you should have done!"

I don't say *Watch out for what?* I say, "I can understand this is hard for you, Niklas."

"Shut the fuck up! You don't hear one single . . ." He shouts, "Get out!"

And that, finally, is what I do.

Alone in the kitchen, I feel good about letting him give his emotions free rein. I can take it. A glimpse, a state, his little hand in mine as I walk him home from first grade.

Maybe I'll be able to get a little sleep tonight if I eat something heavy. The best thing now would be some cold oatmeal with skim milk and banana. I look down into my meal. The color of ghosts, I think, of something unreal: semen.

...

When I open the front door for them, I feel oddly relaxed. I know it's not the real Frederik they're coming for. And it's as if it isn't the real me who invites them in either.

The two polite young men walk into the living room, where Frederik is sitting at the dinner table, reading from a stack of advertising circulars.

"Frederik Halling?" one of them asks. "It is 10:15 a.m. You are hereby under arrest, charged with embezzlement and falsification of documents. It would be best if you remained seated while we go through the house."

Frederik says nothing and, equally silent, I sit down in the chair next to him and hold his hand.

After listening to the front door open and shut a couple of times, I can hear the policemen rummaging around in Frederik's office. I get up and go in there. His computer lies in a moving box with a pile of DVDs and two external hard drives. The officers put files and folders and all kinds of papers into boxes, while they allow me to stand there and watch.

An hour later, they turn their attention to Frederik again.

"Now then, sir. We would like to ask you to accompany us to the station."

Frederik gets up, and I put some crackers and apples in my bag. I put on my coat and am ready to go when the first officer says, "Sorry, ma'am, you can't come with. Only Mr. Halling."

"But Officer, they think I helped embezzle the funds. They've accused me too."

"We don't know anything about that."

The second policeman takes over. "We suggest you wait here at home. Later today, we'll call and tell you whether he's going directly to jail."

"Directly to jail?"

"Yes ma'am. With a charge like this, one doesn't go home to sleep."

Something breaks inside of me. I see Frederik in a fight with other inmates; I see him attacking policemen in an uncontrollable burst of anger and being beaten with batons.

"But he's *sick*! His brain is sick! I have to come. You don't know how to talk to him."

"Sorry, ma'am."

"But you don't understand! He gets fits of anger, he'll start hitting you!"

"We're sorry."

"You can't just do this, the man isn't well! You'll end up having to charge him for assaulting an officer!"

"Ma'am, it can't get any more serious than it already is."

I make an effort to breathe calmly, but the air comes in long noisy gulps as I plead with them and follow them out to the cruiser. They won't budge. Meanwhile Frederik sits peacefully in the car, looking blankly at the seat in front of him and eating the package of crackers I gave him.

As soon as they've driven off, I run into the house and call Laust, who doesn't answer. I leave a message on his machine about him being a psychopath who's killing his best friend.

I call Helena, but she doesn't pick up either.

I call Thorkild and Vibeke. They've had time to digest the news, since I already called them this morning at half past six. Vibeke answers and hands the phone to Thorkild.

"You need a lawyer," he says.

Of course we do. I call Gerda from the support group and ask if anyone in the group knows a lawyer who's familiar with brain injuries.

"You should call Bernard," she tells me.

"He knows one?"

"He's a lawyer himself, and in that field he's the best there is."

Bernard's the only member of the group that I didn't feel completely at ease with, but of course I call.

"Your husband has the right to have counsel present during questioning," he says. "The police should have informed you. If you want, I can be at the station in twenty minutes."

"I'd be tremendously grateful if you could do that. He might start hitting people, and he's—"

"Okay. I'll call you later."

I collapse on our bed, but it smells wrong—of Frederik's new smell. I try to rest, but I cannot. So I lie down on the air mattress instead, pull the comforter over my head, and hope I can drift off.

...

Niklas comes home from school early; he skipped his last classes. I tell him I understand, and give him a quick, watered-down version of what happened.

"Are you very upset?" he asks.

"Yes." It feels oddly still here in the entry. "Yes, I am."

"But not as upset as . . . that other time?"

"No! Not at all. You don't have to worry about that, I'll never do that again."

He clears his throat. "Is there anything I can do?"

"No, it's not really you who's got to . . . you don't really have to . . ."

It's hard to believe how considerate Niklas can be, especially since he's been on my case so much these past few weeks. Angry about the most trivial things. Now we converse as if he never yelled at me last night, as if he never screamed at me three days ago when his bike lock wouldn't open, or before that, when Frederik put a Danish essay Niklas hadn't turned in yet at the bottom of our pile of already-read newspapers.

71

On the debate forum at braindamage.com, I've read that if Frederik does get better, he'll go back and forth between being affectionate and normal, and being irrationally testy and emotional—"like a teenager," they say. There will be good moments, but they will disappear instantly without warning.

Niklas says, "I could show you my new pictures."

He knows that I love to look at his photos with him. And lately I haven't been allowed to.

I hug him and fetch a chair from Frederik's office so we can sit next to each other in his room.

Whenever Niklas does come home, he sits at his computer and edits pictures and videos. Mathias composes the most unbelievable electronic music, and their latest plan is to project Niklas's photos on a screen above the stage while Mathias's music plays as a warm-up for a concert at the gymnasium.

There's no bra in the laundry pile—I checked while he was in school— nor was there anything else white that might look like a bra in the dark. Niklas quickly exits a bunch of programs as I sit down, and I think I see the name Sara listed as sender in a bunch of chat messages, but they fly by too fast to be sure. I do know who Sara is: she's in Mathias's homeroom, pale with long dark hair and freckles, and she used a lot of bookish phrases during the few moments we spoke at Niklas's sixteenth birthday. He's changed the subject the couple of times I've mentioned her name since then.

Niklas brings up Mathias's latest composition and clicks PLAY. A wave breaks against the coast. It breaks again. And then again. And with each crash, it sounds more and more like a person falling down a flight of stairs. Heavily; she must have broken a bone. The falls—the wave-crashes—come more quickly, a great dance rhythm. A melody wriggles in on a piano, and then the wind on the beach in Sweden.

"Our theme is water," Niklas says, showing me a sequence of enigmatic black-and-white patterns. "What do you think this is?"

"No idea."

"You see something round, don't you?"

"It looks like the entrails of a dead animal," I say, thinking it could be a brain, though I don't want to say that out loud.

"It's a glass of water with ice cubes, with the light playing on it. It was standing on the kitchen counter one day, and I took a whole series."

He goes through the pictures explaining them, almost as if I were a little kid and he were reading to me. As if he were my dad. His hands dart quickly across the keyboard; there's hair growing on them, a thin patch from the base of the pinky to the wrist. Lots of men would fantasize about what Niklas and Sara might be doing with each other. Would dwell needlessly on them in their fascination. That's the way men are: they want youth, they think they can screw themselves younger, or marry themselves younger. Yet no matter how much they humiliate themselves, they're just poor wretches, halfway to death. Just like me . . .

The heat's always incredible in this room. I've got to take off my blouse if I'm not going to sweat too much. The water pours down over the screen and up across the screen and presses against us and disperses like steam. Mathias and Niklas are adults now, they're artists.

I slip into Mathias's sea of sound and Niklas's drenching photos, and my son may be doing the same. When my phone rings, we both start. We would laugh if we weren't so frightened.

9

It's Bernard on the phone: the hearing went well. Frederik wasn't jailed after all. They're in Bernard's car now, headed home.

Niklas has turned off the music and is watching me expectantly. I tell him what Bernard said, then turn my attention back to Bernard.

"Thank you so very, very much! What did they say, did he lose his temper? How serious are the charges? What did they say about him being sick?"

Surrounded by the sounds of urban traffic, Bernard's voice is composed. "Unfortunately, I can't tell you anything—client confidentiality. Frederik will tell you whatever he chooses to himself. I'm handing him the telephone now."

"Frederik, tell me! How'd it go?"

"It went fine."

"What did they say?"

He doesn't answer.

"Frederik, are you tired? How are you doing?"

"I don't know."

"You're probably real tired now, aren't you?"

Still no answer.

"Isn't there anything you want to tell me about your hearing?"

"I don't know."

"Something, Frederik, just say *something*. Are they planning to take you into custody at a later date? Was Laust there?"

Again he says nothing. Then Bernard gets back on the line.

"A long hearing's always rough; anybody would be exhausted. We'll be back at your house soon."

Niklas and I hurry down the stairs and out to the street, while I describe for him Bernard's word choice and tone of voice. During the course of the afternoon, it's turned into one of the first mild days of spring. The sun's starting to warm everybody up, and our leafy street is just as seductive as the first time Frederik and I met a realtor to look at the house. We stood at precisely the same spot on the sidewalk; the realtor arrived in his red car, a young man, and a few moments later this was the only house I could imagine living in. Now Bernard's white station wagon comes driving toward us, and through the window I can see Frederik sleeping on the passenger side.

We help him out of the car, and he leans on Niklas and me on the way upstairs, where we lay him on the bed, fully dressed. I kiss him on the forehead but get no response, and then we go back down.

Bernard's sitting on the sofa in the living room. Nearly invisible blue pinstripes run along his creased grey trousers; the top buttons of his white Oxford, with its slightly thicker stripes of light blue, are unbuttoned. He is grasping the couch's arm and appears to be studying a seam in the leather. This Wegner sofa was never put into regular production and it's quite rare, my greatest treasure. He must understand furniture.

Niklas and I remain standing. "Bernard, thank you again. I know that they would have kept him in custody for months if you hadn't made some sort of special effort."

He smiles, and I can see I'm right.

"But you can't tell us what you did," I say.

"No."

In a few months, Frederik might be better—nobody knows, but the doctors say it's possible. Yet the legal case is another matter entirely; we'll be stuck with it till we die. None of us will ever be able to *make great strides* or *rehabilitate* our way out of it.

I try again to get Bernard to say just a little bit about what happened, but he deflects my attempts in friendly fashion by talking instead about general case law pertaining to financial fraud—and in this way he manages to tell us about Frederik's case indirectly, without violating confidentiality.

He does so skillfully, thoughtfully, pedagogically. Maybe it's just because he's a seasoned lawyer, but it feels more like his personality, like he's genuinely concerned for Niklas and me.

As Bernard talks, I look around the living room and think about how it must look to an outsider. The speaker drivers have all been unscrewed from the cabinets, leaving behind gaping black holes. Frederik doesn't think our stereo system sounds good enough and wants to repair it, but now the drivers, along with various snipped cords and small brightly colored electronic components, have lain on the carpet for a week. Two posters also lie on the floor because he's been wanting to hang them up but can't decide where, while the shelves with all his classical LPs have been pushed out from the wall because he was going to do something or other with the electrical socket behind them.

"You'll have to excuse the mess," I say.

"I like it; it's homey. And you have remarkable taste in furniture."

"Thank you. What can I offer you? You must be famished after such a day."

"Well . . . yes."

"A sandwich, rolls? Cheese, ham, pâté, jam? Coffee, tea, beer?"

He smiles. "It all sounds great."

I set out rolls and various fixings on the dinner table, along with beer and water. Niklas sets out three plates without asking, but I know I won't be able to eat a thing.

Our lawyer eats in a controlled, almost dainty manner, despite the evident hunger in his eyes. Perhaps he had a strict conservative upbringing in France. After he's eaten the first half of a roll, he carefully finishes chewing and wipes his mouth with a napkin before speaking. "Of course, now you're both completely confused, and you have no idea what's going to happen to Frederik—or to you either."

"Exactly."

"First you need to collect yourselves. In cases involving financial fraud, it takes the police months to get a general overview of all the accounts and set a court date. In the meantime, Frederik has plenty of time to decide on a lawyer."

"But I thought we had you!" My voice rises to the point of shrillness. I glance quickly at Niklas, but apparently he doesn't find me embarrassing today.

Bernard's voice remains calm. "Frederik has to choose his own lawyer. That's critical, even though he's ill. And although I was with him at the hearing today, he might very well choose someone else."

"But you understand brain injuries, and you have experience with such cases, don't you?"

"That's something Frederik will have to judge for himself."

It gives me a brief moment of calm to discuss something so obviously nonsensical. All Frederik's decisions are made by me now. Having him sign his name to anything is just a matter of form.

As he chews, Bernard's jaw muscles move distinctly beneath his skin. It's amazing that his body's so lean and athletic, given his age—but then again, Gerda said he's actually my age, something I keep forgetting.

"Meningiomas grow very slowly," he says. "So Frederik's was definitely present already when the embezzlement started. It may have affected his actions in a way that he couldn't help."

"Of course it was the disease! Everybody knows that he could never have come up with something like this!"

Still the same easy voice. "The question is whether it affected him enough that you can say it was the *disease* making his decisions. In cases involving neurological damage, there is one question that determines everything, a question that family members need to consider right away. Did the personality of the accused change markedly in the period leading up to the crime—whether or not anyone thought it might be due to illness?"

I find myself shouting with relief. "Oh but yes, three years ago he changed radically!"

For the first time, Bernard's composure breaks. "Fantastic! That's utterly crucial! Congratulations!"

"For the first time, Frederik was coming home from work at normal times, for the first time he took the time to—"

I grasp the arms of my chair. Squeeze them tightly and fall silent. And then run from the room.

In the kitchen I stop and lean over the counter, gasping for air, slumped over the outstretched arms that are propping me up. I don't want to cry while Niklas is sitting in the living room with a guest. But I can't help myself.

The best years we've had together. Years that were going to sustain me the rest of my life. Were they just a by-product of a tumor?

Frederik and I walking down the narrow wooded path along Lake Farum, remodeling the house together, cuddling in the yard and sitting up late in the hanging sofa. His high spirits, regardless of what we had to deal with in our respective jobs; his impulsiveness, which was so life-giving after all those years of sense and discipline; the way he horsed around, the way he suddenly relaxed about work obligations. Where'd it all come from?

In the living room, I hear Niklas assume his most adult voice. "It can get to be a little too much for her. It's hard for everyone."

He clearly doesn't understand what I understand. Because our three good years also gave Niklas his father back.

I hear Bernard reply, "That's something we're all allowed to do. After my wife became brain-damaged, I can assure you I had to leave my share of rooms too."

It's strange to hear a sensible adult male talking to Niklas. The calm deep voice and words of wisdom, in contrast with Frederik's prattle. And to hear how Niklas listens. How good for him to be with a healthy man. It seems so long ago that our home was ever like this.

...

I have to lie down. And I can't go into our bedroom, where Frederik is. The only place I can be is Niklas's room. I lie down in his bed with my clothes on, even though maybe that's wrong of me. Pull the comforter up to my nose.

I mull over details from the best years of our marriage. Frederik coming in from the yard barefoot one Sunday morning, he chases me around to tickle me, I run away, both of us laughing until we tumble onto the sofa together. Frederik arriving home from work jubilant after he bought that expensive camera for Niklas on the spur of the moment. They were my memories of the best we've had. What are they now?

Bernard drives away without me going back down and saying goodbye.

A little while later I hear Niklas open the door to the room. My eyes are still closed.

He must be surprised to see me, yet he just comes over to the bed, as if to look down at me. Then in a concerned voice, he asks, "How are you doing?"

I remain prone, eyes closed, in the same position. "I'm sorry, Niklas. I can't go into our room right now."

"I understand."

"You were really great down there. With the lawyer."

"Thanks."

"Is it okay if I lie here for a little while?"

"Of course."

When Niklas wakes me, this time I open my eyes. I can see from the light that I must have slept several hours. He's standing again by the side of the bed. He asks, "Do you think I should stay home tonight?"

"That might be a really good idea. We don't know what's happening. Or what could—"

"It's just that Mathias and I were going to meet at his house about our show. It's actually really important."

I can recall bits and pieces of something I must have dreamt; Frederik riding a dinosaur.

"But of course," I say. "That's what you should do then."

The inside of my mouth feels sticky. I need something to drink, and as soon as I can I need to text the parents of my fourth graders to say our parent meeting tonight is canceled. I should really call our friends too before they hear about Frederik on TV. And we don't have any food in the house.

I don't have the energy to call anyone, but I'm just going to have to slip out to the mini-mart to buy something for supper.

I get up out of bed and check to see that Frederik's still asleep. As I walk from our yard out to the street, wrapped in more clothing than I perhaps need, I discover Niklas's friend Sara. She's standing a few yards from me, almost hidden beside the neighbor's hedge, busy peering at something on her cell phone.

I'm exhausted, but I pull myself together for a smile.

"Hi," I say. "Do you want to come in? He's home."

She looks almost alarmed. "I was actually . . . I'll just wait out here."

"Well, he's heading over to Mathias's."

"Yeah, I'm going over there too."

"So you make photo and sound shows too?" I ask.

"Nah, we're just going to hang out."

Niklas calls out from his window, behind me. "Stay right there! I'm coming down!"

I call back up to the window. "Niklas, you're welcome to invite Sara up to your room!"

Immediately she loses all interest in her phone. "*Sara?* You thought I was *Sara?*"

"What? No, not at all! I don't even know who Sara is!"

"Has Sara been here?"

"No! Nobody's been here."

I wince under the weight of her probing gaze, as if *I* were the teenage girl and she the grown-up. "There hasn't been *anyone* called Sara," I say a little too quickly, feeling as though I'm still waking up. I add, "You can go inside if you like. Until he's ready."

"We actually agreed . . . I think instead, I should . . ."

The front door opens and Frederik comes out. He looks fresh and cheerful again. Fresh and cheerful, as he pretty much always is, regardless of whatever he may have left in ruins around him. He looks like a man who's just gotten a big raise.

"This is Niklas's friend," I say.

Frederik smiles happily. "*Damn* you look good. To think that you're Niklas's friend. I've got to hand it to him!"

"We're on the social committee together."

He reaches out to touch her arm. "I'd really like to get inside your pussy!"

I slap his hand away. "*Frederik!*"

He snaps at me. "But it's something she should be proud and happy to hear—that men want to get inside her pussy."

"Stop it! Just stop it!"

Niklas comes storming out of the house and immediately sees his friend's face. "What's going on here?"

"I think you two should leave," I say. "Go now, and I'll get him inside."

Niklas and the girl who isn't Sara hurry off. Frederik and I yell at each other. Then I run into the house, and he follows me in so he can keep arguing with me.

Once we're inside, and the neighbors can no longer see us, I throw him facedown to the living room floor, where I straddle his lower back and pin his arms.

"You big piece of shit!" he shouts again and again. "Big piece of shit!"

He thrashes around so much that he bangs his shinbones against the doorframe and knocks over a lamp, and I can see blood soaking through one of his trouser legs.

"Shut up, God damn it!" I shout, struggling to hold him down on the floor.

He succeeds in twisting a hand free, which allows him to pinch me hard on the thigh. I grab the little stainless-steel bowl standing on the coffee table and hammer it down on his back so that he roars in pain.

Who the hell is he, this strange man who's broken into my house? Who's invaded my husband's body, his head?

Once I strike him I can't stop. I bang the bowl down on his back again and again while he writhes and yells that it hurts, that I'm a piece of shit.

I stop to catch my breath. *I cannot live with a man like this*, I think, waiting for him to settle down. *There's no way anyone can expect me to. There's just no way.*

Beneath me, his body grows tired and limp. I've still got him pinioned down when he begins to speak, in a sad voice that I haven't heard since he became sick.

"The words just rushed out," he says. "I knew I shouldn't say something like that to her. I can't understand why I did."

I let go immediately. For he sounds like the real Frederik. The "voice" is gone. I want to help my poor husband, I want to lift him up. Who is he now? Has he been set free?

We stand in the middle of the floor. The room grows bright, and it feels as if all the anger was flushed from my body after I hit him. I'm appalled that I could have done that. *A sick man. A poor sick man.*

I can't stand to look him in the eye. Instead I glance around, trying to find the best place to sit him down.

"Well, it's certainly good that you know it's wrong," I say.

"I do know. It's utterly, utterly wrong!"

His eyes are desperate, and opened wide. As if he's just this moment discovering who he's become, and everything he's done these past months.

"It's utterly, utterly wrong! Utterly, utterly, utterly!" Suddenly he's shouting. "It's awful! Why do I say such things?" And he's crying at the same time, so that tears or snot gets caught in his windpipe and he starts coughing as he shouts. "Why do I do it?"

In seconds his cheeks are sopping wet. He's no longer a human being; more like some animal that bellows. A long-limbed, bony animal. He's a moose, standing alone in the forest and bellowing its grief.

"Too awful! Too awful! I don't know why I say those things!"

"No, you don't know why."

"I don't want . . . I don't . . . I . . . too awful!"

And then something new happens: the tears grow less animal. Without thinking I reach out my hand to stroke his cheek, and he doesn't push it away. It's the first time he's let me touch his face while he's crying.

Immediately I start weeping too. It's such a change—that I may touch him when he's sad. I press myself against him, and he lets me do that too.

"Frederik, I know that you think everything's awful."

"It *is* awful!"

"But you're making progress."

"No, no, no!"

"You are. You're beginning to get better."

"No, it's just too too awful!"

"Yes, you shouldn't say things like that to Niklas's friends, but now you know that. Now you know when you're doing something wrong."

"No I don't!"

"Yes you do. And I'm also allowed to hold you and touch you. That makes me very happy."

"You *are* allowed to! I'm so wretched!"

"Yes, you're wretched. But it's good that you know you're sick. That's a very good thing. And it's good you get unhappy when you've done something wrong. That's very good too."

"No, no, no!"

Fifteen minutes later, his sobbing suddenly ceases. We sit down on the sofa, and from other times I know just what he needs. I go out into the kitchen and spread jam on four pieces of bread, which he then bolts one after the other.

To think that I struck him, just a short while ago. I don't understand. *I'm* an awful person. I've just struck my sick husband. Battered him. With a small stainless-steel bowl. And I don't have any brain damage to blame.

The telephone rings. Then the cell rings, and then I hear a text come in, and then the phones ring again. I don't answer them. I know what they've all heard. The news. Something on TV about the charges. I turn off the phones.

Later, another kind of peace falls over him.

"So maybe I'm sicker than we thought?" he says.

"Yes, maybe you are."

"But I was really looking forward to going back and working at the school. Do you think I'll have to wait a couple more weeks?"

"Yeah, I think that'd be a good idea. You should wait a little while."

We rest our heads against each other, and I drape an arm over his shoulder. That's how we sat in the old days. That's how we sat during our three good years together.

Mia Halling

Dear Mia,

Everyone is welcome in church! That applies equally to people who usually only come for "weddings, confirmations, and funerals," as you wrote.

I understand how difficult it must be for you to write that you feel as if your beloved husband is already dead—that his soul is dead. You have promised to stay with him "till death do you part." But what if his real self is already dead, and only his body remains behind?

Your question has a philosophical history that goes back several thousand years, and there are different views on the soul's relationship to the body in the New and the Old Testaments. There are also differences between Catholic and Protestant beliefs.

It is hard to discuss such serious matters via e-mail, so I sincerely hope you will come by for a chat sometime during the week. I can see that you wrote to me at 2 in the morning. If you are too busy to meet during the day, I'm sure we can arrange another time.

It is clear that, during a time like this, you must be feeling profound grief and great loss, and perhaps that is something you would like to talk about as well.

You're also very welcome to call me at 70 27 25 95.

Best regards,

Else

Else Vangkær
Pastor
Farum Church

10

At a quarter to seven the next morning, I run from the sculpture park behind the senior housing units and down the path through the woods. The path is still full of potholes from the winter, and for a long stretch it skirts the lakefront, just a few yards from the water.

As I run, I think about Niklas. How he no longer dares to bring friends home. And I think about Frederik, who wants to have sex with one of his son's friends. Has he always been like that? Are all men that way? Maybe the only difference between Frederik and other men is that the others keep quiet about it because their inhibitory mechanisms are still intact.

As my feet find their way around the potholes and slush on the path, I think about Frederik during the years he was unfaithful. I think about Hanne's boyfriend, who drove her to jump from a high-rise. About my father *just wanting to ball hippie chicks*. About the married men who made passes at me in the weeks after I'd thrown Frederik out, and my tennis coach, all those years ago when I was in gymnasium. They're everywhere. I think about all the drunk married teachers running around, potbellied and red-cheeked, during faculty Christmas parties. How can a woman ever have a trusting relationship with a man?

Through the low-hanging branches I can see the mist over the lake, which is itself the color of thickened mist. That's what it is after all, I think, and I stop by the pier. I walk quickly out over the water and suck the air deep into my lungs.

I had thoughts like this before Frederik became sick. And I've spoken with Helena about it often. Her attitude is *Yes, all men are like that. But in a few years it'll all be over; we should enjoy it while we can.*

That's where we disagree.

Still in my running clothes, and with sweat pouring down my face, I pop into the mini-mart at the train station. I only have a few minutes before I need to be home and shower, but we've run out of milk, since I never went shopping yesterday after all.

There are already people here. I grab two quarts of milk and stick my credit card in the terminal.

The girl behind the counter says, "Didn't go through. Try again."

I remove the card from the slot and slide it back in.

The display says it's not working. The girl doesn't say anything.

"You know what, I have another card," I say. "Let me try that one."

I fish Frederik's card out of the inner pocket of my damp sweatpants, stick it in, and enter his PIN.

"It says on my screen to confiscate it," she says.

"Confiscate it? Why?"

"I don't know. You stole it, maybe."

She stares at me with big blue eyes that might have been beautiful if the rest of her pale face wasn't so listless. You'd think it must be all she can do just to sit upright.

"Of course I haven't stolen it!" I say. "It's my husband's card."

"Give me it," she says.

"What if I don't want to?"

"I don't know. Hasn't happened before."

She wants me to think she's an idiot. That's what she wants. She wants me to think she doesn't give a damn about me or the store or her own future. Doesn't give a damn about anything but TV, fries, ketchup, and a boyfriend who's as dumb as she is.

"I need it, really," the girl says. "You've got to give me it."

Two men are now standing in line behind me. One of them lives on our street, and I know he's a sales manager for a discount shoe chain. I suppose he's seen the item about Saxtorph on last night's news. In front of the milk fridge we nodded at each other, but now he pretends to examine something in his basket.

The girl's face is as wrinkle-free as a blow-up sex doll's. I find myself talking with much too much volume and emphasis. "I have *no* idea what this is all about."

I force myself not to look away from the men. I'm determined to look as if our family hasn't done anything wrong. The second man sends me a frightened little smile.

"I'm going to try the other card again," I say, a little too quickly. "Are you sure there isn't something wrong with your machine?"

She doesn't answer.

It's only a matter of two quarts of milk, but what else are we going to have on our cereal?

She looks at her screen. "Now it says I've got to take that card too."

"What! *My* card? You also want *my* card? It didn't say that before!"

"Does now. Maybe you stole that one too."

"Stop saying I stole it! I haven't stolen it! It's *my card*!"

"Well maybe, but hand it over."

I don't answer her, I keep the cards and leave the store without any milk. I run back the way I came—toward the woods. It's impossible for me to go home now, I have to keep running in order to flush this from my body. Even if it means I'm going to be late for my first math class.

How long can the bank freeze our accounts? A month, a few months, a year? Some of our friends will have to lend us some money. But will they?

The rhythmic strike of my feet against the wooded path, my panting breath, the big crooked black branches between me and the sun; the light scratching me in the eyes. I'm standing before my seventh graders. Tons of light:

After taxes, the Hallings receive 23,000 crowns a month from a disability pension and a teacher's salary. They owe 10 million crowns that Mr. Halling embezzled from money entrusted to him. How long will it take the Hallings to pay the money back if:

  a) they spend 2,000 crowns a month on food and clothing and move into a one-room apartment, enabling them to reduce their fixed expenses to 10,000 crowns a month?

  b) they move together into a rented room and cancel all their subscriptions,

*memberships, and insurance, cutting their fixed expenses to 6,000
crowns a month?*

c) *they say screw it and live as they're accustomed to, even though that
gives them a shortfall of 8,000 crowns a month?*

*Now calculate a, b, and c again, based on the understanding that the family finds 6 million crowns of the embezzled funds in an account that the father
has forgotten about because he has brain damage.*

I'm going to have to call Bernard again. Is it too early? Definitely. Yet
he'll be up now, won't he? No, I don't know him that well.

I leap to the side to avoid three big wet furrows, and Anna, who sits
right in front of my desk, raises her hand.

*May we assume that the Hallings borrow a lot of money from their friends,
and that they never pay it back?*

No you may not. Other questions? Kevin?

*May we assume that the parents of the brain-damaged father give the
family a large advance on their inheritance, to use as a down payment on a
condo?*

I enter a stretch with lots of spiderweb filaments streaming over the
path; no one else has run here today. The filaments are the color of the
lake mist, the lake, my sweat. They cling to my forehead and cheeks and
mouth, and when I pass trees standing right by the path, I lift my arms
and try to bat away the invisible strands. I run and strike out with my arms,
grimacing as yet another filament drifts through my defenses and sticks
to my eyes.

...

It was late when Niklas came home last night, but I went to his room
anyway and insisted we talk about prison, about his father on the evening
news, and about the poor girl on the street, who I found out is called Emilie. I said it would be okay if he needed to stay home for a day before seeing
everyone at school again. That was what I wished I could do myself, yet
it was as if he almost couldn't wait to go back. He didn't want to put off
having to face them all, my strong son. I gave him a hug, and when I left, I
told him to just wake me up during the night if he wanted to talk about it

88

some more. I placed my hand on the top of his head as I said this, though I'm not sure he liked that.

Back from my run, I set out breakfast, still in my sweaty running clothes. Niklas tromps down the stairs and looks at me in that teenage way—as if he doesn't notice anything and yet is justified in being annoyed.

"Why haven't you taken a shower?" he says right away.

"I was held up."

"Are you going to eat breakfast in *that*?"

"Yes. I'll take a shower afterward."

"I don't want to sit and eat breakfast while my mother's sitting next to me all sweaty and gross."

I want to say that he's going to have to, that I'm not gross, that he needs to show some consideration when he speaks to me. But his tone and his entire manner remind me too much of his sick father. Niklas isn't himself—and he has every right not to be.

Then he pours muesli in his bowl, concentrating deeply, as if I'm not there; but today there's no milk. Niklas looks around, appearing not to notice the big glass pitcher of water that, for the first time ever, stands on the table in front of him.

"Where's the milk?"

"Today we're going to have to eat our muesli with water. It's no big deal, people did that all the time in the old days."

"I don't want to eat this shit." He's already shoved his chair back from the table and stood up.

Make room for his anger. I have to accept it, his anger and my anger both. Accept everything he feels. Of course he's angry, of course he's self-absorbed, of course he doesn't have any extra energy to be considerate of his mother. Don't I have room for that?

Yes, I do . . . And besides, I remember reading a few nights ago, in one of the many neurology books I now have from the library, that teenagers aren't fully developed, orbitofrontally. It turns out that you aren't until the beginning of your twenties. No matter how clever teenagers can be, according to the books they'll always have a trace of Frederik's dramatic symptoms: the poor self-control, the wild mood swings, the lack of concern for others, and the limited ability to plan very far into the future.

I don't say anything other than, "Well, what would you like then?"

"Not *this* in any case. It tastes like shit."

"You don't know that, Niklas, you haven't tasted it." My voice sounds mild when I speak. I feel unbelievably maternal. Room. Give him room.

He roots around in the fridge, using large rough movements. Like his father. Again I say, "I can understand if you want to stay home today. Just go ahead and stay."

"How many times do I have to tell you I don't want to stay home?"

"No, you should just . . . I think I only said it once last night."

He doesn't respond. I have a wild urge to stay home myself, to quit and never see my students or colleagues again.

"Maybe it'll be mostly just the younger kids," I say. "That's probably right. Yes, the parents think they're so clever. They'll get the kids to ask *for* them."

He must register something in my voice; he's finally looking at me as if I'm a human being. He stands there with half a loaf of dark rye in one hand and a block of cheese in the other. "Well, are *you* going to school today?"

"Yes," I say.

"What are you going to tell them?"

"Maybe I'll say that it isn't true."

"But they saw it on TV last night, didn't they?"

"Yes . . . I don't know."

...

For the first time in a long time, I don't bike to work. Instead I take the car, which none of my colleagues or students will recognize, and park behind the school. From there, a back door leads to the stairway going right up to my seventh-grade classroom.

The office knows that I have problems at home, and when I rang this morning and said I'd be arriving an hour late, the secretary was kind and said they could find a sub on short notice.

I turned off my cell phone to avoid talking to journalists. Now I switch it back on for a minute, not checking messages, and call Bernard. When I called before from home, he didn't answer and so I rang up his office, but no one was answering the phones there yet. He's still not answering his cell, but this time when I call his firm a secretary picks up.

"Berman & Friis, Bernard Berman's office."

Her voice is friendly, her pronunciation straight out of a 1950s film.

My words tumble out in the wrong order as I try to explain that I know Bernard, that all our accounts have been frozen and I don't know when we'll be able to access our money again—if ever.

"Mr. Berman is in court right now, but I shall tell him that you have called. May I ask if he has your number?"

I give it to her and go in to my class.

The quiet in the classroom seems tense, but no one says anything about Frederik being on the news last night. As I teach, I wonder if it's only my imagination, or if the knowledge that their math teacher's married to a big-time swindler is making them uneasy. I also try to think about who the hell we can borrow from so we can make it through the month—and who we can borrow a lot more from if we still need money in the months to come.

The obvious choice would be Thorkild and Vibeke, of course, but even without any debt, it's already hard to keep Vibeke from taking over the entire family. I understand that she wants to do whatever she can to help her sick son, and that as a retired nurse she has some caregiving experience that I do not. And there's no getting around the fact that I do need their help. But when she insists that Frederik and I have to save money now and refuses to buy the organic goods I've written on the shopping list, or when she moves the vacuum cleaner to a closet where she says it's easier to get to and replaces all my cleaning agents with other ones, or when she starts talking about staying overnight, then I have to put my foot down.

The psychotherapist training that she embarked on after retiring has made her more irritating than ever. One day I found myself losing it as she sat in my armchair, fiddling with the big piece of amber in her necklace while trying to convince me that the reason I wasn't letting her move in with us was the immature nature of my relationship to my own mother.

The next person I think of in a situation like this is of course Laust. Until the day before yesterday, there was no question that he'd be there for us if we had a problem—and be there with money too. And then there's

Helena. I could ask her during lunch break, though I know that she and Henning are having trouble with their bills these days.

I'm in the middle of going through some problems in perspective drawing. "Can anyone tell me how to find the two vanishing points?"

Anna, who sits right in front of my desk, raises her hand.

"Is it true that your husband's going to jail?"

Have they planned this? Have they talked to one another about who should ask? She looks so sincere—regardless of how rehearsed this might be—and ignoring all the responses I cobbled together last night in half sleep, I blurt out the truth.

"He might go to jail. We don't know. He took a lot of money, but that's because he has a disease. He couldn't help it. His brain is diseased."

We talk about it briefly, and they accept my explanations. It's surprisingly easy, and then we turn back to math. During recess I send Niklas a text, telling him that I've been telling people the truth.

I'm late to my next class because I try to avoid the halls and the schoolyard between bells. I also avoid the teachers' lounge, but during lunch I have to go in.

I texted Helena beforehand, saying that I want to go in with her. We meet outside the bathroom and we hug. A little later, she's the one who opens the door to where all the other teachers are and quickly, with a dismissive air, leads the way over to our usual table, right by the window.

Here I go, the swindler—or maybe just the swindler's wife, they have no way of knowing—in any case, half of the married couple that has destroyed one of the most highly respected schools in the land.

"It'll work out."

"It's lovely the way you keep supporting Frederik."

"If there's anything I can do, just let me know."

The teachers at our table are hugging me, they're flashing me smiles. Others come over to say a friendly word, or wave encouragement from the other end of the lounge. Helena must have talked with some of them earlier, during one of the breaks. They don't think I'm a criminal. They think that I'm staying to support my sick husband.

"*That's* the way to do it, Mia. I only hope I'd have the strength to do the same."

It really catches me off guard, and Helena can't have spoken with all of them. I feel that I'm *liked*, and I find myself crying at the table a little, where everyone can see.

On the way out to the next class, I say to Helena as a joke, "I ought to call up the women Frederik had affairs with. I could say to them, *Now the fun is over. Now it's time to bear your share of the burden. For the time being, what we need from you is 20,000 crowns, here and now.*"

Helena doesn't laugh.

"Well anyway, I do know that I shouldn't ask you for a loan," I say. "That you guys are having a hard time right now."

She pulls me over by the teachers' mailboxes, and in a low voice she says, "I don't think you should go to your next class."

"What? I feel marvelous about the way they all took it so well! I could teach until . . . all the way until . . . for a really long time."

"You should go home now. It's great that you came. But you're not yourself today."

11

Did Frederik really want to have affairs with those women? In everything else, he was the most reliable person in the world, but when it came to our relationship, it was as if he had an opposite set of rules.

I remember his callousness when I confronted him with what I had discovered. The indifference in his features, the complete disengagement and lack of empathy. Was his coldness pathological—something wrong in his brain? It was in any case a far cry from his ordinary self. It might have been an incipient phase of his disease.

And in our first years together, he didn't bury himself in his work. Since then I've learned that a tumor can make it harder for someone to multitask, that it can lead to monomania. Medically, it's definitely possible that it took root at the beginning of our marriage, transforming my marvelous charming husband into an unfaithful workaholic. That it then stopped growing until he learned to compensate and, for three good years, became more like himself again. And that at the end of that time, it started growing again until the seizure and operation.

I followed Helena's advice and left school early, so now I'm home three hours earlier than planned. Are reporters and photographers standing outside, lying in wait? No.

On my way into the house I can see that my in-laws have been with Frederik in the front yard, getting it ready for spring. They've trimmed the bushes and raked twigs, leaves, and the last half-burned remains of the fire into two piles. At the sight of their gifted son, Thorkild and Vibeke have always been fit to burst with pride. Now I remember Thorkild standing in our kitchen and saying, "If only I were dead, so I didn't have to see this!" But that must be something I dreamt, because when they came to take care of Frederik this morning, it was the first time they'd been here since the arrest.

I let myself in, and already as I open the door I can hear Frederik's mechanical sobbing from above. I rush upstairs and find Vibeke and Thorkild in the hallway outside the bathroom.

"He won't come out. We've tried everything."

"What happened?"

They hesitate, and I walk over to the bathroom door.

"Frederik, it's me. I'm home now."

Maybe he can't hear me.

"Frederik, I'm home. It's me here now. I've been looking forward to seeing you."

Still no answer.

"We had a . . . discussion," says Vibeke.

I don't say anything, just look at her until she finally goes on.

"He peed on my pile. In the yard."

"Peed on your pile?"

"The pile I was going to pick up with my hands and carry to the street."

"Did you yell at him?"

Vibeke draws a breath and is about to launch into a long explanation, but I ask in a low voice if they would please go down below, and Thorkild squeezes her hand and leads her to the stairs.

"They're gone, Frederik. It's just me now. May I come in? I'd really like to."

I end up sitting for a long time with my back against the door, making small calming remarks. And then suddenly his sobbing ceases.

Through the door he says, "I didn't do anything."

"No."

"Word of honor, I didn't do anything. I didn't pee on her pile."

"No."

"And then Mom got angry."

"I can understand how that would upset you . . . May I come in?"

"No."

"Well, it's just as easy for me to sit out here. It doesn't matter."

After a long quiet wait, I say, "I'm going to go down and talk to them. I'm sure it'll be all right. Just call if you want me to come back up, okay?"

In the living room, I fall into my armchair and sigh deeply. But I don't relax, not a bit. Vibeke can hardly wait to tell me everything she has to say; she shakes one hand so that her heavy bracelet slides up her arm, and I can tell she's frightened of me. She has reason to be. My head feels cold; everything in me is ready to explode.

"The yard work was going so well," she says. "Frederik and I did the trimming and raked up all the yard refuse, each of us making our own pile. I had to go in for a minute, and when I looked down from the bathroom window, I could see him standing there, urinating on my pile. The one I was going to put my hands into and carry out to the street!"

She pauses and looks inquiringly at me. I must be doing a good job of keeping my emotions in check, because she keeps talking.

"I became furious! And Mia, you can go ahead if you want and just tear my head off. But it's not because I'd get urine on my hands. I've had plenty of urine on my hands—I'm a mother and a nurse, after all. Rather, it's what it signifies. Why did he do it? It's as if he's urinating on me. There are so many symbols in such an act: the phallus, of course, that ridicules the mother . . ."

Vibeke's psychotherapy training and the way it's been teaching her to think have really gotten on my nerves in the last few months. But I control myself and listen.

"The burnt branches—are they death and decay? Does it mean that he doesn't care if I'm old and will die in the not-too-distant future? That he mocks my mortality? Does he wish for me to die?"

"He's hardly putting that much thought into it," I say.

"It's so obvious that he's angry, that he feels this overwhelming grief that lies behind everything and every once in a while bursts forth. And that's something we can all find perfectly understandable. That's how any of us would react. But it feels deeply unjust when he lets his anger spill over on Thorkild and me. We don't deserve it—not when we're here almost every day, just to help him!"

"But there's no way he can—"

"Mia, has anyone ever urinated on something of yours? Urinated? Really urinated on it?"

How can she punish a sick man, I wonder. Frederik can't help it! And now he's hiding upstairs, feeling miserable. I already know that in a few moments, when I finally permit myself to tell her what I think of her, I won't ease up until she cries.

Just as I'm about to let rip, Frederik comes down the stairs. I hurry over to give him a hug but stop halfway; his body language tells me he wouldn't like it.

Before I can turn my attention back to Vibeke, Thorkild says, "Mia, you haven't seen the papers."

I never would have thought that articles about Frederik embezzling would have been able to defuse a tense situation. But Thorkild pulls it off. *Børsen, Jyllands-Posten, Politiken, Berlingske*—he's found articles on his son in all of them. Thorkild and I sit side by side on the sofa and read them, his tall thin body reminding me of Frederik's. It gives me the same feeling of warmth—of something fundamentally right—to sit next to him. To sit next to Frederik thirty years from now; a future we'll never know. As I study the articles, I glance occasionally at my father-in-law's composed features.

The shame in his cheeks, the old skin drooping over his shirt collar. I think of the large office he had as headmaster at North Coast Private Grammar, the office where naughty boys were sent to be punished. Thorkild and Vibeke never found anything strange about Frederik's obsession with his work. When Frederik was little, Thorkild was basically absent all the time.

The urge to put Vibeke in her place dissipates. She's sitting in my armchair now, catching her breath and sending me timid looks.

"Don't you need a bite to eat, Mia? After your long day at school?"

On her way to the kitchen to put on some tea and get the things for sandwiches, she pats Frederik's hair gently.

"Sorry," she says. "I'm really sorry, Frederik."

He shakes off her hand as if it were an insect that landed on him.

When she comes back, Thorkild and I look up from the papers.

"Frederik," I say. "Did you pee on your mother's pile because you were angry with her?"

"No."

"Are you sure?"

"Yes. That's definitely not the reason."

"Well, then why did you do it?"

"I don't know."

"Do you think you peed on it because you're sick?"

"Oh no! Are you going to talk about that again?"

"Yes. But you *are* sick, aren't you?"

"I know perfectly well that I'm sick! But that has nothing to do with it."

These days, he's been saying that his memory has gotten poor since the operation, but it hasn't. He also thinks the operation has affected his bodily control, and that's why he falls down the stairs all the time and bruises himself by bumping into everything. In truth, it's because he runs around the house, fearlessly and all too quickly. But other than those two things, Frederik's convinced that he's the same as he's always been.

…

Was Frederik himself two and a half years ago when he came home driving a used orange-red Alfa Romeo? We'd agreed that we should get a new car—but *that* car? So much extra money for style and speed? That's something we hadn't agreed on, and such extravagance wasn't like him—or me. Back then neither of us had heard about impaired inhibitory mechanisms, much less orbitofrontal syndrome, and we rapidly became fond of the car. Months later, we even got to the point of thinking that Frederik had done exactly the right thing in buying it.

I'm like Vibeke. I can't stand it either if there isn't some meaning behind all the strange things that Frederik does.

He's completely stopped closing windows, doors, cabinets, and jar tops. Our jam jars have all gotten sticky, and one day when I knocked over some gherkins in the fridge, the pickle juice got over everything because he hadn't screwed the top back on.

I've asked several specialists, and they all say there's no separate system in the brain that controls whether you can close things. There *is* a directional center, which is often defective in patients with damage to the right temple. But if Frederik's damage had spread all the way to that region, he'd be having a hard time finding his way around the rooms of the house, he'd unzip his trousers instead of zipping them and start putting his shoes on the wrong feet.

If his recent aversion to closing things isn't due to brain damage, perhaps we should understand it psychologically—as Vibeke's therapy teachers doubtless would. Maybe he doesn't want to close off his possibilities, regardless of whether they lie before him or behind him. Maybe it's something to do with being unable to stand his present state.

Every minute of the day, I hope that he's getting to be more like himself again, and so I'm constantly on the lookout for signs. If the sun is shining as I put the last plate in the dishwasher, he won't lie to me in the next few hours. If the next person who walks past the window has a blue jacket on, Frederik will want to eat a steak like in the old days, not just bread with jam or honey. If the light at the intersection turns green before I pass the parking sign, he'll say something nice to me of his own volition.

I've never been superstitious before. And of course I read more into Frederik than into black cats and ladders, than stars and stoplights. That glint in his eye—isn't that the old Frederik? The way he looks distractedly into the air as he buttons his shirt, that's the way he buttoned his shirt when he was well! It's just like him!

...

"The soul is not born, and it is not created. It has always existed, independent of matter and the formation of the universe." That's what it said on one of the many odd pages I came across on yet another sleepless night when I googled *soul* and *orbitofrontal*.

Was Vibeke yelling at a diseased brain that couldn't help itself—or at a person with a soul and a sense of responsibility? Can you be responsible if you don't have a soul? Or can you have a soul without being responsible? Responsible for ruining an entire school? For wrecking your wife's and son's lives, for being lewd to your son's friend?

Yet Vibeke's anger can hardly compare to me beating him yesterday with the stainless-steel bowl while he lay defenseless underneath me on the floor. I would give anything for the chance to do it over. Last night, I could see that besides the many bruises and swellings he already had, new ones ran up and down his back. He draws me deep into a wilderness of inexcusable behavior, and there's nothing for me to blame but myself.

Vibeke makes me an open-face cheese sandwich, like I sometimes make for Niklas as comfort food. She places it before me, but I can't even choke down a mouthful. So she pours tea in my mug and sits down in the armchair.

She fiddles with the amber chain around her neck and the cuffs of her woolen jersey. Once she settles down, she says, "When I look for psychological meaning in his actions, something besides brain damage, it's also about showing him respect. In nursing, that's something you always strive for. He's a human being—much more than just a diseased body. It's important that you try to listen—"

I'm on my feet before I have the chance to think. "Don't tell me I don't show Frederik respect!"

"Pardon me, no, no, Mia. I didn't mean that at all."

"You don't show him any more respect than I do—not with all your silly psychobabble!"

"No, of course not. I don't—"

I throw the cheese sandwich against the wall. "Get out now! Out! Out!"

"Mia, you can't just kick everyone out! We're the only ones who will still come and take care of him."

Thorkild positions himself in front of Vibeke. As if he's seen the marks on his son's back. "Mia, please. Won't you sit down?"

I can't. I can't sit down, I can't go near Vibeke, I can't even speak.

"Mia, I would like to have you sit down," he says again.

Behind him Vibeke is crying, and so I sit down. I sit down slowly while Thorkild remains standing, calm and ready for action, like a retired animal tamer.

"We're all very angry," he says. "But we need to stand together. We need to live with the fact that Frederik can no longer love us."

With theatrically large tears falling upon her cheeks, Vibeke gasps, "It's so difficult. He doesn't love me anymore. I feel it all the time. It's so hard."

I glance over at Frederik, who's fallen asleep in his chair.

Vibeke looks at me. "And you must find it hardest of all, Mia. Don't you? Him no longer loving you?"

. . .

The following day, I explain to Thorkild my thinking about when Frederik stopped being himself. We're standing in the hallway; he and Vibeke have their coats on and are on their way out the door. They're actually in a bit of a hurry—they're going to the emergency room to see if Vibeke might have broken something in her right hand. She maintains that she accidentally struck her knuckles hard against our dinner table.

Thorkild says, "If anything, the opposite is true. Frederik was his real self when he was working sixteen hours a day. Then the tumor started affecting him, and he began getting tired more quickly. And because he wasn't healthy anymore, he needed to relax with his family. He was most himself when he was working a lot."

Vibeke's anxious to get going; her face is twisted in pain.

"Yes, yes," Thorkild tells her without moving toward the door. Instead he keeps talking to me. "The disease made him weak and turned him into a family man."

"But the last three years he was the most present he's ever been—the most normal!"

"I'd think it over again. A judge isn't going to buy a story about a defendant being himself during the day and then at night being some brain-damaged gambler."

"But that's the way it was!"

"Then Frederik will go to prison for four years, and you'll lose your house, your pensions, everything."

He shoots Vibeke a quick sideways glance and then he says, "We have to go now."

101

12

"How old were you when you first came here?"

"Twenty-one."

"Did you meet a Danish girl, perhaps?"

He laughs. "Everyone knows that all the foreign men here immigrated because of Danish women."

"No, but I didn't think—"

"And you're right! Lærke was an au pair for my parents in Paris. I followed her when she went back home, and it changed my life."

Two weeks have passed since Frederik was arrested and released. I've taken the day off work, and Bernard and I are in the living room, waiting for the school's new lawyer to show up with an assessor, who will appraise the sale value of our house, car, furnishings, pension savings, et cetera.

Bernard shows me a picture on his cell phone. "Here we are on vacation together."

In the photo he looks much younger, but it must have been taken within the last ten years—around the time of the accident—because his twin boys look pretty big.

"She's really lovely," I say. And she is: she has big blond curls and a broad happy smile. Bernard was dark-haired then, lean without being quite as thin as he is now. They stand with their arms around the two boys in some southern European village, with peaks and forests in the background.

"I know what you're thinking," he says. "I've aged a lot in the last eight years."

"Was it on that vacation you had the accident?"

"No, that was two weeks later, back here on Lyngby Road. Fortunately, the boys weren't with us in the car."

I get goose bumps from looking at her; now she uses crutches and goes to a handicapped center all day because she's mentally incapacitated. While he's marooned in a foreign country, without the support of his family or boyhood friends. What's prevented him from leaving her? How can he stand it?

"Her disability is general," he says. "Bodily control, speech, thought, energy."

I look into his dark eyes but he doesn't return my gaze.

"The odd thing is that she's still the same. She's still my Lærke." He almost looks proud when he says it.

I don't understand him. I shudder to think of what his days and nights have been like for the last eight years. And yet the very moment I think that, my own spouse lies brain-damaged and our house is being taken from us.

It's been one week since Bernard called and warned me about the assessor's visit. "In accordance with Danish law, Frederik will have to pay back as much as he possibly can of what he embezzled—regardless of whether the court finds him criminally responsible for his acts or not. So the school will seize all of Frederik's possessions—and half of what you own in common."

"But why don't they simply look at everything we own and take half?"

"No, we need to have receipts for everything. Whose name is on which receipt? Where did the money for each purchase come from? Did you receive any large gifts from Frederik that were paid for with embezzled funds—or with his income? Are there things that are in reality yours, even though his name's on the receipt? Things like that."

Phone in hand, I'd closed my eyes and let myself fall back in the armchair. There was a hollow under my right buttock and a nick in one arm; it was my chair. No doubt they would take it too.

Could he hear me fall?

"It's awful, I know," he said. "Really awful, but you're going to have to do it."

Around me stood the furniture I had bartered and haggled for and restored and pampered over the course of fifteen years, starting from scratch. They'd probably take the coffee table that my feet rested upon. The carpet beneath the table, the lamp that lit it. Everything. *Every*thing.

I needed to clear my throat, but Bernard cleared his first.

"Mia, I know you can do it."

"How do you know that?"

"Because it isn't as hard as supporting your sick husband—and you do an amazing job of that."

When I spoke on the phone with Helena, she became quite insistent. "At the very least, you've got to hide the Wegner sofa at my place before they come. You need something you can count on. *Some*thing in your situation. Would anyone blame you if you hid a couple pieces of furniture?"

"Actually, I think a lot of people would."

"Just let me come over and get something. The lamp! The Arne Jacobsen lamp, I can take it with me in the car."

Again I had a desire to flop down in my armchair, land on the hollow under my right buttock, finger the nick in the arm. But I was sitting there already.

...

They are nothing if not precise. At the stroke of nine, Bernard and I receive two men out in the scorched front yard. The sofa and the lamp are still both in the living room, and I don't know if it's because I'm honest or because I'm tired. The school's new lawyer is young and dark-haired, with a broad jaw and a shiny pink tie. He couldn't be more different from the previous one, the chubby man whom I danced with for years at Saxtorph parties.

The assessor is someone I could run into on the street a couple of days from now and not recognize. His clothes, his features, his haircut—everything—run together in my mind with those of other men who don't want to be noticed or remembered. *He probably picks up hookers*, I think as I proffer my hand. The papers always say that johns are completely ordinary men, and he's so without character as to be almost striking.

"Is this your car?" It's just about the first thing the lawyer says, extending his hand toward the blue Mercedes parked in front of our house. I can already see the delight in his eyes.

"No, ours is over there." I point down the street.

We start walking over to our little orange-red Alfa Romeo. It's sunk down to the asphalt, the tires flat and spreading out to the sides.

"What happened?" asks Bernard.

"Somebody slashed the tires."

"Did you report it to the police?"

I don't answer.

"You should report it," he says. "You haven't done anything wrong."

"We're married."

"That's no crime. You don't deserve this."

Perhaps I feel a fury somewhere inside myself. I think I do. And I wonder whether it's kids who slashed the tires, or a teacher—maybe one of our former friends. But I observe the fury with an overwhelming exhaustion. Lazy and passive, as if I had one of the brain injuries I've read about, just a notch higher up behind my forehead than Frederik's. The car's stood this way for a week, and I haven't done anything about it.

Frederik no longer cares about the car, despite the progress he's been making. The interval between angry outbursts is getting longer, yet he still weeps a lot—and what makes him most unhappy is that he no longer derives any pleasure from music. The notes don't add up to melodies for him; they're simply sounds, without any glint of beauty.

Which is why he's become obsessed with the principles of speaker construction and with building speakers that are better than the ones we have. I took him over to the neighbor's so he could hear that the problem doesn't lie in our stereo system. But he just ran their system down while they stood there and listened. Niklas also tried to play music for him on his computer headphones, but Frederik thought they sounded terrible too.

In the evenings, I enter the access code to our computer so he can visit online forums where they discuss optimal crossover frequencies and the control of impedance curves—and more generally, how to construct the ultimate speakers. Meanwhile I sit next to him and correct math assignments or fill out new forms from public agencies about his illness. In this way I can monitor him and make sure he doesn't go onto sites where he can make investments or other kinds of trouble.

The day before yesterday, he went with Vibeke and Thorkild to a building supply outlet, where they bought some immense sheets of fiberboard.

The two men cut them into pieces with Thorkild's circular saw in Frederik's office, which they've refurbished as a workshop. Since then, he's been holed up in there by himself with his sketches, calculations, glue, and dowels.

Out by the car, the school lawyer asks, "Do you want to keep it?"

"We want to keep everything."

"Yes, but what I mean is, we're going to have to sell the house. But this here doesn't look to be worth more than ninety thousand, max, so—"

"They can certainly afford to keep the car," Bernard interposes, "and they'd *like* to keep it."

"Fine. Good," the lawyer says. "We'll send an expert out to appraise it, but we won't put it up for sale."

Once we've gotten back to the house and I open the door for the men, the lawyer asks, "Is your husband home?"

"Yes, but he's busy."

"Just to be clear, our meeting today will determine how much money you will have, from now on through the rest of your lives. The things we decide here cannot be renegotiated."

"I know that."

"And your husband knows that too?"

"Yes, he does."

The lawyer coughs slightly and tenses his broad chin, as if he's making an effort to look away from me and not ask anything else.

I lead them into our living room. The anonymous-looking assessor sighs with relief and smiles, as if he wants to turn on the TV and sprawl out on my sofa with a beer. "You always get a good sense about whether a house is sellable by asking yourself, *Could I imagine living here?*" he says. "With this one, I certainly could."

The lawyer also appears pleased. "The location is ideal, isn't it, considering that it isn't any larger. I'd think that there are a lot of young couples who are looking for something charming—"

The assessor interrupts him, saying, "But there isn't as much light as young people like these days."

"Yes, we'll have to remove some of the furniture before we have the pictures taken for the listing. That'll create more of a feeling of light and space."

The lawyer raises the small stainless-steel bowl from the coffee table, examining the hallmark on the bottom. I place myself in front of my costly sofa and stand there perfectly still, watching.

"You people sure live the life of Riley," the assessor says.

The lawyer lets his thumb slide appreciatively over the leather on the backrest of my armchair. "Fantastic furniture. Is there any of it you want to keep?"

I glance hesitantly toward Bernard. "As much of it as we can," I say.

I remember distinctly when I bought the armchair. I'd just guided a ninth-grade class through their final exams. It'd been the first time I'd been homeroom teacher for a graduating class, and it had gone swimmingly. They were so happy, their enthusiasm infectious. *So this is how it'll be*, I thought, and I embraced my life and my calling and felt satisfied—felt in fact ready to resign myself to Frederik's absence. And then in the online classifieds that week I found a worn old armchair that sounded promising. I drove the seventy-five miles to Korsør with the trailer to see it, and it was just as I'd hoped: it had been made in the late '40s by a furniture designer from Funen who was essentially unknown, but whose style I'd already fallen in love with.

"This chair here," the lawyer says. "Have you had it appraised?"

"No, but it's not by a name designer."

I glance up at the wall, where there's a luminous suggestion of a rectangle next to the shelves with Frederik's LPs. Until recently, a drawing hung there that Niklas had made in third grade. When he entered gymnasium, he insisted that it no longer hang there, and now all that remains is the light patch of wallpaper.

Where are we going to end up living? It'll probably be an apartment building full of welfare recipients and mental patients—just like us. Far from Old Farum.

"My husband worked in the evenings and on weekends," I explain. "So I had lots of time to deal in furniture. It was my hobby, mine alone. Buying and selling. He didn't have anything to do with it. You'll see that all the receipts are in my name."

The lawyer positions himself on the exact spot where, less than a year and a half ago, Laust stood on a chair and raised a toast to Frederik at his birthday party.

"Yes," he says. "Let's talk then about how we're going to divide this up. If your husband worked on those evenings and weekends, and the two of you were using his larger income for your daily expenses, then Saxtorph Private School also has the right to half of what you earned during those same working hours."

Instantly I feel adrenaline pumping through my veins. I manage to speak calmly though I start gasping for breath. "But it's furniture that I've traded my way up to, on my own. It's taken me years."

"That doesn't change the fact that my client has right to one half—at least—if your husband was earning other money that you used."

"But surely you can't just—"

Bernard steps in front of the lawyer and says, very evenly, "Shouldn't we wait and take this up later?"

And so the confrontation is postponed, apparently. Bernard smiles at me. I exhale noisily, ready to fight but no longer having an outlet for my belligerence.

The assessor sits down in each of the chairs, examines the tabletop, studies the books on the shelves, kneels and turns up the corner of a rug. The lawyer stands still, watching him; I stand and watch Bernard.

Is this what it feels like when someone looks out for you? When's the last time someone looked out for me? The three years before Frederik's seizure were peaceful—there wasn't really anything he had to protect me from. Then there were our first years together, before Saxtorph swallowed him whole, back when I felt he wanted to take care of me. Before that I'd have to go all the way back to when I was twelve, in the years before my father moved out.

Bernard sticks his hands in the pockets of his jacket, then he takes them out, then he puts them back in. Two weeks ago, when I met him for the first time, I felt something wolfish in the combination of his evident solitude and his grey-haired physical presence.

But now I see everything differently. After nearly twenty years, it's clear that he's still besotted with his wife. More than any other man I've met. And now I can see that it's not a wolf he resembles so much as a family dog who can't find its way home. The prominent cheekbones, the intense eyes belong to a dog who restlessly roams the winter streets, hunting for the family and the warm hearth it once knew, while each day its bones grow more and more visible beneath its fur.

We all go up to the second floor and enter the bathroom. There's no sawing or drilling noises from the workshop; Frederik must be marking cutting patterns on the fiberboard. I've been slowly finding traces of personality in the assessor's features. He's a bit more round-headed than most men; his lips are a bit thicker, his eyes a bit smaller. If I bump into him on the street in a couple of days and don't acknowledge him, it'll no longer be because I mix him up with all the others in my mind, but because I don't want to.

Our bathroom's too small, and it feels even more cramped because we don't have anywhere else to put the stacked washer and dryer.

"Hmm; hmm. Well, this is disappointing," the assessor says. "It could easily knock a couple hundred thousand off the price."

"But we've just redone it!"

"I hope you haven't paid a lot of money for it. This remodel only reduces the value."

"You can't be serious."

"Look at this row of tiles. A buyer would want them straight."

"Well, that's part of the charm—after all, the tiles are sitting . . ."

Suddenly I realize: the man who laid the tiles was definitely not the real Frederik.

Two years ago, Frederik and I spent a lot of weekends here. We had perhaps the best time of our best years—flirting and laughing and puttering about among the tools, grout, and tiles. Frederik's never been good at maintaining the house, that's more my department, but he wanted to put up the row of green glass tiles himself, and every time I sit on the toilet and stare up at them, their skewed aspect recalls our happiness.

But the real Frederik would have kept at it till everything was perfect—especially with something he wasn't good at. The real Frederik would never have tolerated anything crooked.

The play of light from the halogen lamps on the tile surface merges with the smell of the open packages of laundry powder, the humid air, and the odor of Frederik's wet towel. I feel like vomiting on the bulging linoleum, with its uneven cut in the corner. Two years ago, the temperament of the sick Frederik was unfamiliar to me—the temperament in which everything is uncomplicated and fun, in which nothing has depth. I must have let his humor rub off on me because I didn't know any better.

...

"Let me stay here for a minute," I say when the assessor and the lawyer are ready to go out and survey the rest of the upstairs.

Bernard looks at me—an inquiring look, straight in the eye. He wants to know if I can manage. Right away he's able to see that I can't, but what can he do? He asks, with a carefree air that I can hear doesn't come natural, "Do you think you'll be here for a while?"

"Nah."

I lock the door behind them and sit down on the toilet lid, my head in my hands. How I detest the stench of our wet towels, laundry soap, and standing water.

Does Bernard and Lærke's bathroom smell like this? I can't imagine it does. Does it smell in a way that's even reminiscent of this? Without being conscious of it, I must have sniffed Bernard during the course of the morning, for to my surprise I have a clear sense of how he smells—and therefore of how his bathroom smells. It smells good.

When I come out, the others are in Niklas's room. The assessor has Niklas's camera bag in one hand, and he's about to root around in it—just as he roots through everything else.

"Don't open that!" I exclaim from the doorway. "It isn't ours, it's our son's."

"Do you have a receipt?"

I rush over so I'm standing right in front of his face. "Could you leave my son's bag alone! It's his, you can't take it!"

But he's not supposed to care about what I say. "Then you need to have a receipt in your son's name," he says. "Gosh, it's a splendid camera."

Bernard's voice is soothing. "They're not going to take it, Mia. It's not Frederik's. They just need to know . . ."

He falls silent, and the other men do too. They're looking toward the door in back of me.

Frederik's come out of his workshop.

110

"Frederik, they want to take Niklas's camera!" I shout.

"That's not really what they want," says Bernard quietly. "What they want . . ."

Frederik studies the three of them, then he ignores them and looks at me. I gaze right into his cheerful eyes. That blank expression. That indifferent pleasure—just like when he's lying to me. Just like when he takes a walk, when he watches TV, when he eats.

"Mia, we have to go out and buy more fiberboard."

"We don't have to go out and buy more fiberboard. They want to seize Niklas's camera. So can't you see that—"

"But I need more fiberboard. I've revised the construction plans."

"Are you listening to what I'm saying? They want to take your son's camera!"

"I think we should go out and buy it this afternoon. Then I can take a nap first."

"God *damn* it, Frederik! Can't we focus for two seconds on someone other than you?"

Something shifts in his eyes. As if a personality is emerging somewhere within. Tentative attempts to figure out how he can get his way. To figure out how I'm thinking and feeling, and what he has to say to get that fiberboard. It's the same look, deeply focused and oddly distant at the same time, as when a little boy—the new neural pathways forming—practices sitting on the pot.

"And if I don't let you decide for me, then you'll just start hitting me, won't you?" He looks hesitantly at all four of us. "Then you'll just beat me hard on my back, right? If I don't let you decide, then you'll beat me with that bowl from the coffee table."

Iowa Gambling Task

It has long been a riddle why people with orbitofrontal brain injuries make such disastrous choices in daily life, when the same people can appear normal in conversation and on conventional psychological tests.

The phenomenon can be explained if we assume that we utilize different areas in our brains when we are going to make an important decision than when we are going to choose between a cappuccino and a café au lait.

We must also assume that there is a marked difference between the brain areas we use when we *talk* about critical life decisions, and the brain areas we use when we actually *decide*.

Orbitofrontal damage is easiest to discover when the affected person has the freedom to make his own decisions. However, such injuries can be quite difficult to observe in situations with well-defined rules—which is precisely why traditional IQ tests and ordinary conversations do not register them.

In addition to satisfying scientific curiosity, the development of an effective test for orbitofrontal injuries is of critical importance in determining how the affected people are treated by doctors and social workers, whether they can qualify for accident insurance and disability pensions, and a host of other practical issues.

But how do we construct a psychological test that will mimic fundamental life choices in all their emotional complexity and lack of rules?

Antoine Bechara, who worked in the department of the famed neurologist Antonio Damasio at the University of Iowa, developed the Iowa Gambling Task for exactly this purpose in 1994.

In the test, the investigator places four piles of cards in front of the research subject. The subject is not told anything about the piles or about the rules of the game, other than that he has the possibility of winning or losing money. Neither is he told how long the game will last. He has to figure these things out for himself.

In two of the piles, the research subject receives $50 for every card he turns up, except for occasional cards that require him to pay $250. If he keeps drawing cards from these two piles, he will make a profit.

In the other two piles, the subject receives double the reward—$100—for each card he draws, except when he turns up an occasional card that costs him $1,250—i.e., a rather substantial penalty. If he continues to draw cards from these two piles, he will lose a fortune over the long run.

Experimental subjects who are healthy (or have brain injuries that lie outside the frontal lobes) will begin by taking cards from all four piles while they try to determine a pattern in the game. After just a few cards, they will prefer the $100 piles, but before they have drawn 30 cards, they generally learn to keep to the low-risk piles. They will thus earn money from the game. They cannot say exactly why they choose the low-risk piles; they just have a vague (but correct) sense that they are profitable in the long run.

The orbitofrontally damaged subjects also begin by preferring the high-risk piles. But they never learn to shift to the other piles. Instead, they focus more and more on the losing high-risk piles. After 50 cards, they have lost everything and want to borrow money so that they can play even more.

Sometimes they can even explain rationally and persuasively that they should choose the other piles, or the investigator can simply inform them of that fact and bring them back in a few weeks to try the test again. And then they will again lose a fortune.

If we measure the subjects' stress level by attaching electrodes to their skin (popularly known as "using a lie detector"), we can see that both the healthy and the ill subjects react to losing and winning money. There is no difference.

But the experiment shows that when a healthy research subject has played for a short time, a stress response is also detected when his hand merely approaches one of the high-risk piles. Although the subject is not yet conscious of the pile being risky, his body sends him a signal of danger and unease when he considers drawing a card from it. The longer a healthy subject plays, the stronger this signal becomes, until finally he is able to explain the system behind the game.

The Iowa Gambling Task strikingly and unequivocally demonstrates that subjects with orbitofrontal damage never develop this unconscious physical signal about approaching danger.

Similarly, if a researcher shows them photos of natural disasters, wars, or other scenes of human suffering, they do not show any fluctuation in galvanic skin response, such as is found in healthy subjects. Neither do they get gooseflesh when healthy subjects do, e.g., while listening to certain pieces of music.

These results led to Antonio Damasio's Somatic-Marker Hypothesis, which he argues for in his book *Descartes' Error*.

It is only when a healthy subject has been experiencing such corporeal signals for some time—about which action will be most advantageous— that he is able to explain the choices he makes. The Somatic-Marker Hypothesis says that a rational choice depends on first an emotion, then a physical reaction to the emotion, and finally an intellectual explanation of what the reaction signifies.

The title of Damasio's book, *Descartes' Error*, reflects its main thesis: a refutation of René Descartes (1596–1650). One of Western philosophy's most influential figures, Descartes is known for, among other things, his theory of the separation of mind and body, and for his assertion "I think, therefore I am."

According to Damasio's theory of somatic markers, Descartes was mistaken in isolating the mind from the biological body. Damasio maintains that rational thought and ethical assessments cannot exist independently of the body and its physical reactions.

13

"This article explains everything!"

I run up to Niklas's room to share it with him, but of course he isn't home. From his window I look down the street to see if he's on his way. But nobody's there.

I hurry toward Frederik's office to tell him but stop in the hallway. He won't care, I'll become unhappy, we might start arguing.

I could call Vibeke and Thorkild, but I can't muster the energy. Then there are our friends, but many of them work at Saxtorph, and the vast majority are siding with Laust and the new administration; they hope that, if Frederik does get well again, he'll be handed a heavy sentence.

One of the teachers we still talk to, and who doesn't question Frederik's innocence, told me that one day the male teachers started fighting during a faculty meeting because some of them referred to Frederik as a criminal and others wouldn't stand for it.

Sometimes when I'm out shopping, random people come over to me and declare their support, while others shout "Swine!" if I take Frederik with me to the Irma supermarket in The Square, Farum's one major mall.

I'd particularly like to phone Laust and tell him about the Iowa Gambling Task; maybe he can understand now how wrong he's been. Yet I can't bring myself to call him again. The few times I've tried, he's slammed down the receiver—even though some nights he still calls me and drunkenly rants and weeps about his school. He keeps on saying that Frederik hasn't just destroyed the lives of students and staff; he's also made meaningless the lives of Laust's father, grandfather, and great-grandfather.

I go down to the living room and look out the window again to see if Niklas is coming home yet. Though why should he?

Three boys run from our yard. Something about them tells me they're not just out playing. I walk outside to find that they've spray-painted our house. SHITHEAD LIVES HERE! it says. I go straight for a stiff brush and a bucket of soap and water.

Half an hour later, dusk is falling and I've scrubbed off as much as I can. The air is chilly and damp, but I'm heated with the effort and walk around to the backyard, where neighbors and passersby can't see me. Here I can also escape from the sight of the burnt grass and the faint hovering shadows on the front wall of the house, where the soap has removed old grime in a pattern that vaguely says SHITHEAD.

I sit down on the naked springs of the hanging sofa. How long ago is it now that Frederik and I blew off the neighbor's summer party and sat here with a bottle of wine before going up to our bedroom? Was that about the same time we were doing the bathroom remodel?

The metal wires press against my buttocks, and I look up at the window of Frederik's office workshop. It's still dark; I ought to go in and turn on a light for him. He forgets to, every evening, and it's wrecking his eyes.

My cell phone rings.

"Hello, it's Bernard. Am I bothering you?"

"No, not at all."

"You sound like you're freezing."

"Nah, not really. Has something happened?"

"I got an e-mail from Andrea in the support group. She said we should google *Iowa Gambling Task*. I did, and it makes a convincing argument that when Frederik was playing the commodities market, he wasn't his real self."

As he speaks, I can almost see the dew descending in the half darkness among the branches of the shrubbery. It falls and falls, it soothes without ever seeming to land. Bernard's voice is that way too: deep and steady as it settles over me.

"She sent that to me too. I just read about it on the web—just now!"

"So you must be happy, right?"

"Yes." I choose not to mention the graffiti on the wall, to say that even children hate us now. And it's too complicated to explain that even when I'm "happy," I still have an underlying angst, a feeling that if I exhale deeply and really relax for half a second, the world will collapse. Hopefully, if Frederik is acquitted, the anxiety will stop.

"You and Frederik should celebrate." He notices my hesitation almost before he has a chance to draw a breath. "Well, Frederik might not be so interested. But when he's better . . ."

"Yes . . . then he'll realize how important it is."

"Are you sure you don't want to go inside? Because you do sound like you're freezing."

"I'm going in now."

As soon as I'm in the house, I discover how cold I am.

"I'm going to lie down on the sofa," I say into the phone. "I've got to enjoy it as much as possible before we have to sell it."

And then we both laugh.

...

"What happened to the house?"

Niklas is speaking to me, and I struggle to figure out where I am. The sofa in the living room, still mine. He stands in front of me. It's dark; I must have slept for several hours. Where's Frederik? Did he run outside? And where's Niklas been—what was it he said?

"What happened to the house?" he says again.

Yes, what *did* happen to the house? I sit up. How dark it is! It starts coming back to me.

"The house? The house? Somebody wrote on it this afternoon. Can you see it in the dark?"

"It looks like big clouds on the front."

"That's where I scrubbed off the spray paint. The surface is lighter there, isn't it?"

"From the street it looks like there's ghosts floating around the yard."

"Have you had anything to eat?"

"Yeah, of course."

"Is it late?"

"After nine."

I stumble up to Frederik's office. He isn't there, but I find him sleeping in our bed. So I go down to the kitchen to throw together a bite to eat. I imagine that his brain heals better when he's asleep, so I never wake him unless it's absolutely necessary.

On the kitchen counter stand a half-empty carton of milk and half a pear pie I bought on my way home from work.

"Niklas!" I shout.

He doesn't respond, so I go out into the entry.

"Niklas!"

"Yes!" The voice comes from his room.

"Would you come down here, please?"

The potatoes are boiling by the time he appears. His shirt is buttoned wrong; it wasn't before.

"What's up?"

"You're old enough to set the milk and pie back in the fridge when you're done with them."

"I forgot. Why didn't you do it yourself, since you were here already?"

"Because you need to learn to do it. We have to save money. We can't let food go bad."

"Dad forgets the butter on the table all the time."

"Yes, which is why it's even more important that the rest of us remember to put things away. Dad can't help it."

"I can't help it either. *My* orbitofrontal region is also—"

He breaks off suddenly when he catches sight of something behind me. I wheel around, but I can't see what he's reacting to. There isn't anything there, just one of Frederik's typical piles of speaker clutter. I step closer: electronic components soldered together, a soldering iron, a coil of solder, some sort of meter. I haven't seen the meter before. It looks highly technical, and expensive. I lift it up; engraved on the bottom it says PHYSICS LAB / PROPERTY OF BIRKERØD GYMNASIUM.

"What's this?"

"It's for Dad's speakers."

"Did you take it from the school?"

"I borrowed it for him."

"Did they give you permission to?"

He doesn't answer.

"Have you started *stealing*?"

"Everything Dad does is just *fine*. All the time, no matter what. You don't give him a hard time for stealing twelve million crowns! But if I borrow just one little tiny thing that isn't even for myself—"

"Niklas, your father is gravely ill."

"Yeah, but *my* frontal lobes don't function the way they should either."

Something here isn't quite right, but I can't put my finger on it. He's not yelling at me as loudly as he usually would; his shirt is misbuttoned; he's taken a double portion of pie. Does he have someone up in his room with him—Mathias? The girl that Frederik was so rude to, Emilie? Is she up there now? My thigh bumps into the counter so that the soldering iron tumbles over the edge and dangles on its cord, three-fourths of the way to the floor.

A note of Frederik's indifferent, unsympathetic tone creeps into Niklas's voice. "You should also show some concern for *my* brain. *My* impulse control and long-term planning aren't—"

"What are you talking about?"

The thought of Emilie in his room: myself once, in Casper's room. Sixteen years old. He let his fingers slide lightly—almost floating—up the length of my forearm. And down again, back and forth, floating. That's what we did—for an eternity. The darkness and Duran Duran. On the captain's bed in his room with our clothes on.

"There was an article about it lying on the coffee table."

"An article about what?"

"Something you printed out. About how when you're sixteen, you're just as smart as a grown-up, but some parts of your brain still need to develop and won't finish till you're twenty."

Casper thrust a hand underneath my blouse, and afterward down my pants. The thin pale boyish skin of his cheeks, still hairless.

Niklas regards me defiantly. "They're in the frontal lobes, same place as Dad. So *I'm* just as—"

"Niklas, you can't think about yourself that way. It doesn't give you permission to do whatever you want."

"But it's true!"

"Yes, it might be true enough. But you should think that way only about others. With other people, it can help you understand and forgive. But with yourself . . ."

We discuss the matter. I've never caught him taking something from school before, and I want him to understand how serious it is. But the whole time, I see before me Emilie and Niklas. She's such a beautiful girl, pale and freckled. And Niklas is better looking than Casper was . . . Are they girlfriend and boyfriend? Niklas lets his hand glide across one of her breasts while she lies on the captain's bed in Casper's room. Duran Duran. Culture Club. Niklas's own music.

He's anxious to leave the kitchen.

"Did you bring someone home with you?"

He hesitates, tilting his head slightly as he answers. "I might've."

"Is it Emilie?"

The way his face freezes, eyes wide open. He's in love, I can see it in his fright.

"You're *not* going up there."

I find myself smiling. "No, of course not."

He's in love. Frederik and I went in for an ultrasound; the heartbeat, his first day of school, the day in the yard when we played badminton. I've got to stop myself, to act adult. Niklas is in love; am I smiling too much? He looks so incredibly serious. Theft, responsibility, pregnancy.

"Do her parents know where she is?"

"Of course!"

And then he's on his way back upstairs.

. . .

Every day, I try to empty my head of thoughts about how different my life would have been if I'd stayed with one of the men I knew before Frederik. Niklas would have had less amazing genes, been less intelligent, less creative, looked different. But perhaps he'd have wanted to play tennis and go running with me. Perhaps we would have been closer.

We'd probably have been something of a sports family, since all the men I was with before Frederik were interested in sports. And maybe Niklas would have had siblings. The fertility specialist said that the problem lay with me, but with another man you never know.

At one time I lived for a year and a half with Søren, who was studying public administration. We were sure that it would be the two of us for life, and we both sobbed on the foam mattress in our dank, noisy apartment on Pheasant Road when it became necessary for me to tell him I'd met someone else. But I was too obsessed with Frederik to stay—Frederik was so much fun, so attentive, he knew everything, he was so honest and could share his feelings. The problems I'd had with Søren, and which I'd thought were problems with me, weren't there with Frederik. No one could compete. No one came close.

A few years ago, Niklas and I were standing in line for the duty-free shop on the ferry to Germany. We were going on vacation, and Frederik was standing up on the deck talking with Laust on his cell, just as he'd done in the car. Suddenly I realized that the father in the family in front of us was Søren. I hadn't seen him since when he wouldn't stop writing me letters about how he'd never be happy if I left him.

On the ferry, he told me that he still played tennis twice a week. He was working in the Department of Sport within the Ministry of Culture, and he wore his age much better than Frederik. He proudly presented his beautiful fit wife, who had the same blond ponytail as me, and their three lovely girls. And Niklas met the man who would have been his father if Trørød Elementary hadn't decided that Frederik and I should both attend a school camp in Sweden where it would be raining on a broad deserted beach.

I told Niklas that Søren was my boyfriend before I met his father, and he regarded Søren with a look that was astonished and intensely blank at the same time. I'd never seen such a look before, though since Frederik's operation it's become a regular part of my life. It's the same expression Frederik gets when someone mentions that he's sick. There's no pigeonhole in his brain where he can file that datum. It simply doesn't exist.

...

So much would have been different if I'd stayed with Søren. My husband would be healthy. My children's father would be healthy.

...

At twenty past ten, I hear a soft click from the front door. Niklas and Emilie did a good job of stealing down the stairs.

They walk a little ways down the street before she mounts her bike; he doesn't kiss her goodbye, doesn't give her a hug either, and I think I manage to step back from the living room window before he turns around.

I hear him go to bed, and even though I must have napped at least three hours, I'm ready to lie down too. For almost half a year now, I've slept alone on the air mattress on the floor, but I usually lie on my side of the bed first and read for a while. I've discovered that I have fewer nightmares if I read a women's magazine just before falling asleep, and there's no lamp over by the air mattress.

A few hours later, Frederik wakes me as he shuffles around, toothbrush in his mouth, and sets his clothes out on the dresser. The alarm clock says half past two. I've fallen asleep in our bed with the night lamp on.

It's the worst imaginable time to start a serious conversation, but I find myself saying the first thing that crosses my mind. "You shouldn't try to get Niklas to steal things for you."

Already as my mouth blurts out the words, I grow apprehensive. Now the rest of the night's probably destroyed; I might have to listen to him yell at me for hours on end. And I have to go to work in the morning.

But all he says is, "That's something I could never do."

He smiles and then suddenly perks up—perhaps because lying stimulates him.

"That would be a terrible thing to do," he says. "I think that would be utterly, utterly, utterly wrong. And I *haven't* done it." He persists with this lie, though I haven't contradicted him. "You'd have to be a real shit to have your son steal for you. That's something I'd never do."

He stands quietly on the floor right in front of me, fixing his gaze upon me with unusual intensity.

I've read enough neuropsychology to know the medical term for what he's doing: he's *perseverating*—meaning that he continues the action he's in the middle of, long past what's necessary.

"Do you really believe I'd try to get Niklas to steal?" he asks. "I swear to you I wouldn't. You can be one hundred percent certain that I wouldn't do such a thing. One hundred percent. Because I think it's wrong. One hundred percent."

I just want him to forget about it without going berserk. We'll have to discuss it some other time. "No, I do know that," I say. "Just come to bed now."

As he returns to the bathroom to spit out the last of the toothpaste, wearing a T-shirt and nothing else, I think about how easy I find it to shelve my impulse to talk about Niklas. Twenty seconds ago, the words just tumbled out. Was that due to poor blood flow through my frontal lobes as I was waking up? Did the blood start to surge then with fear and stress from the prospect of an argument? From what I've read, it seems very likely. Maybe this is as close as I can get to feeling how it is for Frederik all the time.

Frederik settles down next to me with an auto-racing magazine that Thorkild bought him.

I turn on my side to face him. "Sorry for saying that. I'm really glad that you had the strength not to get angry. You're making progress all the time, and I appreciate it."

Irritated, he smacks his magazine down on the comforter. "Feelings, feelings, feelings! We always have to talk about the things *you're* interested in! When can we talk about something *I* think is exciting?"

"Well, but we talk about your speakers every single evening."

"That's not so very much, is it? There's also something called morning and noon and afternoon, and also night. And noon and morning." He's perseverating again.

"Fine. So let's talk about the speakers."

After I've listened once more to him go on about baffle plate density, harmonic overtone series, and Q factors, he calms down. I'm desperate to talk to someone about how I can support Niklas through all this in the best way possible, but Frederik's started reading his magazine again. So I send Bernard a text message, figuring he'll read it tomorrow.

I have to think a long time to achieve the right casual tone. Whatever I do, it mustn't sound desperate.

Hi Bernard—if you have the time, I'd really appreciate talking to you about living with a teenage boy when you're married to someone with brain damage. Not so much a lawyer talk—more of a support group talk. Thanks, Mia

Within a few seconds, the display on my cell phone lights up. I take the call before it manages to ring.

"I think about that a lot," Bernard says. "I'd be very glad to talk it over with you."

"Were you awake too?"

I can hear him hesitate, and then we both start laughing.

"It's not a big deal."

"We can talk tomorrow—or whenever it suits you."

"Yes, let's do that. But we could also talk now." His voice sounds gravelly, in a way it doesn't during the day. "Was there something particular that happened between you and Niklas today?"

I have to draw a deep breath while I consider how best to formulate it. "He's never stolen before, but . . ."

Behind my back, Frederik grunts irritably. "Isn't it time for you to go down to your own bed now?"

I turn over so I can see him. He looks at me over the top of his car magazine.

I switch off my bedside lamp and gather up my comforter. In my ear I hear Bernard's voice. "Was that Frederik?"

"Yes, I'm disturbing his reading. Hold on a sec, and then we can talk."

Dear Mom and Dad,

Mia has asked me to thank you so much for the money you're loaning us so that we can make it through this period while I'm not allowed to work. I'm writing to tell you to give us more.

It would be easy to think that ordinary, inexpensive particleboard would be just as suitable as high-density fiberboard.
   That's WRONG!
   A large percentage of the distortion—and with it the obscuring of microdetails—of the musical essence of music itself!—of the reason that we listen to music at all!—of the subtle musical communication we hope to achieve!—of the joy of once more being able to listen to great art!—originate not with the speaker driver but the cabinet. The heavier the cabinet, the fewer the resonances. That is why some of the world's most-respected and well-reviewed speakers weigh a great deal more than 200 pounds. A quick internet search should convince you of this point.

Normal particleboard would be TOXIC for the sound quality that is the whole point of my endeavor. With such material, all my efforts in speaker design would be wasted.

Concrete is heavier than high-density fiberboard, and many DIYers have therefore imagined that it would be ideal to cast their own cabinets in concrete. HOWEVER, its natural resonance has a higher frequency than wood's, so even though a concrete speaker weighing hundreds of pounds has less resonant energy, the resonance will be more annoying because it lies in a tonal range where the ear is more sensitive.
   For more than a decade, concrete has been DEAD! as a material for the serious DIYer.

Therefore, you can clearly see that you should give me more money. At least 20,000 crowns!

Love,
Frederik

Frederik Halling

PS. *Niklas got an A+ in his social studies project.*

PPS. *You CANNOT solve the problem by constructing the cabinet asymmetrically to avoid standing waves!*
Standing waves are a problem inside the cabinet, and you can design your way out of it by being meticulous in your blueprints, but it doesn't solve the problem with resonances that penetrate the cabinet walls.

14

Monotony is sometimes the only thing you want: the ball coming at you. The stroke, the exhale, the balance. Three quick steps to midcourt. And then the ball coming back. Stroke, exhale, balance.

Stroke, exhale, balance.

I'm playing with Helena. The stroke and the breath, the sweat on my face, the balance; the sun low in the sky, the crunch of crushed stone underfoot.

As I play I concentrate with everything I've got. And at the same time I dream. I dream about playing tennis: another game with Helena. We're on the same court, the balls strike at other angles, the sun perching a bit lower in the sky. And in that game I dream of a third game. The sun even lower. The balls harder. The skid marks longer on the clay.

Stroke, exhale, our hour is up and I wipe my brow, gasp for air. This utter physical exhaustion is the closest I come to happiness. We saunter back to the dressing room and junior players run toward us in the passageway, some of whom I taught in PE. The passage rings with their shouts, we say hello, and Helena knows how much our playing means to me.

After showering, we sit on the club terrace, where we're used to drinking our homemade smoothies. While Helena pulls out glasses, straws, and a thermos of banana-and-forest-berry smoothies from her bag, she tells me of her friend Clara, who for years has confided to Helena her deliberations about whether to leave her husband or not.

It's only at Helena and Henning's parties that I've met Clara and Poul, but over time I've heard quite a bit about them, and their marriage sounds infinitely better than what Helena and I have had to put up with over the years. Yet Clara doesn't find that her sex life meets her expectations.

I'm sure I sound cranky, but it does seem out of proportion to me, her dissatisfaction with trivial problems. "Who splits up because the sex is subpar—at our age, after twenty years? Otherwise everybody'd get divorced."

"But people do in fact. They really do."

"Well okay, men do."

"Not just."

We watch the other players in silence awhile, and then Helena speaks up again.

"It sounds to me as if everything's pretty normal for them. Clara's only problem is that before she got married, she had this boyfriend who set an erotic standard that no one's been able to meet."

We squint over at the players sitting closest.

"So what did he *do*?" I lean in across the table as I stir my smoothie with my straw.

"From what I understand, it never stopped being like the first couple months. He kissed and massaged and licked and stroked and was completely obsessed with her and . . . I don't know. When she describes it to me, she gets all agitated just from talking about it, but it's still hard to get a clear sense . . . Apparently he was quite playful too, but in a natural way—not that porno stuff."

I nod as if I have some idea what she's talking about. We laugh nervously.

Helena takes a sip of her smoothie. "Pretty good, huh?"

"Excellent."

"I sweetened it with cranberry juice this time—and no yogurt . . . Anyway, it's obvious that Clara's never gotten over those early nights—even after having three kids with Poul. That's where the real problem lies."

"But it couldn't have been just what they did in bed," I say, feeling naïve. "He must also have been the love of her life, right?"

Helena shrugs.

It's devolved into a rather pitiful tale, I think. "So why'd she break up with Superlover?"

"He found somebody else. One day it was just, *J'en ai assez.*"

"What?"

"Yeah, he was a Frenchman."

"What was his name?"

"Hmm . . . Can't remember."

Silence.

"Really, I can't." She looks at me quizzically. "Why? Do you know any Frenchmen?"

"Nooo . . ."

She starts laughing a little and says, "Tell, tell!"

"There's nothing to tell."

"But you've met *some* Frenchman, someplace or other. So what's his name?"

"It's just Frederik's lawyer, the guy I'm going over to see later to talk about Niklas. His name's Bernard."

"Jesus! That was this fellow's name too! Could be, he's—"

"It is? Really? That's just—"

"Ha-ha! You should see your face!"

Helena doubles up in her seat with laughter. Three teenagers at the far end of the terrace turn around and look at us with disapproval, though they can't possibly hear what we're talking about.

"I did say I couldn't remember his name."

We turn the conversation to other things. Only in the parking lot, when we're about to take leave of each other, do I say, "You don't recall hearing anything else about that Frenchman, do you?"

Helena no longer looks amused. She shakes her head as she studies my features a little too closely.

...

Bernard is no doubt a busy man, so I suggested we have our chat at his house. That way I'd take up as little of his time as possible.

"Sounds good—and then you can meet Lærke," he said right away.

As I drive to Brede, I speculate about what his wife's secret must be. A partially paralyzed, mentally handicapped woman who, eight years after their auto accident, still makes her husband dizzy with excitement. How does she do it?

Once I've parked, I check how I look in the rearview mirror. I gave it everything today, so that Helena wouldn't beat me too badly—I'm not at all in shape after taking a couple of months' break when Frederik got sick. My skin's still flushed from the morning's effort, and my pores still open, but my eyeliner sits okay. I've already opened the car door when I discover damp patches under my arms. I do happen to have, on the backseat, a white short-sleeved blouse that I picked up from the cleaners. Nobody's on the street, so I do a quick change in the car.

Bernard's low white house looks exactly as homey as I imagined, and the woods at the end of the street can't be more than seventy-five yards away. I can smell dank soil and the Mølle River; everything seems so lush, even though here I'm closer to Copenhagen than when I'm home in Farum.

But it's not Bernard who opens the door. Instead I find myself standing before a striking older woman with an upright bearing and impressively upswept grey hair.

"Hi. Bernard called to say that he's been slightly delayed."

"Oh, but that's all right."

I already know that she's Lærke's mother, Winnie, but we introduce ourselves anyway.

"Lærke's in the yard," she says. "Can I get you anything?"

"If you have any cold juice, that would be lovely."

"You bet. Just go out to her and I'll make up a pitcher."

My eyes are drawn to a photo on the wall of the entry, the same holiday snap that Bernard showed me on his cell phone the other day: all that happiness, all those smiles. It's odd that it stayed with me, for I only saw it briefly, yet I have the sense of having dreamt about it since.

Winnie follows my gaze. "Yes, simpler times," she says.

We both stand there, looking at the picture.

"One can get so angry," she says. "But he's dead now—the driver."

I keep staring stiffly at the photo, but not from curiosity anymore; I just know I can't bear to look into Winnie's face.

"He changed lanes and rammed three cars into each other," she says. "There was nothing they could do. Two seconds, and it was all over."

As we walk through the living room, I take in everything I can, trying to get a reading on their home without drawing too much attention to myself. Low ceilings, quite cozy, and lots of framed black-and-white art photographs on the walls—just the thing for Niklas. And thick art books on a set of shelves that cover an entire wall.

They've clearly done something with the space, a bit like I have, but more inventively. More French signs and fun things they might have found at a flea market, less Danish design.

The backyard is decidedly larger than ours, and it slopes gently down to a large impenetrable thicket. Perhaps that's actually the woods extending all the way to here.

Seated at a table in the middle of the lawn, Lærke looks, with her flowing blond curls beneath a broad-brimmed hat, as aristocratic and dreamy as her yard. She's hardly aged in the past eight years. Blue tits dart about the blooming honeysuckle halfway down the slope.

I walk all the way over to her before she notices me.

"Hi, I'm Mia."

She smiles but doesn't get up. I can see the grips of her crutches sticking out from the darkness under the table. "Oh yes, welcome. Good that you could come."

"What a magnificent yard you have!"

"Thank you, we like it a great deal too."

"And it's so well maintained! Are you the one who takes care of it?"

"My mother does."

"I've got to say, it must be great having a mother like that."

"Yes, we like it a great deal."

I sit down. "Your mother's coming out with some juice for us in a little bit."

"Well now, juice. That's something I really like."

Everything is so inviting, so tempting, so marvelous, yet I feel like the healthy person whose hand approaches a dangerous pile of cards in the Iowa Gambling Task. I can't say why, but there's something about her replies that gives me a strong urge to retreat. Instead, I make an effort to find my cheeriest and most relaxed tone of voice. "We were just standing and admiring the picture of the four of you in your entryway."

"That's from the Cévennes." A long curly lock of blond hair has fallen across her forehead, but she leaves it there. "We love those mountains, they're in France. Bernard's family has a house in a village there, Aumessas. It's our favorite place."

"I've never been down there."

"It's lovely." She smiles and says, "You've been tennising?"

"Yes."

"Just like Bernard."

"Yes."

"I also tennised. Or . . . it's not called that, is it?"

"You also *played* tennis."

"Ah yes. Ha-ha!" She has a sweet, girlish laugh. "I *plaid* tennis."

"But you can't anymore?"

"No, and it's really too bad."

"Yes."

I keep discovering new aspects of the garden. An azalea bed in a far corner blossoms in several colors, and when I look back toward the house I catch sight of three camellias. I certainly haven't seen many of those in Denmark. I once tried to get one to grow in my yard.

"Have you been to the day-care center today?" I ask.

"Yes."

"And you like going there?"

"Yes, I like it a great deal."

"So what did you do today?"

She sits silently for a long while before she answers. "Imagine, do you know what? I can't remember." She laughs. " 'Do you know what,' that's a good pression, isn't it? I love good pressions. Our language is so rich! It's rich in good pressions, in . . . ex- . . . ex-pressions."

"Yes, it is. I really like good expressions too."

" 'Do you know . . .'; 'do you know . . .'—what was it now?"

" 'Do you know what?' "

"Oh yes. Ha-ha! I said, 'Do you know . . .—what . . . ?' And you said, 'Do you know what?' "

"Yes, that's funny."

"Ha-ha! Language is so rich."

Winnie comes toward us from the house, bearing a tray with a pitcher of juice and four glasses. When she's still some distance away, she calls out, "You'll have to pardon me! I was delayed."

"Don't worry about it," I say. "We're sitting here enjoying your lovely yard. I could stay all day."

132

"Thank you, we like it a great deal. Actually, I was in the middle of playing mah-jongg online with my sister in Sydney. She was sitting there waiting for my next move, so I just wanted to—"

"That's fine, you should go back in then and finish playing."

"Thanks, I'd actually like that. Just give a shout if there's anything I can do."

She leaves again, and Lærke says, "You and Bernard are going to talk about your son Nelkas, right?"

"Yes, that's right."

"I'm sorry."

"Thanks."

"Tumor."

"Yes."

Through the bushes at the bottom of the yard, I glimpse a couple running past in sweat suits. There must be a path back there. So Bernard and Lærke used to be able to go running in the woods right from their yard.

...

Bernard's suddenly standing behind us. He's in a suit, and when he bends over to kiss his wife, his white-grey hair catches the sun.

After embracing her and exchanging endearments, he glances over at me. "You'll have to excuse me. I try to always be punctual, but sometimes when I'm in court . . ."

"Of course."

He looks at Lærke again and touches her shoulder. "Why isn't Winnie here? Is she in her room?"

"She's mah-jongging."

Bernard explains, "My in-laws have their own room here, with a computer and everything. So they can overnight when we have a special need for them."

As I nod, smiling, I try to imagine Vibeke and Thorkild keeping a room in our house. It sounds horrific, but I suppose not everyone feels that way about their mother-in-law.

"We've been sitting here enjoying ourselves," I say. "Lærke told me about the Cévennes."

"Ah, Aumessas. Every year we set a few days aside so we can be there on our anniversary."

"Such a romantic couple!"

"Yes. In recent years, Lærke's parents have come along too. It's more practical that way." He must see something in my face, for he immediately adds, "But in the evening on that day, we go out and dine without Winnie and Knud!" His voice rises on *without Winnie and Knud*; those few hours, on that one evening, must be a high point of their year.

This time I think I manage to disguise my pity.

"We like it a great deal," Lærke says, and Bernard gives her shoulder one last squeeze before leading me to their living room to talk about Niklas.

It wasn't dark when I passed through here before, but now it strikes me as almost gloomy. Of course, that's only because we've been sitting in the backyard soaking up the sun.

Bernard waits for me to sit down on the sofa, and then he sits at the other end.

"Some people find it difficult to be with her in the beginning," he says. "Naturally, that's only until you get to know her and see past the surface. For she's still got a great sense of humor and is just as loving as in the old days."

He grows lost in thought staring at my empty glass, while I think that he'll never get his old Lærke back. No matter how much he dreams and lies to himself, there's no rehab that can bring her back after eight years.

With a start, he catches himself. "Sorry about that! Would you like something more to drink?"

"Please. I seem to be just pouring it down my throat."

"Come out to the kitchen with me and we'll see what we can find."

On the way through the door to the kitchen I go a little too quickly and catch his heel, falling into him. We laugh and find some elderflower cordial in a cupboard.

The ice cubes clink as he tips them into the glass, and I see before me how he sits wedged in the car, screaming with pain and horror as the love of his life lies unconscious at his side, blood soaking into her fair hair, the color disappearing from her cheeks. The scent of blood and burnt rubber rises around me and presses against my palate.

I have a strong urge to ask, *Was she unconscious? Did you think she was dead? Were you trapped there beside her?*

I know I shouldn't, but my inhibitory mechanism must be impaired, and of all the things I want to ask, one piece slips out. "Were you injured too, that time in the car?"

"Yes." He stares deeper down into the elderflower juice than need be. "Is it okay if we don't talk about it?"

"Of course! Of course, that's totally okay!"

We walk silently back to the living room.

I start telling him about Niklas. "Often, I try to get him to tell me how he thinks things are going. But with a teenage boy, actions say more about how he's doing than words, don't they? And then when his father has him stealing from the school . . . It's also incredibly difficult when you have to set limits . . ."

I know I'm talking about everything at once.

"Yesterday Frederik set some fiberboard sheets on the floor in his office and then drilled through them," I say. "He knew he would make holes in the floor, but he didn't care! I swallowed my anger, because it was so trivial, in comparison to the embezzling. And it's all due to his sickness. But then what about when Niklas leaves a plate on the coffee table after eating something? Isn't that even more trivial? And I only yell at Niklas! So of course he gets grumpy."

Bernard talks about his boys. No answers to what I'm asking him, if I could even say what that was, just personal experiences.

It's a weird sensation: a glimpse of how it could be to raise kids as a couple. I hear myself speaking more calmly now, and my thoughts become clearer; only now do I realize how jumbled they really were.

After listening to me talk some more about Niklas, he leans forward. "I don't know why, but I was just wondering: has Frederik met some of Niklas's friends, or perhaps a girl your son is interested in? Maybe he behaved inappropriately toward her?"

"No way! How could you—"

I don't finish; he sees something through the window and hurries soundlessly to the back door, where he stands concealed in the edge of the doorway, as if he's caught sight of a deer that's come up from the woods to graze in the yard.

Instinctively I know we mustn't spook the timid creature. Cautiously, silently, I sidle toward the window.

But I don't see anything but Lærke, who's lurching across the lawn on her crutches.

"Winnie should see this too!" whispers Bernard, his eyes boyishly wide with excitement.

He heads toward the hallway, and only when he's by the hall door does he turn around and whisper, "She hasn't walked that steadily on the grass since the accident! Look at her! What willpower! She's getting back her will!"

Then he's gone.

She does look lovely out there. She struggles, and her hat's flown off, while behind her lurks brush, thicket, woods, bog. Yet I don't see anything other than her slow lurch across the lawn. I don't see what he's seeing.

Headmaster's wife still not charged

EMBEZZLEMENT. Every week brings new revelations in the case against headmaster Frederik Halling, who was charged with embezzling from Saxtorph Private School one month ago.

Halling's wife, Mia Halling, has not been charged in the far-reaching embezzlement case, although the tabloid *Ekstra Bladet* reported yesterday that she was in jail and had confessed to transferring 4 million crowns to a private bank account in Spain. That report turns out to be false.

There has been widespread speculation in the media about Mia Halling's role after it was revealed that her signature appears on several key documents in the case.

The lawyer for Saxtorph Private School, Tom Jørgensen, has stated that his client finds it indefensible that neither of the Hallings has been detained while the investigation is still ongoing. Several independent legal observers have said that it is indeed highly unusual for a defendant to avoid pre-trial detention in such a large embezzlement case. But they also emphasize that there may be mitigating circumstances that are not public knowledge, including details of a serious operation that Frederik Halling underwent recently.

In addition, Frederik Halling's lawyer, Bernard Berman, succeeded in convincing the court that Mia Halling's signature on key documents was, beyond a reasonable shadow of a doubt, falsified by the defendant himself.

Laust Saxtorph, chairman of the board for the bankruptcy-threatened school, said in a press release that while the school cannot at present prove that Mia Halling signed the documents herself, he awaits the results of further investigation. *(MT)*

15

My cousin's husband, the younger sister of the hardware store owner, the neighbor's ex—everyone, everyone. Every single one of them has their own unpredictable reaction. I get to the point of being antisocial, then I open myself up to them anyway, only to regret it when they find some new way to catch me out.

The former treasurer of our homeowners' association is suddenly standing next to me in front of the fish shop in The Square. She smiles, and I think that of all people she at least will say something kind. She's been fond of Frederik, who helped her out at one point with the accounts.

She's wearing a short red jacket, with a belt strap dangling from either side and a gaily colored scarf around her neck. "That was terrible what happened to Frederik—and on top of his illness!" she exclaims.

"Yes, it's been rather awful."

"It's so obvious it wasn't him. I can't understand how they don't see that."

The fishmonger points to me, but I wave another customer forward.

The treasurer grasps me by the arm. "But surely they'll find whoever really did it soon, won't they?"

"Whoever really did it?"

"Yes, the person who embezzled from the school. Since it wasn't Frederik."

"But it *was* him, you know. It's just that he was ill, and not himself."

"Who?"

"Frederik, yes. But he was ill. *Very* ill."

She lets go of my arm and glances around quickly, as if she's suddenly not sure she wants to be seen with me. "But it *couldn't* be Frederik. I told all my friends that I *knew* it wasn't Frederik."

"No, it wasn't Frederik—not the *real* Frederik. When it happened, his tumor had already changed who he was."

"What! So it *was* him? But I mean—has he confessed to it?"

"Yes, he—"

"What! That can't really—"

"It's complicated. He's had a brain tumor that's been growing for many years, and each year it's made him less and less himself, and as a result it's not—"

"But he was still running the school, wasn't he?"

"Yes, he was able to do that well enough."

"But he was too sick to keep from stealing from the till?"

For the thousandth time, I try to summarize in a few seconds all the books and articles I've been poring over for months. But she hurries off, and it's clear that I've yanked the rug out from under her. She'll be talking about it for the rest of the day to her husband and all her friends.

...

Before our case, I never realized that sometimes a verdict isn't decided by a judge or jury. Frederik's will be determined instead by a small group of state-approved psychiatrists, and it can't be appealed.

We'll still go to court all right, months from now, but the proceedings will be essentially pro forma. For the judge knows that he doesn't have a clue about neuropsychology, and he'll let everything hang on the psychiatric report. If the report says that Frederik embezzled the funds of his own free will, the judge will sentence him to a minimum of three years in jail. If however the report says it was the illness that drove him to it, Frederik will have to undergo treatment instead. Since the treatment is actually the operation he's already had, he'll be able to leave the courtroom a free man who doesn't have to feel guilty about having destroyed an entire school.

It's possible to find "experts" who will say anything for money, so to avoid that American state of affairs, the government has established a special group of forensic psychiatrists. It pays them to keep abreast of the latest findings in forensic psychiatry, maintaining a level of knowledge that judges, lawyers, and ordinary psychiatrists cannot.

Frederik's psychiatric report was prepared by the Clinic of Forensic Psychiatry in Copenhagen. It was based on four examinations: two by psychiatrists, one by a social worker, and one by a psychologist. In the waiting room before each exam, I was as nervous as if we were about to appear before a judge—and with good grounds, it turns out. For the four of them have been compiled into a psychiatric report that goes against Frederik.

You can't appeal a psychiatric report, nor even register a complaint about it. But Bernard requested that Frederik's report be submitted for approval to the Medico-Legal Council, which is as high in the system as you can go. In Danish law, there's no other body above it.

Today, nearly two months after Frederik's arrest, and plenty of phone conversations with Bernard later, Frederik and I are sitting in the waiting room of neuropsychologist Herdis Lebech. The council has appointed her to conduct a new psychological examination before it makes its final ruling.

Between Frederik's operation, his rehabilitation, and his embezzlement case, I've become a seasoned user of the waiting rooms of neurologists, neuropsychologists, neurosurgeons, and neurological clinics large and small. I always take along a bag of required reading for the wait, but this particular appointment is too important to let me read. I get up from my chair and sit down again with an agitation that'd make a casual observer think that my calm husband had accompanied me here and not vice versa.

The man in the chair next to me is in his sixties, slim and dressed in an elegant suit. It's easy to imagine he keeps a yacht in some expensive slip north of Copenhagen.

"I want to go home now," he says.

His wife is tanned and slathered in some odd glistening grease, and she answers him dully, like a tired receptionist.

"But you can't."

"But I want to go home."

"Yes, but you can't."

"I'd like to go home now."

"First we have to have the exam."

"But I want to go home."

"You'll have to wait."

"Now I think we should leave."

"You have to see the doctor first."

"But I want to go home."

She falls silent and gazes straight in front of her. It isn't for long.

"Erica! You could answer me when I speak to you! It's the least one could expect!"

"But you can't go home now."

"But I want to."

"You can't."

"I think we should go now."

Twenty minutes of listening to them, while I alternate between sitting and standing with a cramp in one leg, and I'm ready to go round the bend.

"Now I think we should go home."

"Just wait here a bit."

"Let's go home now."

"We have to go in for the exam."

"But I want to go home."

I smile at her and try to pass the time by making a little amateur diagnosis. He must be suffering from a frontal lobe injury too: he's got the deficient apprehension of how much time he spends continuing to do the same thing—perseveration, of course—and then the absolute lack of initiative. After all, he could just get up and go. Nobody's forcing him to stay.

I'm only beginning to form a vague sense of how the brain functions, but I wonder if his extreme lack of initiative doesn't mean that his injury lies more dorsolaterally than Frederik's. In addition, his cheerless monotone makes me think that the damage extends farther to the left.

Perhaps I should have taken Niklas along to one of these examinations, so that he could see what I have to put up with for our family's sake. On the other hand, I'd like to spare him this world.

Frederik slumps in his chair with eyes closed; perhaps he's asleep. He's storing up for the exam, I think. I can't even stand still anymore but have to shuffle about with annoyingly small steps because my calves keep cramping up.

Like an old lady who's peed her pants, I toddle down the long corridor, with all its identical closed doors. When I glance back at the waiting room, I note that the elegant yacht owner is sitting motionless in the same position as when he first sat down. He reminds me of a story Birgit told during support group last night. A week ago, when she went to fetch her husband from the day-care center, the staff couldn't find him. It turned out that he was still sitting on his stationary cycle in the workout room, even though he had finished biking two and a half hours earlier and everyone else had left the room. His initiative has been affected to an unusual degree. If no one tells him to get off the bike, he'll just keep sitting there. And he doesn't say anything because no one asks him. He probably would have sat there all night long if Birgit hadn't found him.

When our old friends see Frederik, even the best of them might say, "If I ever get a brain injury, I'm going to exercise like mad every day to get better." I get so irritated when they say things like that, for it shows they're only pretending that they think Frederik's innocent. They haven't understood anything.

If man had a self located outside the brain, and that self could stick to a decision to rehabilitate intensively, even after the brain was damaged, it could also stick to a decision to not commit crimes. Then Frederik *would* deserve to rot away in some jail. And then if he ever came out, we wouldn't be able to look ourselves or our friends in the eye; we'd have to take new names and move far away. But we have no such self. Outside the brain, there's nothing.

That's also why it's such a relief to go to support group. Everyone there knows the score. They're not just pretending to.

After I've shuffled around the same area for more than half an hour, I venture farther down the hospital's deserted corridors. There I meet a petite dark-haired woman with a pageboy. I say, "They'll come out and call us in, won't they?"

"Come out and call us in."

"Yes. It's just taken so long that I've started to have doubts."

"Doubts."

"Yes, we got a letter saying we were going to have an examination with Dr. Lebech."

"Lebech."

"Right. She's a neuropsychologist here."

"She is, right. She's a neuropsychologist here."

I feel like an idiot, looking at the small woman sweetly smiling up at me. How do I extricate myself?

I say, "Thank you for your help."

"But thank *you* for your help."

I've read about echolalia—when someone with brain damage can't help but repeat what another person says. Perhaps she suffers from echopraxia too? A cold impulse makes me raise my right hand and wait. But she doesn't raise hers; it's only words that she mimics.

Behind one of the doors a toilet flushes, and a grey-haired, even more diminutive woman emerges.

"I was just standing here talking to your daughter," I say.

Behind me I hear a voice. "Talking to your daughter."

"Do you know whether they'll call us, or do we go someplace first and let them know we're here?"

I try not to listen to the daughter while the mother tells me we've done exactly what we should have. We just have to keep waiting. "Then a secretary will come and call you."

"A secretary will call you."

A few months ago, I never imagined that this secret world existed, tens of thousands of homes where there was brain damage in the family. Pigheaded people I've argued with in the supermarket, irrationally angry folks on the sidewalk, blockheads at public meetings—now I realize that many of them are literally sick in the head. And lots of them have friends and families who love them, and who meet up like we do in my new group.

It's as if I'm in some film, where suddenly I can see and hear all the ghosts who walk among us. People with brain injuries have been here the whole time. I've met them, spoken with them, argued with them—and suspected not a thing.

...

By now, I've read lots of stories about people who have undergone neurological changes without anyone noticing. It could be due to a fall from a ladder or a bike, or to a slowly growing tumor.

We don't normally go around diagnosing each other. Even after a thousand arguments and a divorce, it rarely occurs to a person that it might be brain damage that transformed their engaged and socially adept spouse into someone cold and stubborn. It's only when you look back that all the pieces fall into place.

So when did what the doctors call *insidious personality changes* begin with Frederik?

In the case of an orbitofrontal tumor, the first signs typically appear when your partner begins to make choices that you don't understand, and he becomes more adamant about these choices than usual. The neurologists use the word *rigid* for this lack of flexibility. They say that word a lot.

In addition, you should keep your eye on whether he becomes more easily distracted by immediate pleasures and impulses. For example, he might be getting lazier and worse at honoring agreements.

You should also monitor any changes in his emotional life. It could be that he starts to always be in the same unvarying mood—or conversely, that he starts experiencing dramatic mood swings.

Then of course there's increased self-centeredness. And finally, another danger signal is alterations in your partner's sexuality—if he exhibits markedly enhanced or diminished sexual energy, or if his sexual interests change.

Looking back on the last few years with all this knowledge, I can see now that yes, Frederik was starting to make poor decisions more often. But in fact I thought that the change was in me—that I was getting older and smarter and less youthfully uncritical in my adoration of him.

A few times, he also acted impulsively in a way I doubt he would have before—for instance when he bought Niklas's camera or the Alfa Romeo. Yet it's hard to say exactly when it wasn't just a normal development in his old self, but him actually becoming another person.

And compared to the husbands of all my friends, he didn't grow lazy, though with respect to his own standards he certainly did. In the old days, he shirked his domestic obligations plenty of times; the difference was that when he did so then, it was always because he had more important things to do at school. Now he'd do it sometimes just so he could loaf around at home. And I thought, *Finally!* We started kicking back together on the weekends in a way that I'd begged for in vain for more than ten years. Never mind that I had to cut the grass after we'd agreed he would. I didn't care.

Did he start having a harder time controlling his emotions? Yes, he probably did. In the last couple of years before the operation, he occasionally became angry or upset like he never had before. But I found comfort in that too—because it meant we were together. Because I no longer felt he was hiding his feelings from me. At last he was letting me in. And it didn't seem pathological. None of his changes seemed the least bit pathological.

I've read that an increase in the number of arguments is often the warning signal you notice first. That's because in a family context, where everyone's evolving and interconnected, it can be hard to single out changes in one person. And Frederik and I did begin to argue, in the car; I'd tell him that he took alarming risks in traffic, and he'd shout back that I'd gotten more chicken since we first met. The truth probably lay somewhere between—or so I thought until recently.

Yet by and large we argued less than before. In the old days we would argue a lot about his absence from our family. And that stopped.

So when did the insidious changes begin—when exactly? Among all the thousands of chaotic little conflicts and oddities that make up everyday life in a family, what's the first episode, however minor, that I can point to and say *Frederik wasn't himself*?

The earliest one I can come up with and date precisely was on our anniversary six years ago. As his gift to me, Frederik bought a cheese. I was furious—especially because I still felt bitter about his affair with the English teacher that I'd uncovered a few years earlier.

"I'm sure you didn't buy *her* a cheese!" I yelled.

And he was, yes, perfectly rigid in insisting that it was a fine romantic present. "A *delectable* cheese!" he said, again and again. "It was expensive! We'd never buy a cheese like this if it weren't our anniversary. We'll have a great time eating it and savoring it together."

And he persuaded me that I was the one being rigid, though of course we didn't use that word. That I wasn't being open and modern if I couldn't see how romantic it would be for us to enjoy ourselves with that cheese and some fine wine.

Now I think differently about every single detail of our eighteen-year marriage . . . It *is* a weird gift for an anniversary, isn't it? A *cheese*? Would a perfectly healthy Frederik have come up with that? I'm genuinely convinced that he wouldn't have. And that was six years ago.

...

I've lost all sense of dignity and am standing doing stretches up against the wall, to get rid of my leg cramps, when a secretary calls Frederik in.

Herdis Lebech, who will now pass judgment on us, turns out to be a small, smiling woman with an enormous pelvis. She ushers us into an office with overflowing shelves. It could easily belong to an accountant or an insurance agent if it weren't for the plastic model of a brain that stands on a table right in front of my chair. The brain's wrinkled surface has been painted neon red and pale blue, so that it resembles the face of a mandrill.

"The Medico-Legal Council has sent me the reports from your earlier examinations. In addition, I have here the scans from before and after your operation," she says, addressing Frederik. "What I'd like to do first is have the three of us talk together. After that, I'll ask your wife to leave, so that you can concentrate on some new tests I have for you. And finally, I'd also like to speak alone with your wife, if that's all right with you."

Frederik sits calmly in his chair. "That's quite all right with me. No problem at all."

"Good. As a starting point, can you tell me how you felt about the other examinations you've had?"

Frederik starts talking, and he sounds perfectly healthy! It's in his tone of voice, his choice of words. It's that he himself takes the initiative and talks about more than he's been asked. He's the old sensible Frederik.

I'm overwhelmed, and after a couple of minutes I can't sit still any longer, I feel compelled to interrupt him. "Frederik! This is fantastic, really fantastic! I haven't heard you talk like this in an eternity! You've gotten so much better!"

"Yes, I'm getting better all the time. But I was actually about to tell the doctor about this test."

Frederik goes on talking, until a little later when I feel the need to break in again. "I'm getting a bit worried now that Dr. Lebech will get the wrong impression of how sick you really are."

He replies with the easy charm he used to be praised for. "Mia, you need to trust the doctor. Dr. Lebech is a neuropsychologist. You should have no trouble assessing my condition, right, Doctor?"

"That's right."

I look at Frederik and the doctor in turn. "But perhaps you should also show Dr. Lebech how you usually are—how you've been at home with me during the last few months."

"I'm not going to act like something I'm not! That would be dishonest. And besides, Dr. Lebech is going to report on how sick I was then, not how sick I am now. The postoperative swellings have been exerting a pressure on my brain that is distinct from the pressure exerted by the olfactory meningioma they removed. So my symptoms after the operation should in any case differ from my symptoms before—right, Doctor?"

"Yes, that's quite correct."

"Good," he says. "So if I could just be allowed to continue . . ."

My friends have told me it can be obnoxious, all the neurological terms I've started using in conversations on almost any subject. Frederik has never lain awake at night and read the scientific literature like I have. Nevertheless, he's apparently picked up some technical expressions even I wouldn't use.

I make an effort to sit quietly, but a few minutes later I simply have to interrupt again. "Frederik, why are you so well all of a sudden? It's wonderful, of course—but why just now?"

"No need to exaggerate my illness, Mia! I feel in fact that I've been healthier the whole time than you make me out to be."

"There, now you sound sick again."

"I had better interpose here," the doctor says. "It's completely normal for someone to function better during an examination like this than in everyday life at home. If you've been anxious about this exam, the right level of stress in your brain—not too little, not too much—can eliminate your symptoms temporarily."

She looks at me, and her pale round eyes twinkle in her pale round face. "Mia, of course you wish that Frederik could be like this all the time. But he can't. It isn't something he can control. And if he does have some hours when it goes well, then he may also become terribly tired afterward. What you and I find normal is an Olympic performance for him."

I'm extremely impressed by this moon-woman. I came in here thinking I'd have to argue in some Kafkaesque show trial, yet after just a few minutes she's displayed more understanding for my situation than my friends. It's almost like when I talk to Bernard.

"I know," I say. "And I've seen it come and go many times, but I've never seen . . . And I hope you don't get the wrong impression."

"You can trust me not to. That's also what Frederik's court case is about. A year and a half ago, you were much, much less sick than you are now, Frederik. And you seemed to be healthy nearly the entire time—though perhaps you needed to leave work earlier than you were accustomed to, didn't you?"

"That's right, I did."

"Yes, you needed to relax with something that wasn't too demanding. Maybe you watched TV, maybe you sat in your yard a bit to unwind?"

"Yes, that's what I did."

"Did you have headaches very often when you were relaxing at home?"

"I did."

"But my male patients don't ever tell anyone about them—so you probably didn't either, did you."

"No."

"And so if one day you were feeling especially tired, or had a couple glasses of wine, or perhaps had been brooding about something that had worried you all day, then you'd experience the opposite of what you've been experiencing today with this exam, right? Your symptoms would manifest themselves. And then you couldn't be trusted. Or could you, Frederik?"

"No, I couldn't. I did some terrible things."

"Yes. With the type of tumor I've seen on your scans, you might end up making some mistakes you would otherwise never make. And that would put a serious strain, wouldn't it, on a marriage—or a work environment. But then of course it'd only be due to the disease."

I sit up with a start. Her words just seemed to spill from her mouth, but didn't she say what I've dreamt of ever since Frederik was arrested?

I strive to maintain composure. "You say it was due to the disease?"

"That would normally be the case. But now of course I just need to speak more with Frederik."

She gazes at me with large sparkling eyes. She smiles again, and when

148

she blinks, she does so slowly. As if she wants to tell me something she mustn't say before she's conducted the entire formal examination. I get goose bumps and can't stop staring at her.

"From what I've read about Frederik, and the scans . . ." Her voice sounds just as relaxed as it was a moment ago. And then she repeats what she said, just as quietly. "It would normally be due to the disease. It wouldn't be something he could help."

She gives me a box of tissues she has standing behind the plastic brain. While I cry, Frederik doesn't say anything, he just puts his arms around me and holds me like in the old days.

I don't know how much time passes before I feel somewhat coherent again. I'm enveloped by Frederik's body heat and he's whispering small calming words in my ear, so that I feel his breath against my temple and throat. I look over at the doctor and say, "Thank you."

I try to explain. "Everything else is so difficult. Just trying to cancel the subscription on Frederik's phone or getting a plumber to come out. I thought that here I'd also have to argue and complain and . . . and I planned all kinds of things I was going to tell you about the Iowa Gambling Task."

"I know that study quite well. Neurophilosophy is my great passion."

"Neurophilosophy?"

"Yes—applying the methods of neurological research to questions of theoretical philosophy. Just as Damasio does with Descartes."

Then Frederik resumes his account and I try to collect myself, staring into the convoluted folds of the plastic brain before me. Small letters on the region closest to me say INTERPRETATION OF SMELL, while alongside there stretches a belt composed of many small areas: INTERPRETATION OF TASTE, ABDOMEN, THROAT, TONGUE, TEETH.

16

Dr. Lebech's test of Frederik's neurological function lasts only ninety minutes, but she's chosen tasks that challenge him where he's weakest, and when he emerges from her office, he's so beat that he can barely walk straight.

Twenty minutes later, after I've been in to talk with her too, he's asleep in the waiting room, half reclining and half sitting across two chairs. I let him sleep, and I walk out to the parking lot to call Niklas.

"The doctor said Dad's innocent!"

On the phone, it sounds as if Niklas is surrounded by friends speaking in loud voices. Apparently, his meeting of the social committee for the gymnasium isn't over yet. He speaks in a low voice, his mouth pressed to the receiver. "But wasn't it going to be in a few weeks that they—"

"Yes, this wasn't the actual psychiatric report for the court case, but the examination that the Medico-Legal Council will use to make the report. It's a step on the way—a huge step! And Dad was much more himself today too. I think you should stay home tonight so we can celebrate."

Silence.

And then his voice, still almost a whisper: "Do I have to?"

"No, you don't *have* to, Niklas. But this could be one of the most important days of our lives. Shouldn't we spend it together?"

"But it's not today that's the most important day, is it? You just said that it isn't until—"

"But maybe today's the day that decides it. Maybe it's the day that determines that Dad's innocent!"

"Then of course I'll come home. I will. We ought to . . ." I can hear from his tone that he's changing his mind again as he speaks. "But you did just say it isn't the actual report. It's only maybe . . . And besides, all of us who did something for the spring concert were going to meet tonight."

"So you'll just have to cancel your plans and celebrate with your mother and father. This is something worth commemorating."

After we've hung up I call Bernard, but he's in court. I must sound a bit silly in the message I leave on his phone, yet if Frederik can be as well as I saw today, anything is possible. Then I ring up my in-laws, Helena, and some of the others in the support group. They all sound happy for my sake. I feel so exuberant I even leave a message on my mother's voice mail.

It feels wrong to force Niklas to stay home, so I'll make an extra effort to ensure that his evening with us is a special one. After driving Frederik home, I shop for Niklas's favorite meal: large steaks and then chocolate macaroon meringue from an old fattening recipe of Vibeke's. We agreed that he'd be home at seven. I start waking Frederik half an hour before and try to get him into some festive clothes.

It's seven thirty when Niklas shows up, but I don't mention the time. I serve virgin cocktails in the living room, and I almost feel like clanging a spoon on my glass and making a speech. We've won two major victories today in the struggle for Frederik's health and freedom.

But Niklas is grumpy. I try to get him to laugh, I compliment him, ask how he's doing, fill up his glass; apologize for pressing him to stay home. And I explain once more that since a family's forced to weather the worst times together, it's important we remember to enjoy the best times together too.

Maybe he's trying to be nice—because surely he can see all I've put into the evening, with the fine cloth and the silver candlesticks on the table. But he doesn't succeed. I wonder if there might be something wrong between him and Emilie, but I know it's not worth asking. Are they girlfriend and boyfriend now? Have they quarreled? Instead, I ask how his committee meeting went, and I tell him about the other patients in the waiting room today, trying to make it as funny as I can.

In the end, I say I'll leave the two men by themselves in the living room for a few minutes while I see to the last things in the kitchen. In truth, I don't need to do anything except broil the steaks, but once in a while Niklas has more fun being alone with his dad.

It seems to work. From the kitchen, I can hear them talking about some boxing clips they've seen on YouTube. A week ago, Frederik suddenly stopped being interested in motor sports. Now he's into boxing, and he gets annoyed if someone starts talking to him about race drivers.

When we've seated ourselves at the table, Frederik wolfs down his steak in a couple of minutes—that's how he eats when he's tired. As soon as he finishes, he gets up and walks away without a word. I could shout after him, but nothing good usually comes of that.

I wonder if Niklas is going to say, *When he leaves, I leave too.* I prepare myself to answer him, but he doesn't say it. Yet my brain keeps coming up with needless reasons for why he shouldn't go. It won't stop picturing our argument.

We have a standing agreement that dinners are to be cell-free, but his phone emits a TEXT RECEIVED beep and he starts tapping out a reply.

He's managed to keep me at a distance from Emilie since I called her Sara out on the street, yet I imagine all kinds of things about her. At night before I fall asleep, I wonder what she's like. She must be gifted since Niklas is in love with her, and she must like the sort of art films that Niklas and Mathias do. Yet she doesn't take photos, she said, and she doesn't make sound collages or music like Mathias. Other than that, I don't know anything about her except what I've nosed out online: that during her first year of gymnasium, she was already on the editorial staff of the school paper, and that she's written a good article about a school in Burma that their student charity supports, as well as three short poems about her best childhood friend, who developed multiple sclerosis.

Sometimes at night when I'm dozing, I confuse her with the beautiful pale long-haired girls from my time in gymnasium. If she's a poet, she must also be sad and alone at times; maybe she has a difficult relationship with her parents, maybe I could be the kind of mother neither of us has had. And again I think of the children—the ones I lost after Niklas. Daughters, sons, siblings. The tumor we had instead.

"Why doesn't Emilie come over tonight?" I ask. "It'd be really nice if she did."

Something detonates overhead. We both start but remain seated, even though it feels like the house and the whole street continue to shake. Frederik's managed to knock over one of his great big sheets of high-density fiberboard again, onto the floor of the workshop directly above us.

"I think it's fun that you and Bernard are interested in the same photographers," I say. "He's got a book on Denis Darzacq that I borrowed. I thought we might look through it together. Then I can hear what you think about it, as a photographer."

Niklas isn't interested. And I thought I was so clever bringing the book home.

The ceiling booms above us again. I can't understand why Frederik can't see that the sheets will fall over. Niklas is texting again, and I slowly compose myself to say what I'm about to say. I'm sure he doesn't notice anything, since it was already quiet here before.

When I see that he's clicked SEND, I take a deep breath and say, "Niklas?"

"Yeah."

"I've been thinking a lot about something."

"Mm-hmm."

"I think that we need to talk about our anger."

"What anger?"

"The anger we've been feeling."

"I don't feel angry."

"I was hoping you *wouldn't* say that."

"I'm not angry!"

"Listen to yourself. You're shouting at me."

"God damn it, Mom!"

"It's okay to be angry. I'm angry too. In fact I'm furious about everything. Both of us have a great deal to be angry about."

"Aarghh!"

"It just shouldn't come between us. It doesn't have to come between us. That's too sad, all too sad."

He sighs loudly and stares down at the table. "I'd really like to go to that meeting tonight."

"Do you think *I* like to talk about this? Do you?"

Niklas's voice grows calm again, and for a moment he's the old Niklas. "No."

"I told you about the twelve appointments you can get with a psychologist, if someone in your family—"

"So you think I should go to a shrink because I don't want to stay home with you tonight?"

"No. But because you're so clearly full of sorrow and anger. Because you run away from me. And because something goes wrong every time I try to talk to you about it."

"I just wanted to go to the meeting."

"When I say *psychologist*, maybe it makes you think about your grandmother, because of the training she's doing. And so you think that it wouldn't be anything for you. I'd feel the same way. But a real psychologist is something completely different."

"I'm not thinking about Grandma."

"Did I ever tell you that when my father left us, I was angrier with my mother than with him?"

"Yes, you've told me a thousand times!" He gets up from the table. "Dad *isn't* well! And there *isn't* any psychiatric report that says he isn't going to jail! There's nothing at all to celebrate, and there's nothing nice about being here! I'm going now!"

"Won't you please just stay for five minutes?"

"But five minutes always becomes an hour, and then the whole evening."

"You're not really going to go before we've become friends again?"

"Stop saying that I'm angry at you!"

"But you *are* shouting."

"I'm shouting because you say that I'm angry."

"Let's just talk until we're good friends again. Just five minutes."

"Mom, you're lying to me! It won't be five minutes. It's *never* five minutes."

"Five minutes!"

"You're lying."

"Five minutes, Niklas! This time I swear."

"Mom, it won't be five minutes. Because things'll never be fine in five minutes. They won't be fine even if we sit here and talk all night long."

He runs up to his room and slams the door.

I hear Frederik storm out into the hall, shouting that he can't concentrate with the noise. Niklas yells back that just a couple of minutes ago *he* was banging his fucking fiberboard on the floor. I don't have the energy to go up and sort it all out. I turn on the TV and boxing comes up on Eurosport. Frederik must have been watching it today. I surf around until I find a program with some beautiful happy American women.

A few minutes later, Niklas comes down. He's changed clothes and mussed up his hair; he obviously wants to leave now.

"Sorry about yelling at you," he says.

"I'm sorry I yelled at you too."

I'm allowed to give him a silent hug.

"Are you okay?" he asks.

I recognize the look he gives me. It isn't love, but a bitter worry I might do something dumb. He's probing, to see if he can go and join his friends. He casts a brief sidelong glance at the wineglass on the coffee table.

I lie. "I'm fine."

I'm sure he sees that it's not true, but he also must see that I'm not on the edge of a breakdown.

"I'll be at Kira's," he says. "I'll be back before eleven."

From the kitchen window I watch him ride off.

And so you ride away from us; from Frederik and me. It feels so decisive, like it marks the end of an epoch, this very minute. How I envy your ability to find out how not to stay those five minutes that always turn into more. That's what I never figured out—or dared to do—with my own mother. I envy your ability to bike away from me.

The beautiful women on TV get to be too much in the end, so I click back to boxing. The Mexican's penalized for ramming his forehead into the Romanian. Sweat, the clang of the bell, towels and bloody lips. I ought to go up to Frederik, try to talk with him about Niklas. But I can't summon the energy that would require. So many things we ought to do; we ought to be able to trust each other. We ought to be able to support each other. And he ought to be completely different, so that I might feel the smallest fraction of desire for him.

Instead I prop my feet up on the coffee table. Boxing's never caught my interest, but Frederik's been forcing me to watch it these last few days, and I've started to develop a taste for it. They pound away at each other—I can see the pleasure in that. And then there is their technique and speed, their fantastic physiques.

I'm enjoying the fight and the men's grunting, gently relieving a bit of stress, when the phone rings. I quickly turn off the TV and yank my hand from my pants.

I hear Bernard's voice. "Am I disturbing you?"

"Uh-uh. No."

"I just wanted to say congratulations."

"Well thank you."

"Such a great day."

"That's just the way I feel."

In no time, I'm transported to the festive evening I'd been dreaming of. We congratulate each other again warmly, and Bernard tells me that he also has something major to celebrate. The doctor from Lærke's day-care center confirmed what he saw the other day on the lawn: Lærke's still improving, the coordination in her right leg is better, and her willpower's getting stronger.

"In fact, I'm sitting here pouring myself a glass of wine," he says. "Lærke's gone to bed. Do you have a glass so we can toast?"

"I do. Good idea."

Frederik isn't allowed to drink, so I settled for buying myself a half bottle for our celebratory dinner. I raise the glass before me.

"Cheers."

"Cheers."

We talk about how much better both Frederik and Lærke might get. I'm half reclining in the armchair with my feet up on the coffee table, and as I listen to Bernard, I turn the boxers back on, this time on mute. I ask him whether he knows anything about neurophilosophy—Dr. Lebech's word—mostly so I can listen to him some more without having to talk myself. The better sculpted of the two boxers, the Mexican, sits down in his corner, sweat sheening his torso. His abdominal muscles bulge beneath his skin, nicely defined, and he gasps for air. I slide down in my chair even farther, work my hand back into my pants, and start relaxing again to the sight of the boxers—and especially now to Bernard's deep voice.

After his neurophilosophical review, he says, "This has been very hard on you, but you haven't been thinking about leaving your husband. I find that admirable. It's one of the first things I noticed about you. Your loyalty is really remarkable."

"And the same with you, Bernard—I feel it's amazing how you always support your wife and take her part. It's unusual for a man."

"I just feel that once you've chosen each other—"

"My feeling exactly."

I take a swallow from my glass and can hear that he does the same. It seems like we've said everything there is to say on the subject, but he continues. "That's something you and I have in common. Lots of other people wouldn't have been as faithful as we've been."

I start to laugh.

"What's so funny?"

"I don't know."

Neurophilosophy

Neurophilosophy is a rapidly advancing branch of philosophy that uses neurological research to shine a new light on classical philosophical problems.

The 1986 publication of <u>Patricia Churchland</u>'s modern classic, *Neurophilosophy*, was the first major breakthrough in the field. Since then, a number of prominent philosophers and neurologists have contributed to new knowledge of the subject. Among them, <u>Daniel Dennett</u>, <u>Antonio Damasio</u> (*Descartes' Error*), <u>Daniel Wegner</u>, and <u>Benjamin Libet</u> have had the most impact.

They all base their research on the scanning technology developed in recent decades, which gives us the ability to peer into the brain while it works. The ongoing revolution in neurological monitoring equipment enables us to observe and measure fear, love, substance dependence, empathy, egotism, decision-making, daydreaming, and numerous other mental phenomena as they manifest themselves in the human brain.

In *Brain-Wise: Studies in Neurophilosophy* (2002), Churchland writes:

> . . . if we allow discoveries in neuroscience and cognitive science to butt up against old philosophical problems, something very remarkable happens. We will see genuine progress where progress was deemed impossible; we will see intuitions surprised and dogmas routed. We will find ourselves making sense of mental phenomena in neurobiological terms, while unmasking some classical puzzles as preneuroscientific misconceptions. Neuroscience has only just begun to have an impact on philosophical problems. In the next decades, as neurobiological techniques are invented and theories of brain function elaborated, the paradigmatic forms for understanding mind-brain phenomena will shift, and shift again. (p. 32)

A New Renaissance

The most radical neurophilosophers believe that the next 30 years of neurological research will bring about greater changes in our shared notion of what it means to be human than what has been achieved by the last 300 years of philosophy.

A comparison with the late-European Renaissance and the scientific revolution is germane. Until 500 years ago, physics, biology, and chemistry were considered part of "natural philosophy," not "natural science." Great minds who wanted to explore the natural order of the universe had no other means to do so than logic and reason, since their observational equipment was extremely limited. The major philosophers had concluded that the world consisted of four fundamental elements: fire, earth, air, and water. They were also of the opinion that the earth lay at the center of the universe, while around it floated the planets and stars, and beyond that the angels and God. Their entire system of thought comprised a cosmology that was complex yet logically coherent.

The rapid development of telescopes and microscopes around the year 1600 changed everything. Suddenly, one could observe and measure many aspects of the world that had been previously hidden. Essentially every explanation that philosophers had arrived at for the physical world through the exercise of pure reason turned out to be wrong. And not wrong in a trivial sense, but in fact tremendously misleading.

Today we have witnessed the arrival of machines that can monitor the brain as it functions. New instruments and methods are being developed each year at lightning speed, with enormous consequences for our understanding of classic philosophical concepts such as free will, responsibility, determinism, consciousness, language, identity, and the mind-body problem.

Our time's new instruments will usher in a wholesale upheaval in everything that philosophers, psychologists, and scientists think they know about human beings, corresponding to a new Renaissance. In time, this changed conception of humanity will spread to the judicial system, education, literature, art, and the very way we conceive of ourselves and others.

17

"The acoustics would be perfect except for this wall. It'll create reflections that might diminish the stereo perspective, but we can just hang up some Rockfon sound batts."

Frederik beams with delight, contemplating the possibilities of the claustrophobic apartment the realtor is showing us. I hate being in here. "You mean blankets of rock wool on the inside wall?"

"Yes."

"I don't want rock wool hanging on our wall!"

"Ha-ha!" He laughs his noisy mechanical laugh at the thought. "Is that so? Well it won't really be that way! I'll wrap the batts in felt, so they look almost like lawn-chair cushions."

"I don't exactly want lawn-chair cushions hanging on the wall either."

"Well, we're both going to have to compromise there. It's important to me. And there are two of us."

It's the first time since the operation that he's said *compromise* or *two of us*. There's progress all the time. Now I can leave him home by himself—he stays in his workshop anyway, pretty much from when he wakes up till when he goes to bed—so we no longer have Thorkild and Vibeke at the house every weekday. And when he's rested, strangers think he's healthy—that he's just an unusually self-centered man with an obnoxious laugh.

We're accustomed to living modestly. But what we can afford now—on his disability pension and my teacher's salary—is *very* modest. We're look-

160

ing only at two-bedroom apartments. Somehow we'll have to manage the lack of space. But I'm going to miss my yard something terrible. I'm looking for an apartment I can be happy to come home to after a day at work, an apartment that despite the lack of square footage is light and inviting. An apartment where I can imagine a future.

The one we're looking at now is horrible. Even though it's one of the larger apartments on my list, the layout is so ill conceived that regardless of where I stand, it makes me feel trapped. Even the realtor looks as if being here is making him ill.

"I could have this room to myself," Frederik says happily when we're in the only large room, which also happens to face south. "My desk could stand here, my workbench here. I could have a bed here, and the armchair could stand here. On this wall I want my large poster, and over here I want a bulletin board."

"What'll we use for the living room then?"

"The room next to this one."

"We can*not* share our bedroom with Niklas!"

"He's a big boy now and will be moving out soon. You have to think of the long term, Mia. This is an apartment we'll have for years and years after he moves out."

"But we're also going to have it now, while he's still living at home."

"He can move in with Emilie. He'd be happy to, I'm sure. Then *he'll* be happy and *we'll* be happy. See, it'll work out great. I could have the TV here, and then I can watch it from the armchair and the bed and the desk. It's a fantastic apartment. I think we'll take it."

I try to avoid the agent's gaze. "Frederik, it's simply out of the question."

Every minute we're here, I despise this apartment more. The view on either side is wretched, looking straight into other apartments, and the staircase is squalid, almost disgusting.

Frederik acts as if he doesn't hear me. I canceled two earlier showings because I only want to look at apartments when he's rested. He's rested now, but this showing has brought out the worst in him.

It's also hard to know how much I should listen to him. He's right, that we'll end up keeping the apartment for a long time after Niklas leaves home. But who'll Frederik be in two years? Who'll he be in two weeks?

Will he lose all interest in acoustics and stereo equipment from one day to the next, just like he did with motor sports?

The realtor tries to fake some enthusiasm for the possibilities. He talks about the lovely shared party room in the basement and the excellent soundproofing of the windows.

But I have no idea if Frederik will get any better than he already is. The doctors said his progress would be rapid in the beginning, but that after the first three months it'd gradually stop. And no one can say when it will stop completely.

Frederik stands with his head in the breaker box. "It gets better and better!" he exclaims. "Look, there are two separate circuits for the electricity to my room. So we can connect the lights to one and the hi-fi to the other. That could make a *huge* difference."

I tell the realtor that we'll think about it, and drag Frederik away.

On the way home, I decide that from now on, it should be just Niklas and me who choose the apartment. But I don't know how much I should listen to Niklas either. He hates being home anyway, and in a couple of years he'll be moving out. Then I'll be stuck with the apartment and Frederik all by myself.

When we get home, Frederik goes up and takes a nap, and I start to text Niklas, telling him the apartment wasn't anything for us, and that I have an appointment to look at another one a little later.

As I stand there, cell in hand, Bernard calls. The prosecutor's misplaced some of the files, and Bernard wants to hear if we have a backup somewhere. I'm sure we do. When Frederik still had his act together, he always backed up our most important files on an external hard drive. It's over at Vibeke and Thorkild's, in case of fire or theft at our place. I promise to make him a copy.

"Now that I've got you," I say, "are you doing anything forty-five minutes from now?"

"No . . ."

"Any chance you want to go with me to look at an apartment?"

"Yeah . . . Sure, I can do that."

. . .

162

The apartment's on the second floor of an old house on one of the residential streets nearby. The ground floor has large bricked-up windows and must have been a store once. From the outside, it all looks a bit run-down, but that's also probably why the apartment's affordable.

Another realtor from the same agency lets us in. His colleague must have said something about Frederik, for the realtor looks at Bernard oddly, as if he keeps expecting him to act weird.

An old narrow stairway leads up to an apartment that is darker than the one I saw with Frederik. A converted attic, but I can see right away that it's got character. We walk around wordlessly and look. From the small bay windows in back, I look down on a hidden yard that is larger than the one we have on Station Road. It's neglected and overgrown, but it looks like it has some interesting plants, suggesting that at one point, somebody invested some effort in it. In a few summers, it could be very nice.

The agent follows my gaze. "The yard has potential. You'd be sharing it with the tenant downstairs, but you can see they haven't had the time to use it very much or take care of it. You can put your own stamp on it, and most of the time you should be able to use it without being bothered."

Without saying anything, I turn to see what could be done with the central room. If we tear down the wall it shares with the kitchen, we could have a large open room for cooking and eating. We'd probably spend most of our time there, and then the other two rooms could be bedrooms.

The outside wall between this room and the backyard also catches my eye. Apparently, Bernard sees the same thing I do, for he asks the agent, "Would it be possible to put in some large windows and a balcony here?"

"It's certainly possible. If you wanted to put in a full balcony, it'd block some of the light for the downstairs tenant, so you'd have to get permission from them. But there shouldn't be any problem with putting in windows and a French balcony."

"And this wall here," Bernard says, indicating the wall between the central room and the kitchen. "It doesn't look like a load-bearing wall."

"No, you could knock that out if you wanted."

I catch Bernard's eye: French balcony doors on an open kitchen and living room, looking out over a yard that's all but our own. There'd be a flood of light up here, and a view. We could eat, relax, sit in the balcony opening, and watch the sun drop behind the trees.

Then Bernard says, "The garage that the listing mentions—is that the one I can see down there?"

"Yes."

"There wouldn't be any problem using it for a workshop, would there?"

"You can do what you want with it."

I have to sit down. This is much more than what I resigned myself to: Frederik would have his own workshop. I struggle to keep my cool so that we can push them on the price.

Bernard walks past me and his fingertips brush my shoulder; I think it's a signal, to warn me that my excitement is a bit too obvious. He turns, and his face expresses calm, but when the realtor looks away, I can see Bernard's relieved on my behalf.

On his way into one of the other rooms, the agent says, "If you made this the master bedroom, you'd get some fantastic morning sun."

At some point, I suppose we'll have to tell him that Bernard isn't my husband.

"The stairs are *very* narrow," Bernard says, with convincing dissatisfaction.

He's well aware that I'd be only too happy to have a narrow stairway. It would create a little psychological distance from the street in case the Medico-Legal Council report goes against Herdis Lebech's recommendation, and lots of people continue to despise us.

The realtor's phone rings. He excuses himself and goes down the stairs. After making sure he's out of earshot, Bernard comes over within whispering distance.

"This place—it really is you."

In my relief I could almost hug him.

"Your dinner table could stand here, right next to the balcony doors."

"Yes, and the paneling's from the same period."

He walks over to a corner of the main room that would make a nice quiet nook. "Your armchair would be perfect here."

I place myself at his side and try to see the corner the way it would look after we arranged the furniture.

"And then the two chairs you used to have in Frederik's office could stand here."

"Yes," I say, "but there's not much room for my coffee table. Yours, however, would be narrow enough—and work great with the chairs."

The words just fly out of my mouth. I wasn't thinking of anything except how perfectly his table would fit.

We look into each other's eyes. Is it my imagination, or could we kiss now? What would he do if I brought my mouth closer to his?

I allow myself at last to look at his face, long enough to take in the curl of his eyelashes, the pores of his skin, a broken blood vessel on his temple; the crow's-feet in the corners of his eyes. I see everything.

So aren't we going to kiss? Isn't he going to come closer? Isn't there going to be an exchange of glances and small advances, a drawing of breath, a dilation of pupils?

"The slanting walls here make for great acoustics!" the agent's voice exclaims.

I turn around and find him looking at Bernard.

"And it shouldn't be any problem to install extra electrical circuits," he adds while the corners of his mouth tighten slightly, as if he's suppressing a smile.

I clear my throat. "There must be some misunderstanding," I say. "Bernard's just a good friend."

"Ohhh." Now it's me the realtor stares at.

"I need to see the bathroom too," I say, leaving the room quickly. Inside the bathroom, I lock the door behind me.

Maybe I've also become unbalanced; maybe Frederik infected me. Two of the women from support group say they feel as if they've contracted their husbands' disease. They become confused just like their men, take the initiative much less often, fumble for words.

And maybe, just like Frederik, I believe that I'm fully rational and well when in reality I'm doing something crazy. It's not something I'd be aware of. I wouldn't realize it any more than he does.

I fall into my usual escape fantasy about playing tennis. The sultry heat, the low sun. The strike of ball against racket; the sweat running into my eyes. A stroke. The sweat reaching the bridge of my nose now. Skidding on the crushed stone. Another stroke. I glimpse my opponent, and it's Bernard I'm playing. He's good. Athletic, power in his strokes. A handsome profile in the evening light. The fantasy's mine, but Bernard has followed me here. Stroke on stroke. I've got to get away from him.

Another fantasy: my happiest years with Frederik. Sitting in the hanging sofa in our yard. We've blown off the neighbor's garden party to be by ourselves. I rest my head against his chest. The sun still coloring the northern sky. His strong arm around me . . . but wait, Frederik's arms aren't strong! I turn my face and find myself looking up at Bernard. I'm not resting my head on Frederik's chest; it's Bernard I've run off with. I've been to the neighbor's party with Bernard. I've got to leave again.

Walking along Lake Farum: Frederik and me in the sun. He wraps a strong arm around my waist. We meet the parents of some—

"Mia?"

I hear a knock on the door, and Bernard's voice.

"Mia?"

I open the door. He stands close, right outside the door. *Now* I feel it. He comes even closer. The exchange. Our breath, our pupils.

I grab him, pull him into the bathroom, close the door, and kiss him. He kisses me. He presses me to him, so that for a moment I can't breathe. Our tongues, our lips, our skin and spittle. I encircle his shoulders. Our eyes and noses, bellies and groins. It'll never stop, we'll keep on and on. So it was true. So there *were* signals from him. It'll go on forever. So it'll be the two of us now.

He gasps for breath, and I pull my face back a little so I can smile at him.

But now he's gasping too much for breath. He tears himself free and stands doubled over, his hands on his knees as if he's going to throw up.

I've been in a state of alert for months and I don't even think, I just shout for the realtor before I know what I'm doing. "Call an ambulance! Damn it! Damn it! Call an ambulance!"

The husbands of my friends in support group keep having strokes. Strokes right and left. The men drop dead. The real estate agent's steps sound on the far side of the bathroom door. He knocks over something with a crash and swears under his breath.

I'm not sure if I should reach out to touch Bernard. May I hold him?

"Bernard? Can you say something?"

"I'm not ill," he says. "Or rather yes, I am ill, but I'm not . . . He shouldn't call for an ambulance."

I drop to a knee so that I can see his face. "What is it? What's the matter?"

It takes time to get such wet cheeks; he must have been crying while we kissed.

"Bernard? What's wrong?"

The realtor enters the bathroom with his phone to his ear. "They're asking what happened. What's wrong? What should I tell them?"

We both look at Bernard, who doesn't answer.

"Bernard?"

"It's nothing. Just hang up. We don't need an ambulance."

But he's speaking with Frederik's voice. The toneless voice from the weeks after the operation. My friends' husbands. *My* husband.

I find myself shouting. "He himself doesn't know! That's one of the symptoms—apoplexy! His brain!"

Now Bernard is weeping—again, almost like Frederik. "It isn't apoplexy. I'm sorry!"

I know what the eyes of a stroke victim look like.

"Sorry, sorry, sorry," he repeats.

"There's no reason to . . . can you move your right side? Can you say your name? Do you know where we are?"

"I have to go now," he says.

He straightens up and heads for the door.

"You can't go now!"

"I've got to."

I run after him down the narrow stairs.

"But you can't drive a car," I say.

"Yes. I can drive just fine."

He's walking quickly, so I have to run around the parked cars and back onto the sidewalk, where I plant myself in front of the station wagon door. "You aren't allowed to get in. This is for your own good."

"Mia, stop it now."

And now he's speaking in his own voice again.

Maybe it's me who's sick. He isn't, in any case. Maybe I just can't deal with kissing another man. I step aside, and he gets behind the wheel.

167

"I'm really sorry," he says. "I'm really, really sorry."

I want to go closer. Lean into the car. But something tells me I shouldn't. And then he drives away.

The real estate agent and I are left standing there.

The agent leads me back to the apartment, and now it's myself I don't dare to let drive. With solicitude, he guides me over to an armchair in the middle room, the room we wanted to open up into the kitchen. And then he gets me a glass of water in what might be Frederik's and my new home.

18

Soon we won't be living here anymore. I look at my white house. The black-stained timbers, the light shadows on the wall where I scrubbed away the graffiti. I take it in as if I'm not looking at a real house, just paging through an old photo album.

Someday, years from now, I'll point to this page and say, *We used to live here.*

It looks so charming, so homey, a future acquaintance will say, sitting beside me on the cheap ugly couch I'll have then.

Yes. We were happy living there.

And then a stillness will descend between us. She won't say, *That must have been before it all went south*—and really, what else could she say? And I won't say, *That was when I kissed another man.* What else would there be for me to say?

The house back then, the photo poster you can faintly make out through Niklas's window, the wicker enclosure I built around the garbage cans with my own hands.

I continue to leaf through the album as I walk down the flagstones to the front door. Yes; we were happy living here.

Before I pass the FOR SALE sign, I wipe my lips off on my sleeve one more time. Bernard also wanted to, didn't he? Should I call him, text him? Have I done something awful? Have I wrecked the good working relationship we have with our lawyer?

In the living room, Eurosport is on with the sound turned down. I switch it off. On the floor lie three books, two of them open. I leave them lying there but pick up the plate with the jam sandwich, one-fourth eaten.

I place it in the kitchen, where I find another plate with bread and jam, this one half eaten. I yell up to Frederik, who's in his workshop, no doubt. "I'm home now! It was a lovely apartment—just the thing for us!"

He doesn't answer.

Our folding clotheshorse is also in the kitchen. For once, Frederik's remembered to hang up the clothes that don't get tumble-dried, just like I've asked him to.

"It's great that you've hung up the laundry!" I shout. "I really appreciate it!"

Back in the living room, I see some circulars spread out on the dinner table. A plate protrudes from the top bookshelf, and when I take it down I discover a jam sandwich that looks like it's been there a couple of days without me spotting it.

Then I notice that one of the papers on the table is damp. I lift it up and see my cream-colored Odd Molly blouse lying beneath it. Frederik must have gotten distracted when he was about to hang it up. I walk back into the kitchen and hang it on the clotheshorse. Some of the printing ink has rubbed off on it, so it'll have to be washed again. Perhaps it can still be salvaged.

"Niklas?" I call out.

There's no answer.

Upstairs, I knock on his door. I look inside, but he's out. Of course.

So I go into Frederik's workshop, but he's gone too. On the floor is a rolled-up poster that used to lie in my closet. Frederik must have been meaning to hang it up, which would also explain the hammer I saw in the kitchen.

I find him in our room. He's lying in bed with his clothes on. I've found him here often enough, but today he's pulled the comforter up over himself and drawn the curtains.

"How are you?" I ask.

He doesn't say anything, just stares at a spot on the wall. He's different, I can tell right away.

I sit down on my side of the bed and wait.

At last he says, "Mia, there's something I've been thinking about."

"Yes?"

"Something I'd like to ask you."

"Yes."

Another long pause. The curtains in here are pale, with a rather loose weave; they don't do a very good job of keeping out the light. One of them trembles slightly. The light in Majorca, I think, early one morning.

"Do you think it was wrong of me to invest that money?"

I don't know what to say. This is so major, so different. I stretch out a hand and touch his hair. And he lets me.

"Yes. I think it was wrong," I say in my mildest voice. I smile at him, though he doesn't see it.

"But I would have gotten the money back when the markets went up, you know. Then I'd have given more back to the school than I borrowed. We could have fixed up the B wing."

"But it really wasn't certain that the markets would have gone up, Frederik. It wasn't a sure thing, was it."

He doesn't get angry with me, nor does he start weeping. He listens. The curtains, like in Majorca. It grows a shade darker in the room.

Then he asks, "Do you think Laust is very upset about it?"

"Yes, I think so."

"Is that why he doesn't call anymore?"

He pulls the comforter over his head and curls up in a ball, and I can see by his breathing that he's crying. He's trying to hide from me; it means something to him that I don't see his face. Laust and me and the school and all of us; we exist for him again.

I want to lie at his side and cry with him, from sorrow and guilt over what he's done to his school. And from sorrow and guilt over my own betrayal.

I press myself into his foreign scent, his foreign body. I haven't been so close to him since he became sick. Perhaps the same images are flooding us both: Saxtorph on the last day of school. The flag waving, the happy children, the staff, and all the teacher friends that we still talk to. Frederik making a speech up on stage, and pulling it off so well that everyone praises him afterward.

171

And the prison where I visit him: electronic doors slamming, guards behind tiny glass windows, Frederik slumped over when I arrive; him shriveling up and slowly going to pieces.

And him getting better—so that perhaps we take a walk like normal people, perhaps we can have friends to dinner like in the old days.

And Bernard's lips. His body pressing against mine. He was doing the pressing too. He was kissing.

...

Early in the evening, Bernard calls.

"We can't see each other anymore," he says.

"What are we going to do about the case then?"

"I'll help you find a good lawyer."

I hold my tongue. From what I've learned about him in the past two months, I should have known that this was the way it would have to end.

"I'm sorry," I say.

"There's nothing you have to apologize for."

"But can't we continue to talk on the phone?"

"It won't work."

"But just about the best way to support our sons?"

I can hear the stiffness in his voice; each word carefully chosen before he called. As if the least nudge in an unexpected direction might break him.

"I'm sorry, Mia."

"It would be better for our kids, we really don't need to—"

"I can't do it."

"We *were* friends," I say. And now I hear in my voice that we no longer are.

"Yes."

"I'm going to miss you."

"What do you want me to say?"

"So now you won't call me anymore?"

"No."

"And I shouldn't call you either?"

"I'm asking you not to."

My fingers feel stiff as soon as I hang up. I have to stretch and flex them several times, just to verify that I still can. It feels slow, it feels strenuous. My arms and legs; I can hardly move. A jeep in the desert, a jeep that's driven thousands of miles but whose engine has seized up. It rolls along slowly in neutral, then stops somewhere in the dunes.

Without tears, without expression, without any stops for little tasks on the way, I manage to fight my way up to our bed. I'm going to lie here a long time, I think to myself. I lie down in the same position as Frederik. I'm going to remain here for months, looking at the wall, at that sign on the ceiling.

It's dark when Thorkild calls. I haven't slept, haven't stirred, haven't gotten up to eat dinner. And Frederik, who in the meantime has gone to the workshop, hasn't noticed.

Thorkild always sounds serious. I think he was that way before his son became ill, but I'm no longer sure.

"Frederik sounded quite upset on the phone this afternoon," he says. "I just wanted to hear—"

"Yes, we're pretty upset," I say. "The school and everything, it's just devastating him now."

"But in a way that's good, right? A sign that he's still getting better?"

"Yes, it's good."

"Something to celebrate, right?"

"Yes."

The conversation doesn't last much longer.

The next day there's a letter from Bernard's firm, informing us that we now have a new lawyer by the name of Louise Rambøll. I manage to make it through the school day. I don't know if my students notice anything wrong with me, but as soon as I'm home I go back to bed.

Frederik is already lying on his side of the mattress. I start to console him but have to stop; I can tell that it'll only make me bitter, for I need solace as much as he does, and I never get any. We lie under our respective comforters with our backs to each other, the air still; it's stuffy in here.

I get up, cry, go to bed, cry, take some Tylenol because the roof of my mouth hurts so much from crying, get up, take a shower, cry, go to bed again.

I'm down in the kitchen making a jam sandwich with the cheap jam from the blue plastic bucket I bought for Frederik when I hear laughter out in the street. Through the window I see Niklas and Emilie. She has a sweet way of laughing with a single tone, like the signal call among some pygmies I once saw a documentary about.

They grow quiet as they approach our front door. Will she come in here again after her experience with Frederik? Yes, I can hear them in the hallway. Brave girl.

They mustn't see me in this state. I slip into the unlit living room, just in case they want to get something from the kitchen, and I sit down in the armchair. My sight adjusts to the darkness of the room, my hearing to the silence.

Some of my friends have told me about their teenagers having sex at home. When we were their age, we too would have sex when our parents were elsewhere in the house, but we were quiet. My friends' kids aren't; there are moans and grunts and smacks regardless of who's nearby. Youngsters have gotten so unself-conscious, though I can't imagine Niklas being that way.

Have the two of them done it before? Of course they have. Has he done it with other girls? I don't think so, but what do I know? Are they going to do it tonight? Of course they are.

And you can't help but see it unfold before your eyes. The smooth young bright faces, the lean bodies, the swelling red-brown genitals pumping away at each other. You can't help but see their laughing, kissing, and groping, or the quiver of their faces in orgasm.

In the darkness here, I can't hear a thing. I listen but no, there's nothing. I've got to make sure that Frederik doesn't try to barge in on them. I have to protect them.

Quickly I tiptoe up the stairs. Outside Niklas's room, I remain standing a little while, and again I hear Emilie's laugh—softer now, more of a giggle, while Niklas speaks with a mild adult voice that I've never heard before. The voices stop—and then?

I ought to walk away. I hear a light clattering noise in there. What'll I say if the door opens? My mind goes blank. I should definitely walk away.

The sounds are so muted now as to be almost inaudible—a YouTube clip? Some synthetic-sounding voice? Is that Niklas speaking again? Silence? Breathing? Gasps?

A few steps down the hall, I open the door to Frederik's workshop. The light here is cold and overwhelming after the darkness of the hallway and the room downstairs. He sits at his desk, bent over some technical diagram. He doesn't react when I come in; he probably has no idea if Niklas is even home.

I remain silent too, standing just inside the door. How different it would all be if it were Bernard who sat there, in the same posture and the same clothes, bent over the same sheet of paper. I'd walk over to him without speaking, take his head in my hands, turn his face up to mine. And then I'd do it again, the thing I mustn't—I would—I'd kiss him.

He would laugh, speak, do *something*. And it would be something that had meaning, something that fit the occasion, that fit him in particular and me in particular—because he's a real person and not just a diseased brain with a body attached.

Or no, no words. I would let him know that with just my eyes, and immediately he'd understand. And then he'd rise, and we'd press our bodies together, in a way I haven't pressed my body against anyone's in more than half a year.

He won't get sick. He won't call later and say that we can never see each other again. This time we can keep going. And we'll unbutton each other's pants right there on the desk that stands in front of me, there where my foolish, sick husband sits with nothing but speakers in his head.

I look at Frederik's face. He's gotten small pimples on the top of his forehead these past few months, and fat deposits on his cheeks; all that unhealthy food. What'll he do if Emilie's noisy when she comes? He must be just as starved for it as me. Will he try to go in there? Will he throw himself on me? Will he become aggressive and unbearable so that I have to hit him again?

"Come, we're going for a walk," I say.

He stares at me, only aware now that I'm in the room. "Now? It's night-time! We never go for walks at night."

"No, but tonight we're going to."

"I'm sitting here in the middle of deciding whether—"

"It'll have to wait for another time. Come. We're going now."

"Why?"

"We just are. Come."

"But I don't *want* to go for a walk."

Since the operation, it's been me who decides everything here at home. Which friends we're going to call, and when; what we're going to eat, and when; which websites we visit, and when. He grouses about it all the time, but he always does what I say anyway.

"Let's go," I say, pulling him out past Niklas's room. I still don't hear any sounds from in there. Downstairs, I throw Frederik his jacket, the lining the color I imagine Bernard's pubic hair must be, and then I drag him out onto our small residential street, with the high hedges standing there so peaceful and lovely in the night. This is where we live.

Which Alcoholic Would You Prefer as a Son-in-Law?

TOM BUCHMANN

Our society risks becoming much more callous in its treatment of deviants.

Tom Buchmann has an MS in sociology and serves as a senior researcher at the Center for Future Studies.

IN 2009, AFTER IT WAS revealed that Tiger Woods had had at least 11 extramarital affairs, it didn't take long for the golf star to be admitted to a rehabilitation facility for the treatment of sex addiction. Woods *wasn't* a mendacious, egotistic person—no no, he was merely the victim of an illness.

After similarly embarrassing public episodes, other celebrities have explained that they too suffer from disorders, including various forms of dependency and the inability to control anger. We're inclined to shrug off these statements with a quick laugh and not think any more about them, but in point of fact the celebrities are right. They haven't *wanted* to take drugs, or to destroy their marriages and careers with angry outbursts. They've never consciously wished for lives like that.

In recent years, science has found genetic and neurological

explanations for a host of human weaknesses, including:

- alcoholism and other forms of substance abuse
- lack of concentration
- poor social skills
- excessive fits of rage
- timidity
- self-centeredness
- loss of initiative

The latest research has shown that all of these character traits have a physiological basis—and that if it's at all possible to change them, it isn't simply by "pulling yourself together."

As a result, we live in an era when our shared sense of what it means to be human and exercise responsibility has been changing at breakneck speed. The way we think about our impossible son (ADHD), our boozing uncle (addictive personality), and our killjoy mother (hidden depression) is shifting. Who are these people really? And how should we relate to them if they're not to blame for their own actions?

IN THE COURSE OF the next few years, many other human traits will become closely associated with neurological functions and dysfunctions. This is something that can be stated with complete confidence, since it's an unavoidable consequence of the huge breakthroughs in brain research.

If someone is lazy, for instance, soon we may be able to measure what it is in his or her brain that is causing the laziness. And perhaps all lazy people will be able to address this trait merely by taking a pill—just as we've seen with the tremendously widespread use of anti-anxiety drugs and antidepressants, and of concentration-enhancing drugs for children with ADHD.

The causes of numerous other personality traits will doubtless be determined in the same fashion; the only thing we don't know is the exact order in which they'll be identified. They may include the reasons for things like compulsive lying, pigheadedness, and poor long-term planning. And we'll be able to address some of these traits pharmaceutically.

Accordingly, human personality will become something one can increasingly design and purchase. Certain coveted personality traits will require the newest, most advanced treatments—perhaps even surgical or electromagnetic intervention in the brain. In this way, these characteristics will become status symbols in the course of a couple of decades, just like costly cosmetic surgery has been in recent years.

This development isn't an abstraction or something that belongs to the distant future. It's already happening now, and in a few years it will pick up a great deal of speed. Consider for instance how rapidly the ways we think about depression, childhood hyperactivity, and male impotence have changed after having stood essentially still for millennia.

OF COURSE IT IS DIFFICULT, if not impossible, to predict how our culture will react to new knowledge about how we really function. But the following thought experiment may provide a clue.

Imagine that you know two men who both have serious drinking problems, and who both hit their wives and children when they are drunk. You find the way they treat their families deeply disturbing. Brain scans reveal that one of the men is neurologically normal. They also show that, neurologically, the second man is highly disposed to alcoholism and violence—and in fact, on the basis of his scans, the specialists expect him to behave at least as terribly as he does.

What is your attitude to each of these men? Would you be more forgiving of one than the other? Would you be able to be friends with one and not the other—and if so, which one? Take your time mulling it over, for the answers to these questions are far from straightforward.

Your reaction to the man who is neurologically *normal* is probably reminiscent of the way many people regarded violent alcoholics 20 years ago, when few people knew that alcoholism could be considered a disease. This man has made some despicable choices and quite likely attracts your greatest moral condemnation.

By contrast, your reaction to the *man who is neurologically abnormal* should provide some indication of where our culture will stand in 20 years—and not only with respect to violence and alcoholism, but also with respect to countless other human traits that will be mapped out in the brain by that time.

Many of us would feel a certain sympathy for this man if we knew he was an unwilling victim of his neurological flaws. (How awful it must be, to be relentlessly compelled to hurt the ones you love!) We would be inclined to forgive him—for after all, the doctors have said that he can be expected to behave *at least* as horribly as he does. Perhaps it has required an extraordinary effort on his part simply not to murder his family. He's pulled himself together and done the best he could.

AT THE SAME TIME, the matter is more complicated than that. If no pharmaceutical treatments have been developed yet for *the neurologically abnormal man*, we will do everything we can to keep him away from our workplace and prevent him from marrying into our circle of family and friends. For his brain will not permit him to get any better.

The opposite is true of *the neurologically normal man*. Maybe he speaks the truth when he says that he deeply regrets the way he has been and that he has turned over a new leaf. We cannot know, for the brain he has *could* get him on the right track. Should he not have a chance?

In this way, our society risks becoming much more callous in its treatment of deviants—and only because we are learning more about ourselves and our brains. On the surface, this inevitable evolution in our view of human nature is making us more generous. Yet underneath

it we risk becoming merciless and incompassionate. If we no longer consider some people to have free will when it comes to beating or not beating their spouses and children, do we still think of them as human at all? Can't we just expel them then from all social contexts—families, workplaces, etc.?

GRADUALLY, as we become accustomed to new ways of looking at ourselves and others, it also becomes natural for us to think that there must be some hidden reason for why the second man hits his wife and children. No one really wants to be that way voluntarily, does he? Might he be a victim of childhood trauma, a personality disorder, or some neurological deviance that science simply isn't capable of showing on a brain scan yet?

And aren't the two men subject in the same degree to neurological processes beyond their control, even though the processes can only be detected in one of them? Surely that must be the case. Don't both of them deserve the same forgiveness and compassion?

And what about us?

Aren't even the most apparently healthy people simply unwilling

(cont'd on p. 64)

19

I'm on my way home from school. In a little while, I'll find Frederik in our bed. He's been lying there for more than a week with the curtains drawn. He might lie like that for months or years to come.

As soon as I get home, I'll drink a couple of cups of tea, eat a couple of open-face sandwiches, and lie down beside him. That's what I've done every day of the past week, and every day I remain there until the world forces me to get up again.

But I'm not home yet. My car is stopped for a red light on Mayor Jespersen Road, and I'm thinking about the days Bernard and I have spent together: the phone conversations, the texts, the brief meetings.

One day we walked through Østerbro from the office of the public prosecutor for serious financial crimes. The sun was low and the light sharp and red, making the quarter's monotone rust-brown high-rises seem luminous. Why does everything light up that way? That's what I remember wondering. Why isn't it just reds that get a boost of color from the afternoon light? The wrapper of a chocolate bar, a dark green bench, the remnants of a dandelion between the paving stones—why does everything *glow*?

Bernard was wearing one of his grey suits, and he talked about his twin sons. At the boarding school they were attending for the final year before gymnasium, one of them had developed a passion for astronomy. There was a telescope at the school, and three of the boys and the math teacher were using a computer program to look for signs of life in the universe.

While Bernard spoke, he forgot all about Frederik's case, he forgot about me, he forgot the streets. There was no doubt in my mind that he was a good father.

And besides the things we talked about, besides the luminous buildings around us, there were our bodies. Their harmony as we walked together down the sidewalk at an inconspicuous distance. The even rhythmic click of our heels on the paving stones. The feeling that spread throughout my body: that it was good to walk like this, next to his body.

Just think if Niklas had had a father like Bernard. Then I wouldn't have needed to keep secrets from him when he was small, about his father's lechery at school. I wouldn't have needed to throw his father out on his ear or drink myself blind. Niklas wouldn't have found me and had to call to have my stomach pumped. It's impossible to imagine what our relationship could have been like.

I'm on the overpass that crosses the freeway, almost home now, and I recall another time sitting here in the car on my way from work, talking to Bernard on the phone about my day. He told me about his own day, on his way home to Lærke in his car, and just as I reached Station Road, we started talking about a trip he'd taken once as a student. Three law students traveling together, staying in a cottage in some community garden outside East Berlin. They were into the local raves, which were huge back then in the years after the Wall fell.

"I was pretty wild when I was young," he said.

"Wild?" Perhaps I sounded startled. "But you were already with Lærke back then, weren't you?"

"Well yeah. Not wild in that way."

...

I throw my school bag onto the small table in the entry and call out, "I'm home!" like I usually do.

Frederik doesn't answer. I turn on the electric kettle and go upstairs.

The bed's empty. I walk quickly, almost at a run, to the workshop. He isn't there either.

"Frederik! Frederik!"

Has he left a note behind, a letter? I run back to the bedroom, down to the living room, back to the kitchen, out into the yard. No letter, no Frederik.

On our patio I stand completely still, listening to sounds from the neighboring yards, feeling the pulse in my temples. Will today be the day I've been fearing, ever since he began lying in bed and moaning for hours at a time? Since he first said that he'd destroyed everything and just wanted to die?

The yard's as still as I am. The silver-white undersides of the leaves on the tall poplars next door don't so much as stir.

And just the way you always hear cops state the exact time when they arrest someone, I hear the basic facts being recited in my ear: *There is no wind, it is cooler than normal for the season, there is moisture in the air. I am standing on the patio of our silent yard. Frederik is dead.*

No one can know how it must've felt for him, for the first time in ages, to reproach himself for something. For the first time since a tumor changed everything. How does guilt feel the very first time? Or empathy for another person? How does it feel to realize in a blinding flash that you've ruined the lives of everyone around you?

I call Niklas, who is at Mathias's with some friends, but he hasn't seen or heard from his father. I manage to sound calm on the phone, though I can hear the thudding of my heart. Niklas sounds calm too, and I don't think it's an act. He has no sense of the danger; he hasn't been home during the afternoons when Frederik's at his most inconsolable.

Then it's my in-laws' turn.

"Is it possible he might do something to himself?" Vibeke asks.

I hesitate too long, and Thorkild has to take the receiver. "We're coming over there now," he says.

"I'd rather you wait. If I don't find him in the next half hour, I'll call you again."

Back to the yard. I shout his name and get no answer.

And just then—at the same time that I'm searching and calling and feeling desperate—just then, it's not simply despair I feel. What was it that Ulla said at my first support group meeting? *It would have been better if Kirsten's husband had died this time.* The group smiled afterward; we all felt a bond.

I run down the wooded path toward the lakeshore. No sign of him on the small pier that extends from the woods out into the water.

Thorkild calls again. I tell him they should wait another hour before they come, but he says they're already in the car and on their way.

I call the police. They haven't heard anything.

Vibeke calls again from the car, and while I have my weeping mother-in-law on the phone, I hear the beep of another incoming call. I hang up and suddenly Laust is on the line. "Will you come and get your husband!"

"He's at *your* place?"

"He just shoved his way in, and I can't get him to leave."

Relief. And then not, after all. What was it Ulla said? And everyone smiled. I'm relieved. I *am* relieved.

I picture Frederik standing erect and sobbing in Laust and Anja's classy Copenhagen home, his thin body amid their vintage furniture of Swedish birch, with its lovely patinated stain. The moose in the forest.

"May I speak to him?" I ask.

He comes on the line, but he isn't crying. "There's nothing to say," he says in a pinched voice before falling silent. He sounds like a lonesome hero in an old western.

"But you're not going to leave?"

"No."

"You have to. It's Laust's apartment."

"It's him who needs to talk to me. There are two of us. He's being so unconstructive."

"How did you get all the way over there?"

The receiver's torn from his hand and Laust is back. "I'm calling the police if he isn't out of here in two minutes."

I try to convince Laust to wait and I run back to the house and car. Once I'm on the freeway I call Niklas and then Thorkild and Vibeke, who are headed toward me on the same road.

Frederik and I have been to lots of parties and dinners in Laust and Anja's apartment, which lies a few hundred yards from Saxtorph. I know where everything is, in their rooms and kitchen cabinets. I know which photos of their kids hang by the door in the living room and which ones hang in their bedroom. I know the reflection of the window onto the long white dinner table, and the bookcases with Anja's blue-grey folders of teaching materials for her gymnasium English classes. And I know, from one of the few Saxtorph teachers who side with us, that Laust and Anja have to move. The board's personally responsible for the school's finances—something that nobody gave much thought to because the finances were always rock-solid, but now four of the board members have to sell their homes.

All my life, whenever I've encountered men who are grieving, I've observed a certain restlessness in my body. Unhappy women weep and talk and spew their sorrow over everything. Grieving men, on the other hand, shuffle dumbly about and seal up all the chinks in their houses until they're ready to gas themselves or ignite some catastrophe for whoever happens to be nearby. They commit suicide and murder and monstrosity, while we only make sobbing attempts that aren't really meant to succeed. The grief of men is a vast, silent world that's never revealed itself to me.

And yet I may be starting to understand a little anyway. These last few days in bed, as I've finally begun to glimpse my new future, my eyes have been completely dry.

...

Laust opens the great carved oak door of his and Anja's apartment. He looks just as I expected, his pale round head bleak and brooding. And Frederik, standing in the hall behind him, looks the same way. Not a peep. There's nothing to suggest that they've been talking to each other at all.

I don't know what to say to Laust, who until a few months ago was one of best friends. Now I don't even want to talk to Frederik in front of him. Lacking a better alternative, I decide to be like the men: I hold my tongue and look annoyed. The three of us proceed silently into the large corner living room, with its stucco ceiling and the view over Saint Thomas Square. Then we just stand there.

FOR SALE signs block part of the windows. Several of the old paintings are gone; perhaps Laust and Anja had to sell them. The ceramic bowl I picked out for Anja's fortieth, as a gift from us and some friends we had in common, is also gone from the dinner table, though probably not to be sold.

Why is Laust home in the middle of the day? Is he on sick leave?

At last Frederik speaks up. "You change your accounting methods the way I've told you; you sell the gym, and the other premises that we rent out after school hours, to an independent firm, and the school can lease them back during the school day."

He speaks quickly and coolly, summarizing something he's evidently already been arguing for.

"You contact the sixteen parents of former students whose names I wrote down on that list. You speak with Aksel at the bank about dealing directly with him and Jørgen—*not* with Anette on any account. And I'll e-mail you the letter for the Friends of Saxtorph."

He can sound so persuasive. If anyone can rescue the school, it's him of course.

I find myself blurting out, "Is this a plan, Frederik?" I turn toward Laust. "Is that what it is? A plan?"

"Naturally, we've tried everything like that," he mumbles, not looking me in the eye. "We aren't idiots."

Frederik's agitated, but it might not be just his illness, since he's also dedicated his life to the school. "That's not true!" he shouts. "I talked to Kim yesterday, and he hasn't heard from you!"

Laust finally raises his voice too, and it's as if I needed him to. "We've tried everything. *Everything!* To save us from all the shit you dumped on us! The party's over, like I've told you a hundred times."

"You haven't talked to Kim! Have you talked to anyone else on the list I gave you? They're precisely the people you should be talking to."

Something now about how to position myself—body language and facial expression—I should show that I'm backing up my husband. Or should I? Should it be the opposite—should I show Laust that I know Frederik's a nut the two of us have to appease?

Laust enters a short number on his phone, no doubt the police. "Your coming here didn't do much good, eh Mia?"

Frederik continues, undeterred. "It has to be *them*. All sixteen."

I don't know if I should step toward Laust, or back, or . . . "Laust, will you let me talk to him alone? Two minutes?"

He doesn't answer, just turns his back on me and puts his phone in his pocket. He's giving me a chance.

After Laust has gone out in the hall to the kitchen, I slowly get Frederik to sit down on the sofa, seated at my side. He's still worked up; I hold his hand. "Frederik, what's this plan?"

"I've figured out how we can rescue the school."

Laust sticks his head back in the room. "Mia, I'm holding you responsible if he smashes anything."

Then he's gone again.

Assuming my gentlest voice, I ask, "Why didn't you just ask to call Laust and suggest your plan on the phone? Wouldn't that have been a lot easier?"

"I did call him. Often. But he hung up on me every time."

Now I know he's lying again. Shit. Only Niklas and I know the codes for the phones. Why do I keep having these moments where I believe him? They just wear me out.

Softly, I say, "Fine. Come along, Frederik, we're leaving now."

"I'm not going before Laust says he'll save the school."

"Yes you are. Come, we're leaving."

"No."

I'm used to him fighting me tooth and nail until finally he does what I say anyway. I get up. "Come Frederik, we're going *now*."

"I won't. I'm not leaving."

"But you never called Laust, damn it. You can't, after all."

"I got permission to borrow Niklas's phone, as long as I let him hear what I said."

Right away I know he's telling the truth. And the repercussions of what Niklas has done are enormous. "But we're involved in a court case, God damn it! Neither of us is supposed to talk to Laust unless we've agreed with Bernard first about what we're going to say."

Frederik looks up at me. "Bernard? But he's not our lawyer anymore."

"No no, I know that. Not Bernard. The new . . . Neither of us is supposed to talk to Laust unless we've agreed with the new lawyer . . ."

It comes to me in a flash: the strong urge to be done with it all. As if it were unfolding before me, I see how I take quick long strides out to Laust and Anja's kitchen without letting anything distract me. How I find Laust's carving knife on the left side of the fourth drawer from the top. How I—before I myself or anyone else has a chance to think or feel a thing—draw it across my throat. Freedom. Joy. It's over.

The silence, the sense of purpose, the knife.

One of Frederik's psychiatrists told me that when she's making a diagnosis, it's important for her to listen to her own feelings. If a patient makes her nervous, it might be because the patient is afraid and can ease his fear by spreading it. Or if a patient makes her confused, perhaps it's because he finds life chaotic.

Frederik sits at my side. He's tensed like a boxer waiting for the fight bell to ring for the next round, but I have to take these suicidal impulses seriously. Only by listening to them will I be able to understand him.

And it comes to me that when we get out of here, we need to drive to the psychiatric emergency room at Hillerød Hospital. I'll have to put up with sitting by myself again in some sad waiting room while he's being examined—this time for life-threatening depression. But if he's going to give me such vivid fantasies, I don't dare shoulder the responsibility for him alone.

...

It's Sunday. For four days, Frederik's been in the hospital, under observation for depression. I've lain in bed since Friday afternoon. The curtains are drawn. The blackbird outside the window lacerates my ears, and nothing'll stop it.

In another hour and a half, the realtor's coming by with three families to see the house. Everything's a mess, and I need to wash my hair before going out. I can't put it off any longer.

While I'm standing under the showerhead, I hear my cell phone ring. Could it be Bernard, wanting to take on our case and see me again? I run to the bedroom and find the phone on the dresser, but the display doesn't show any calls. For a moment—perhaps longer—I sit naked on the edge of the bed, though it makes the mattress wet.

Back in the shower. It smells bad in here, I think. I need to air it out before the buyers come—better that it's too cold than that it stinks. Now the cell's ringing again. Or is it? There's an echo of distant melody, my ringtone, but it might just be the shower water splashing on the floor and the crooked green tiles. The tones could be arising spontaneously.

I run back to the bedroom anyhow. Once more there haven't been any calls, and once more I sit down on the bed.

This time I leave the cell on the table in the bathroom while I finish showering, and when I've dried my hair, I bring up his number. It's something I've been doing often, each time with some convoluted new pretext in my head, and each time I stop myself before the decisive depression of the CALL button. The pretexts are all too transparent anyway.

Now I've found the simplest, most watertight excuse yet. I press the button, and when he answers I assume my most innocent voice.

"Hi Bernard, it's Mia. Sorry I didn't take your call, but I was in the shower."

"What?"

"Yes. You called, but I was in the shower."

"I didn't call."

"Well that's weird. I must have been looking at a list of old calls . . . Well, uh, you'll have to excuse me."

It's quiet for a bit.

His voice. "How are you doing?"

The voice is deep, it booms from my cell's tiny speaker in a way that it doesn't boom in person. I know both timbres so well. We actually don't need to talk anymore. That was all, I just needed to hear his voice. Now I can relax, now everything's better.

He asks again. "How are you, Mia?"

"Not that great."

"What happened?"

"Frederik's in the hospital. They think he might be suffering from depression."

"But that's good, isn't it? Isn't that a sign of progress?"

"Yes, it's good. I don't know . . ."

Then it's quiet again.

"I don't know," I say once more. "What about you?"

"To be completely honest, things here aren't going so well either."

"What's *wrong*?" I find myself shouting, as if he's suffered some disaster.

"Well, it isn't—"

"Yes?"

189

"No, it isn't so . . . It's just Lærke, she's been struggling with some stupid sores she gets because she sits so much."

I see vividly before me the spongy sores she might be getting from poor circulation in her buttocks.

And then without warning: he says it in the space of a second, and the tone of his voice is something I'll replay again and again in my head. "I end up saying too much to you, Mia. It just slips out. I'm not cross, but you shouldn't call me again. I need to hang up. I'm sorry."

Hastened. From one moment to the next. And then a click. Then three short beeps, and quiet. I memorize the sound of his voice—and the click—and the three beeps. They all fuse into a single sound: the last I'll ever hear from him.

20

A wan diffuse light lies upon the maze of small and rather deserted streets of low yellow row houses. Andrea lives here, and the support group is meeting at her place tonight. Three times I think I've found a parking spot, and each time it turns out to be reserved for disabled drivers. Perhaps the buildings here have been especially designed for wheelchair users? Petals from a cherry tree speckle the lime-green surface of the car in front of me, which has a handicapped sticker in the window.

As I maneuver my car into a tight space a little farther away, I catch sight of Kirsten; she stops and stands waiting for me. Two weeks ago, she told me on the phone that her husband had been admitted to the hospital again. The doctors say she might get him home in a couple of months, but it could also be that he'll never return.

Together we walk over toward Andrea's house, and on the way we meet Gerda and Anton. They've already heard from others in the group that Frederik was only in Hillerød for a few days, and that he's been home again for a week now. Gerda tells us she's finally gotten a new caseworker from the local authorities, but Merethe already told me.

Andrea lets us in, and she gives me a great long hug. She's the group member I talk most to on the phone. Every time I call her, I feel a strong desire to take care of her—to protect her from her hard life with two small children and a husband who has multiple handicaps. But in reality, she's the one who looks after me. Despite a demanding career as a biologist, she always has time to pose the right questions, to listen, and to come up with new suggestions about neurological research—like her tip about the Iowa Gambling Task—that might save Frederik in his court case.

While she ushers the others into the living room, I act as if I'm going to use the bathroom. She won't mind me walking around a little and seeing what her house is like before taking my seat with the group.

Quietly, I walk to the bathroom, which is large and fitted out for a wheelchair user, with lifting equipment like in a hospital. I know that a home caregiver comes twice a day to help Ian with hygiene. Then I poke my head into the kitchen, which looks more ordinary. The walls are mustard-colored, '80s-style, and the kitchen cabinets cheap, but Andrea has hung up lots of kids' drawings and paper chains and photos. There's so much color and life here that it makes you just want to sit down and hang out with your family.

The biggest picture is of Ian seated in his wheelchair and grinning, while their youngest crawls on his lap and their eldest stands at his side, thoughtfully leaning her head against the backrest.

I'd like to poke my head into the bedroom too, but Andrea has stacked two moving boxes in front of the door. They'd be easy to get past, but they may signal that she wants to keep the bedroom to herself.

In the small entryway, I stand quietly and listen through the door to the living room. Lissie's telling them how she tried explaining to her husband this afternoon where Andrea lives. " 'It's just north of Hillerød.' 'Ohh, in the direction of Køge?' 'No, up along King's Road past Birkerød.' 'Do you go past Kolding?' "

I can hear them laughing in there, Lissie loudest of all. Kolding's on the mainland, some three hours in a completely different direction. " 'You drive up along King's Road, and then north of Hillerød you take a right.' 'Ah, now I understand! You head toward the airport!' 'No, no, toward a small town called King's Meadows.' 'And then past Roskilde?' 'No, no, no!' 'Well then I'm completely confused. Do you drive toward Gilleleje?' 'Yes, at the start you could actually say it's toward Gilleleje.' 'Okay, and then you turn off at Odense?' "

They keep laughing on the other side of the door. Lissie has the healthiest spouse of the group. She and her husband still see their friends, travel together, and I dare say enjoy life on his pension, but he suffers from spatial disorder and can perseverate as well. When he has a bad day, he can ask questions about directions for half an hour at a stretch without realizing that time is passing, and in the end he gets to be tremendously annoying.

Lissie told us once that she laughs a lot with her husband. But by now I've heard plenty of women say the exact same thing, only to find out later that they actually laugh *at* their husbands, who laugh along without really understanding why. It might sound harsh to say that the best thing you've got left from a long marriage is laughing at how stupid your husband is, but if that's the only way to keep your spirits up . . .

I open the door to where the others are sitting, just as Andrea says that Bernard's been delayed a bit. I stop in the doorway. "Delayed? But I thought he wasn't coming today. That's what Merethe said."

"Yes, he was supposed to have a meeting at Lærke's day-care center, but it was rescheduled."

Do they notice anything in my reaction? They must be deaf and blind if they don't.

But nobody reacts, and I sit down quickly without a word, staring at the table. Bernard must think I'm not coming tonight, because I sent Andrea my regrets and only found out today that a meeting at school had been canceled.

I should leave now. I should definitely leave. Bernard's been in the group much longer than me.

The others talk about the relationships they have with their in-laws—ancient mothers and fathers who are helping take care of sons over sixty.

The doorbell rings. Andrea gets up and the others chatter on, oblivious.

Faint noises in the hall. Is he hanging up his jacket? Andrea's friendly chuckle. The door opens.

He catches sight of me and slumps, and hunched over he retreats backward to the hallway.

"Bernard, Bernard! What's the matter?" the women all call in chorus.

"Nothing!" he answers from the far side of the door.

"Yes, but . . ."

They look anxiously at one another.

And then he enters again, erect and smiling. It took only a few seconds.

"I get stomach cramps once in a while," he says, avoiding my gaze. "It's the stress. Don't worry about it."

They fall on him. "That's awful! You should do something about it."

"Werner had the same thing, but he got over it." "Have you had X-rays?" "I know a good specialist." "Carrot juice, have you tried that?"

"Sorry to frighten you. It's nothing, I feel better already."

At home in bed, I've tried to explain to myself that he can't really look as handsome as I remember. But he does. Silver-grey, lean, smiling broadly. And already he's able to look at me, cheerful and energetic, as if there's nothing between us. The others can't possibly notice anything. I'm not sure how sincere his charm seems to me, though it convinces the others; these last few months I've gotten to know his facial expressions better. Tonight he inhabits the expressions in turn and then, as if he wants to withdraw into some solitary reverie, abandons them. But the others don't see it.

We discuss differences in municipalities and how much rehab they'll subsidize for people with brain injuries and physical handicaps. Gerda's animated. The hair on Bernard's hands isn't as grey as on his head, and I wonder, *Is all his body hair dark?* I can see the vaulted musculature beneath his shirt. I think of rowers, tennis players, and hundred-meter sprinters—their shoulders, their arms, their chests. That's how they look; and they're not old.

Ulla talks about her doubts. "The more years we spend supporting our husbands and wives," she says, "and the more we learn about how to do it really well, the longer the road back to what we wanted to do with our lives. Aren't we really just helping each other veer farther off course, down some dead end?"

The fine creases in the corners of his eyes form patterns in constant motion. Kirsten tells us more about her husband's admission to the hospital and cries. The corners of Bernard's eyes are trees, a forest, the two of us, the hands, the slender fingers. Now Ulla's crying too, and he drapes an arm around her. The creases become bushes in the mist, a light on the far side of a cliff.

And then the meeting's over.

We all crowd into Andrea's small entryway. We hug each other and look Ulla and Kirsten in the eye, and a couple of minutes later I'm sitting in my car in the dark, not turning the key in the ignition. Kirsten drives past, Anton drives past, Ulla drives past.

Bernard's car is parked farther up a ways. It doesn't start up either, and I can faintly make his silhouette out through the window.

I think of how Lærke was kind to me. She trusts me; and the marriage they have is a lovely one. I don't owe Frederik anything, because I've already given him more than anyone could expect. But Lærke—I have to look out for Lærke. I will give Bernard energy, so he can stay with that poor sick woman even longer. I must promise myself to stop if I ever start detracting from her life instead of contributing to it.

I get out of my car and walk toward his. He remains seated. The streetlamps are intensely orange—more so than the lights in Farum or Copenhagen—and they make the outlines of the handicapped vehicles light up against the black hedges and the smooth bright pavement.

Bernard gets out of his car. I don't say anything. He doesn't say anything. The orange light. I raise my mouth and kiss him. He collapses a bit—like when he saw me in Andrea's living room—and his hands gather up my hips. Now we're alone, with the cherry blossoms in the dark treetops above us and scattered upon the asphalt beneath our feet.

We kiss for a long time while his hands find their way under my shirt and mine find their way under his. His fingers stroke my lower back and run along the inside of my waistband; I shiver a little. His lips sink down to my throat, and I want to press him against me while I still feel the hovering touch of his lips and fingers. In the wrinkles that extend from the corners of his eyes I see once more the trees, the forest, his hands and slender fingers. He sees something in my eyes too—what? what? I want to possess it, to know what makes him smile as he slowly undoes the button of my pants and fingers the upper part of my zipper.

"Mia, Mia," he says.

With my pants off, I sit down on the hood of the lime-colored car parked behind his. I feel the chilled automotive paint and the fallen petals from the cherry tree against the skin of my buttocks.

The streetlamp swings overhead, and its reflection bobs in the paint beneath us—or does it? And all the little yellow-brick houses of the disabled bob around us.

I look up into the light as I draw him in. The trees now a dark jungle, an elephant that stamps and trumpets to drive its enemies off.

Branches before my face. The bellowing grows harsher and quicker and still fiercer and the elephant attacks, it comes blowing toward me, trampling tree trunks and huts, villages, fences, all things in its path as if they were twigs.

And then I hear more stomping: another elephant. It likewise bellows and thunders this way. The sounds of both pounding equally loud in my ears and eyes, through my lips and my fingertips.

For a moment I feel Bernard slide out of me and the sounds vanish, I don't have time to think.

"No!" I shriek, much too loudly.

He's already inside again. The elephants stomping toward me again from their respective sides of the forest, the rhythmic booming, the shattered trees, and at last the all-embracing flutter as they crash down over us on the gleaming hood of the handicapped vehicle. Shards of shining ivory and splintered skulls in the moonlight.

21

Am I absentminded as I stand before my sixth graders the next morning, with a tender crotch and a chin abraded pink by Bernard's stubble? Decidedly, and in high spirits. I don't have a clue what my students are asking me.

No one complains; but then again, I've been absentminded for months, and at least today my distraction is cheerful.

"Yes, Molly."

"Why's negative times negative positive?"

"That's because . . . because . . ."

The beam from the orange streetlamp falls upon us, lighting up the outline of his hair as he leans in over me and I gaze into his features, colossal and blurry, rubbing my face around in his and smearing him over me so he can't be washed off.

A boy in the back row closes one eye, raises his left arm slowly, and with a quick flip of his right launches a metal lunch box that whizzes a couple of inches past my head, smashing into the wall and tumbling to the floor.

Silence.

I look at him.

"It wasn't on purpose," he says hastily, looking confused and a little fearful. "I didn't know it would go that far."

The eyes of the class: the girls waiting for him to be chewed out, the boys more inscrutable, as usual.

But I smile at him. "I know why you did it."

He doesn't say anything.

"Do *you* know why you did it?"

"It went too far. I didn't realize it would fly so far. I'm sorry."

"Yes. But do you know *why* you threw it?"

"I just wanted to try—" He stops.

I'd recognized the movement, right down to the closed left eye. "You saw *Iron Man* on TV two days ago, didn't you?"

"Yeah."

It's copycat behavior, it's so obviously copycat behavior. That's the way Robert Downey Jr. throws in the film, and now Mark's done the same thing without being able to explain why.

Anna raises her hand. "Aren't you going to scold him?"

"Mark and I will talk after class. Won't we, Mark?"

"Yeah."

In some respects I've become a poorer teacher since Frederik became ill—not as well prepared, and often distracted during class by thoughts of my miserable home life. Yet in other ways I've gotten better.

So much of what kids do and say takes on new meaning when you know a little neurology—for instance, that teenagers' ability to control their impulses isn't fully developed yet, which inevitably leads to brief episodes of mild copycat behavior, when they unthinkingly act out something they've seen. A watered-down version of the genuinely pathological cases of echolalia and echopraxia.

It also leads to what the textbooks refer to as *utilization behavior*. If a person with serious damage to the frontal lobes stands in a station waiting for his train, he might find himself entering the first train that stops at the platform, for he has an automated sequence of actions associated with train trips and it's impossible for his brain to interrupt that sequence. If he sees a bed, he might crawl in under the comforter—even though he knows full well that, at this very moment, he and his wife are shopping in Ikea's bedroom department.

The frontal lobe deficit isn't so pronounced in teenagers, but if some cherries are sitting in a bowl they're not supposed to take from, you risk having them eat the fruit without consciously deciding to do so—even if they're not hungry. If there's a ball lying on the lawn, you risk having them kick it, even if it isn't their ball and some glassware's standing on a table right behind it. It's an automated sequence of actions, and once in a while the inhibitory mechanism fails.

Last week I tried to explain this to Helena, but she cut me off. "I actually called to hear about Frederik."

"Helena, it's all part of how he's doing. Don't tell me that now *you're* going to say I talk too much about brain research?"

"Of course not."

But her voice wasn't convincing. Helena and my colleagues can't always follow what I say, and sometimes it's just easier to talk with Andrea and my other new friends in the support group.

On the phone, Helena and I both hesitated, and then she said, "Tell me about it, I want to hear."

I tried again. "The kids don't know themselves why they eat the cherries or kick the ball. When they try to explain, they're full of rationalizations— exactly like people with frontal lobe injuries who refuse to admit they're ill. It's what the doctors call *confabulation*: when someone with brain damage tries to cover the gaps in their train of thought with fantasies they actually believe."

Helena no longer sounded impatient on her end. "Okay, I can see how that's interesting. And I can also see how it's a big part of what you've been experiencing during this shitty year."

"Good, I'm glad to hear it."

Helena gave a little snort, which meant she was about to say something she thought was funny. "But Mia, can I tell you something?"

"Yes."

"If you start using the word *confabulation* as much as you do *perseverate* and *inhibitory mechanism*, I'm going to ask Frederik's doctor for a lobotomy."

...

The rhythmic booming, the shattered trees, and finally the all-embracing flutter when they collide. During recess, I stop in the middle of the stairs to text Bernard on my way down to the teachers' lounge.

Last night he again requested that we not see each other anymore, but I didn't feel devastated. I was in a silly Frederikian mood and giddily promised to stay away from the next support group meeting.

My Frederik mood's persisted till this morning. What harm could come from a single text?

All I write is: *Thinking of yesterday. M.*

In the hallway in front of the teacher's lounge, I bump into Niels, a math colleague. He's a handsome fellow in his thirties with a passionate engagement for the subject, loads of ideas, and a charming laugh. When you first meet him, it's hard to imagine why neither students nor parents respect him. Yet on three occasions, the principal's had to find a new math teacher for one of his classes because the parents were up in arms.

And for two of these ravenous, extra-demanding classes, the principal felt I should be the one to take over. ("I know it's difficult, Mia, but their next teacher *has* to make it work. And I can tell you, confidentially, that you and Tove are the only ones who fit the bill.")

For two years I worked unpaid overtime, slaving away at work that Niels had already received a salary for. But when I started hating him, it wasn't because of the extra work—Frederik was always gone anyway, and Niklas was often playing elsewhere—but because I grew fond of the students. If not for me, they'd have had trouble getting into gymnasium and college, because they never would have learned math. Niels is one of the few people I've met who's made me fall asleep on many a night with the thought that the world would be better off if he were dead.

Yet when we see each other today, he smiles at me. He often acts as if he doesn't know what we think about him.

"I've gotten some of the books," he says. "I just need the ones from Germany and Norway."

"Good," I reply, though I know he's lying. Of course he hasn't ordered the books, and he'll just come up with some new strained excuse about when we'll see them.

Several eternities ago, I made the suggestion at a math teachers' meeting that we procure copies of textbooks from the other Scandinavian countries plus England and Germany, so we could see how they go about teaching math. Niels jumped in right away and said he'd make sure to order the books.

We all knew what would happen, but it was me who said, "Tove could do it too."

"Don't worry, I'll take care of it."

"Or maybe each of us should take a country and try to get the textbooks from there?"

"No, let me do it, I really want to. It's a great idea."

We all hesitated, until finally I said, "But Niels, it's just that back when you promised to look into that course facility, you never did—and then we never went."

His big happy smile, his enthusiasm. There's no doubt that he fully believed what he was saying. "I'm really sorry about the slip-up that time." He cast his eyes downward, and a note of seriousness entered his voice. "There were reasons for that, which I'd just as soon not get into now." He exchanged a confidential glance with one of the other teachers. "I'd really like to make up for it."

I could see that the others felt we should let him.

"So you'll order them then?"

"Yes, of course I will. Definitely. *I'm* the one saying I want to do it."

Half a year later, in the days leading up to our next math teachers' meeting, I began to remind him about it. One day when we were in the coatroom about to put on our jackets, he said, "It's because you've been pressing me like this that I've completely lost the desire to do it."

"So if I hadn't reminded you, you'd have done it already?"

"Yes, no question."

"Well then, I'll leave well enough alone."

"Thank you. *Anyone* would lose their motivation with you taking that role for yourself."

I let his comment slide to keep the peace. But in the following weeks, I pulled each of the other teachers aside and asked if they thought I was too domineering. No one agreed with Niels, and in fact I received a lot of praise. And yet his confabulation made me put a damper on new initiatives.

Of course he didn't get the books during the subsequent half year either. A few days before the third meeting, when the two of us happened to be alone in the teachers' kitchen, I said, "Niels, you don't have to worry about it anymore. I'll order the books myself."

Again he became aggressive. "I thought we agreed that you wouldn't press me."

We started arguing. "Well if you'd only done what you promised to . . ."

Yet just a few days later, he showed his sweet, charming, somewhat flighty and befuddled side—the side that everyone who doesn't know him falls for.

"I'll definitely do it. I've just been delayed," he said.

"Okay. So I *shouldn't* do it?"

"Nope, not on any account."

Now a fourth meeting is in the wings, and this time I'm not saying a word. Not only that, but in the last few months I've actually begun to feel a connection to him. For I've read about his symptoms hundreds of times on the internet, heard about them in support group, seen them in the clinics. And they're quite common.

The impulse to execute an action is formed in an area of the brain that is distinct from the area that determines what we plan and say. Even a quite minor injury to the frontal lobes will often weaken the connection between the two areas, and that means that an affected person may seem completely healthy as long as you're just talking to him. Yet it's disturbing how few of his fine words and plans ever lead to anything—again, just like with some teenagers. There's simply no neural contact between word and deed.

In the teachers' lounge, when the others are hanging out and enjoying themselves, I've begun to feel alone. Even if I took several weeks to explain to those I'm closest to how different everything's become at home, none of the teachers would really understand. Niels certainly wouldn't understand either, and yet I have a deep sense that he and I are on the same team.

I don't know if his injury's congenital, or if he perhaps hit his head at some point. No one's ever mentioned brain damage when they talk about him or why the hell the administration doesn't fire him. But I'm sure they can't imagine how different things are for him at home either.

. . .

The doctors have been saying for a long time that I shouldn't expect Frederik to ever become completely well. The best I dare hope for is that, someday, his symptoms will be just as difficult to detect as Niels's.

202

After the next class, Bernard hasn't replied to my text. I pay it no mind. But after the third class he still hasn't answered. And then it hits me: he *isn't* answering.

He doesn't intend to answer.

He'll never answer.

The goofy mood I've been in since last night vanishes from one moment to the next, and just like I've seen teenage girls from my older classes do, I lock myself in the bathroom. Fortunately it's lunch break, and then I have a free period, so I can weep in peace. When the free period is about to end, I call the school secretary from the bathroom and tell her I've become ill and have to go home. She knows it's not true, but she's kind and wishes me a speedy recovery.

As I'm driving home, the realtor calls; a buyer has signed the contract, and we have to be out within a month. We still haven't found another place because it turned out we couldn't afford the apartment I saw with Bernard, and since then I haven't had the energy to look elsewhere.

At home, there's already a message on the answering machine from the estate administrator: now that the house has been sold and no longer needs to look good for potential buyers, they're going to come on Monday and take possession of their half of the furniture and household effects.

I just want to crawl into bed. Frederik's lying there already, just like he was before he was admitted to the psych ward.

In bed, I toss and turn at his side, I can't fall asleep, yet I don't feel awake either. Again and again I check my cell, to see if I accidentally turned it off or set it to mute, to see if the text to Bernard was sent. The sign on the ceiling: are we really cursed? Is it our own fault? I threw Frederik out a long time ago, and Niklas found me unconscious on the kitchen floor. Something a son shouldn't have to experience. Yes, cursed. A righteous punishment.

And the odor in here: my father home from prison, the smell of his two-bedroom flat as he sat with a blanket across his legs and slowly went to pieces. My visits, the months before he died. He was definitely cursed.

The doorbell rings. I'm not up to answering it, but then Frederik gets out of bed and goes downstairs.

I can hear that it's the neighbor. A letter for us, delivered to them by mistake. I've explained to them that they shouldn't give letters or messages directly to Frederik. I'm worried that they won't reach me, but I can hear she's doing it anyway.

They're talking down below. I hate getting letters. As a rule, they just pile more work on top of what I'm already behind on. Forms to fill out for the municipality, the union, the insurance company; new appointments with Frederik's doctors. It never lets up.

Frederik comes back in. "Not good," he says.

"*What's* not good? God damn it, what is it this time? What mess have you dragged me into now?"

He hands me a letter that he's already opened, and I twist myself up into a sitting position.

It's from Frederik's new lawyer.

Dear Mr. Halling,

I have attached the psychiatric report from the Medico-Legal Council.
Unfortunately, it is not as positive as we had hoped. As you can see, the council chose to disregard the opinion they commissioned from the neuropsychologist Herdis Lebech.
As you will recall, it is not possible to appeal the case any further.
I am at your disposal for any questions you may have, starting on Tuesday. You may call my secretary and request an appointment for us to speak on the telephone.

Sincerely yours,
Louise Rambøll

I read the opening lines of the attached report and skim the other pages: . . . *finds the assertion that Frederik Halling was mentally unstable at the time of the crime not proven . . . fully acquainted with the consequences of his actions and therefore responsible . . .*

Back when Frederik was himself, I would have talked to him about a matter as critical as this. I also would have tried to in the first months after his operation, because I still couldn't conceive then how meaningless my efforts really were. But I no longer have the energy—the energy to struggle with the case and at the same time attend to his needs.

My cell phone lies on the night table, still without a text from Bernard. I punch in the new lawyer's number. Her secretary doesn't want to transfer me, but I press her and at last she puts me through.

"I don't understand . . . but Dr. Lebech said . . ." I find myself crying.

Louise Rambøll's an idiot—just as she's been in my previous conversations with her. The only thing she can say is that I've understood the letter correctly: Frederik will receive a sentence of at least three years. After he's served his time, his criminal record will prevent him from ever working with children again or for a public employer, regardless of how well he becomes. If he doesn't qualify for a disability pension, he'll have to go on welfare, and there's nothing we can do about it.

Frederik asks, "What's she saying?"

"She hasn't got a clue about anything!" I shout at him, with her still on the line.

I hang up without saying goodbye and call Bernard.

His secretary doesn't want to put me through either. But I don't stop crying while I tell her to tell him that Frederik's psychiatric report has come.

He takes the phone and his manner is formal—hardly that of a man whose limbs were entwined with mine on the hood of a car last night.

"This is Bernard."

"Bernard, you're going to have to take on the case again. Louise Rambøll is totally impossible. Frederik's going to jail now."

"Louise is very clever."

"No! She's about to send Frederik to jail!"

"I'll have a talk with Louise, and then—"

"You know full well that you're so much better than she is!"

It's true, so there's nothing he can say.

"Frederik's going to jail because you didn't want us. People will keep on blaming us for everything, they still won't talk to us. And Frederik will simply shatter in there. He'll get even sicker."

"I'd like to help you as much as I possibly can," he says. "I really feel

205

terrible about this. I'll have Louise send me a copy of the psychiatric report, then I can give you some suggestions over the phone. And I'll have a long talk with Louise."

"But that won't change a thing." Now I'm sobbing into the receiver.

"But I think we'll both regret it if I take on this case again."

Now Frederik is standing next to the bed, looking at me with eyes wide. I avoid his gaze as I say, "If Frederik can't get the best lawyer, he runs a greater risk of going to jail. He *does*!"

Bernard pauses. A pause is a good sign; I keep my mouth shut.

He clears his throat, and then he asks, "Don't you think you should think this over?"

"No."

"Hmm."

Another pause; longer this time. I'm no longer crying, just listening in silence. I want to hear his breathing over the phone, but my own breath is still making too much noise.

"Okay," he says at last. "But remember that I'm Frederik's lawyer—*not* yours."

"I understand."

"Frederik's the one I'll meet with. If he's amenable to it, you may come along on occasion. But it will be he and I. You and I will not be having any meetings alone together."

"Of course. Of course. That's the way to do it."

"Okay. Good."

Again a pause. Now I think I can faintly hear the background noise where he is. The cars on the street outside his office; perhaps his breath.

"Thank you so very, very much, Bernard," I say. "Thank you. It means the world to us."

"Okay . . . Yes. Okay. Frederik will naturally want to know as much as possible about the consequences of the new report, and as quickly as possible."

"Yes."

"If he could be here in forty-five minutes, I'll see what I can do."

"I can't thank you enough, Bernard. It'll make all the difference. I'm so glad to have you back."

His tone becomes formal again. "You mean *glad that Frederik has me back.*"

"Yes. Of course." I try laughing, but he doesn't laugh with me, and then I can't either.

After we hang up, I get up out of bed. It would be natural for me to give Frederik a hug now. But I can't anymore; I just look at him.

"Now we still have a chance, anyway," I say.

I put on some clothes and reapply my makeup, while Frederik goes down to make some sandwiches to take in the car—ham, cheese, and tomato, since he no longer eats only jam sandwiches.

I drive fast, staring straight in front of me at the freeway. Neither of us is hungry after all, so he sits with the lunch box in his lap. He says, "I've started to think about some of the things I remember from after the operation. Some strange things. Did they really happen?"

"Yes," I say, "it was a strange time."

"But I'm thinking—did you use to call Bernard up at night while I lay next to you in bed?"

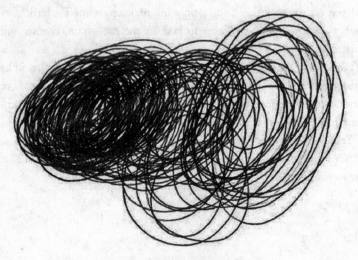

Figure 23.2. Test for perseveration.
The subject has been asked to draw a circle.

22

If Frederik is going to go to jail because I couldn't control myself around his lawyer, I'll never forgive myself, and it simply sucks to be having this conversation right now, heading down the freeway at eighty miles an hour.

But he keeps interrogating me.

"Stop it! God damn it, Frederik, it's your fault I'm even in a support group. I talk to *all* of them."

"But you don't talk to the others in the middle of the night, do you?"

"Yeah, actually I do."

"No you don't."

"Stop it!"

"So which of the others do you call? Do you call up Andrea at two in the morning?"

"Frederik! You're going to end up in jail and will never get another job if our meeting with Bernard goes down in flames."

"But what's all this about Bernard not wanting my case, and then you call him up and he takes it on anyway?"

"Frederik, stop! You're perseverating!"

That gets him to shut up. He sits there grumbling, staring at the airbag panel in front of him.

...

Bernard's office is situated in an old half-timbered building on Great King Street. The reception area is small, but modernly furnished and bright.

I've been here a couple of times and know that all the rooms are like this.

Before we kissed at the apartment viewing, Bernard often alluded to his first year after the car accident, a watershed year when he had to figure out how to deal with everything being different. Till then he'd had a brilliant career in one of Copenhagen's largest law firms, but if his eight-year-old boys were to have a healthy parent in their everyday lives, and if Lærke were to have the support he wanted to give her, he had to sacrifice his future with the firm.

For a while he tried using a nursing aide and an au pair to help him balance his work and home life. He also got permission to cut back on his hours at the firm, though otherwise he would have soon made partner. But it couldn't be avoided; he had to make a choice. He chose to quit and join forces with an old classmate to start a small firm that would bring in a lot less money. During law school the friend, Alex, had kept to the periphery of parties and student life; for a few months each year he'd be away paragliding or visiting tropical islands no one had heard of. Yet even though most students seldom saw him, Alex made an impression, for he did surprisingly well whenever he finally showed up for exams with his long sun-bleached hair.

Now Alex lives with four kids and wife number two in Amager, where they share a large rambling house with another family. He still has lots of friends in Africa, and he spends long hours each week doing pro bono work for a fair-trade organization.

As I understand it, they became the subject of intense speculation by old acquaintances when they started the firm seven years ago. Hadn't the industrious Bernard always been Alex's opposite? Or were they, beneath the surface, really cut from the same cloth? Some lawyers maintained that they'd always thought Bernard and Alex ought to start something together.

It's the end of the working day when we arrive, and both the receptionist and secretary have gone home, so Bernard comes out and lets us in.

He shakes hands with Frederik, and afterward with me. Everything in his expression and body language is polite and serious. I wish I could look so composed, but I doubt I do.

Frederik looks at him, then back at me, and then again at Bernard.

Perhaps he sees something that surprises him—but if so, he doesn't know how to process it. It's still a novelty for him to be interested in other people at all, or to think of them as having lives when he doesn't see them.

Bernard leads us down a short hallway to a conference room with expensive but bland furnishings, where he starts reading through the psychiatric report.

The room grows quiet. I can still feel the way his hand clasped mine a short while ago. A large hand, a dry hand—a bit like Frederik's, but younger and warmer. I can also feel my buttocks and thighs against the seat of this skinny little Arne Jacobsen chair. Hand, ass, the hand between my legs; the lingering sense-memory of him inside me. Almost as if he's still there, and I let out a small gasp that he must be able to hear. A brief twitch crosses his face, but he doesn't lift his eyes from the report.

I wonder what Lærke's doing now. I can't stop myself from imagining her at the handicapped center. No doubt she's sitting with a group of other disabled people at some round table where they're weaving baskets or painting with watercolors, while she waits to be picked up by her amazing husband whom she's too brain-damaged to appreciate.

I see them come home from the center in their white Volvo station wagon—Bernard opening the door for her, getting out the wheelchair or the crutches, helping her over to the magnificent yard that slopes down toward the woods. There they sit, contemplating the mild summer evening. It's true that I don't know her that well, so in my fantasy she says the same thing as when I visited them: *We like it a great deal.* She smiles sweetly and beautifully beneath her large hat. *Language is so rich.*

And I see how Bernard was standing last night in the orange light with his pants down. His large erect cock; the feeling that every cell of my body is excited and alert.

"The Medico-Legal Council finds that even though you were somewhat impaired mentally at the time of the crime, it shouldn't have been abnormally difficult for you to resist selfish impulses." Bernard gazes intensely into Frederik's eyes, as if I weren't here. "That's because before you had the tumor, you were unusually intelligent, structured, and focused in your thinking."

That might be the only thing that gives Bernard away—the fact that he isn't sufficiently attentive to me. After all, I *am* the wife of the accused.

He's kind to Frederik, and he's always been—also back when Frederik was much sicker than he is now. Bernard's shirt lies a little taut across his shoulders; I know how it feels to squeeze those shoulders tight.

"There have evidently been some problems in using the Iowa Gambling Task diagnostically," he continues. "In brief, people with orbitofrontal damage are not the only ones who exhibit the irrational behavior that the test detects. There are also many healthy people who make precisely the same mistakes when they sit before the stacks of cards. They too will gamble all their money away, flouting common sense—and the strategy they expressly state they should be using. And that certainly doesn't exempt *them* from punishment."

Frederik asks, "But then what can we do?"

"Louise was correct in saying that there isn't any higher court to appeal the ruling to. But the ruling is not a verdict. It's perfectly acceptable for us to contact the Medico-Legal Council and argue that they've overlooked something in their report. But that only makes sense if we can point them to facts that they haven't been aware of."

"I've told them everything."

"If for instance your secretary were to declare that your personality underwent a dramatic change—or if others who've worked closely with you for a long time were to say so."

"But they're all at Saxtorph. They work for Laust."

I break in. "Are you suggesting that we try to get employees from the school to speak up in defiance of the new administration?"

"Yes."

He looks at me only very briefly before turning his attention back to Frederik. "If the truth is on our side and you *did* undergo a transformation in the period leading up to the crime, it *may* be that some of your former staff members will acknowledge it."

In the moment he finally met my gaze, I saw how capable he is of shutting me out of his life. How he's a noble person who puts his sick wife before anything else.

We do not flirt. I do not try at all to be charming, and he doesn't try to look good in front of me either. That's it. It's over.

"Is there anyone you worked closely with, who you think we could interview?" he asks Frederik.

"There were three secretaries in the office. If we're going to ask any of them, we should begin with Trine."

...

No longer can any of us—Niklas, Thorkild, Vibeke, and me—avoid understanding what's happened. Niklas is always out with Emilie and his friends, while the rest of us lie around in our beds or in front of the TV, sprawling like mournful dogs anywhere there's a little warmth and space.

Since the auction house has taken my most expensive prints and pieces of furniture, I move around our home bumping repeatedly into big patches of empty space—places where there used to be something I was fond of, where now it's utterly bare. In a way this feels more real. Frederik's soul has disappeared, and now everyone can finally see what we've known for so long: that the contents of our lives have been torn away.

But we need to get hold of at least a couch and a dining table and chairs, so on Sunday afternoon Frederik and I drive the trailer over to Thorkild and Vibeke's to get some surplus furniture from their basement.

In the old days, Vibeke would have baked a nice cake for our visit, but she's been lying sick in bed this past week. In the old days, I would have then baked a cake to take along, but I don't feel up to it either, so I buy one at the bakery.

When we sit down to afternoon tea, Vibeke sets out my cake with one she bought. Hers is much more expensive.

"But you knew that I would buy a cake," I say.

"Yes, but I fell for this one, it looked so tempting. So we have two."

Fortunately, my inhibitory mechanism is robust enough that I can behave as if nothing's wrong. But is this the way it's going to be now? Am I going to be humiliated the rest of my life just because her son ruined me and not her? We've only been in their house five minutes, and already I feel the need for a few moments to myself.

"I'm just going to run down to the basement and look at the dining table," I say.

Seconds later I'm halfway out of the living room, but in the doorway I hear Frederik behind me. "Shouldn't we all go down there together?"

I curse his obliterated capacity for empathy as they all troop down behind me.

Easy now. Easy. Easy.

I'm playing tennis, the balls on the clay court, the low sun. I want to enter my daydream. I'm sitting in the hanging sofa, it's evening and we've come from the neighbor's garden party. We're happy, me and Healthy Frederik. That's key. It's Healthy Frederik I want to be alone with. We go on a walk around the lake. And it's Healthy Frederik.

But the fantasies no longer open up for me. They don't invite me in—not with Frederik beside me in the hanging sofa, not with Bernard.

In one of the basement rooms, Thorkild and Vibeke have piled up all their old junk. Someplace in the very back are buried a dining table and chairs.

"It's great that you can use them," Vibeke says to Frederik. "It's a good thing we saved them. They aren't anything special, but it's the first table your father and I owned as a couple."

Was I crazy when I accepted this offer? It must be possible to borrow furniture somewhere else. I sure as hell don't want their furniture in my house after all. It'll be torture.

The table is hidden behind so much clutter as to be invisible. Frederik brings out some chairs that stand right behind the door. Then he grabs hold of two large moving boxes that also go into the hall, then two suitcases and a food mixer.

Vibeke says, "Stop, stop. We were just going to come down here to look. The tea's hot upstairs."

There's a restless energy in Frederik's eyes. "But aren't we going to look at the table? That's what we came down here for."

He starts struggling with an armchair. Then a freezer chest.

"Come, we're going upstairs," Vibeke says. "Frederik, come along."

He doesn't answer, just continues to heave on the freezer.

"*Now*, Frederik. Come upstairs!"

But he doesn't join us, and so I have to sit alone with Thorkild and Vibeke.

"Your cake looks delicious," Vibeke says after we've sat down.

"Not as delicious as yours," I say. "Anyone can see that."

None of us believes in Bernard's plan for saving Frederik. Prison awaits, and then the dole. The only one who puts any stock in the plan is Frederik. Then again, it's impossible to know what's really what in his inner mire of depression and antidepressants, lack of empathy and ill-timed elation.

My gaze drifts out of the dining room and into the living room, where two of the walls are covered with dark wooden shelves. I've paged through some of Thorkild's books on past visits, when I was trying to disappear from these rooms. A large part of them are history books, with a focus on eighteenth- and nineteenth-century Denmark. Despite a brilliant career as an educator, Thorkild sometimes upbraids himself for not pursuing a university career as a historian.

"Wouldn't you like to try this other cake too?" Vibeke has the cake knife in hand, ready to put a slice of her cake on my plate.

"No thanks, I'm not that keen on raspberry these days."

Again silence, broken only by the faint sounds of Frederik pottering about in the basement. He and I haven't left home on this Sunday outing; we've brought the mood of our home with us.

Thorkild's spoon clinks against his plate. His voice is breezy. "You know who your best friends are by the fact that you can be silent together."

Vibeke doesn't give up. "I could cut the raspberries off—"

"No!" I say it with too much emphasis, I know.

Then Frederik's back, and he places on the table a book, on the history of European philosophy. "I found this."

Vibeke's already putting food on his plate. "I'm sure you can eat two big pieces."

Frederik looks at his father and says, "Mia leaves neurophilosophy articles lying around at home, spread out everywhere. So I need something to read as a bit of an antidote."

"*I* leave things lying around? Am *I* the one who makes such a mess? How many times have I had to take your speaker boards and—" I stop mid-sentence, despite my fury; it all seems so pointless.

But Frederik continues unabated. "She's convinced that new brain research is going to invalidate twenty-five hundred years of philosophy. But the question of free will was the same back then as it is today. Nothing's new. Nothing at all in twenty-five hundred years."

Thorkild reaches for the book and grips it firmly, regarding it with fondness.

"If you're interested, I've got some others you can borrow as well. How on earth did it end up in the basement? It really shouldn't be down there." He gently strokes the dust jacket, and it occurs to me that I've never seen him touch Vibeke that way. He leafs through it and leans over, suddenly engrossed.

Vibeke sets Frederik's plate before him. "Well, what do *you* think, Frederik? Do human beings have free will?"

"It's a complicated question. For the time being, my only thought is that one should try not to say anything stupid."

Thorkild nods approvingly. It would be impossible to articulate his creed more precisely.

They are like three peas in a pod. The Halling family tone of voice, the conventional, frosty self-righteousness, the cultivated hostility that they've thrown in my face for twenty years.

What am I doing here? Why in the world have I agreed to be present at their family's private party?

Frederik eats quickly and then heads back to the basement. The rest of us follow, and we see that he's dug all the way through to my in-laws' first dining table and chairs.

"I remembered this furniture being somewhat different," I say. "I don't think we can use it after all. But thank you so much for the offer."

"Do take it," Thorkild insists. "Then you can keep it until you find something better."

And Frederik's too ill to twig anything at all. He's got his hands on his hips, just like his father. "Yes, we could keep it till we find something else."

We go back upstairs with three philosophy books that Thorkild found for Frederik in the storeroom, including one by a contemporary Spanish philosopher. Then we sit down in the living room. I'm aching to get out of here.

Thorkild says, "Speaking of Spanish, Vibeke and I were wondering if there was something we could do for Niklas."

I didn't see that coming!

Niklas got Ds in both written and oral Spanish, but all his other grades have been good. When Frederik was a boy, Vibeke and Thorkild coached him to a top GPA; now that their son has failed so utterly, Niklas is evidently supposed to be their next golden boy. And that means accusing me of being unable to raise my own son.

Vibeke says, "Maybe Niklas could use a little peace and quiet, what with the moving and all. Maybe it'd be good for him to live someplace else for a few days."

I fly out of my chair. "Stop it now! How many attacks do I have to sit here and listen to before the two of you will let it rest?"

Vibeke looks frightened again. "Is it because of the cake?" she mumbles. "I was wondering if it was wrong of me to buy it, but then—"

"It's *not* because of the cake, God damn it! Can't you ever listen to what I say?"

I'm on my way out the door. "And Frederik! Couldn't you for once in your life stand up for me when your mother runs me down?"

My cell phone rings. I glance at the display and find myself saying, "It's Bernard."

Everyone grows quiet. As if that's what we've been waiting for all along. As if what we thought were life-or-death struggles were just minor distractions till we heard from Bernard again.

My fingers fumble with the button.

"Hello, Bernard."

I can hear a faint wind, and his voice in the distance. "Do you have a few minutes?"

"Yes."

No one moves. The others are seated; I'm standing up.

"Can you talk right now?"

"Yes."

"I'm in Aumessas with Lærke."

"You're in *France*?"

Surprise in the others' faces.

"Yes."

"But we just saw you at the office."

"After you left, I canceled all my appointments. Lærke and I have gone to Aumessas for four days."

"Is it your anniversary?"

"No."

217

He sounds so serious, so different from how he's sounded to me before. I have the sense that something terrible's happened.

"Is it Lærke?"

Frederik and my in-laws are still staring at me. But they're far away now. An old faded photo I quickly flip past in the pile.

Again his grave voice.

"It's not going so well down here. Not as well as it usually does . . . It made a deep impression on me, seeing you again at our meeting."

I don't look at the family for long. I've got to get out of here. I run out into the hallway; I'll have to come up with some story for them later. But that isn't far enough away. I run out to the driveway. And then farther, out onto the street.

They shouldn't be able to see me anymore from the house; I check. What should I tell them when I return? I'll find something—and otherwise screw it.

"What's going on there?" Bernard asks. "Should I not have called?"

"Yes. Yes. You should have called. Nothing's going on. I went outside."

We fall silent.

"But I was just so . . . at the meeting," I say. "After all, we didn't *do* anything."

"You were good. You're trying! We're both trying. That's something we have in common. And you seemed to me lovelier than ever."

There are a thousand things I ought to say. I can find no words.

Again he says, "Was it wrong of me to call?"

"Not at all." I'm still tongue-tied. All I can manage is "Bernard." It's a new way for me to say his name. "Bernard." I'm getting used to saying it like this. From now on, I'll say it this way often. "Where are you?"

"In Aumessas."

"Yes, but I mean where? What are you looking at right now?"

"I've walked a long way from our house. An hour. It's the first time down here that I've needed to be alone. Up a wooded path on the mountainside. There are chestnut and mulberry trees here, and I'm looking out across a valley."

On Thorkild and Vibeke's street, the steel half-roof over the bus stop has something of the color of the sidewalk pavement, of the sky.

"I'm looking at a bus stop three houses down the street from my in-laws," I say. "It looks like rain."

We laugh. Something within me is shaking free. The little laugh at almost nothing feels so deep and right. It's falling into place. It's all falling into place.

"Thank you for calling, Bernard. I'm really glad you called. Really, really glad."

INTRODUCTION

In the 60 pages that follow, you will find articles addressing one of the most highly debated questions in metaphysics (which is itself one of the most controversial disciplines in 2,000 years of Western philosophy).

Almost every major philosopher has expressed an opinion about how much we decide our own actions ourselves. If everything is predetermined by an almighty God or by the laws of nature, how then can the individual be free? Regardless of whether we conceive of our actions as being immutably arranged by a god, by our genes and upbringing, or by the fundamental physical laws governing the atoms we are comprised of, the essential nature of the question remains unaltered.

Yet the opposition between everything being predetermined and man being master of his own actions is not so simple. Many philosophers do not consider the two ideas to be in conflict at all.

In 1814, the French astronomer Pierre-Simon Laplace imagined a vast intelligence that knew every natural law as well as the precise location of every constituent of the universe, and he wrote that such an intelligence would be able to calculate every event at every juncture in time, past and future.

This thought experiment has been known ever since as Laplace's demon, and it encapsulates the problem of free will. For someone to act freely, most people would agree that two conditions must be fulfilled:

1. The person must have the possibility of acting differently.

2. The person himself must choose how to act-–he cannot merely be the last link in a chain of events that has already been set in motion and that can only occur in one way.

Even if an individual attempts to wrest himself free from his upbringing and the immediate expression of his genes, the impulse to do so must itself come from somewhere. Nothing arises from nothing, for that would violate the very nature of our universe. Every single choice he makes is made in an interaction among countless influences of varying strength—and nothing more. He is in no sense master of the struggle among these influences, so how can one say that he acts freely? Or that it would be just to punish or reward him for what he chooses to do?

Most people have an intuitive sense that they act freely and that others do so too. Yet if these same people seriously consider Laplace's demon and the way the universe is constructed, they normally conclude that it is impossible for us to possess free will. And that it may very well be possible that what we so convincingly experience as our own freedom is in reality an illusion.

The philosophers on the following pages are some of the most influential in the modern debate on the subject, and they represent a broad spectrum of opinions. The following diagram provides an overview of their positions.

	Everything is predetermined (**Determinism**)	Everything is *not* predetermined (**Indeterminism**)
The individual possesses free will	**Compatibilism**, or **Soft Determinism** Free will can exist in a deterministic universe (Daniel Dennett) (Harry Frankfurt)	**Libertarianism** Free will cannot exist in a deterministic universe, but the universe is not deterministic (Robert Kane) (Peter van Inwagen)
The individual does *not* possess free will	**Hard Determinism** Free will cannot exist in a deterministic universe, therefore the individual has no free will	**Hard Incompatibilism**[1] The individual has no free will, regardless of whether the universe is deterministic or not (Galen Strawson) (Derk Pereboom)

1. Hard incompatibilists hold that the question of whether the world is deterministic or not has no bearing on the question of free will. In the diagram, this position should therefore cover both of the bottom fields.

LIBERTARIANISM

Within libertarianism, there are two major strands:

1. Metaphysical libertarianism. The individual possesses a soul independent of the physical universe and its laws of nature. This strand is sometimes bound up with religious belief.

2. Science-based libertarianism. This strand has found support in the field of atomic physics—specifically in Bohr's quantum theory of subatomic particles, which states that not everything in the universe is determined. Electrons move randomly and unpredictably. Questions then arise about whether the movement of electrons can have any effect on human thought, and

23

Everything before us. Nothing behind us. Nothing, nothing, nothing! Bernard and I are twenty-one, we're beautiful: on the street people turn around behind us, the smooth skin on his chest almost without hair, my breasts taut against him. We talk at the same time and so quickly, even folks in their thirties can't understand us. We both moved from home to the city a few years ago, and at night we leap fences into parks and look each other in the eye, letting the sounds and gaps in our voices rub up against each other till they merge into one.

And then we sing loud. Really loud! Because everyone at my school's gone home. And if anyone can hear us anyway from the basement corridor that goes past the teachers' small break room, with its cot, its large yielding cushions and pyramid poster, they'll never be able to guess who's singing and giggling and moaning and making the cot creak.

For I am the very picture of virtue. Have always been. The door here is locked. And if they can guess anyhow, we don't care, because life stretches out before us as long as Bernard's hard-on keeps pounding away inside me. The fall from his nostril to his upper lip, the valley between earlobe and cheek, the piers of his lashes. I grasp his lower back more tightly. Our faces are so close that we're singing into each other's mouth:

Twenty-one years old
And burning gas on
Hans Christian Andersen Way

We put the seat back
The window down
The volume up
Let summer air in
Just me and him
Our skin it glistens
And damn it's hot

We float up from the break room in the basement, we dive down from the cloudless sky toward the school's squat buildings, we swim naked in Lake Farum surrounded by all our twenty-one-year-old friends. Slender tanned bodies melt into the dark. Pale buttocks catch the light in the blackness and bounce around on the bank, appear and disappear. Like us. We appear and disappear, Thursday, Friday, come and go, Saturday, Sunday, his balls against my inner thighs. Appear and disappear.

Down the basement corridor and up the school stairway, letting the summer air in. Damn, it's hot.

In the parking lot behind my school, I point.

"What?" he asks.

"Zipper!"

He tugs it up and laughs too.

We don't give a shit.

And I just *know* that Bernard and Niklas will be great together, as soon as Niklas gets over the shock of it. Bernard can get along with anyone. I can see them before me, playing badminton in our new yard, bent over Niklas's laptop and sharing computer tips, sitting by themselves in the twilight and talking about which photographers mean the most to them.

And what about Bernard's boys? Will I be able to get along with them? He's shown me pictures and e-mails. They'll still want their sick mother—just like Niklas will still want his sick father. The wrath; the desire to protect. But his boys are grown now. Just like Niklas. I'll figure something out; we're canoeing on the Mølle River. We live in Bernard's house, and Lærke's at a home where trained caregivers can see to her. She's thriving there. And my divorce from Frederik is easy; from a legal point of view, I get everything that remains behind—the money, the car, the furniture—since the bank determined exactly what his half was and took it. But I want to be nice; I'll give him something or other that I don't have to.

All the happy plans buzz around in my head night and day. And they're buzzing there as Bernard and I cut across the parking lot behind the school on our way home from the break room. He gets a text; his alert sound is the sea, the crashing of a wave.

"Lærke was helping make dinner and knocked the milk over," he says. "I've got to buy some on my way home from the office."

He says this with sorrow in his voice, as if only in this instant does he realize what he's done. If only he'd taken himself in hand and resisted temptation even longer! If only he could last another eight years without enjoying sex, intimacy, and equal give-and-take with a healthy woman. Then everything would be as it should in their little family.

Eight years! I think again. Eight years with a wife who has multiple handicaps, eight years before he's had the least little something on the side. And it hasn't been due to any lack of libido, I now know.

I want to say something to alleviate his suffering: *If you're doing well, Bernard, it's better for her.* Or something along those lines.

But I always have the sense that if I say one wrong word about Lærke, it'll be over. He lights up when things are going better with her—and nothing can make him more unhappy than when she's having a hard time. He'll never leave her. And I accept that. It's what makes him such a remarkable human being. I don't want to destroy anything; I just want to make their lives better. To give him renewed energy to be an even better man.

"I know it must be hard for you" is the only thing I say.

...

Saturday morning, I'm wakened by Frederik bounding up the stairs and shouting, "It's saved! Saved! It worked!"

He sits down on the edge of my bed. (We've agreed that from now on he's the one who sleeps on the air mattress, while I sleep in the bed.) He shows me today's *Politiken*, with the headline SAXTORPH PRIVATE SCHOOL RESCUED.

And down in the article: "A group of affluent parents of former students have joined together to present Saxtorph with a large gift. In addition, after intense negotiation, Danske Bank has agreed to slash the school's debt by several million crowns."

"That was my plan! The school's been saved! I've saved Saxtorph!"

Frederik hasn't been so happy since his manic period.

"We'll have to celebrate," I say.

And even as I'm saying it, even as I'm feeling happy on his behalf, on our friends' behalf, on my own behalf—even as I'm full of all this, I see before me Bernard's naked body, as if an immense pornographic poster of him were plastered from floor to ceiling on our wall. As if he were plastered on every wall I turn to face.

"I'll rustle up something special for breakfast," I say, thinking about how incredibly happy I feel, and how my joy feels nonetheless strange; about how happy Niklas will be when we wake him, and what I should make for breakfast. And then too about whether I'm now going to be too late for my afternoon assignation with Bernard in the break room, and about Bernard's body: his ribs, lines, and curves, his hair, his wrinkles. Always and especially his body.

The things I have in the freezer are few and cheap, but I decide to make American pancakes from an old package of cornmeal mix, and I set out some grapes and a particularly fine cheese I'd reserved for tonight, for the farewell dinner for our house that I invited Helena and Henning to.

For most of our celebratory breakfast, with a very sleepy Niklas, Frederik's on the phone with old friends and employees. I can hear how some of them still slam the receiver down when he calls, while others now speak to him for the first time since the embezzlement came to light. They tell him things the paper's neglected to mention: which employees the new administration has fired to satisfy the bank's demands for austerity, and which board members are, like Laust and Anja, losing their homes and pensions.

I still don't have any sense at all of our own financial future—or even of how long we have a future together at all—so I've decided that for now, we'll rent an apartment in Farum Midtpunkt. It's a jump straight to the bottom rung on the social ladder in our town, but it's only temporary, which makes the thought easier to bear. In less than a week, all our things have to be packed up and out of the house.

Later, an hour before Helena and Henning are supposed to arrive, I'm toiling away in the kitchen while Frederik sits in the living room, talking on the phone again. He knows what time it is, and he can see that the table isn't set yet, but it doesn't occur to him to come in and offer to help.

I wait until fifteen minutes before the guests are due to step into the room and interrupt him. "Come on, it's high time you get going! The table needs to be set and the wine uncorked."

A short time later, Henning's booming voice and penetrating laugh reach us from all the way out in the street. For years he's had his own contracting firm. He's proud of the way he gets along with the tradesmen he hires, and he evidently has a talent for earning pots of money. In any case, he and Helena live in a house twice as large as ours, with a view of the lake to boot. But the house has been for sale now for four months. The financial crisis and the drop in housing prices have meant that Henning's lost everything he earned in the past decade.

Frederik pours out the wine, and for once I give him permission to have a glass. It's the first time since the operation, but today, the day we learn that he's saved Saxtorph, he deserves it.

We tell Henning and Helena the fantastic news and touch glasses ceremoniously as we listen to the shots and explosions from upstairs, where Severin, their thirteen-year-old son, is already playing a computer game with Niklas.

I'd like to take a brief moment to toast and bid farewell to the house we've had so many good experiences in, but Frederik interrupts me. He wants to tell us more about the school, about his brilliant rescue plan, about the book on the history of European philosophy that he's reading. In the beginning, what he says is clever and interesting, but after a while the rest of us lose interest without him registering it.

The first time I met someone with mild orbitofrontal damage in one of Frederik's hospital wards, I didn't realize she was ill. I listened to her attentively, despite a couple of minor angry outbursts and some oddly out-of-place jokes in her torrent of speech. But then she kept talking. And talking. And talking.

She wasn't speaking in any way she hadn't already spoken during our first minutes together, and yet the mere incessancy of her speech made it obvious that she wasn't the lively, cheerful, somewhat whacky type I'd first taken her for. She was very ill. Listening to her at length would take the wind from anyone's sails, and I was obliged to invent some excuse to escape.

When Frederik and I eat dinner, he pretty much talks the whole time, but now that Henning's had a couple of glasses, our guest keeps right up with Frederik. Sometimes they talk at the same time, other times Henning forces Frederik to take a breather simply by raising his voice.

There's nothing new about seeing Henning like this, and in fact Frederik and I have always had a hard time understanding how Helena can stand being married to him. Every time the four of us are together, he drinks too much and drowns out everyone else at the table.

When we're nearly finished with the first round of lamb meatballs and Greek salad, Frederik pours some more red wine, first for us and then for himself.

I ask, "Are you sure you want more to drink, Frederik?"

He doesn't reply, just avoids my gaze and finishes filling his glass.

The two boys disappear back upstairs to resume their shooting. I had Niklas promise to stay home until Severin has to go to bed, since Severin looks up to him and loves spending time with him so much.

Such a lot is happening in our lives right now—and not just Frederik's and mine. Where are Henning and Helena going to move? What'll Henning do now that he can no longer build and sell houses? I try asking him but have to give up. And Helena tries to engage Frederik in conversation, but she gives up too.

After listening to the men go on for a little too long, we lean toward each other in order to create our own little tête-à-tête of real talk on real matters. But we have to abandon that too, for when Henning and Frederik notice that they no longer have our undivided attention, they grow even more vociferous, until they're once more in the center.

If it's so important for them to have our attention, why can't they pose a couple of questions and start a conversation that we can feel we're also contributing to? But they couldn't care less what we think or how we're doing—just as they clearly have no clue what the boys are doing when not in the room, and just as they don't offer to help collect the plates from the main course or serve dessert.

Dessert is my red-currant cheesecake. Helena calls the boys down from their computer game; since they know my cheesecake, for once we don't have to shout several times before the roar of explosions from Niklas's room dies out.

A white dab of cheesecake is sticking to Frederik's upper lip. I point discreetly to my own lip with my pinky. But he doesn't notice. I do it again. Still no reaction.

"Frederik!" I say. And then I point to my upper lip.

He glances at me for a moment and goes on talking.

In the end I'm forced to be explicit. "Frederik, you have something sitting on your upper lip."

He finally scrapes it off, with a quick, somewhat casual movement—and without making the least bit of eye contact. His lecture is unstoppable.

We don't manage to talk to the two boys very much before, stuffed with cheesecake, they clear out.

How often have I suffered through this at some dinner, with half- or completely drunk men on either side of me? Sitting surrounded by men who look at me and talk to me, while at the same time I feel strangely ignored beneath their aggressive gazes—and strangely desirous of going home and watching TV by myself.

But Helena and I simply refuse to put up with it. We'll set the tone here. I ask the table about back when we were all living in cheap apartments in poor neighborhoods: wasn't there also something nice about it? Was it only because we were twenty-one and the world still seemed wide open?

I haven't managed to finish what I'm saying when Henning interrupts me to talk about how he plans to earn enough money to get out of construction and sail around the world in his own boat. The first ten or fifteen times I heard him talk about this fantasy, I found it charming, but for years now I've had the desire to shout in his ear, *So sail away, God damn it, or shut your trap! Stop interrupting others to talk about it for twenty years in a row!* And I know Helena's other friends feel the same way.

Henning seems to feel more at home here than he usually does. He also seems to feel more affection for Frederik than he ever has before, but maybe that's because he's drinking more. Or perhaps he's drinking more because he feels more at home.

He reaches out and takes more than half of the cheesecake that remains. With the big slice on the cake server halfway between platter and plate, he suddenly hesitates. He looks over at me.

"You folks are good, right? Okay if I take this?"

"You should just make yourself at home," I say in a voice that, in the old days, would have made Frederik, in any case, put the piece back.

Henning sets the slice on his plate, stuffs a generous bite in his mouth, and then plunges into a joke about a woman who does yoga in the nude. One day when she's doing the splits, her crotch gets stuck to the floor like a suction cup so that she can't get up again.

In the old days after a dinner with Helena and Henning, Frederik and I would load the dishwasher together. And as we buzzed around the kitchen, synchronized and efficient, we'd express shock at how crude Henning would get when he'd had something to drink. After we both ran him down for a while, I'd say, *But he's good for her.* I'd say that not because I actually knew it to be true; it was more that I'd begin to have a bad conscience about vilifying our guests just a few minutes after they'd left.

But now . . .

Henning goes on with his joke. The woman's husband fetches a neighbor who's a bricklayer, and together the men attempt to pry the woman loose from the quarry tile she's sticking to. But it's as if she's glued fast to the floor. In the end the bricklayer says, "We're going to have to break the tile in pieces." The husband says, "Are you out of your gourd? These tiles cost five hundred crowns apiece!" "Well, what you should do then is make her good and horny until she gets all wet. Then we can slide her along the floor and out into the kitchen." "You think that'll get her loose?" "No. But the kitchen tiles only cost five crowns."

Henning doubles up with laughter, and only at the last instant do I manage to move his glass from the path of his elbow, while Frederik guffaws with glee. The two men pound each other on the back, tears in their eyes.

I find myself compelled to turn away. It's just too depressing to remember everything that Frederik used to be. Everything he no longer is.

Helena catches my eye and I see the gentleness of her look; she feels for me. At least I have her, I think.

She grasps my hand and says, "It's so good to see Frederik well again."

"*Well!* What do you mean *well*?"

"Yes, to see him healthy again. It's much more important than that you have to move."

I can hear the hardness in my voice. "He's not well at all. He's a far cry from well."

Does my best friend really not know Frederik any better? Can't she see that he's become a foolish, vulgar shadow of himself?

She grows nervous, and she should be. In this moment, it feels as if I can never see her again; she hasn't understood a thing about my life.

The men of course notice nothing. Henning is droning on again about circumnavigating the globe. He completely drowns out Frederik's lecture on his half-finished speakers, and I know it's going to end badly, even before Frederik brings his fist down on the table and yells, "Shut your mouth already about sailing around the world! Everyone thinks it's totally ridiculous!"

"What?"

"It'll never happen. I've talked to Mia about it a hundred times!"

"It *will* happen, whatever you say! Helena and I are going to sail—"

"I told you to shut up about it!"

"First we'll start in the Caribbean, then we'll head south and—"

"No one here wants to hear another word about it! In any case not Mia or me."

I try to calm him down but can't talk over Henning, who's shot up from his seat. "Don't fucking speak to me like that!"

Now what—is it going to come to blows? Are they stupid enough for that? Henning could whip all of us at the same time, but Frederik shows no fear. "Go and shit in your ocean!"

"What?"

"Yeah, just sail over and do it!"

I say, "Frederik!"

Helena says, "Henning!"

They're two big dumb dogs we've brought to the park who don't know what's best for them. We ought to have kept them on much shorter leads. We pull and pull at them, but now it's too late.

Niklas stands in the doorway. Has he come to protect me? Incredible how quickly he always shows up.

How can I live with Frederik for even one more week? How's Helena been able to stand twenty years with Henning?

Without any warning, Henning's mood changes. The next moment he's laughing loudly and has his arm around Frederik. "You should have another glass of wine! Ha-ha-ha!"

Frederik hugs Henning back. "You should too. Ha-ha-ha!"

"I certainly will. But you first."

I break in. "I'm not so sure it's a good idea for Frederik to drink any more right now."

Frederik looks at me, irritated. The run-up to a brawl a few seconds ago has already blown clean out of his head. "Oh, come off it. I've hardly had anything."

"Frederik, you're sick!"

"Well, in that case I really *should* have something."

"I'm simply going to have to put my foot—"

"Our guest wants some company," he says laughing. "You can't say no to our guest! Especially since I've offended him so terribly!"

And Henning adds, chortling, "Yes! You can't refuse me when your husband's just offended me! You really can't. He's offended me *dreadfully*. Ha-ha-ha!"

Frederik's already on his way out to the kitchen. "I'll find the wine myself."

Henning places a big paw on his shoulder. "I'll join you."

Helena and I remain sitting behind by ourselves; Niklas has left again too. I take a slow deep breath, and so does Helena.

Then she says, "Why exactly is it that both our husbands have had leadership positions, and not us?"

I try to laugh along with her, though I still have the sense that I'm completely alone in my new life.

There's no way we can resolve our conflict with the preschool rapidity of the men, but we make an effort. And meanwhile I think about a brain-damaged man I once read about. He'd always been rude with customers in his small corner grocery, but he acted that way with warmth and a twinkle in his eye, so they patronized the shop in fact *because* of him. After he suffered a minor stroke, he still thought he could kid his customers affectionately, but he'd lost the fine motor skills he needed to be disarming—the brief hint of a smile at precisely the right moment, the way he turned his head and looked down after speaking. The customers grew annoyed. His wife kept telling him that he'd have to act like a normal boring shopkeeper, but that just made him furious. And the shop went bankrupt.

Which makes me wonder: why has Henning's contracting business been running in the red these last few years? They've said it's the financial crisis, but is that true?

I try to sound friendly and conversational when I ask. "Was Henning always so glad to go to dinner parties back when you first met?"

But Helena's quick as lightning. "I know *exactly* what's going through your head right now. But just because you force everyone else into that box doesn't mean you can do it to Henning and me."

"Of course not. I'll make sure I—"

"That's just the way men are."

I object. "Not *all* men."

She answers with a glint in her eye that's supposed to indicate a joke, but it doesn't come out very funny. "You must not know men very well."

"But before Frederik got sick, he certainly wasn't like that."

We fall silent. The men are still shouting out in the kitchen.

Helena leans toward me. "Mia, I don't know how to tell you this . . ."

"What?"

"Maybe Frederik wasn't always the perfect man you remember."

There's no way I can have this discussion with her tonight. "But Bernard's not that way either—and that's not something I remember. That's right now."

"Oh, of course! I'd forgotten Bernard. Bernard, the great shining exception to everything in the whole world!"

I've got to be careful about what I say. One wrong word, one wrong pause or facial expression and she'll know that Bernard's a source of more than just legal deliverance.

"But other than the supernaturally magnificent Bernard," she says, "that's just the way men are." She takes a large gulp from her wineglass. "Get used to it. Or be single."

In the kitchen now, the men are laughing uproariously as they argue over which male politician in Denmark has the biggest nose. And it sounds to me as if there are *three* men's voices in there. Has another guest shown up?

I get up, and Helena follows.

In the cold light of the kitchen, we can see Niklas sitting on the counter between Henning and Frederik. His large hairy hands upon the countertop. He doesn't look like my Niklas anymore.

His new deep voice roars with laughter. "Have you guys seen the schnozz on Bertel Haarder? Ha-ha-ha!"

24

I'm kissing Bernard in our new kitchen, which is both larger and better equipped than the one in our old place.

Farum Midtpunkt is a strange ghetto—and not just because, as an architectural experiment, the façades of its apartment blocks were fabricated from great plates of rusted iron. The Midtpunkt apartments are modern, with luxurious private patios and outdoor common areas that are green and well maintained. But the rent's so high that the people who can afford it bought houses of their own long ago. Most of those left behind have all or most of their rent subsidized by the municipality: people on disability, immigrants, and single parents.

In the flat suburban idyll that is Farum, constructed from bike paths, yellow bricks, and thousands of lawns, the Midtpunkt complex towers over everything else. To judge from the crime stories and letters to the editor in the local paper, its apartment blocks are the tarry smoker's lungs that make our young blond suburb gasp for air. I know from my job, though, that that's not the whole story; lots of Midtpunkt kids come from well-functioning homes, and lots of parents are happy to live here. Their only problem with the place is that friends are nervous about visiting them at night.

Bernard presses his groin against mine, and I can feel his erection through his clothes. I prop myself against the counter with one hand, next to a high stack of dishes.

The front door opens. Niklas's and Frederik's footfalls move slowly toward the living room; they're carrying something heavy.

Bernard and I release each other, and I step into the hall. "Super," I say. "Wasn't that hard to get up the stairs?"

"That's why it took us so long," Frederik says. "What have you two been doing?"

"We've been getting the kitchen sorted. It's going to be nice."

Niklas doesn't say anything. I asked him if he could get some of his friends to help us move, but he didn't want to.

Frederik is too sick to see through us; his suspicions come only in flashes. It's not too bad, and I can generally maneuver him back into the naïve thought that Bernard's our new friend who's lending a hand to get things organized.

But does Niklas notice anything? Teenagers are so unpredictable; sometimes they see everything, other times it's amazing how oblivious they are—especially when it comes to their parents' love lives, right?

Besides Bernard, Andrea from the support group helped us pack things up two days ago, and Helena and Henning were here yesterday with a couple of other friends who haven't defected yet. And then of course my in-laws have been here a lot.

Bernard and I have to pass each other in these unfurnished rooms without giving ourselves away. But if he raises his hand someplace in back of me, I notice; if he takes a step toward the bookcase, I sense it. I know when he's about to take a breath before he lifts a moving box or calls out to my husband or son.

Back in the kitchen I tell him, "I was thinking we should put the globe glasses on this shelf."

He leans back slightly, to counterbalance the box of plates and glasses he's bearing. A cord of muscle bulges from the top of his forearm as he stands there holding it. "Do you use them more than the tall glasses?"

"Not really."

"I could put them there, of course," he says. "But if I put the tall glasses there instead, they'll be easier to reach."

I pull aimlessly at the dust rag I happen to have in hand. "Yes, that'd be better. Will they all fit on the shelf?"

"Hmm. What do you want on the shelf underneath?"

"Plates."

He sets down the box and squats, holding the top edge of the cupboard door with one hand. A lovely hand, and so close.

"But the plates won't take up all the space, will they?" He peers into the cupboard, and I know that he's making an effort not to look directly at me.

"Then we can set the plates on the right," I say, and I realize I'm speaking too quickly. "And the rest of the tall glasses next to them." I'm blabbering, I need to pull myself together. "No, we'll put the tall glasses over here instead." It's completely impossible to dial it down. "And the globe glasses here. And any glasses we don't have room for, we'll set all the way over there."

"And then the small plates here?" He's pointing to the side of where the large plates will go, but I find myself looking at his arm instead of where he's pointing. I know what it's like to bite into that bare wrist, to rub the thin pale skin on its inner side against the sensitive skin of my belly.

"Exactly, exactly. The small plates should go there."

Exhausting! If I could only sit down on the kitchen floor next to him. For just one moment.

Niklas pokes his head into the kitchen. "Dad and I are going to bring up the speakers now."

Bernard says, "I'll go with you."

Then they're gone, and I sit down on the floor as if he were still here.

If we'd moved any place other than Farum Midtpunkt, we couldn't have afforded for Frederik to have his own room, and I saw how I'd have to put up with even more of a mess with electronic widgets and sawdust than in the house on Station Road. But now we have an apartment with three bedrooms; Frederik will sleep by himself in one of them, and all his speaker-building clutter will move in with him.

Yet building speakers doesn't play the same role in his life that it once did. He rarely talks about it anymore—though on the other hand, he won't admit it was the illness that got him started on it either. When once in a while he does work on the speakers, it's easy to think he's merely trying to maintain his dignity and preserve the illusion that something about these last months has been positive.

The men's voices return to the hallway and I hurry to get up.

"I can understand," Bernard is saying. "It must be wretched not being able to enjoy music. Naturally, you'd want to do anything you could to get that pleasure back again."

There's a bump as they set the one speaker cabinet on the floor in Frederik's room. Frederik sounds so calm, he sounds oddly like the old Frederik.

"If you contrast what other people do to make their homes *look* good, what I'm doing to make my home *sound* good is actually not that much. All the emphasis on visual appeal—what's with that? Gorgeous mansions with unpleasant odors and awful-sounding stereo systems?"

I've heard him deliver this little lecture on good sound before, but his voice sounds so sensible now. Bernard brings out his most coherent and healthy side, talking to him as if they're equals. And Bernard apparently knows a great deal about speakers too.

"Have you considered building ribbon speakers or electrostats instead?" he asks.

"Yes! I certainly have!" Frederik isn't so well that he can control the urge to raise his voice in excitement when posed a concrete technical question. "It's a difficult decision, and it may be that I'll come to regret mine. But there have been a lot of advances in the field of dynamic drivers during the past ten years . . ."

Then they're out the door and heading down the stairs again. I can hear from their footsteps that Niklas is with them. This is the kind of male conversation I'd like to expose him to. Men formulating themselves cogently. He shouldn't be soaking up the side of his father that Henning brings out.

I drop the kitchen, though it's far from finished, and go into the living room. Here's where the men have set most of the things they've hauled up, but they haven't put them where I think they should go. As I place a small bowl holding ballpoints, loose change, and other pocket detritus in a cabinet, I find a wad of thin white paper that looks as if it's gone through the wash. I unfold it. It's a supermarket receipt, with all my usual purchases—plus a tray of sushi and some filled chocolates.

It'd take so little. I could talk my way out of having bought some sushi that Frederik remembered nothing about, but at some point it'll go south:

Niklas or Frederik will answer my phone when it rings, and then I'll yell at them with terror in my voice to just let it ring. And as soon as they don't trust me anymore, it'll all come tumbling down.

What else is there that could flush us out? Hundreds of things, if you think about it—and that's exactly what Frederik's doing, more and more with each day that passes.

Perhaps more than anything, there's my mood on a day like today. Why don't I seem devastated by having to rip my life up by the roots and move here? For the same reason that our seventeen-year-old son isn't: because I'm somewhere else entirely, so head over heels that it's only on the outermost surface that I register anything that's happening.

So mostly it's my smile. It's revealing. It reveals everything if you think about it.

My smile, which is like Niklas's, like Bernard's. The only one who isn't in love is Frederik—and he's clueless.

...

In someone else's house, the party is over.

It's three thirty a.m., and the last exhausted guests hang about the empty rooms, unable to move, ghosts who can find neither rest nor life. Light sifts slowly through the windows and exposes the dust where people once danced, the empty spaces where furniture stood before being moved out of the way.

That's how it looks at twilight in our old rooms on Station Road, though it's not three thirty in the morning but ten in the evening. Bernard has long since driven off, Niklas has gone over to Emilie's, and Frederik and I walk around the house and stare at the naked walls and the traces on the wallpaper of where a picture once hung or a bookcase once stood. The light doesn't sift into the rooms, it recedes. In the trunk of the car are a broom, a vacuum cleaner, and a couple of small items. Our last night here.

I walk out into the garden, which is about to lose all color to the incipient dark. I take a farewell tour, stopping before each of the plants I've nourished, cultivated for years. Will the new owners let the yard sink back to wilderness?

I start when I feel a hand on my shoulder. It's Frederik, who's followed me outside.

I say, "There's no need for you to pretend you understand."

"But I do understand."

"Haven't you finally gotten well enough to recognize that both your empathy and your emotions are impaired?"

"I'm trying to—"

"Frederik, your brain makes it so that you can't really be here."

"I really *am* here!"

"That's what you say, of course."

"I *am*!"

"The inability to acknowledge one's illness, Frederik."

"But I *am* here."

"You're perseverating."

And then I watch his face disintegrate. How these crying jags wear me out, how they're rammed down my throat! Far beyond what any human being could tolerate. In a second he's going to dissolve into bestial sobs and make me feel even more isolated.

Quickly, I usher him into the empty living room and close the door behind us. He collapses blubbering on the floor by the wall farthest from the window.

I have absolutely no desire to hold him; absolutely no desire to comfort him. But I try to stroke his back as best I can, simply because I am, after all, his wife—or in any case, I was married to the man he used to be. I don't know how to, but I strive to be for him what he can't be for me.

The room grows dark. Almost all the lamps are in the new apartment now, but a pair of wall sconces we don't need are still mounted in the hallway. I go and turn them on, leaving the door ajar so that the living-room floor is lit indirectly.

"Why don't you just become Bernard's girlfriend?" Frederik asks, weeping. "Then the two of you can be happy, and I can just kill myself. Then *everyone* can be happy."

I take a deep breath. Here we go again. I hesitate perhaps a fraction of a second too long. "You mustn't say such things!"

"You're well matched. I can see that. The two of you suit each other remarkably well."

"Stop saying that!" It feels weird to say this while at the same time feeling I already need to talk to Bernard again, and planning how to best steal away and call him.

Later, when Frederik's crying has abated, he says, "I really understand if you don't feel you can ever sleep with me again."

"Well, let's just see how—"

"What I did that night was awful. And then Niklas coming in . . . I don't know how I could have. I can remember it, but I'll never be able to explain it to you."

"No, you won't. I know."

"It was terrible. Just like what I did to Saxtorph. That was so awful, wasn't it."

We've talked a lot about his embezzlement, but this is the first time we've talked about the night I had to lock myself in the bathroom.

And it's the first time he says, "We have no future. We don't, do we, Mia? The things I've done. To you in bed. And the money. And soon I'll probably go to prison. I just want to die."

His eyes are huge as he gazes into mine.

"You've got to leave me! I'm dragging you down."

"We'll talk about it later," I say.

" 'We'll talk about it later'!" he shouts. "You say, 'We'll talk about it later'! But then you *have* decided to leave, haven't you! You're doing it, you're getting ready to leave me!"

"No, no—I'm not!"

He rolls over on his stomach and hides his face from me. As if he's only talking to himself, he mutters, "You have to leave me. It's the only right thing to do. And I can just die."

"But I don't want you to die."

"It couldn't be any worse than this."

"Yes it could. You can have a good life. A very good life."

While I try to dissuade Frederik from killing himself, a fantasy begins to run through my head about what Vibeke will say when he's well enough for me to leave him. In the fantasy we argue, and she shouts that I'm a self-obsessed egomaniac; that that's what I've been our entire marriage.

No doubt Frederik noticed that I said *You can have a good life* and not *We can have a good life*. But he acts as if he didn't, and I tell him again and again that I'll stay with him, until maybe he can believe there's a small chance that that's what'll happen.

"You're right, we should talk about it later," he says at last. "Now isn't a good time. Not tonight when we're moving. I'm sorry."

"You don't need to apologize."

"I'm sorry, sorry, sorry, Mia. Sorry!"

"You couldn't help it."

"No, I couldn't help it."

We lie there in the darkness, in a spot where once there was a rug, and on top of it a floor lamp and a coffee table.

Many suffer hidden brain damage

One out of every eight people over 45 has a brain injury without realizing it, according to a Dutch study reported in *The New England Journal of Medicine.* Two thousand healthy subjects took part in the study, in which researchers from Erasmus Medical Center in Rotterdam scanned their brains. The researchers found a surprisingly high number of undetected brain lesions.

The most common form of lesion was what is known as a brain infarct—dead tissue arising from an insufficient supply of blood to the brain cells.

Other abnormalities included aneurysms, minor cerebral hemorrhages, and benign tumors.

However, the researchers do not recommend that healthy persons be scanned at the present time. The procedure is quite costly, and doctors cannot treat most of the injuries anyway. *(MLJ)*

25

I'm back in our home on Station Road. The colors in the kitchen sparkle like a Christmas tree: the glint of the cabinet handles, the golden stain of the wood shelves, the red and light blue of the plastic bowls. I'm setting the dishes we've eaten from back in their places, and the sugar bowl we inherited from Frederik's grandmother catches my eye, with its chased silver and its blue glass so dark, it's impossible to see through.

And then suddenly it's late evening and Niklas is still up, unloading the dishwasher with Frederik and me. We've been putting things away and washing the serving dishes and glassware after a dinner with Laust and Anja and some of the others from Saxtorph. The three of us joking around and enjoying ourselves after the guests have left.

Once that was something we did often, having our friends over for dinner. It's been a long time. I have a vague sense of why we don't do it anymore; I step over to Frederik and embrace him from behind. I hug him longer and harder than I normally would, resting my head against his back and shoulders.

Niklas looks up at us happily, and it's obvious that Frederik really enjoys the attention too. He sounds a little shy when he asks, "Now what have I done to deserve this?"

But I don't know yet. I only feel the warmth, the joy of the three of us together.

Frederik's tipsy and quite silly now, the way he can get after a party. He says, "Did either of you notice I have an extra willy?"

I lean around him and see a large, oddly shaped bulge in his trousers.

He says, "I got it when I was out peeing."

Then he takes out of his trousers an empty beer bottle that he must have stuffed down there. He laughs happily; he finds this funny.

We continue taking things out of the dishwasher and putting them away. In the living room, we wipe the tables and set the chairs back in their usual places.

And in the meantime I begin to weep, for I'm slowly analyzing this dream as I dream it. I'm dreaming that I understand why our dinners and parties are now a thing of the past. Why we can never be together again as a family.

I dream that I'm drying off glasses the dishwasher didn't get completely dry, that I don't utter a word, that the tears just run down my cheeks. At some point Niklas sees me. He asks what the matter is, and I say, "He's dead, of course! This isn't real at all! We're having such a lovely time, but of course he's dead. In reality he's no longer here. Tonight he's just visiting."

…

The teachers' break room at my school was furnished in the '70s. The walls are still covered in burlap, the cot's still a captain's bed, and the poster next to the door even depicts a pyramid. Who in the last twenty-five years would even think of buying a pyramid poster? It's as if the room was simply forgotten by the administration. But it certainly hasn't been forgotten by amorous colleagues when the annual Christmas party takes place upstairs, or by the odd teacher who seeks refuge here after a bad class. There are so many downward-spiraling fates bound up with this room, so many teachers who failed to get a grip in the months before they were fired or quit, or who did their best to reconcile themselves to a disability pension on psychological grounds.

Since Bernard and I are here every day, now that summer vacation's begun, I brought in a vase yesterday and a bouquet of flowers I picked by the ditches beside the bike paths. Last week I took thumbtacks and hung up some unused postcards of fine photographs. And in the closet I've hidden a locked suitcase with linen and a quilt of our own, so we don't have to lie directly on the old spread.

Here we lie, naked and still a bit sweaty, Bernard resting his brow against my cheek. And he tells me once again about Lærke.

I doubted before whether he really understood how serious her brain damage was. But he knows. He's fully aware how little of her remains.

During these past months, he's described the real Lærke as a remarkably charming and generous woman. Every single weekend, she'd take the family on some new adventure. Treasure hunts in the woods that took as their theme the last cartoon the boys had seen; long songs with lyrics of her own invention; forts they built together of old cardboard boxes for the boys' toy monsters. I have a hard time believing that anyone could be so relentlessly full of fun and passion for family; it must be an idealized memory. Yet what can I say? Perhaps I do the same thing myself in the way I conceive of the Frederik I once knew.

"I still enjoy being with her," he says. "It's difficult to explain exactly why. But she's still my Lærke."

"I understand that," I say, though it's not true.

He lifts his brow from my cheek and rolls over beside me on the narrow foam mattress, staring up at the ceiling.

"It's odd how one can find people who make really clever remarks so terribly boring. And yet love to spend time with people who speak only in banalities. So what is boredom anyway?"

We discuss this. We have the strangest long conversations while lying half on top of each other and eating the pastry and fruit we bought on our way here. And then we look again into each other's eyes, not talking, or we explore each other's bodies.

It's hard to say which classroom lies directly above the break room, as there are no windows here, and you can only get here through the maze of shelving in the textbook storeroom. But as far as I can tell, we're lying entangled and sweating right beneath one of the eighth-grade homerooms.

Ten days after Bernard and Lærke's accident, Lærke still hadn't come out of her coma. Bernard sat by her side. The nurse he confided in most told him he should lavish all that attention on their eight-year-old boys instead. They needed every hour he could give them, while for the time being, Lærke wouldn't notice the difference.

He knew that the nurse was right, yet he couldn't keep himself from staring all day long at Lærke's unmoving face behind the oxygen mask.

He held her hand, he stroked her forearm where there weren't any tubes or tape. And also where there were tubes and tape. He spoke to her, trying to say calming, cheery words.

Jonathan and Benjamin weren't with us in the car, he'd say, since she probably wouldn't be able to remember what happened right before the accident.

They're doing well, he'd tell her. *Your mother's taking care of them. You're in the hospital, sweetheart. We've been in a car wreck. We weren't the ones at fault. He suddenly changed lanes. There was nothing we could do. I'm well—and you will be too. It'll all work out. We'll be fine.*

And when she still showed no signs of life, he'd say, *Yes, that's good. You shouldn't let me wake you. That makes the most sense. Just rest. That's the best thing you can do.*

But in fact it hadn't been going well for their eight-year-old twins. The fourth time they visited their mother in the hospital, Jonathan screamed so convincingly about stomach pains that the nurses called a doctor in. Jonathan was positive he was going to die, and when the doctor's examination didn't calm him or get rid of the pain, Bernard had to take him down to the emergency room, while his father-in-law drove Benjamin home and Winnie stayed with Lærke.

The consultation in the emergency room didn't turn anything up either, and when Jonathan continued to yell about his stomach, the older female physician asked Bernard if she could give Jonathan a sedative on top of the painkillers.

At that, Bernard's brain seized up. He couldn't say *yes* or *no* or *I don't know*; he couldn't utter a single word. And he wasn't able to give his son any of the support he needed either. The emergency room staff had to ring up to the neurointensive ward and ask to speak with Winnie. She immediately told them to give Jonathan the sedative, then rushed down to the emergency room, got Bernard and Jonathan into a taxi, and rode home with them.

There were so many decisions to make about the boys during those long days: Should they return to visit their unconscious mother again? Where should they stay when they weren't at the hospital? What was the best way to protect them from the desperation that everyone around them was feeling? All decisions that depended on whether Lærke was going to die in the next few hours. Or whether she might wake in the next few hours. And every one of them, a decision that made Bernard miss terribly being able to consider it with Lærke.

The doctors had told him waking from a coma doesn't happen like in the movies, from one instant to the next. It's a sluggish affair, and every single patient must fight their own way back to life.

"Look forward to it—it'll be an amazing moment," said a nurse, who appeared to be completely convinced that things would be looking up for Lærke now.

Half past five in the morning. Not a sound to be heard on the ward except for the faint hum of machines. The sky outside the tall windows beginning to lighten a pale blue. It was Day Thirteen, and in the last couple of days Lærke had had recurring convulsions while still comatose. Now her right leg and arm went into spasms. Bernard held her hand as it twitched between his hands. He whispered that there was nothing to fear, that he was there to take care of her; that he loved her. For she always looked so terrified when she went into convulsions.

"Can you hear me?" he asked, just as he did every single time he was there. "Can you? Lærke, can you hear me?"

Her head lay still upon the pillow, turned toward him, and then her eyelids trembled. He was on the point of shouting; this was so major, so unexpected. Her eyelids trembled and they opened and suddenly, for the first time in almost two weeks, he was looking straight into his wife's blue eyes.

"I'm right here," he said. "Your husband."

Her eyes regarded him for what felt like several minutes.

"Can you hear me, Lærke? Can you understand me?"

Her eyes that were only half open; that were far, far away. He sensed that she had no idea where she was.

"I'm Bernard," he said. "Your husband."

"Watch out!" she said—or in any case that's what he heard it as, her speech nearly unintelligible, as well as muffled by the oxygen mask.

And then she disappeared again.

Bernard wanted to call everyone he knew, he wanted to get up and run out to the nurses, he wanted to squeeze Lærke's hand. Everything. He could feel his body shaking, just like hers. He wanted to jump up and run into the corridor, but he couldn't leave her; she might open her eyes again.

He called a nurse, and after she left, he sat and gazed at Lærke until the first nurse on the morning shift came in, one hour later.

Then he went down to the parking lot, where he was allowed to use his cell phone, and called his parents, who had flown up from Paris and were staying at a hotel in Copenhagen. They'd been very fond of Lærke ever since she'd been a teenager working for them as an au pair. He also called his in-laws, and the parents of the twins' best friend from school. The twins had been sleeping there so that they'd be as unscathed as possible by the family's disintegration.

The grandparents all arrived at the hospital an hour later, but nothing more happened that day. To wake up and try to warn Bernard about some unknown peril had required a huge effort from Lærke. She remained completely unconscious for another twenty-four hours.

Because Lærke might be about to wake, the doctors cut back on her morphine and replaced the oxygen mask with a thin tube that ran from her nose. It was odd to see her without the mask; she was starting to look more and more like herself.

The next day she woke again, and this time the boys were in the room too.

"Jonathan," she said. "Benjamin."

Her speech was still very indistinct, but there was no doubt she recognized them. Jonathan climbed up into bed with her, and Bernard let him. After his attack, Jonathan had said he didn't want to go back to the hospital, and now Bernard was glad he'd insisted. Benjamin crawled into the bed too. Lærke said both of their names several times, and then a minute later she was gone again.

Bernard lifted the boys down, explained to them that their mother was very tired now, and took them out into the common room, where he unpacked some of the many lunches that their friend's mother had packed them.

So Lærke could speak, and she could see, think, and recognize them. Good news. Just that she was *in* there, in her apparently dead body. Yet as Bernard was trying to make the shared meal a pleasant experience, he was also thinking of something he'd have to ask the doctor about: Lærke hadn't smiled when she saw the boys. There was no joy on her face when they climbed up to her—only something that looked like wonder. The whole thing felt so new to him that he didn't yet know what to think about it.

In the days that followed, she woke up for a few minutes every couple of hours. It was clear she didn't understand where she was, regardless of how many times Bernard explained it to her. But he was patient, and he told her she'd get well, and he told her he loved her. The wonder was still in her face, though without a trace of the gentle smile she would have smiled if it'd been a movie. As if he were some math problem to her; as if she didn't see him as a person.

Then, late one evening as Bernard listened to the sounds of a family out in the hallway—the family of a teenager who'd just died in the next room—Lærke said her first sentence.

"Ah luh ooh."

He sat in his chair for a long time and gasped for breath in the half darkness. She closed her eyes again and he kept sitting there, stock-still, even though he'd read enough about brain damage in the last few days to know she was probably just echoing the words he'd said to her.

...

In the following months, the whole family began to founder. Lærke's parents moved in to help take care of the boys.

The doctors at the rehab center were quick to say they didn't expect Lærke would ever be able to return to her job as project manager at the ad agency. They also doubted she'd be able to walk again. Bernard had to relinquish his career plans and his hopes for the boys and himself.

But everyday life at home with Lærke was more draining than anything else. Her injury was distributed across her entire brain, which basically meant she had less of everything: she lacked emotion and was indifferent to herself and others; she got tired after a few hours of mere conversation and couldn't concentrate on anything for more than a couple of minutes at a time; she couldn't make decisions or deal with the most ordinary trifles; and she usually couldn't remember anything Bernard or the kids told her.

She used to pump so much energy into the family, but now her dominant trait was utter passivity. She never took the initiative or said anything of her own accord, and it seemed like she didn't even think or imagine anything on her own. Her face hung dead from her cheekbones, without those tiny twitches that in a healthy person indicate life beneath the skin.

The boys started getting into a lot of fights, because they felt the other kids were teasing them about their mother. Sometimes it was true, but as a rule it wasn't. And no matter how much Bernard and his in-laws tried to give them the support they needed, the boys' close friendships began to fall apart, simply because the twins were fighting their best friends too much.

So this is my family, Bernard would think as he headed home from yet another parents' meeting where the other parents had brought up the issue of his sons. *This is what we've become.*

He tried to be constructive in their new situation, to come up with something that would improve the boys' lives, and above all to avoid destroying anything else. Jonathan and Benjamin mustn't notice how he felt like he'd lost his way, every day, though he still lived with them in the same house on the same peaceful-looking residential street.

On one Saturday, around lunchtime, Bernard came home hauling five bags of groceries for the week ahead. Lærke was waiting in the hall. She always was when he came home, though she never opened the front door, even after a ramp was installed so she could roll herself outside.

"Hello," he said, but she didn't answer.

He tried to edge his way around her wheelchair in the narrow hallway.

"Do you think you could back up just a little, so I can get past?"

She backed up.

"Now then, Lærke. This bag has only frozen goods, so I thought you might be able to put it away in the freezer."

No answer.

"Do you think you could do that?"

"Yes."

"Great."

She remained where she was, parked in front of him. Her long golden hair fell across her shoulders. Bernard brushed it every morning, a ritual he genuinely enjoyed. And it seemed to him as if her skin had gotten smoother and younger after the accident, perhaps because she no longer tensed the skin in her forehead or around her eyes.

"Then you should go out to the kitchen now, over in front of the freezer," he said.

So that's what she did.

"Here's the bag. Look. Try to set the new things farther back in the freezer, so that the open packages are easy to get at. Okay? Can you do that?"

"Yes."

"Good."

Bernard put away the groceries in the four other bags and then came back to Lærke and the frozen goods. She still had a long way to go, but it was good for her to do it by herself.

He stood behind her and said, "Try to set the open packages on top. Then they'll be easier to get at."

"Oh, right."

"You understand why, don't you?"

She didn't answer.

"Look, sweetheart, this package has been opened. If you set it in *front* of the unopened package, then we won't end up having both of them open at the same time. Does that make sense?"

"Yes."

"Good."

He remained standing there.

After a little while, he said, "Look, this package isn't open, while this other one is. Now if you set the new one in back . . . It'd be great if you did the same thing with all of them."

"Did what?"

"If you set the *new* packages in back."

"Yes."

She did it with the one she had in her hand, but then she forgot to do it with the next one.

"Well, maybe you should just do it the way you want to," he said. "You're the one putting the frozen things away, so you should decide where they go."

She didn't answer, and he started to perseverate.

251

"So you should decide where they go, right? When you put them away?"

She looked up at him and said, "First the back ones should go first, because then the first ones . . . First the new ones should go in back, because then the old ones can first . . ."

Lærke could usually express herself more clearly, but when she got into a bad rut, she had a hard time getting out again.

She started to scold herself, while at the same time trying to say it correctly. "Not in back—front! By the door! The front ones shouldn't first . . . the door."

He gave her shoulders a little squeeze and said, "Yes, that's where they should go."

She didn't answer.

On Saturdays, Winnie would drive the boys to and from soccer. Ordinarily they were back by noon, and now it was twenty minutes past. Bernard felt a mild unease, which he knew he ought to resist. Otherwise, where would it ever end? But Winnie wasn't so young anymore; her eyes, the cars, what happens in traffic . . .

"Did your mother call?"

"I don't know."

"But did she call just before I got here?"

"She called."

"Well, what did she say?"

"I don't know."

He went to the phone to see if there was anything on caller ID. Next to the phone was a scratch pad, where they'd tried to get Lærke to write down all the messages.

Winnie *had* called. He called her back and heard from her that practice had been delayed a little, and there was no need to worry.

He began setting the table, with Lærke at his heels, rolling back and forth between kitchen and living room so that she blocked the doorway every time he went back to get something new. Since she was following him anyway, he gave her something to take out to the table.

And then he sat down and waited. And Lærke rolled over to his side.

Tired, he stared into the air, and tired, she stared into the air. But at some point he had sat still long enough, and he turned his face to her. She didn't turn hers.

252

He said, "What I wouldn't give to know what's going on in your head."

She made no reply.

"Lærke, what are you thinking right now?"

She still didn't answer.

He grabbed her hand so that she turned to face him. He looked her in the eye and asked again, "What are you thinking, sweetheart?"

"Nothing."

"You're not thinking of anything?"

"No."

"Your mind's a complete blank?"

She continued looking wordlessly in front of her.

But he couldn't let the riddle rest. "Do you see images, or is there something that's making you sad, or happy? Something we could do differently? Are you excited about physical therapy on Monday? Are you remembering something we've done together?"

"Yes, it's completely blank," she said. "Completely."

...

As any family member of someone with brain damage knows, the hard part isn't the initial shock. The hard part comes when the adrenaline recedes and you have to set out down the endless grey corridor of disheartening days, days that look like they'll last the rest of your life.

The daily grind in which companionship is lacking. Where you find yourself more alone than you thought humanly possible; where you grieve so much, you just want to stay in bed for months. And where you force yourself to get up anyway for your kids' sake—and because your spouse isn't actually dead.

Yet there are joys, too. During the first year after the accident, Lærke became better at remembering, speaking, moving—and she began to get her feelings back. Just seeing the boys could once more make her happy.

And then one day when Bernard was sitting at home, working in what used to be his home office but was now furnished as a bedroom for his in-laws, she came in to him beaming with pleasure.

"I was daydreaming! I lay on the bed, and then I imagined being on vacation with the three of you. Imagined it! There were palms there, and a beach. I just imagined it and it showed up, completely on its own!"

Could anything be more momentous than the return of your inner life? Bernard and Lærke celebrated. And the boys did too. They understood what a big day it was for their mother to imagine things once more.

I press my bare chest against Bernard's as he tells me this, and it's as if my body thinks it's me he's crying for. Rationally, I know that's not true, but my arms squeeze him tighter, and I feel the urge to say, *But I'm here, really. I'm not dead, don't cry. I'm right here.*

And I try to be a little bit Lærke, and it's almost as if he's my old Frederik. And I wish I could just wrap my arms around Niklas like this—with my clothes on, of course—just hold him and weep with him for the real husband and father who now is dead.

For a second, it's Frederik who lies in my arms. We're at Trørød Elementary. We're young again and I'm a student teacher, he the committee chair for teachers of Danish. We're starting our lives all over again. Bernard met me when I was an au pair in Paris, and he followed me here to Denmark. I am his young healthy wife.

26

"Whenever water appears in dreams or fantasies, it symbolizes feelings—particularly feelings of grief and depression. And I must say, Mia, that never in my life have I seen such a huge collection of water photos. I have absolutely no doubt that Niklas is one deeply unhappy young man."

My mother-in-law's on the phone, all worked up. Yesterday she joined Facebook, and since then she's been going through the photo albums Niklas posted.

Since Frederik's well enough to be left home by himself now, his parents no longer come over as often. Yet every day when Vibeke's name shows up on my phone display, I can't help but groan a little before I take the call.

"It's an art project he did last winter with Mathias," I say.

"But why did he pick water as the theme for the project?"

"It wasn't him who—"

"Or if he wasn't the one who picked the theme, why did he take on this particular project, when other people had decided it'd be about water?"

"Can't you just look at the pictures as some beautiful photos where he's simply practicing how—"

"Mia, you're going to have to trust me on this one. It's no coincidence that he threw himself into a project that happens to involve water. Young people today have thousands of other options. There's a reason for everything—even if you may not want to admit it. I'm actually studying for a certificate in this, you know."

I stare down at the pension papers I was about to dig into. What are the rules for withdrawing some of your pension funds before they mature? The tax consequences?

"Water can also represent trauma," she continues. "A sense of entrapment while experiencing volatile emotions, for instance hate or feelings of inadequacy. Quite often, water symbols can be traced back to a parent who makes it impossible for a child to express his feelings."

"Vibeke. Can't you ever let it rest?"

"There might be some primordial situation, perhaps several years in the past, in which the child was overpowered by the parents. He felt surrounded—as if it was water threatening to drown him. A new crisis could actualize the repressed emotions."

"So just to be perfectly clear: you think I'm to blame for this."

"Oh, not at all, Mia! I'm only saying how one *usually* . . ."

. . .

After the conversation's over, I gaze out of our big new windows at the apartment block opposite. Beyond it's the sky and more apartment blocks, while behind me looms the large earthwork that's supposed to dampen the freeway's continual drone.

Though I completely disagreed with my mother-in-law on the phone, and though I still consider her psychological "expertise" an utter fraud, her description of my relation to Niklas couldn't be more accurate. He feels I suffocate him—exactly like water that's drowning him. And he feels that way no matter how much distance I keep, how much room I give him. I retreat farther and farther, making hardly any demands on him with respect to his father's illness, and still he feels stifled. Where will it end? Do I have to disappear completely before he can feel free?

For almost four years now, without naming it directly, Vibeke's been circling around the night I had a breakdown after throwing Frederik out. The night that I was sure I was embarking on a happy new life, but that instead made it clear I couldn't manage without him.

I remember how Niklas was then. It's only a few years ago, but he wasn't that big, just thirteen. He was wearing his orange hip-hop hoodie when he came to see me in the hospital. Frederik was there too. Who *was*

I that night? Niklas's thin fair hand in mine, his pale face. How could I have? That wasn't me, was it? Hardly the "real" Mia. Was it because Frederik and I have always been "meant for each other," like he said? Was it because, dream as I might about slipping free from his grasp, in truth I'm nothing without my unfaithful, criminal, brain-damaged husband?

I struggle to concentrate on the documents in front of me, deciding as I do that tonight I'll google the combination of *water*, *symbol*, and *psychoanalysis*, perhaps *neurology* too.

Someone opens the front door of the apartment. Just a few months ago, I could distinguish between Frederik's and Niklas's footsteps, but lately they've started to sound the same.

"Niklas, is that you?"

No reply. Small steps, small heavy steps; he's lugging something large into the apartment, my stifled unhappy son.

"Niklas?"

Frederik enters the living room. He's bearing an enormous wooden box and smiling broadly. "See what I got from Sergei?"

"What?"

"Rabbits!"

"Rabbits?"

"Sergei and Tonya raise rabbits in their apartment. They breed them and sell them. They earn more than seven hundred crowns a month. And he's given me five rabbits because we've gotten to be such good friends. So then we can also—"

"You want to breed rabbits, here in the apartment?"

"Sergei says it's easy and fun, and I'd really like to start pulling my weight around here. Abdul and Nasira from down on the third floor, they've got an allotment garden and raise almost all their own vegetables. One can really save a great deal of money."

"I *don't* want you keeping rabbits here, not under *any* circumstances."

"But Sergei and Tonya—"

"I don't want it! Period! End. Of. Story. There's no need to discuss it."

"You can't just—"

"It's not going to happen!"

"You can't just decide! I'm allowed to have rabbits if I want!"

"It doesn't help to yell."

"But how can you—"

"Frederik, here I was thinking that soon you could have the car keys again, and the password to go online, maybe even a credit card. But you're certainly not as well as I was hoping."

"I'm not—"

"Frederik."

"Everyone else is raising something! Why can't I? We don't have any money!"

I let myself fall against the back of my chair and shut my eyes. "I'm just going to have to let go of this," I say. "I really thought you'd made more progress."

He stomps off to his room and slams the door. A few minutes later he comes out and, not saying a word, gets the box with the rabbits, hauls it into his room, and slams the door again. A little while later it's the front door that slams, so violently the whole apartment echoes. He's headed back to his new friends.

We've only been living in Farum Midtpunkt for two weeks, and already it's as if Frederik's lived here for years. He's joined a bunch of people on welfare or disability who hang out on the lawns and in the other common areas all day long. Unconcerned and unself-conscious, he's told them his whole life story and all his favorite jokes. He eats lunch with Sergei and goes fishing with him, sits at home with Abdul and Nasira or Khayyat and Sheza, drinking tea and watching Al Jazeera. Every day he comes home with new stories about our neighbors and their kids and grandkids, and already we've been invited to two big weddings.

Back to the pension papers. Now I can't concentrate. I try calling Bernard, but he's in a meeting.

...

Both Niklas and Frederik are eating at friends' tonight, but it actually suits me just fine to eat alone. I'm beat. Besides everything that's going on here with the three of us, I've taken a summer job working for Helena's sister at her shop in Ordrup, spending almost every day of vacation selling fabrics and household knickknacks.

At ten thirty, Niklas lets himself into the apartment, and for the first

258

time in eons he comes into where I am without being prompted. It's just a couple of minutes before the killer'll be revealed on the British crime series that I'm kicking back in front of, but I turn off the TV immediately.

There are a thousand things I want to ask him about, a thousand things I want to tell him. He looks at me a bit shyly and sits down on my in-laws' old couch. I want to say that he doesn't always have to act so brave about his father's illness, that he can tell me what he's thinking, that I won't be nosy—I know he doesn't like that—but will listen. And I want to say that I'm always there for him.

And as these things are running through my mind, I find myself, oddly enough, measuring the gap between our knees and the gap between our bodies—his on the couch, mine in the armchair. Why am I doing this? I'm much too conscious of the distance. Of our bodies. Is this consciousness the water that's choking him? Am I being too much, too intense?

I cross one leg over the other, fold my hands and separate them, glance at Niklas, glance down. How can I set him at ease? Maybe I should start by saying something like *I just want to tell you, I feel like you've done a remarkable job of dealing with your father's illness.* From there we can proceed to what's been hardest for him, and maybe he'll even want to share a drop of his sorrow with me.

But he beats me to the punch, and before I say anything, he asks, "Why can't Dad have rabbits?"

"What?"

"Why can't Dad have rabbits?"

"Did he ask you to talk to me about that?"

"No."

"Hmm." I'll let it slide for now. "Niklas, we can't just have a bunch of small animals running around everywhere. To begin with, there's still all this clutter from moving, and then on top of that I have to take care of you *and* a sick husband. There's just a lot to deal with—an incredible amount."

"But Dad's not really sick anymore, is he?"

"When he comes up with ideas like raising rabbits, you can bet he's not quite right in the head."

"I think they're a good idea."

"You think it's a good idea for us to turn our new apartment into a rabbit farm?"

"Yeah."

"And what's so good about this idea?"

"Well, he's at home all day long anyway. He really wants to help you earn some money, and he can't get a job. It's perfect—he has time, and we need the money."

"How much has your father been talking to you about this?"

"Not much."

He looks away, and I try to figure out if he went over to eat at Abdul's, or if perhaps Frederik called him from Abdul's phone.

"You probably don't understand," he says, "but it's humiliating for a man when his wife earns all the money."

"I probably don't understand? Ha! But you do?"

"Yeah."

I stare at him and can't help but laugh. "Want a piece of cake?" I ask.

"Yes, please."

So I walk into the kitchen to cut two pieces of cake and make myself a cup of coffee. Niklas isn't allowed to drink coffee at night.

"And some black-currant juice," he says from the living room.

"You obviously think Dad's gotten better," I say as I cut the cake. "Dad's become a teenager, and you don't realize that living with a teenager can be a little trying."

I hear Niklas's voice behind me. "If I were a boss somewhere, I'd definitely give him a job, now that he's so well."

I don't answer. To avoid admitting how thoroughly changed Frederik is, Niklas and his grandparents have become acrobats of self-delusion. All day long, Thorkild and Vibeke try to come up with little episodes from Frederik's boyhood to prove he isn't sick, since their anecdotes all show that he's always been the way he is now. Thorkild will call, totally hopped up, to tell me how once in a canoe on summer vacation in Norway in 1979, Frederik insisted on telling a certain joke over and over again, though everyone told him to stop. The next day it'll be something else, and I can't even tell if the stories are real or if they're just making them up.

But no one—not any of Frederik's new friends, not Niklas, not Thorkild or Vibeke—is with him enough to know the truth. I'm the only one. And there's no question that he still has problems taking initiative. Again and again, I have to remind him about things that need taking care of in the apartment when he's there alone. And when they don't get done, it's not just because he lacks initiative; there's also evidence of self-centeredness and deficient long-term planning, since he certainly can make the effort to go out with his new friends.

And then there's his impaired inhibitory mechanism. If he's used the last piece of toilet paper, either he forgets to replace the roll, or instead of just taking one roll down from the cabinet, he takes three and stacks two of them on the floor beside the toilet, even though I've told him I don't like him doing that. When he opens a bag of muesli or something else in the kitchen, he makes the hole much too large, and when he's supposed to buy groceries, using the list I write out for him in the morning, he buys too many packages or packages that are too large of whatever it is I've asked him to get, even when I explicitly write a reminder not to on the list.

At least Niklas has been brought up well enough that he comes into the kitchen without being asked, and carries his juice and cake back to the coffee table.

Last week I saw him sitting with some friends down on Williams Square. I was driving past, and Niklas had an arm around Emilie as if they'd just been kissing. Something in their body language told me that they were the alpha pair in the group. And why not? They're both attractive, well dressed, intelligent, they've got everything. They must be the couple the other couples all want to be—sick father and all. So has Niklas shifted his whole life, his whole world over to his friends now? Is he actually happy now? If only I could discover a little bit more about how it's going with Emilie; that must be what takes up the most space in his life these days.

Niklas says, "You also say we can tell Dad is sick because he's over at the neighbors' so much. But in the old days he was always working, right? He didn't have any time to talk to the neighbors. Being at the neighbors' now doesn't necessarily have anything to do with him being sick. In fact I think it's a good thing; there just wasn't anybody who did that on Station Road. Now we've moved, and he's adjusted to the fact that people live differently here, that they're more involved with each other's lives. You're the one the neurologists would call rigid. And the same thing goes for the rabbit business."

261

"Well, I guess I can see that," I say, wishing that for just five minutes, Niklas could be on my side.

But he won't let up. "If you gave Dad his car keys back and let him go online again, it'd also be a lot easier for him and Khayyat when they get old LPs and stuff from people's homes and sell them down by The Square."

"What are you talking about?"

"I really like Khayyat. He sets out the things he gets by the parking lot in back of the mall, and Dad helps him sell—"

"Your father is *not* going to sit in some parking lot and hawk junk! All our friends pass by there! He's a headmaster! Not one of those people who—"

"He just wants to help. To earn some money."

"But he earns squat! In any case *I* haven't seen any money."

"Right now there's only enough for candy and cigarettes. But later—"

"He's started smoking?"

"Not that I know of." Niklas answers too quickly, clipping the words off.

"Have you started smoking too?"

"No."

"But Dad has."

"No, I definitely don't think so. He just buys them for his friends."

"Oh God damn it, Niklas! Why are we talking like this? Why can't we just be honest with each other, you and me?"

"But I *haven't* started smoking!"

"That's not what I mean!"

What have I done that's so terrible? Why are my husband and son both being taken from me like this? I feel awash in self-pity, and that makes me despise myself even more.

But I'm the adult here. Three deep breaths. No sniveling; I pull myself together.

"Niklas, I just want to tell you, I feel like you've done a remarkable job of dealing with your father's illness."

"Really?" Why does he already look so bored and dismissive?

"Yes, you have. But there's no call for you to be brave all the time. It's all right for you to have feelings too, just like—"

"Uh-huh."

"I mean, you're human too, and even though you probably have a great time with Emilie, I'm sure you also must be affected by . . ."

I hate myself as I speak, I sound like such a cliché. It feels as if it's not just him, but also me who's being crushed and suffocated by all this water. I can't tell where Niklas is right now, but I'm deep inside his photographs, I'm sinking, gasping for air, drowning.

Storytelling's Crutch Is Broken

Signe Riis Gormsen

Twentieth-century narratives have become inextricably intertwined with psychoanalysis in their use of structure, characterization, and symbol. Meanwhile, psychiatric research in recent years has exposed psychoanalysis as an unscientific superstition on a level with astrology and numerology.

If the art of narrative in literature, TV, and film does not develop the strength to stand on its own feet without leaning on psychoanalysis, storytelling will be doomed to play a role in our time like that of a dictatorship's doddering old head of state: a decidedly antimodern force that must be circumvented or killed if any form of real cultural development is to take place.

One essential characteristic of the well-told tale is that elements introduced along the way in the story subsequently turn out to have been introduced with a purpose.

Every reader has an intuitive narratological feeling that she obtained from fairy tales, among other things, which enables even a child to distinguish a sequence of random events from a "telling."

I'm reading "Silly Hans," the fairy tale by Hans Christian Andersen, to my 7-year-old nephew, who has never heard the story before. I read about Silly Hans's two brothers riding to the king's castle on horseback to propose to the princess, while Silly Hans rides a goat. I ask my nephew if he thinks the story is over yet.

No.

I read to him how on the way to the castle, Silly Hans finds first a dead crow, then a wooden shoe, and at last some mud, all of which he takes with him. Is the story over yet?

No.

I read how the princess at the castle says that it is hot because the king is roasting chickens. "Then I should be able to roast this crow," Silly Hans says and pulls out the crow. The princess tells him she has nothing to roast it in. "But *I* do," says Silly Hans, pulling out the wooden shoe. The princess says that she doesn't have any sauce. "I've got so much sauce that I can spill some of it," says Silly Hans, and he pulls some mud up out of his pocket.

"I like that!" says the princess, and so they get married.

Is the story over now?

Yes. Now it's over.

A series of random events doesn't become a story until the events have been shaped into a meaningful pattern and the narrative's various threads have finally been braided into a rope. This sense of elementary narrative structure resides so deep in us that even a 7-year-old can distinguish a story from a recitation of personal descriptions and actions.

◻

Let us turn now to the twentieth century's fairy tale for grown-ups: the psychological novel. Let us imagine an ideal type of this novel, a hodgepodge of the hundreds of thousands of psychological novels published in the Western world during the past century.

A man lives in the small port town where his father worked by the harbor and his mother died from her job in the glassworks. He beats his children. The man's oldest son grows big enough to confront him about the violence in their home, and the reader follows the man on a journey back to his childhood. The harbor and the threatening dark water take on a symbolic cast, and the man relives the traumas that continue to plague him—the death of his beloved mother and his own father's violence, which he is involuntarily repeating. He encounters resistance on this journey of realization, and this resistance makes him even more aggressive. But he also experiences inspirational turning points that alter his understanding of himself. By the end of the book, he has recognized the overall pattern of his life. This recognition is sufficient to transform him; at last the violence can cease, and he is liberated.[1]

Regardless of how clichéd this plot may be, it is clearly a coherent narrative and not a chance collection of people and events. As readers, we feel that we get to know new aspects of the characters. We take an active interest in the turning points of their lives and follow along as, by degrees, their self-knowledge develops. The story has an abundance of symbols connected to the traumas as well as their resolution, and readers can feel themselves heartened and enriched in reading the novel by the profound insight they acquire into their fellow human beings.

The author doesn't even need to be particularly skillful in her understanding of structure or

---

1. Of course, not all 20th-century novels take place by a harbor or involve violent fathers. Here it is only the structure that interests me, and in this respect the examples are endless: detective novels where the villain's character is "nuanced" and "rounded" through flashbacks to his boyhood; family chronicles in which childhood traumas have an inexorably determining effect on the rest of life; psychological novels where insight into a primeval trauma translates into behavioral change; etc., etc., etc. There is no end to the stream of novels in which separate events constitute a narrative only because they are pinned to a unity that has been postulated by psychoanalysis.

composition, as the psychoanalytical worldview automatically structures episodes that would otherwise appear disjointed and unresolved. It makes them into a *story*.

Everything contributes structurally to this story. There is only one problem, albeit a major one: The novel is one great big lie! It confirms for the reader an antiquated view of humanity that psychiatrists (and others who have advanced degrees in the human psyche) have long since abandoned. That means that the novel can be considered an indifferent diversion at best, and at worst a patent stultification.

Let us imagine instead another novel.

A man who lives in a small port town beats his children. Many things happen, there are feelings and vivid sensations and dramatic scenes—but none of them lead anywhere. The man tries to understand his own life, but regardless of what he realizes, it doesn't change anything. Several events intrude without direction or purpose. Then one day his doctor prescribes him some antidepressant pills. After that, he no longer hits his children so often.

This cannot be called a story. Everything dissolves into meaningless fragments without consequences, into a bald recitation of facts. This novel undermines the very structure of narrative.

The problem here is that this novel comes much closer to the unmerciful randomness, the immense chaos, and the constant biological vulnerability that constitute the essence of human existence. In short, this "anti-narrative" is more truthful.

◻

The great majority of novelists and people who write for film and TV have never attended lectures about the breakthroughs in the last 30 years of psychology, psychiatry, and neurology. On the other hand, in the course of their high school or university education, pretty much all of them learned about psychoanalysis— which happens to provide the perfect structure for storytelling that is otherwise structurally unreflective.

The damage sustained by modern fiction is colossal. The ramifications are greater than if the authors had been educated in biology before Darwin or physics before Einstein. For it means that the person who watches a lot of TV, reads a lot of books, and sees a lot of movies has probably developed a more outdated and conservative notion of what it means to be human than people who have been able to keep their consumption of fiction at a lower level, and who obtain their knowledge from practically any other sphere of human activity.

Will TV series, movies, and literature then be able to find another paradigm for structuring their narratives? In other words, will fiction—whether found in books, in movie theaters, or on TV screens—be able to survive as anything but a deception and opiate of the people? It is doubtful, for the "psychoanalytical cultural tradition has

27

There's room for no more than thirty boats in this small natural harbor. Even then, that's only if they're moored several boats deep, so that kids playing on board have to scamper across the boats of other holiday visitors to reach land.

The two jetties are crescent-shaped promontories of granite rock, while the harbor's only building is a kiosk, an old wooden shed painted barn red. We parked the car behind it so we could buy ice cream and extra water, but it turns out they also sell fresh-baked heart-shaped waffles with jam, scoops of ice cream, and whipped cream.

Together with blond happy tan Swedes, Bernard and I wait in line to buy our waffles, standing with an arm around each other's waist. We're wearing shorts, sunglasses, and sunscreen. Gulls swoop in low over the boulders beyond the harbor, and we'll clamber around on the rocks as soon as we've had our waffles and coffee. Later we can hike up the path between the fields or walk along the coast to the edge of the woods where cows are grazing.

When a family gets up from one of the tables, I hurry over, draping my pullover across the back of one chair and tipping a second one forward so its backrest leans against the edge of the table. The table's ours now. I trot back to the line and wrap my arms around Bernard, and we kiss as if I'd been gone a long time. The couple behind us smile conspiratorially; perhaps they discovered love recently too.

I've been over to look through the window of the old wooden kiosk, and they have a large selection of ice cream, but the best kind with waffles is plain vanilla.

"One scoop of vanilla," I say to Bernard as we stand in line. "And coffee."

"I'll have the same," he says. "Plus a chocolate-covered marshmallow on top."

I squeeze him tighter when he says this. I don't know why, there's just something about the simple fact that he'd like a chocolate-covered marshmallow that makes me want to fall into him and disappear even more than I already did. Or maybe it's his tone of voice, or the way the strong sunlight falls upon his almost-white hair, or the smell of warm waffles combined with the way he scratches his neck.

It's so clear we were born to be together—there's no avoiding it, it's constantly clear—yet somehow it becomes even more obvious when he says *plus a chocolate-covered marshmallow on top*, or when he gazes out over the glassy Kattegat Sea and screws up his eyes because the light is so harsh, or when he takes another two steps forward in line, with steps I'm learning could only be his.

The couple behind us is smiling again, and though I smiled back at their infatuated, wide-open faces before, now I turn away. I suppose I'm feeling a tad bashful, and Bernard must sense this, for he nudges me over in front of him until I feel his chest warming my back.

We don't say anything else until it's our turn at the counter. Behind the glass stands a thin old man with a large nose. Maybe he's run this kiosk every summer since he was young. By his side is a plump teenage girl, perhaps his granddaughter. Or the daughter of a friend. Will she stand here for another fifty years too?

We get our orders and carry the limp paper plates with the waffles over to our table. The tables and chairs stand directly on the bare granite; they look old, with thin metal frames and wooden seats and backs where the white paint has flaked off.

"See that gull over there?" I ask. "A second ago it caught a fish."

"What, did it dive?"

"Yes. It flew over by that red boat, and suddenly it plunged, straight down. Like a raptor."

"Do you want to sit in this chair? Then it'll be easier for you to see over there."

"No, I'm just fine sitting here."

In this manner we continue to unwind, together in the emptiness.

"You think the people sitting over by that poster are Danes?"

"Did you hear them speak Danish?"

"No, it's just that . . . there's something about them."

Then we grow quiet again.

We're so close to Denmark. But here in Sweden, no one knows who we are.

We walk out onto the rocks, maintaining our balance all the way down to the water, sometimes holding hands and other times proceeding separately and using the rocks for support. We stretch out upon a great flat stone, feeling the sun on our faces, our bodies. The heat, the calm, the distant sound of chattering children someplace behind us. Our bodies dissolve. And then the shadows are long; we must have lain here for hours, my head upon his chest and his head upon mine, my bare knee over his bare thigh, his hairy thigh across my belly, my nose against his . . . my eyes . . . my heel in a puddle of water on the rock.

We walk back toward the harbor and the kiosk. The low sun is golden over the fields and accentuates each rise, each rocky projection here where the Halland Ridge subsides to topsoil and thence to shore and sea. We walk down a path through fields of grain, then up along a rise until we come to a parasol over a table with cardboard baskets of strawberries. A sign says 30 CROWNS. We take two baskets, leave a hundred-crown note and take forty crowns in change from the small pail of money on the table. We'll eat the berries tonight, after we've eaten dinner in the restaurant beneath the guesthouse where we're staying. We can eat them in the dark down by the shore or up among the elderly visitors on the guesthouse grounds.

And so it continues: nothing happening. Nothing at last. Nothing, nothing, transparently nothing.

...

During dinner that evening, Bernard tells me about the first time he took Lærke to a swimming pool after the accident.

Three months had passed and she still had no initiative at all. She essentially remained sitting wherever Bernard or the staff at the rehab center placed her. She never ventured to do anything of her own accord, and her face never lit up because of something she felt or thought on her own.

Bernard arranged with one of Lærke's girlfriends who had stuck with her since the car wreck to help Lærke in the dressing room. He stood outside for a long time, waiting for them to come out, and when they emerged and Lærke saw all the water, she started to flail about, out of sheer excitement—her right arm flew up and down, she squealed loudly and started to run toward the water. She fell right away, of course, but they had a good grip on her so she didn't hit the tiles; they helped her up, and then she started flailing and running and fell once more. Lærke's friend and Bernard both began to laugh, because it was such a relief to see Lærke suddenly as unmanageable as an overexcited three-year-old. Something had finally gotten through to her.

Lærke knew she wasn't supposed to act that way at the pool, but just as it was impossible for her to increase her energy level at home through mere force of will, at the pool it was impossible for her to lower it.

Bernard led the two women out into a hallway where Lærke could calm down before they took her back to the water again. They did that twice. The third time she no longer tried to run, but her right arm was still out of control, flying every which way, and she was shouting with such joy that the lifeguard came rushing over and Bernard—who had decided once and for all to never act ashamed of his wife—had to explain that the only thing happening was that Lærke was happy to be there.

Since then, Bernard's used what he saw at the pool to make Lærke's life easier. He's constantly on the lookout for experiences that might increase her engagement at the right time. He can't take her swimming every time they have to do something important, of course, but less drastic measures also help. Disco music and old video recordings of talk shows with Jarl Friis-Mikkelsen are perfect.

Disco gets put on the stereo fifteen minutes before guests arrive, or before Bernard and Lærke have to go somewhere. If the music remains on for more than ten minutes, Lærke becomes overwrought and agitated, and if it isn't put on, their friends will be disappointed by how listless she is.

They use Jarl Friis-Mikkelsen to create a calmer joy. Winnie will often pop a talk-show tape in their old VCR before Bernard or the boys come home. Lærke has also learned to manage her own energy level with music and other experiences; with time, it's become as natural for her as it is for others to drink a cup of coffee or have some candy to wake up or calm down.

This three-day vacation's the first time since the accident that Bernard's been away from her for several days in a row. Down in the break room at school, we concocted a story about how he had to work for a business client in Aalborg.

As for me, I signed up for a continuing-ed seminar on pedagogical theory, leaving the course materials around on the dining table and then in my bedroom. I'd stand with program and participant list in hand, talking about how I was looking forward to it. Perhaps I overdid it; it's hard to know, as I never really paid attention to how much room such papers took up in our family's everyday clutter.

The stories seemed so simple when Bernard and I planned them, but one lie feeds the next. When Helena heard I was going on a seminar, she naturally asked why in the world I'd chosen to use some of my relatively few days off this summer with these particular teachers, who were so theoretical and impractical. Normally, neither of us would have considered taking a course like that. She wanted to know what I thought I could use their highfalutin theories for in my everyday work—and Frederik happened to hear my reply.

He threw himself into a disquisition on educational theories and challenges, and while otherwise we might have been able to connect with each other through our shared interest in teaching, our discussions now were grounded in lies about what I thought and what I wanted from my job—lies about who I was.

A pall of deceit and alienation settled over our meals and interactions, heavier than before. And when Niklas was there, too.

This must be what it's like to have an affair, I thought—something I'd never tried before. The real Frederik, my unfaithful spouse from before the tumor, must have lived for years like this, inhabiting two realities at the same time. This had been his life.

On the first morning of the seminar, I showed up and struggled to sit calmly in my chair, unable to focus on anything at all due to pure physical anticipation. A couple of hours later, I told the course leader I was feeling ill, and then I drove to the Elsinore ferry to Sweden and waited for Bernard.

In the bright dining room of the guesthouse, each regular has her own white linen napkin and napkin ring, waiting for her at her assigned place at one of the small tables. Everything's just as it has been for half a century, with guests who return gratefully year after year.

Bernard places his cell phone and our room keys on the starched white cotton tablecloth, and then we walk over to the buffet.

The guesthouse was furnished many years ago by the family who lived in this stately manor, just a hundred yards from the beach and even closer to the woods. They've let their old mahogany furniture remain in the rooms and the family pictures on the walls. Over time, the manor and the grounds have only grown more idyllic, though the guests are older now. Around us are several well-dressed women in their seventies and eighties, each seated at her own table with an empty place across from her.

Soon I'm back from the buffet with a bowl of oatmeal topped with stewed apples and cinnamon, evidently a traditional breakfast in Sweden. Bernard walks leisurely around the long table, pondering the eggs, the bacon, the cheese and fruit. He wakes in stages, I now know. And when in a little while the young woman asks me what we'd like to drink, I also know I should order him a double espresso.

While he's up there, I hold his cell in my hand, feeling its smooth backside against my palm, a bit like skin. Suddenly the display lights up: *Winnie calling*, it says, and without thinking I press the END CALL button before the phone manages to ring.

This holiday mustn't end early. But it's about to—or in any case, its unspoiled happiness is. For Bernard's mother-in-law wouldn't call without a reason—and the reason must have something to do with Lærke. I feel the urge to cry. An icon on the cell display indicates that there's been a call, and a moment later another icon appears, to show that a message has been left. Can I erase the message and remove the icon? These are the last good minutes of our vacation. Of a vacation I never thought I'd take.

Bernard lumbers back to the table in his one-quarter-asleep gait with fruit, two croissants, and a little Nutella on his plate. I want to drink him in. To inhale him like air, suck him into my lungs, I want to see every little hair on his face, every little wrinkle, for this is the last I'll see of him before our vacation ends.

Will he glance down when he grasps the arm of the chair to seat himself? Will he notice his phone and pick it up to see who's called?

No, he only looks at me. And smiles broadly.

"Thank you for last night," I say.

"I think it's me who should be thanking you."

We both laugh.

Yesterday morning, we studied all the widows at the breakfast tables around us and imagined their lives. Some were excessively erect of posture while others were hunched over, but they all radiated a certain dignity in their fine summer dresses, pressed and pastel.

Every summer for forty years, we agreed, they've been coming down here from Stockholm—at some point with just their husbands, and before that with their children too, who could play on the grounds. As each man died, his widow had to consider carefully: should she lay this little paradise with him in the grave, this preserved essence of their summers' happiness during the '60s and '70s? In the end, however, each widow insisted on her freedom and her right to go on living life on her own, and she kept making the trip.

But even though each return has been a declaration of independence, a loud exclamation to herself and the world at large that she still has a life to live, yet each summer's visit, each napkin ring lying in the same spot in the dining room, becomes a shadow dance with a man who had once been warm and muscular and laughed when he came home from work, who chewed her out or ignored her or pressed himself into her during sleep. A man who is now dead and gone. And each sunken widow's face moves about this bright dining room as a memorial tablet testifying to a love that extends beyond death.

The love that Bernard and I share is another sort. We've smuggled our deceit into their temple, and I imagine that if the pastel widow ladies discovered our infidelity, right here in the midst of their shrine, they would band together, hang us naked from the fruit trees out on the grounds of the estate, and flay us alive with their old women's claws.

Is he looking down at the phone now? How can I divert his attention? If I try to move it away, it'll only increase the risk of him looking.

Our last good minutes, our very last good minutes; I take him by the hand. He gazes into my eyes, I gaze into his and I say, "Thank you for a wonderful holiday."

"And it isn't even over yet," he says.

I'm not a good person. When I listen to what Bernard has been through for his darling—with his respect for her undiminished, and a love that the widows here would admire—I know I haven't deserved him. He's denied it many times when I mention it, and I enjoy hearing his repeated denials, but I know that they don't really hold water. I know that he still doesn't know me, that I haven't told him everything. For instance I haven't told him about the night when Niklas found me on the kitchen floor, passed out from drinking.

Is he glancing at the phone now? If I'm lucky, I've got three minutes left. I want to swallow them whole—to suck them into my grasping, guilty soul, which laps up egotistical pleasures and neglects my son and husband while stealing a sick woman's future.

"What's up?" he asks. He's remarkably good at noticing if I'm not fully present.

"I'm just thinking about that painting in the parlor."

"She has a dreamy expression, doesn't she?"

The painting he refers to is hardly the largest in the room, but he's absolutely right: That's the picture that's made the biggest impact on me. He's been figuring me out.

He asks, "Do you think it might portray the grandmother of one of the women who looks after the place now?"

"Well, some of the things aren't original. They must have been bought for the place later."

He says, "The napkin ring here . . ."

Don't look down! Don't look down! I lift up the ring, away from its position by the side of his phone. "Oh yes," I say, unnecessarily holding it up to the light. "I do like it."

"But it was definitely a recent purchase."

That's it: nothing! We'll talk about absolutely nothing at all. Denmark and the rest of the outside world can just vanish. I will make love to him, I'll dunk him in the waters of the Kattegat and raise him up again, I'll bike with him down from Halland Ridge with the air blowing into our cuffs and puffing out our sleeves.

"There must be someplace up on the ridge where we could lie down, just you and me," he says. "Just like yesterday. You know—off the beaten track."

He spreads Nutella on one of the croissants and glances down.

"Somebody called."

28

Frederik and I are watching a Danish crime show. It's a rerun, and if I'd cared enough to remember when I saw it the first time, I'd know right now who the killer was.

Frederik made dinner tonight. He set candles out on the table, he asked about the seminar and wanted to hear all about the other participants and what we learned. He spoke affectionately to me all day; leaned over the table toward me and looked me in the eye. I know what he's up to—he's told me more than once. *After all, we're still man and wife*, he says. *We need to make it work again.*

Now he's set the coffee on the coffee table in front of the TV, along with our half-drained glasses of red wine. He scoots closer to me on the couch so that our thighs nearly touch.

But I have Bernard on my mind.

When he called Winnie back, during breakfast at the guesthouse, she told him that Lærke had disappeared. But we couldn't just rush back home, because they still thought he was in Aalborg. Then a couple of hours later he got a call from Tivoli's security office.

Although Bernard and his in-laws had explained to Lærke a hundred times that he was taking a business trip, she got it in her head that he was off having fun somewhere without her. And she thought that that somewhere must be Tivoli, the old amusement park in Copenhagen. She went down to the station in her wheelchair and took the train to the city. She managed to get into Tivoli, but once she was inside, the battery on her wheelchair died, and one of the security guards found her in her chair under some low-hanging branches on a path by the lake there.

Our vacation was never the same after that. Bernard spoke to her on the phone for an eternity, and when the two of us were alone again, I could feel he was elsewhere. Late that afternoon, I suggested that we go back home, and he didn't object.

On the couch I can feel Frederik's hand on my shoulder. He says, "Pretty soon Lars Brygmann will turn up, won't he?"

"He might."

"That scene where they chase him in the mall?"

"Yeah . . ."

If I turn my head, I'll find myself looking straight into Frederik's eyes. I don't, but I can feel the weight of his gaze.

I need to leave him at some point, but how do I do it so that Niklas will suffer as little as possible? And how do I keep Frederik from committing suicide? And will I ever be able to take Lærke's place in Bernard's life? Then there's the finances of a divorce. I've been trying to calculate my income and where I can afford to live. And to calculate what Frederik will have for rent from his disability pension each month.

"See, here comes the mall," he says. "Is your coffee too cold?"

"No, it's fine."

"I can put it in the microwave and zap it for twenty seconds."

"It's just fine, Frederik. No need to bother."

"Should I make a new pot? I could do that too."

"Frederik, it's okay. Why don't we just watch the program?"

I've never seen so much TV as I have this summer, as I try to get some clarity about the best way to leave my husband. I'm nearly up to the national viewing average.

Once darkness falls on Farum, the multicolored light of the TV screen flickers in the window of every single home where a married couple over forty lives. I finally understand why: before all those screens, in solitary silence, men and women are taking out their questions and calculations, holding them close to their chests, rocking them back and forth—questions and calculations they mustn't voice out loud. Should they leave their partners or not? How should they tackle a divorce, practically speaking? The finances and what people will say, the family, the kids?

In front of their screens they ponder the options, year after year.

Tonight I decide to wait till next summer. Niklas needs to be done with gymnasium, and Frederik needs to be more involved with his new friends, so I can feel sure he won't kill himself. And now we have a court date. The trial will start in a month and a half, which means that a couple of months from now, Frederik will probably be behind bars. If I want to ever look myself in the mirror again, I'm going to have to support him until then, and through his initial time in prison too.

I'm the only person now who's 100 percent certain that Frederik's *not* the man I married. A few times he's said—in jest, I suppose—that I act as if I have Capgras syndrome, a syndrome in which a person's convinced that her closest friends and relations are no longer themselves but have been replaced by impostors.

When the crime show's over, Frederik reaches for the remote and resolutely presses the power button, as if he's been waiting for a long time to do so.

"I'd like to see the news," I say.

He doesn't answer. Instead, he takes our wineglasses from the table, handing me mine as he raises his own and gazes into my eyes.

"I'm a very lucky man," he says, his voice calm and tender. "I'm married to a woman who made a tremendous effort on my behalf while I was sick. That's something I'll *always* remember. And as if that wasn't enough, you're just as beautiful and sexy as when I met you more than twenty years ago. I look around at other women and how they've changed, and believe me—I don't take it for granted that you've gotten so much lovelier."

"Is that really the best you can come up with?" I scoff. "How full of clichés can one man be?"

He smiles crookedly at me. "Cheers, darling."

I feel compelled to raise my glass, but I can't stand looking him in the eye and quickly focus on the rug again.

"I've been watching you when you go out on the balcony with the watering can, when you set your purse on the table like in the old days and let yourself fall back in the armchair—all the little things, the things that are *you*. I look at you, and though I don't say anything, I have such a desire to touch you, to kiss you."

I get up. It's impossible for me to remain seated so close to him.

"Can you remember what I told you that time?" he continues. "How it's impossible for us to live without each other—because we're *meant* for each other?"

Right away I know the night he's talking about. The dinner we had just after I was hospitalized.

I grab a cushion from the couch and swing it at him. "So you thought you'd mention the time I had my stomach pumped. Just something we ought to remember, eh? You think it's a good thing to bring up? It won't put me in a bad mood, not at all!"

The wine's knocked out of his glass.

"All your powers of empathy, Frederik, could fit on the head of a pin!"

"I'm sorry! I'm sorry! I just wanted—"

"You want this and you want that! I'm so *tired* of being married to a sick man who can't help *any*thing that he does!"

"But Mia, it was only because I was hoping that—"

"That's enough! It's simply beyond the pale! I can't stand it!"

He doesn't say another word, just gets up and goes to his room. He can't even deal with it anymore; he's gotten to be such a wuss.

I storm up and down the length of the room, waving the cushion in the air, and then I hurl it against the wall. It springs back and knocks his glass off the coffee table and shatters it. Shit!

What's he doing in there? I go over to his room and throw open the door. "Now what? What?"

He's sitting on the edge of the bed, doubled over, his head buried in his hands. "It's true," he mumbles. "And I understand. I do understand. How will you ever again be able to . . . ? And Saxtorph, and Laust, Niklas and our house and—"

"Don't start blubbering about suicide again!" I yell. "I won't hear it! It's not fair!"

I slam the door and go back to the living room, where I start pacing up and down again.

I go back to his room and fling open the door once more. "And how am I ever supposed to have any desire for you when you're such a wimp?" I shout.

He hasn't budged. He sits on the bed in the same curled-over position as before, hiding his face, not answering my question.

"The real Frederik wouldn't act like this! You claim you're healthy—then pull yourself together! Be a *man*, God damn it!"

I slam the door again and go back to the living room. I fling myself into the armchair, turn on the TV, watch it for maybe ten seconds, then turn it off.

Later he comes back out and positions himself across from me, standing with legs slightly spread and arms akimbo. He affects some sort of mechanical, military voice. "You have no right to speak to me in that manner. I was only trying to be friendly. I must ask you to govern your emotions the next time."

In his stocking feet, he looks like Niklas and his friends would in the old days when they put on grown-up clothes and played theater. They thought they were saying adult things and spoke with great gravity and conviction, but that just made the performances all the more grotesque. This is the same thing; it isn't Frederik's real self, and I can't control my laughter. "This is your idea of what a man's like? This is your best effort? Ha-ha-ha! Really? You have no clue, do you. No clue at all!"

"I was just trying to say something nice to you before."

"Yes, and you can bet that you did an excellent job of it."

He continues with the same feigned briskness. "What we need now is for you to be constructive for a moment—"

"Ha-ha! You come across as even *more* ridiculous when you take yourself so seriously. But it's a long mile from this circus to the real Frederik."

For a moment his sergeant's voice seems authentic; his anger animates it, and he actually sounds a bit like a man. "Mia, the reason you can't work things out with me is that you're sick in the head! You have Capgras syndrome!"

"You're the one who's sick in the head!"

He walks toward the wall.

"Watch out, Frederik. There's broken glass there!"

But he doesn't listen.

"*Ouch!* Damn it!"

"Oh Frederik!"

"And I didn't say anything about suicide! I *didn't*!" he whimpers as he hobbles out to the bathroom.

I follow him there, where he seats himself on the toilet lid and raises his wounded foot. I take hold of it to examine it—and he lets me. There's just a small cut on the ball of his left foot, just a little dome of dark, thick blood. I find tweezers. And I grasp him gently by the heel, softly stroking his arch, the ball of his foot. There is a glass splinter there, and I remove it.

It's the oddest thing to kneel on the bathroom floor with Frederik's foot in my hand. His long, delicate, thin-skinned foot, with its prominent network of blood vessels on the upper side. A foot I know so well.

I put an adhesive bandage on it and look him in the eye, smiling at him. I run my finger across the bandage. For a few moments I am nice to him. Once I was that way to him for month after month, and in this moment I am like that again.

He alternates between looking at me inquiringly and looking shyly away. He tries to smile at me, yet I see the weeping there as well. His muscles lose their tension, they relax, but I also see how he gets a grip and pulls himself together. Everything in his face blurs together, like an ink-jet print in the rain, and I feel the same way. Our faces are sludge, both of them, the very same sludge.

I can't help myself; I take care of him. And at the same time I can tell it's been a long time since I've had the energy to.

…

I lie twisted on Thorkild and Vibeke's wretched couch, alone in the half darkness, my torso slung against the stiff armrest, my eyes pressed to my forearm. The roof of my mouth hurts from yelling and crying. And I'm so tired; I can no longer shout, and my muscles are all achy and tender, as if I'd been marinating in my own bitter juices.

Maybe Frederik could come back and take me now . . . I don't know. I might strike him much harder, this time without a cushion. Or maybe I would yield, and that might be the best thing that could happen for all of us—more than twenty years ago, meeting on the broad sand beach near the school camp, having Niklas . . . I don't know.

But he doesn't return for another attempt. He's not *that* sick.

I sleep; I wake; I'm still on my in-laws' couch. Frederik hasn't installed all the lamps in here yet, so the room has a golden light that's weirdly uneven. I wonder what time it is.

This is what Vibeke calls *our first couch*, just like the dinner table is *our first dinner table*. It's a classic, upholstered in blue wool, which also covers its slender sloping arms. Here they sat almost half a century ago and played with little Frederik; here Vibeke nursed him while Thorkild smoked a pipe, listened to Miles Davis, and conversed with his headmaster friends. I can't say that I'm comfortable lying here, yet I can tell I've slept deeply.

On the ceiling, I see a patch of light move. It looks like the sign on the ceiling back home on Station Road, though it can't be the same thing. That sign came from the tree branches moving in front of the streetlight. And it appeared in the embers where Niklas lit a fire on the lawn.

It can't be the same sign, but it *is*; I recognize the pattern, the smoldering sign in the embers that proclaims our curse.

Am I dreaming? I look around the living room. Everything looks unfamiliar because we're still strangers in this apartment, surrounded by strange furniture. But it also looks real, and this doesn't feel like a dream in any way.

I'm running down a sandy road along the Majorcan coast, away from the car accident in which Frederik and Niklas tumbled over a cliff and died.

I'm running down the sandy rainy beach in Sweden where I met Frederik, where we became each other's fate.

I'm running down the sandy path along Lake Farum. I played tennis yesterday, I'll play again tomorrow, the heat, the sun, the sweat on my brow and under my breasts, I'm running. I'm running.

And overhead the sign in the sky follows me, the light that throbs, that smolders, that grows in strength. Surely, everyone must be able to see it now.

But the sign grows much stronger, and its reflections in the Mediterranean, the Kattegat, and Lake Farum are so blinding I have to kneel, my bare knees pressed against the sand and pebbles.

And as I kneel I hear a voice. Booming, close at hand, a voice from the heavens. It's like thunder, and I cannot distinguish the words it says.

"Who are you? Are you Jesus?" I ask.

282

"I'm not Jesus. There is no Jesus, Mia," says the voice.

"Are you God?"

"You know perfectly well that God's an illusion of your prefrontal cortex."

"But who are you then?"

"I'm like you, I have no soul. I am my brain, and my brain's a labyrinth of synapse and fat."

For a moment I dare to squeeze open my eyes to two chinks, and in a flood of light I see a clean-shaven, grey-haired man with a round head and glasses that are much too large, the kind that were the fashion in the '70s. I recognize him; it's Peter Mansfield, one of the physicists who won the Nobel Prize for developing the technique of MRI scanning. He stands quite close to me in the sand, and the light radiating from him is so strong that it's as if Heaven itself has opened. I have to squeeze my eyes shut again if I'm not to go blind.

"Now I know that I'm dreaming," I tell myself aloud.

"Believe what you like," Mansfield says. "But you should only hold on to your belief if you can prove it. The empirical method's the only path to truth."

"What do you want from me? Why have you come here?"

"I've come to tell you that you're blessed by the mercy of science. This is no dream, Mia. It's a gift of grace; all your sins and all your guilt have been taken from you."

"But I've been deceiving my sick husband. I'm sleeping with his lawyer."

"You can't help it. If that's what you've done, it is Nature's will. You're nothing more than atoms in motion. Anything you do is merely part of a process that Nature initiated billions of years ago. Every decision you make could have been predicted back then."

"But I battered him. I hit my sick husband with a stainless-steel bowl from the coffee table. No one could forgive that."

The light from Peter Mansfield is so strong that it hurts my eyes, even though they're closed. I fear I'm going to go blind and want to raise my arms before my eyes, but I can't move them. I want to move my knees off the sharp pebbles beneath them, but I can't move my legs either.

"Nothing escapes the laws of Nature," he replies. "Nothing comes into being unless the laws of Nature want it to. And that also applies to the things that you do to your husband."

"But Niklas—that's the worst. He found me on the floor when he was thirteen. I was drunk, I could have been dead. That's something no son should see."

"If it happened, it was Nature's will for it to happen. Do you believe anything exists that is higher than the laws of Nature?"

"No."

"Do you believe anything has more power than the laws of Nature?"

"No, I don't think so."

"Then you know that if your son sent you to the hospital to have your stomach pumped, it is nothing to blame yourself for. You couldn't do anything else. It was Nature's will; the laws of Nature compelled you to do it."

"Yes, the laws of Nature."

"You may rest now, my child. You are blameless. Nature bears the blame for you, and you are innocent once more."

...

I fall forward upon the sand, unable to catch myself with my immobilized arms, and I kiss the stones on the path, knowing that the spirit of Nature resides in each and every one of them. Just as it resides in me. I can open my eyes now, and I look up into the dust motes that dance in the light of the sign in the sky, knowing that the spirit of Nature inhabits every single speck of dust upon the earth; just as it inhabits me. I know that the motes of dust have no soul, just as I have no soul. We are all children of Nature, and I have been set free.

29

I've been in the support group for half a year now, and this is our second death. I didn't attend the first funeral; at the time, I didn't feel like I knew the widow or the dead man well enough. But Solveig, the brilliant retired woman whose husband died last weekend, has been a font of intriguing thoughts about the situation we all find ourselves in, and I speak with her often on the phone. Several times I also met her goofy, confused husband, Torben, who was a department head in the Ministry of Justice before he suffered brain damage and started piling up trash in their yard.

Actually, we all thought that our next funeral would be Kirsten's husband, who's been hospitalized for months now. But sometime during the night on Saturday, after a dinner party that three of the women in the group had with their sick husbands, Torben had another stroke. When Solveig reached for him the next morning in bed, he was dead.

Lots of us from the group are attending the funeral, and Andrea's been kind enough to offer me a ride. She and Ian have a converted van with a wheelchair lift in the back, so that he can get in the van without having to be lifted out of his wheelchair first, and when she pulls up outside our entry, he's in the back, strapped down in his chair.

Ian's brain injury affects his hormone balance, and one of the hormones must do something to his skin, for it has a strange pink sheen, and it looks as if it's lost its elasticity and might split at any moment. As always, his motionless legs are gathered and hidden beneath a blanket, along with his catheter and colostomy bag. I don't know if he even *has* two legs; perhaps they were destroyed in his mountaineering accident in Norway two years ago. Although I've met him a few times now, I still feel the urge to avert my gaze when I'm with him; I always make an effort to govern myself, and now I wave and smile at him through the windows.

I hop into the passenger seat and feel Ian and his wheelchair looming up behind me. It's like being watched by a gigantic half-boiled prawn.

"Love . . . *krrr* . . . ly to see . . . *krrr* . . . you," he says.

He's got a PhD in biology, just like Andrea, and while he has no problem finding the right word, his muscular control's so compromised that it can be exhausting for him to speak.

We talk about Torben and the hymns Solveig has selected for the ceremony, and we talk about what we think Torben must have been like before his strokes. The obituaries have described him as a powerful figure in the Ministry of Justice under Erik Ninn-Hansen, playing a key role in the Tamil Case that brought down the Conservative government in 1993. It's difficult for us to imagine, as we've only known him as an affectionate klutz.

We also talk about Frederik's coming court case. Andrea's been convinced of his innocence from the start, and her support used to be very important to me. But I didn't quite know what to think of it later, once it became clear to me that she believed all criminals were innocent. She's definitely the intellectual in our group, always able to raise discussion to a higher plane. Now she says, as we drive to the church, "Four hundred years ago, people believed that the mentally ill had made a pact with the devil—meaning they were witches—and so they burnt them alive with the entire village looking on. Episodes like that from our past offend modern sensibilities, because now we take it for granted that of course the poor wretches shouldn't be burnt or imprisoned because they're mentally ill.

"But it won't be very many years before people look back on our time now and think exactly the same thing about how we punish those who are cruel and violent and make foolish choices that end in crime. It's medieval to think that these people want to be the way they are. Their brains just don't function that well, and it's obvious that they should enter treatment. They shouldn't simply be locked up for years like another Natascha Kampusch."

Ian chimes in from the back of the van. "In just twenty years . . . *krrr* . . . we'll look back . . . on this time . . . as . . . *krrr* . . . utterly barbaric."

They both laugh, but I don't understand what's so funny. Perhaps something we drove past?

"We're living in a second . . . second . . . *krrr* . . . a second Renaissance, you know."

"I've read that," I say without turning to look at him.

Andrea parks in one of the handicapped spots close to the church and the three of us get out, but after she busies herself for a while in rearranging the blanket over Ian's legs, she tells me to go on ahead. I get the sense that there's something they'd like to deal with by themselves, so I make my way toward the church.

Solveig's been very active in the Brain Injury Association, and several of her friends from there have come. Out in front of the church door I step to one side, to make room for the walking-impaired, and I say hello to Anton from our group. He's come with his wife, who I haven't met before. Both of them hold themselves upright and sport golf tans, fastidious hair, and expensive taste in clothes.

Anton introduces us, and his wife gives me a friendly smile, gathering her long elegant coat about her and saying, "I'll nip in and take one of them . . . those things you use when . . . with the . . . that you eat with . . . you eat and you . . . here in . . . when you're going to . . . sing with it . . . I'll take one of those."

It took a couple of days at Frederik's rehab center for me to discover that if I wanted to chat with a patient while waiting for my husband to finish his treatment session, I should approach one of the ones who looked the most severely brain-damaged. Sometimes the ones with serious physical handicaps were brighter and more articulate than the personnel, while the patients who moved about without difficulty always had major problems with language or cognition.

After another two wheelchairs have gone in, Anton and I follow his wife into the church, and it takes my breath away. It always does: the vaulted ceilings, the carved woodwork, the chalk paintings. I can't walk into a medieval Danish church without feeling Christianity calling to me. And I've been that way for as long as I remember.

For centuries, people have prayed and grieved here, suffered and celebrated, and I still can feel traces of their presence. In the churches, they abide with us still: the wives of farmers who keeled over in the field, the wives of fishermen who drowned in the storm. All the children and parents of the centuries' departed. They begged and wept before God because their own lives were over now too and maybe they'd have to enter the poorhouse, maybe they'd starve, maybe they'd have to wed some rich old man.

And the joys, the centuries' joys: the christenings, the weddings, the Sundays in August when the harvest was abundant and everyone could feel safe for the winter.

Poverty in Europe till a hundred years ago, less than three of my lifetimes ago—the tattered clothes and the teeth yanked out with no anesthetic, the diseases you got when you shared a straw pallet with rats. Back when there were no toilets, when backbreaking labor from dawn to dusk gave even young people the pain of arthritis all night long. The way life was until just a few years ago; I still feel it, here in the dark.

Christ gazes down from the cross, and Solveig's nephew switches his iPhone to mute. For centuries, spaces like this framed Europe's dreams and hopes and spiritual·life, and now it's all kaput. Regardless of how the chalk paintings and ancestors call to me, I know this funeral is mere show, like when Native Americans perform an ancient rain dance for tourists but no longer believe in a rain god. I'm looking around at something that's disappeared because the fundamental delusion of God and Paradise can no longer convince us.

Is it wrong for me to be here and act as if I believe in God, now that I've converted to atheism? After all, that's idolatry. Is it wrong for me to enjoy it, to let myself steep in Christendom's seductive lies for the interval of an hour? I don't know.

Anton sits beside his wife, and I sit next to him. Seven years ago, she was diagnosed with a tumor and required surgery in her left temporal region, which the doctors said lay on the edge of her brain's language areas. The evening before the operation, they both knew she might never be able to speak again. In support group, he told us how she held him in their bed, looked him deep in the eye, and said, "After tomorrow, I might never be able to tell you I love you again." They both wept. "You're the only man who's ever meant anything to me," she said. "If I can never tell you that again, will you always remember that I told you tonight?"

"Yes," he said.

And only in the group did he say that as he held her and wept, even as he knew that he'd remain with her till one of them died, he couldn't avoid a poison droplet of suspicion that she said what she did because she might become completely dependent on him the next afternoon, and she wanted to chain him to her.

I'm turning around a little too often, looking back toward the door. I'm not sure why I'm doing this, but then Bernard and Lærke enter, and I remember.

I can't imagine that anyone notices anything—we exchange a brief innocent glance as he walks past, and we nod our little funeral nod. Others have lowered their eyes and are leafing through their hymnals to find the right page, while I shift about restlessly on the hard wooden pew.

Bernard and Lærke sit down several rows in front of us. His short grey-white hair pokes up above the other people sitting around him, and I also catch a glimpse of Lærke's impressive locks. I know how his hair feels against my palms, against my cheeks, my belly and breasts, my crotch. I know the feel of his chest hair, the hair on the top of his hands, the hair on his legs.

After we returned from Sweden, Bernard didn't call me, and I felt I couldn't let myself keep contacting him. I had to let him dissolve our relationship, since he was obviously fighting so hard to be faithful. Since he thought it'd be best for Lærke.

But then I had that experience by Lake Farum. I have no clue what happened, but the likeliest explanation has got to be an epileptic seizure in my temporal lobes. It's been well documented that temporal lobe epilepsy can create the sensation of booming voices, blinding light, and paralysis.

Naturally, I've spoken to my doctor about it. But several months ago, I insisted on neurological scans for both Niklas and myself, because our personalities had changed more than I thought was reasonable to expect from a crisis. Nothing showed up on the scans, however, and since then my doctor's refused to spend any more tax money on our brains.

If you approach it with an open mind, there is also of course the possibility that I did experience a genuine revelation—that Peter Mansfield really did reveal himself to me and initiate me into the pursuit of beauty and truth in the true atheistic life.

And the one explanation need not preclude the other. Wouldn't it be consistent with the spirit of atheism if such a revelation *respected* the laws of nature? If it revealed itself to initiates through something so scientifically ordinary as an epileptic fit of the temporal lobes? Researchers have posited that temporal lobe epilepsy is the source of many well-known revelations throughout history.

Regardless of what it was, I now knew that Bernard and I were predestined to meet each other and fall in love. There was nothing we could do about it.

So I called him, and I was such a compelling evangelist on the phone that we met up that very evening, and since then we've seen each other almost every single day.

...

One of the other users at braindamage.com posted a comment saying that women have a harder time than men when their spouses suffer frontal lobe injuries. She said she'd even met men who were thriving with wives who had such damage. True, a brain-damaged wife may not be able to read her husband's feelings anymore, but she's finally stopped nagging him when he's messy, and she's completely forgotten that she's bitter about something he did in the distant past, or that she can't stand being in a room with his sister and mother. And on some things—especially in bed—he finds she's less inhibited and easier to get along with.

The women lose so much more. In particular, they have to live with loneliness; it's draining when their husbands can no longer share their feelings, when they become even less emotionally nuanced than they already were.

Nevertheless, it's usually a woman who will stay with a sick spouse and spend the rest of her life as a round-the-clock nurse, while a man with a sick wife will find a healthy woman to run off with.

There's a wake at Solveig's after the funeral. Lots of people come, and in the throng in front of the hors d'oeuvres, I see Lærke hanging on Bernard. I position myself on his other side. Does she know what a unique man she has? Does she realize?

Yes, you only have to catch a glimpse of them together to see that she thinks he's the most wonderful man in the world, thinks he's lovelier beyond compare; that in fact he's the *only* wonderful man there is. But that's how I feel too. He really *is* the only one.

Lærke tugs on his sleeve. "There are those ones with lox, and those ones with something white, and then there are those with that . . . it's pâté, right? Is it pâté, Bernard?"

"Yes, it's pâté. It looks delicious, don't you think?"

"But should I pick the one with pâté?"

"Yes, pick that one."

She sets an hors d'oeuvre with pâté on her plate and looks around. "But the others are taking two pieces at a time, two different pieces."

"You can do that too."

"But what other one should I pick?"

I consider this other woman whom Bernard loves. Even before we began our relationship, he told me that Lærke had a hard time making decisions, so she needed help. For instance, her mother made a deck of index cards with different combinations of clothes and shoes, and every morning, Lærke draws a new card from the deck and puts on the clothing listed on the card. That way, she doesn't end up wearing clothing that clashes, plus she saves a lot of mental energy that she'll really need later in the day.

And whenever they're at a restaurant, Bernard's trained her to choose the first entrée on the menu. With dozens of little tricks like these, their everyday life has become more normal.

But there's no menu here. "You could take the tuna salad," I find myself say a little too loudly as I point across the table.

She immediately does what I suggest, without answering or looking at me. And without another word, she hands her plate to Bernard, so that she can move away from the buffet on her crutches.

What did I just do? I hold my breath, not daring to look at Bernard. Was I nice to Lærke? Was I mean? Did I cross some line?

I skirt my way around retired department heads from Justice and their wives, around Solveig's and Torben's family members, and around the very different sorts of friends that Solveig and Torben have acquired in recent years: brain-damaged men and their wives.

One woman, who I know is from the Danish Stroke Association, is helping her husband sit down in a corner of the sofa; his injury must have affected his appetite regulation, for his sport coat hangs off him like a flag. Another woman, whom I've seen twice at the Center for Brain Injuries, holds her husband's glass while he drinks from it.

Without Bernard, Lærke's world would crumble. So would mine.

I go up the stairs, peer into Solveig and Torben's large bright bedroom— the queen-size bed with a cream-colored spread, still made up for two— and continue on to the room that was once Torben's office. The walls are lined with dark wooden bookcases, filled with books and folders on politics, economics, and law. But the books have all been shoved to the back, and in front of them on the shelves stands trash that Torben's discovered on his walks around the pleasant residential streets of this neighborhood. On the floor squat some filthy plastic supermarket bags, filled to the brim. In one corner there's a sundial, and on the desk a potted fern that takes up a third of the desktop and clearly doesn't belong. And on the seat of the dark overstuffed leather sofa, he's placed an old TV set.

There's also an empty guestroom up here. Can the door be locked from inside? No, but I try placing a chair so the backrest blocks the handle from turning. It works. I shake and pull on the handle; the door won't budge. Then I remove the chair, open the door, and walk back downstairs.

In the living room, Bernard is now sitting by a coffee table with Lærke, Andrea, and Ian.

As I approach, I hear Lærke say, "I never want to die. Death is so sad, don't you think?" She's addressing Ian's crustacean features. "Torben, who's dead . . . it's so sad . . . yes, really sad, don't you think?"

When she discovers me, she tries to wave me over to one of the seats.

I stand behind Bernard and say that I'll be back later, there's someone I need to talk to from the Brain Injury Association. I walk away, and as I pass behind Bernard, I let my right index finger slide along one shoulder, across his nape, and out along the other shoulder.

Then I go back up to the guestroom without a backward glance.

A short while later he's standing in the doorway.

I hurry over to him, close the door behind him, and kiss him while holding it shut with my foot.

The chair underneath the handle, depress it a couple of times and yes, the chair jams the door fast and then we're onto the bed. A few minutes;

the others outside. Panties off, dress up. Two in the morning and we're in the toilet together in the rear of some small dark dive. Together in broad daylight behind a hedge at Farum Tennis Club.

We can do anything. Anything, anything, anything. We can start our own family and none of our kids will ever become like the people here. We stand with our beautiful children in our sun-drenched yard in Brede, the lawn sloping gently down toward the woods, the skies stretching wide above us, the inevitability of Nature blessing us.

Someone pulls at the door, but the chair keeps them out. It's secure. No, it falls, landing with a quick hard bang. The door opens; a face. It shuts again.

"Shit!"

"Who was that?"

"I don't know!"

"No, no, no!"

Someone's feet clatter rapidly down the stairs. If Lærke hears about this . . . My panties on the floor. Bernard's jacket on a chair.

We rush around the room getting our clothes back on, and as we do we can hear the conversation at the wake stop dead in the living room beneath us.

"Where are you running?" someone asks loudly in the silence. "What's the matter?"

It remains quiet. Everyone must be looking at whoever's rushed down the stairs. "There are two upstairs who are running!" a man shouts.

"They're running?"

"Yes . . . no. They're running! Oh . . . no, no!"

"They're not running?"

"No."

"So what are they doing?"

"They're running! No, no! They aren't. Running . . . running. That's what they're doing! Oh yes! They're running! . . . No, no, they're not running."

"Who?" asks another voice.

"I don't know. I haven't run them before."

"You don't know?"

Someone asks, "Is it Rikke?"

"No, it's not Rikke. It's her that's running and is Rikke, and he's running Rikke. They're running together!"

The man's getting more and more worked up because no one understands him.

"Upstairs! Rikke—running!" he shouts. "No, not running. Not Rikke. They're running! They're not running!"

A woman's gentle voice says, "You end up repeating the words we say, don't you?"

"Don't, don't. I end up repeating them. Don't. Running. I want to say running. No, not running. Oh, oh. Not running they're running."

By now, Bernard and I are out of the guestroom, but soon the man will find his way to the right words. We hear another woman's voice; it must be his wife.

"We just have to be quiet for a bit. Then he won't have any words to repeat, and then he'll find the right words himself."

And the man yells, "Upstairs they're repeating! They're repeating words! Rikke! Oh oh! They're lying down and repeating words!"

30

It's been three weeks since Torben's wake, and I'm starting to think that Frederik might stand a chance in court after all.

The papers say that a jury's sentenced a father who murdered his two children to psychiatric treatment instead of life in prison. In doing so, the jury went against the recommendation of the Medico-Legal Council. If it can happen to a child-murderer, it can happen to Frederik as well.

Bernard and Frederik have always thought such a verdict possible, and now I'm beginning to think so too. From the police, Bernard's obtained logs of all Frederik's phone calls from the past four years. He's had an assistant enter the numbers and call times into several enormous spreadsheets to demonstrate statistical changes in who Frederik called, when he called them, and how long they spoke. The numbers should provide some objective proof that Frederik became a completely different person during these years, whose telephone habits changed radically.

The preliminary data's quite reassuring. In the years leading up to his diagnosis, Frederik made a gradually increasing number of calls, but their average length became shorter each year. One interpretation is that he developed a greater need to call and talk to all and sundry—while at the same time his deteriorating sense of situation made people try to get off the phone more quickly when he called.

His circadian rhythms also changed, as well as his inhibitions about when he called. In the last year before his illness was discovered, Frederik ended up calling parents almost forty-five minutes later than in the earlier years. On the other hand, he completely stopped working in his home office and sending e-mails between 6:00 a.m. and when he'd leave for Saxtorph.

Over the course of four years, the mean duration of his calls fell 32 percent. The question is whether the panel of judges can be persuaded that this proves that Frederik wasn't really himself anymore.

Frederik's also become deeply involved in preparing the case. He's bringing the intense energy he once used on stereo speakers—and later his new friends—to bear on the statistical analyses of his own behavior that he conducts with Bernard.

Soon they should also be able to show trends in the proportion of his conversations that were private instead of work-related—and much more. And from his bank statements, the two of them should be able to document changes in his spending habits. For instance, it looks as if his clothing expenditures rose sharply—which could be because he had a harder time resisting impulse purchases, or perhaps because he wanted to dress differently once he started becoming someone else.

Frederik's been getting so much better. But of course there's no knowing what he might end up doing when he's tired or upset. After all, he seemed just fine in the year leading up to his operation.

What would he do for instance if he discovered that his wife and his lawyer were having sex almost every day? Would he show as little compunction in destroying us as he did in destroying Saxtorph's account balance?

It's actually somewhat of a miracle that we haven't been found out already. Seeing Bernard requires so many lies now that the school year's started again. We can no longer meet in the school break room, and Frederik's grown very observant about how I spend my time. I act as if I play tennis every afternoon, but what'll happen if he chances to talk to someone from the club?

My cell's always on mute, so that no one can hear when I receive a text—since I get so many—and I delete every one, though naturally I'd like to keep them as reminders of my first year with Bernard.

Niklas doesn't notice anything either. The one I feel is really on my trail is Vibeke. She and Thorkild were visiting last Sunday, and we spent the whole afternoon discussing the phone and credit card analyses. When I told them what Bernard was thinking about the case now, Vibeke looked at me with what I would almost call alarm. It'd take only a few unguarded moments—of not being conscious of my voice and facial expressions while talking about him—for everything to fall apart.

And I have yet another reason to thank Andrea. At Torben's wake, she figured out what the man with the speech disorder was trying to say, and she ushered him out of the room before he could find the right words.

Now she knows that Bernard and I have something going, and it's been such a huge relief to share it with someone that I've also told Helena.

Neither of my friends has said that Bernard and I are doing anything wrong. They know that we both give our spouses so much more than we get back.

...

With ten days until the trial, now's our last chance to try to rescue Frederik from prison and a criminal record that'll prevent him from ever returning to the education field. For Niklas, it'll determine whether he's branded for the rest of his life as a swindler's son. And as for me, I'd really like to rid myself once and for all of the endless gossip about whether I was Frederik's accomplice and whether we've salted away millions of crowns somewhere.

It's been a long time since Bernard first suggested we speak with Trine, one of Frederik's secretaries, and find out if she noticed any personality changes in her boss. But Trine's brother who works in Brazil invited her and her husband and kids to stay all summer in his house in Rio, and only now is she finally back home.

In Denmark, it's highly illegal to do anything that could be construed as trying to influence the testimony of a witness. So Frederik mustn't talk to Trine, and it'd be equally unlawful for Bernard to contact her. But if I seemed to bump into her by chance, and we fell into conversation, no one could object to my pumping her a bit.

Every afternoon just after four, she leaves Saxtorph and walks along Old King's Road to the Frederiksberg subway station. There she boards first the metro and then a tram to Måløv, where she shares a row house with her husband and three children.

It's unseasonably cold for August. The sky's asphalt grey, and for the last two hours, it's looked as if it could start pouring down at any moment. As Trine passes by the Netto supermarket on Old King's Road, I step outside with a full bag of groceries, pretending I haven't been standing just inside the door waiting for her.

She tries to walk past me as if she doesn't know me.

We've talked to each other at tons of parties. During the many years he worked with her, Frederik came to trust Trine implicitly, and at home he spoke about her with greater respect than he did about the board members, his deputy headmaster, and almost everyone else on the staff.

"Hi, Trine," I say distinctly, with a smile that I think seems natural.

She stops then anyway. She's tanned but otherwise looks the same: she isn't very tall, has always had a weight problem, and wears her thin medium-blond hair in a bad perm.

It's Frederik's fault that her husband, who taught at Saxtorph, was fired a couple of months ago as part of the bank's harsh austerity demands—and that her closest friend, who also worked in the school office, was fired then too.

I start prattling away about all the ordeals of the last year, acting as if Frederik is still sicker than he actually is, and I say that Trine's the only person who knows him as well as I do.

It's true. In some respects, she knows him even better. Year after year, she spent many more hours with him than I did. And I know that, some-place deep within, she must still be fond of him. She *must*. Just as she must also hate him now too.

"I don't think . . ." she says, screwing up her eyes and taking a step backward.

Of course, her world's been ruined too. The school might limp along for the time being, but it's with a new headmaster she never got along with when he was an ordinary teacher. She must feel the need to unload about a thousand things—and the need to ask about a thousand more.

"You've no idea how happy I am to run into you," I say. "If you've got a few minutes, I'd really like to treat you to coffee and cake at the Métropolitain."

I've planned this too; I know she loves Café Métropolitain.

"No thanks," she says.

I remain standing there, smiling, giving her time.

She hesitates, but then just repeats herself. "No . . . no thanks."

"Look, Trine, I was just as devastated by the embezzlement as you. My life's completely changed now too. We've had to move, our pension's gone, the car's gone, my furniture, everything."

She begins walking away.

Bernard's carefully instructed me that I'm not, under any circumstances, to press her or give her any pretext for saying that I tried to. The laws about this are completely different here in Denmark than in the U.S. or on TV. But I end up not sticking to the plan.

I rush after her, shouting, "Trine! Trine!"

She stops and lets me catch up with her. She speaks to me slowly, enunciating each word with great deliberation. "I trusted him more than any other person in the world."

"But that's the way I felt too. I also trusted him more than . . ."

My despair at this moment is completely genuine. I have *nothing*! Nothing except a clandestine lover and a hope of maybe rescuing my husband from prison.

Perhaps that's what she sees now. She peers calmly into my face, and I see how the muscles around her eyes have gone slack; how she's abandoned them.

The first raindrops strike us and we look up into the sky. And she says, "I know that it was at night that he gambled away the school. Maybe his brain was sick when he was tired . . . I have no way of knowing. But during the day, when we were together? Then he really *wasn't* sick! He wasn't! Why didn't he say anything during the day? We had meeting after meeting. Parent conferences, him and me alone looking through correspondence together, all those trivial things. And yet it was during the day he went to the bank and forged the signatures."

Then the roar starts. Not of thunder, but of water sluicing down upon the pavement. Everyone around us is fleeing toward driveway ports and shop doorways, and we run under a tree. From there we look out silently on the rain.

Frederik often said that if Trine had had another degree, she could have had a stellar career as an administrator. But that was not to be. Instead, in her job as school secretary, she had a crucial part in why Saxtorph became a refuge from the world outside—the refuge it once was. And she knew she played a linchpin role. Everybody knew.

It isn't possible for us to walk out into the rain. I see her weighing how wet she'd get if she left the tree behind and ran into one of the nearby stores.

She says, "Frederik and I were sitting in his office, going through the teachers' scheduling preferences—"

Her sentence grinds to a halt.

I say, "Yes?"

The sound of the rain lashing the city. Pedestrians standing everywhere motionless, under every kind of shelter. She says, "It took almost the entire day, but it was important—or so the rest of us thought. And later I saw in the documents that on that very morning, he'd been in the bank, defrauding the school of another eight hundred thousand crowns. He knew that it would destroy the school. He knew it. Why didn't he say something?"

"He'd become a completely different person, Trine. And now the tumor's removed."

Oops; that just slipped out. Did I just suggest what her opinion should be in court? Can she tell that our meeting might not be totally random? I know she's as smart as a whip.

"We felt kind of sorry for you," she says. "It was clear that Frederik didn't especially want to spend time at home."

"I know that."

"He said he was bored."

"He said that, did he?"

"Yes. You just weren't much of a match, he said, intellectually or emotionally."

I answer calmly. "But that changed, didn't it? The last years before he was diagnosed, he was perfectly fine staying home with me."

She doesn't say anything, which must mean she concedes the point.

But can I take that to court? *Your Honor, my husband's secretary felt that when he was healthy, he found me boring. At the time of the crime I was no longer boring him, so therefore he must have been severely mentally impaired.*

"There was also the suicide thing," Trine says. "He *had* to stay home with you."

"What suicide thing?"

"I mean your attempt. In the kitchen."

"I didn't attempt suicide in the kitchen!"

"The . . . you know, four years ago. In the kitchen."

"Trine, I didn't try to commit suicide! Did he say that?"

She regards me skeptically. It's obvious she doesn't believe me. "I don't know if he said it. But it's something everyone knew."

"Everyone knew—everyone *thought* that I tried to drink myself to death in my kitchen?"

"Yes, and then the pills—"

"There weren't any pills!"

She doesn't say anything.

"Does Laust also think I attempted suicide? And that that's why Frederik needed to spend more time at home?"

No answer.

"Well it isn't true! There weren't any pills! There weren't any pills! No pills at all! There was *one single evening* when I ended up drinking too much. Four years ago! That's it. That's all there was!"

A drenched little woman shuffles in under the tree with us. Sopping wet, foreign-looking, perhaps a beggar . . . southern Europe. She doesn't look like she understands Danish.

Trine remains quiet. I manage to recover some of the calm in my voice. "So you do think Frederik changed dramatically four years ago?"

"Yes. A lot. An unbelievable amount."

"But you thought it was because of me? You thought he got tired and unfocused and weird because he had problems with me?"

"Everyone knew it was you. Your marriage."

"Did you have to help him so he could make it through the day? Did he start getting forgetful and disengaged?"

She won't answer.

"You thought it was my fault? That I took your beloved headmaster away from you? Such a remarkable, responsible person—even toward his boring wife—that he had to take care of me? Even though it meant all of you at Saxtorph had to suffer? And that's why he became different?"

But she just holds her tongue.

"Does anyone know how much extra work you were doing at the office, Trine? Did you keep it a secret?"

The shadows and reflections of the rain quiver upon her face, as if her abandoned eyes were staring into a blue-grey fire.

"Trine, did you know that in cases of slow, insidious brain damage, it's completely normal for a secretary to cover for her boss so that their work-day will function?"

Still silence. But I can see I've hit home. I can see that that's exactly how their days had been during these last years. Her mouth grows smaller, it sort of sucks into itself. I've gotten to her, I've gotten through!

"He was brain-damaged!" I shout into her ear. "That's what it was! Brain damage. He was sick, sick, very very sick!"

She emits a plaintive moan as if I've struck her, hiding her face by pressing it against the trunk of the tree and raising her arms above her head. The little beggar-woman gives me a dirty look.

And I know that Trine isn't crying because her husband and her best friend have been fired, or because no one can say whether the school will even survive another year. I know she's crying because now she understands why Frederik withdrew from her, and from everyone else at school. Because she understands why her hero deserted her and left the empty husk of his body sitting behind in the headmaster's office.

For he really *did* have a luminosity—at least until he began to stay home with me in the evenings and on weekends. An ardor, an idealism, a passion for doing his utmost for the school. A light that made me resign myself to his always being gone, though it went against everything I'd dreamt of for my life and our marriage, light that drew teachers and students together in a vision of making Saxtorph something extraordinary. Until a tumor extinguished it all.

I look out from the tree's grey-green shadow onto the glistening streets, a great flat-bottomed lake everywhere stippled with the impact of rain-drops. I've gotten Trine to remember who the real Frederik was, how utterly different he was. Her perm's going flat, as if tears were oozing out of her scalp as well. In a couple of places the water has found a path through the crown of the tree, one thin jet falling right behind her heel. The water that envelops us and continues to intrude on us, flowing toward us over flagstone and cobblestone, the water that, a few nights ago on the web, I read could symbolize grief in an old-fashioned psychological novel.

Gene makes rodents faithful

RESEARCH. For the first time, scientists have succeeded in altering behavior among individuals of one species by giving them a gene from another species. The journal *Nature* reports that the gene, which was transplanted from prairie voles to meadow voles, changed the latter from polygamous loners to monogamous herd animals.

After the transplantation, researchers at Emory University in Atlanta found major changes in the behavior of male voles when they were placed with females.

While the male meadow voles had previously spent only 5% of their time with females, they now—just like male prairie voles—spent fully half their time with females, and they took good care of their offspring as well. In addition, the males now remained with only one female each, whereas before they had mated indiscriminately.

In the experiment, only a single gene was transferred between the two species—the gene for what is known as the vasopressin receptor. Many other animals, including humans, have their own version of this gene. *(KS)*

31

"There's something you should know."

Helena's on the phone, and she sounds alarmed. I'm in Nørreport Station, heading up the escalator from the metro.

"Yes?"

"I don't know," she says. "Maybe we should talk about it when I see you instead. It's to do with Bernard."

"Well now you *have* to tell me."

I hear how my voice gets hard-edged and clipped. I'm not very good at this, I think. Have we been found out? By Vibeke? Frederik? Who? I've known the whole time that this was coming.

"All right," Helena says. "Where are you?"

"Nørreport Station. On my way home from meeting with Frederik's old secretary."

"Oh, that's right. How'd it go?"

"First tell me what's up with Bernard."

"Are you sitting down?"

"No, I'm walking. Stop it already—spit it out!"

"Umm . . ."

I've reached a packed throng of people in the granite-walled passage between the first and second escalator.

She hesitates. Then she says, "My friend Sissel slept with him."

Helena says this as if it's supposed to be some sort of sensational shock, and then the line goes completely quiet.

304

I let out a big sigh of relief. "I know that's not true."

"Sissel says he sleeps with loads of women. He's a real lothario. He's not at all what you think."

"Sissel must be mistaken."

"I just thought I should let you know."

"All right." A harried businessman with a big briefcase bumps into me. "You're right to tell me, but when you meet Bernard, you'll see that she's definitely got the wrong man. You just have to see him for two seconds around his wife."

"Yes, I know you've said . . ."

I put the ridiculous notion out of my thoughts, and then I ask, "Did you tell Sissel about me?"

"No, of course not."

"Then how does she—"

"I just said *a friend and a lawyer*," she says, speaking more quickly now. "No one would be able to tell I meant the two of you, and . . ." Here she commences on a long, convoluted explanation.

I wouldn't exactly say that Helena and I are about to drift apart. Yet somehow, I feel that Andrea and I are more on the same wavelength, since like me, her understanding of the world is based on a certain knowledge of neuroscience. A little while later, Helena and I hang up.

I'm still hauling around the Netto bag, with the things I bought to make my encounter with Trine look like a coincidence. I stand on the tram platform at Nørreport, surrounded by wet people who all look exhausted, going home from work to the suburbs.

Our friends at Saxtorph all thought that I tried to commit suicide. They thought I ruined their headmaster, and their school. I drove them out of paradise long before anyone knew Frederik was ill.

I call up Bernard, even though I know he's sitting in a meeting for the next forty-five minutes, and I leave a message on his machine.

"It went swimmingly with Trine. She said that Frederik changed *a lot*. There's definitely something we can use." Then it just slips out. "Other than that, Helena just called and said you know her friend Sissel from the Energy Agency."

Should I have kept my mouth shut? But there isn't anything, is there. I keep talking.

"In any case, I'm going to call Frederik now and tell him about Trine. I'm sure he'll call you a little later and tell you all about it."

I call Frederik after boarding the tram to Farum. I sit leaning right up against the window and whisper into my handset, covering my mouth and phone with my hand.

"Did you tell people at school I tried to commit suicide?"

"No, not at all."

"But then where'd they get that idea from?"

"I have no clue."

"You do understand, don't you, that it's not especially nice to hear that old friends have been thinking that?"

"Yes, of course I do."

There are so many faces in Farum that are familiar from the old days. I used to like the fact that it was a small town where I was always saying hi to neighbors' friends or to parents of kids I used to have in class.

But ever since the embezzlement made headlines, I've stopped nodding and smiling every which way. I've withdrawn from the community, and people haven't said hello to me for a long time either.

So that's how I walk home, in my own little bubble. I wonder: how many of the people I pass have heard rumors—not just about how I was mixed up in the embezzlement, but also before that, about how I tried to kill myself four years ago, and how ever since, I've been a millstone around the neck of my husband and his school.

I'm definitely moving to another town. Next summer, when I get my divorce, I'm going to move. And I'll get a job in another town too, and then I can be 100 percent Bernard's, regardless of whether I can get him to leave Lærke or not.

Darkness falls early because of the clouds still hanging overhead, and in no time I'm walking the long paths connecting the apartment blocks of Farum Midtpunkt. As soon as I step into this ghetto of mine, my steps slow and I inhabit my body once more. Here, among the rust-clad apartment blocks, I can relax. Here there are fewer people I know my own age. Groups of young immigrant men are standing around. We've seen each other before, some of them years ago in the schoolyard, others just because now this is my neighborhood too. We greet each other with a glance or a small nod. Maybe they know that I'm a teacher at a nearby school, but I don't think they realize a lot of people suspect me of embezzling. And if they did, I wouldn't mind.

I call Bernard again, since he hasn't returned my call. He doesn't answer the phone. His meeting should have been over a long time ago.

Frederik's made us dinner, and as soon as we've sat down and dished out the fried liver and potatoes, he tells me what Bernard thinks about my conversation with Trine.

I'm very conscious not to interrupt the arc of the bite of potato I bring to my mouth. Not too quick, and not too slow; Frederik mustn't notice anything odd.

"So you've talked with Bernard?" I ask in my calmest, my most restrained voice.

"Yes." And yet he must notice something anyway, for he asks, "What? What? Is there something wrong with that?"

"Not at all, of course not. What'd he say?"

"He thinks that what you've done is great. It could make a huge difference—" He stops. "What is it? *Now* what have I done?"

"Nothing. You haven't done anything."

"But what's the matter then? Why do you look like that?"

"I don't look like *any*thing."

"*Some*thing's eating you."

"I'm just thinking about your case, and that makes me nervous. That's all."

We keep eating, while he looks at me inquiringly and I try to appear natural. I already know that I'll go out for an evening walk tonight in order to call Bernard. Frederik's gradually gotten used to me needing to go on long walks almost every night.

After dinner, I'm back down among the young dark men between the long dark buildings. At night, the Midtpunkt apartment blocks aren't brown anymore but black.

How often does someone get raped here? Never, as far as I know. How often are there attacks or shootings? Almost never. The area's bad reputation is mostly due to teenagers who try to snatch purses or extort money from the sick or elderly in exchange for leaving them alone.

I leave a message on Bernard's machine.

"Are you sick? Is something wrong?"

Maybe his cell phone's broken, or maybe he's left it somewhere.

Still no answer. When I get back home, before I go to bed, I send him a text. I write,

Love you. Do text me tonight if you want.

...

Saturday morning, after a miserable night's sleep, I meet up with Andrea near the local marina. I've promised to show her some of my favorite runs, as well as the spot of my atheistic revelation by Lake Farum. As a pedigreed scientist, she's been much more intrigued by my revelation than I have, and she's discussed it with the other biologists at work.

Andrea's not a very experienced runner. She shows up in baggy exercise clothes and her shoes look ancient, though that shouldn't matter as long as we stick to the soft forest paths.

Right away I can see it'll be easy for me to talk while she gasps for breath beside me, and while we're still jogging through Nørre Woods, I'm already telling her that I feel a bit uneasy about Bernard not calling me back. She asks about the last message I left on his machine. I say it was the one that mentioned Sissel.

Andrea snorts. "But Bernard's been around the block more than any man I know. I thought you knew that."

"What!" I pull up short.

"He oozes sex," she says. "No one's that way unless they've had some experience."

"I simply can't believe that. I know him really well now, and he's the one guy who—he'd never—"

"But I'm talking about before the accident."

It's like a blow to the gut. "Before the accident?"

"Didn't he tell you they were both in the car?"

"Yes. Of course he did."

"Didn't he tell you he was injured too?"

"Yes."

"Well? What kind of injury did you think it was?"

"I don't know."

I'm drawing a complete blank. I can't recall anything he said about it, or that I even gave it a second thought. But he did say it was serious. That I remember.

It's as if I'm taking a final exam in a bad dream; I can't think straight.

"He lay in a coma for days," Andrea says. "Just like Lærke. Everyone thought he was going to die, and his parents flew up from Paris."

I manage to say, "I know they came up, but wasn't he sitting next to Lærke while *she* was in a coma?"

"Yes—*after*ward! He was a totally altered man when he came to. Just like other people who suffer brain damage—their sleeping pattern changes, their body odor changes, their appetite. It's all hormones. Didn't he ever tell you how he had to restructure his life, dropping his career and all?"

I don't answer. I just say, "He isn't sick."

I say that even though I know she's right. Something deep inside me knows that he's terribly sick, just like Niklas is sick and I'm sick too. Everything's so fragile. Our brains are all disintegrating, halfway to some alien state—and only maybe is the alien state death.

The sun reflects off something between the trees and hurts my eyes. I feel as if I can't stand up any longer. Andrea sees this and embraces me, she clasps me to her and prevents me from falling.

"I never heard you could become monogamous from hitting your head," I say in a small voice, speaking into her neck.

"Nor I. But have you ever met another man like Bernard?"

"No."

"Me neither. He's not normal; he's too good to be true. It's all something to do with vasopressin and oxytocin. It's well known that those two hormones in particular are the ones that control monogamy. Compared to a healthy man, Bernard's hormone profile must be off the charts."

"But it's his choice to be kind to Lærke, isn't it? His own healthy choice?" I ask in a voice that I can hardly hear.

The sun's reflection from in among the trees. It ought to be raining. If my story had any symbolic meaning, it ought to be coming down in buckets.

...

Winnie opens the door of Bernard and Lærke's house. I cut short my run with Andrea and had her drive me over. Now I stand here in running clothes that never got sweaty, and Andrea's driven off again.

"Sorry to intrude," I say, "but there's something I need to ask Bernard about our case. Really quick, it'll just take a minute."

Winnie looks a bit skeptical, but she leads me through the house and into the backyard, which the roses during these last days of August have made even more overwhelming than last time. At a long table on the lawn sit Bernard and Lærke, their two boys who I've seen pictures of but never met, and Bernard's father-in-law.

The welcome's not the warmest; Bernard's family doesn't look as if they like having their lunch interrupted. And perhaps they have a sneaking suspicion, an intuition that I'm not just here to take their food—that after I've raided their Saturday lunch I'll plunder their house and kidnap their father, husband, son-in-law. That I'm shameless, that like a swarm of grasshoppers I will consume *everything*.

Lærke's the only one who gives me a big smile when she sees me, waving her arms enthusiastically. "Why Mille! So lovely that you've come. You can sit between Jonathan and Benjamin. There's lots of room!"

The boys have mousy hair and look sullen. They're not nearly as handsome as my Niklas, not by a long shot.

Bernard's on his feet long before I reach the table. "Oh yes, I forgot to give Frederik the documents," he says in a clear voice across the table. "It's good you came by to get them." He turns toward his mother-in-law. "Mia and I just have to pop into the office. I have some charts she and her husband are going to use this weekend."

He walks quickly around the table.

"The papers should be inside," he tells me loudly.

"But Mette, you'll come back out and eat with us afterward, won't you?" asks Lærke.

Bernard answers for me, saying, "Not everyone has time to sit down and hang out all afternoon like we do."

"I'd love to," I say. "Unfortunately, I need to bring these charts back to my husband."

As Bernard walks across the lawn, it's as if he's grasping my arm and dragging me away, though of course he doesn't actually touch me. We march over to the house. As soon as we're out of the others' hearing, he hisses, "You should *never* come here without calling first!"

"But I *did* call! I called you again and again!"

We step into the house, and he leads me toward his little office, saying, "What the hell were you thinking of, coming here?"

Looking at him, I can tell he's not so much angry as afraid; his family's nearby. My voice is louder than it should be. "You lied to me, you lied through your teeth! You said you'd never been with anyone since you met Lærke, and here I find you were screwing the whole town! You don't return my calls! And you deceived me! I'm married, and you—what the hell were you thinking, Bernard? What the hell? You deceived me so that—"

"But I *didn't* lie!" He raises one hand a little, as if to place it on me to calm me down.

I do my best not to shout. "You said you'd never been with anyone else!"

"And I haven't—not the person I am now. That was someone else, Mia. You have to believe that! And I don't like that man. I hate that man! He isn't me."

Mia Halling

From: Solveig Jansen
To: Mia Halling
Date: Mon, August 22, 2011, 3:09 pm
Subject: Our recent phone conversation

Dear Mia,

Now that we've been together in support group for half a year, and you met my family and friends at Torben's funeral, I feel we're close enough for me to send you this e-mail.

Ever since you joined the group, I felt we thought the same way about many things, and I found it very troubling that I made you hang up on me so quickly the other day. I suppose you tried to control yourself because it's only a few weeks since my husband died, but I could tell in any case how much I upset you.

Let me try to explain what I meant.

I know you think that Frederik was free when he was healthy. And that he wasn't free when he was ill and embezzled from his school. But you should remember that the sick Frederik was no more inhibited in his thinking than lots of normal people who've never been diagnosed as sick. They just weren't born with Frederik's exceptional abilities.

Do you really think that these people are free, when Frederik wasn't?

Who says the ability to think clearly is developed to the same degree in every adult? That can't possibly be true. For example, even though the intelligence of teenagers is fully developed, their frontal lobes are still deficient. That means they have a hard time pulling themselves together and doing what they've decided to, and they're too easily distracted by short-term temptations. And surely adult brains don't all attain the exact same level of development beyond the teenage brain.

Which means that, biologically, the amount of free will varies from person to person. That's the "nuancing" of the free-will debate I was talking about. Only a small number of especially gifted people are 100% free.

Before Torben fell ill, he and I often discussed this question with his best friends from the Ministry of Justice.

Take China for instance: the reason it'll achieve world domination before long is their one-child policy, plus the way they've kept their exchange rates so low that the ordinary Chinese live in utter poverty. When it comes to the country's long-term interests, these decisions are absolutely the right ones to make—but can the man on the street think that far ahead? Hardly; only the Chinese politburo can do that. If China had been a democracy, it wouldn't be on its way to owning most of the Western world.

In the U.S. it's the opposite. Millions of people who lack the necessary qualifications have the right to vote—which means that politicians have to allocate so much to tax relief and spending that in fact, because of the national debt, the country's already doomed to fail. If it had been ruled by a council of experts instead, things would never have gotten to this pass. And again, there's no question that that would've been in everyone's interest— from the poorest to the richest.

It's distressing to watch the U.S. being run into the ground by the majority— people who in point of fact have no more free will than Frederik when he was sick—when the country could be governed by a small committee of people who are as free in their thinking as Frederik when he was well.

I had the sense that what really set you off was when I said it was theoretically possible that free will might be less developed among certain races or in one gender. I did NOT say that that's the way it is—I only said that it's a possibility.

Remember, Mia, I'm not saying this to be a bad person. I want the best for us all, just as much as you. You should know that when you use a word like "fascist" in connection with my positions, which are carefully thought out and scientifically based, it can be very upsetting to a woman of my age, who is old enough to have experienced the all-out war on fascism in Europe.

I still think that, in time, your way of looking at the world will inevitably bring you around to my position. Then perhaps you'll want to take part in some of the meetings we hold with the most intelligent of the retired department heads from Torben's ministry.

With hope for a good, long friendship—and a more positive conversation next time,

Solveig

32

Now I have no one.

...

Of course, I *had* seen that photo in their hallway. Bernard's hair has gone white since the accident—also due to the hormones. And he's gotten thin, losing his appetite like so many other brain-damaged men. Lærke looks like herself, but Bernard's unrecognizable.

Finally I found a good person, I thought. A person who deserved to be trusted. And then it turns out it wasn't Bernard who was self-sacrificing—it was his sickness. I was head over heels with a brain injury instead of a man.

I start running the entire distance home from the argument. I receive the first text before I get very far: *Mia, I know I was being unreasonable. You haven't deserved this.*

And as I run through Vaserne, the bird sanctuary that lies about half the way home, I get more. *I'm sorry I yelled at you. I do understand that you had to come see me. I swear I haven't lied to you about the man I am now.*

But I suppose it's the brain injury talking. I don't know that much about vasopressin, but I seem to recall that besides making a man more faithful, having lots of vasopressin receptors would also make him less aggressive.

It's obvious that Bernard's sick. I only need to think about my father, about Frederik, about Hanne's boyfriend and the whole fetid herd of men, with their long ugly feet and bony bodies, their pricks the color of entrails and their backs covered in long black hairs. Bernard's a freak.

I gasp for breath, shoving my legs forward harder and harder. As if with each step, I'm kneeing someone's belly. Sweat pours down my brow and temples, it runs into my ears and I can't get it out, even when I shake my head—and even after I stop, leaning forward with hands on thighs till my head's horizontal and I'm shaking it like a lunatic.

I resume running, but the sweat stopping up my ears makes my pulse sound much too loud. As it booms, I see before me Frederik in prison and can almost smell the sour reek from beneath the foreskins of the other male inmates—the stabbers and child-murderers, the rapists and school swindlers.

Up the stairs to our floor and then down the hall; I can already hear Niklas playing techno inside the apartment. Our front door buzzes in time to the bass; I unlock it and noise fills the corridor.

I hammer away at his door, on the offbeat so he can hear me banging over the bass. As soon as he opens it a crack I say, "I cannot deal with that today."

"Oh, it's you," he says, shutting the door.

I hammer away again and shout, but he doesn't open up. "Hey! Don't you talk to me that way!"

As a rule, when I ask him to do something, he lets a few minutes go by before finally doing it. That way, he can act as if it's something he's decided to do of his own accord. I figure that today as well he's sure to turn it down after a little while, and I go out to the bathroom, thinking about Bernard whom I've lost, Bernard who was never anything more than a hormonally modified dick.

I wonder what's wrong with Niklas. He usually uses his oversize head-phones when he plays that kind of music. The times when he decides to use his speakers instead, he's angry about something, and he finds comfort in annoying us.

More likely than not, his anger has nothing to do with Frederik or me and it's something with Emilie, or maybe Mathias or another friend. And regardless of what it is, his day can't possibly be as wretched as mine—I'm sure he hasn't just found out that Emilie's brain-damaged like his dad.

When I turn on the water, he still hasn't turned the music down. His music feels more unbearable than ever, pounding an alien beat into my body. I twist the handle, test the water temperature, and gaze at the halogen spot in the ceiling, all the while a foreign beat thudding inside me. As if his music has taken my heart out and installed another in its place. The rhythm pounds and pounds, the heart no longer mine, the blood no longer mine.

Back out of the shower stall. I throw on my bathrobe and return to the hall.

Again I bang on his door, hard. He doesn't open up. I pull on the knob but the door is locked.

"Open up! Come out here! Turn it down and open up! Come out!"

At length he opens the door a crack. "What!"

"Niklas, please turn it down!"

"And what'll you do if I don't?"

He's never spoken to me like this before. He wants to take the fight to a new level. And today of all days. He's challenging me, and I just don't have the energy. Then I ask myself: what right do I have to order him around? I, who have cheated on his father?

Does he know? I have a sudden strong hunch that I've been found out. Something's clearly changed, and I have no idea what it is. I don't dare make a stand against him just now, and instead I hurry back toward the bathroom, yelling, "I said I've had a hard day! You're so self-centered!"

"*I* am?" he shouts. "Am I the one who's self-centered?"

The techno pulse continues as the shower's hot hard stream strikes my forehead, my throat, my breasts. Is he turning it down yet? I stand still and wait.

No.

Something's very wrong.

...

It's impossible to hear myself think in the apartment, so I go outside to one of the common areas and find a distant bench where I can be alone.

Will Niklas tell Frederik about Bernard and me? Does he realize how fragile his father is? Thorkild, Vibeke, and I have agreed that Niklas shouldn't hear about his father's suicidal thoughts, but maybe I need to start telling him.

Maybe it's already too late. Or is he actually ignorant about Bernard and me—am I just imagining things? I call and text Niklas several times, but he doesn't answer.

And then new messages arrive from Bernard. Should I reply? Does it make any difference whether it's his real self that I've fallen in love with? His hormonal changes could be a gift. In fact, I may be the luckiest woman in the world, to find a man who's brain-damaged in precisely the remarkable way that Bernard is.

I can't deal with any of it.

I read his texts for what seems like hours. I don't send him any myself.

Frederik calls around seven to say that dinner will be on the table soon.

When I return, Niklas's music has stopped. I check my appearance in the hall mirror. Nothing to see. And Frederik seems calm and happy, so Niklas can't have told him anything.

I sit down quietly at the dinner table. A little later, Niklas comes in; he doesn't say anything either. I try for a bit of eye contact, just some form of recognition, but it's a lost cause.

Frederik's spread a cloth and done a nice job of setting the table; he's been making an effort every day to win back my love and respect.

"Now let's enjoy ourselves!" he says with a bright smile. I watch Niklas, who looks just as angry as this afternoon, though more tight-lipped than ever.

Neither Niklas nor I answer.

One beer stands next to Frederik's plate and another next to mine. Seeing his I say, without really thinking, "That's not very good for you. And we can't afford it either."

He gets up and takes both beers back to the fridge. Halfway there, he stops and holds one out toward me. "Do you want it?"

"No thanks."

He knows that if he claims he's no longer sick, it can be interpreted as not acknowledging his illness. And the inability to acknowledge his illness is such a key symptom of his injury that an even longer time would

317

pass before I let him go online without sitting beside him, or go shopping without checking all the receipts.

We're having homemade moussaka and salad. Frederik's really made the dinner into something nice—as much as he can, considering there isn't much money and he basically never cooked before a few months ago, when I gave him responsibility for all the household work.

When Niklas and I don't say anything, he looks at us with disappointment. "What's the matter?"

Niklas doesn't answer.

"I thought we could enjoy ourselves tonight," Frederik says. He looks over at me. "Did you have a good run with Andrea?"

I finally have to tell him. "Niklas and I were fighting about his music."

"Oh, so that's why."

How did Niklas find out about Bernard and me?

The other day, he barged into the bathroom while I had my tennis clothes in the sink to make them wet before hanging them up to dry. They were supposed to look as if I'd been playing tennis all afternoon. But did he really know that was what I was doing?

Or did one of his friends see Bernard and me swimming in the sound the other day? What went wrong?

Niklas gets up without saying a word and walks out to the kitchen. I hear him open the fridge, and he returns with two beers.

"I don't think you should . . ." I start to say. "It's not a good idea for either of you."

And then for the first time tonight, he looks me in the eye. It's not a pleasant experience. He comes closer, sets one beer in front of his father, and opens the other for himself.

Frederik hesitates, and I can see that he's thinking about showing his solidarity with me by telling Niklas to listen to his mother. Perhaps he wonders why Niklas can twist me around his little finger today.

"Is this okay with you?" he asks me.

I sigh resignedly, and Niklas takes a big gulp of beer.

"You should listen to your mother," Frederik says in a subdued voice.

Other than that, not a sound.

Frederik doesn't open his beer.

He says, "Well, *I* for one have no idea what's going on around here." All too quickly he corrects himself. "Or yes—of course I do. Obviously, you've been fighting about Niklas's music—that's clear."

Silence.

"Yes, it's difficult," Frederik says. "We all have to live here, don't we?"

In the end, I make an effort to pull myself together.

"What have you been up to today?" I ask Frederik in my most controlled voice.

He lights up. "Well, I was trying to find more evidence in my old bank statements."

"Find anything interesting?"

"Yes, in fact I was looking forward to telling you. Just one new thing: in the years before my tumor was discovered, I signed up twice for fitness classes without ever going to them. And once for fencing, which I never went to either. Before that, I *never* signed up for exercise. It was my impaired inhibitory mechanism that let me sign up, of course—and my inability to focus that kept me from following through."

Niklas looks up at the ceiling, as if to say he thinks we're hopeless.

I find myself sounding a little grumpy, though I don't mean to. "There are tons of people who sign up for all kinds of things that they never end up doing."

"But that's where Bernard is fantastic. We're gathering lots and lots of these sorts of facts."

What goes through Niklas's mind when he hears his dad use the word *fantastic* about the man he knows to be my lover?

This past year, a wall of manhood has risen up around Niklas, and I can't see through to his real self. My boy's still there within the wall, I know he is—the boy who'd come running to me from the yard if he found a small animal or an oddly bent branch, the boy I could once embrace and lift into the air when he was unhappy. But now his real face hides behind a broad jaw and a coarse complexion, his real body under strange muscles.

"Yes," Niklas says. "He can do a little of everything, that Bernard."

I scowl into his bottomless, grey-blue man's eyes. I do what I can to signal to my son that he should stop now.

"Yes, he can," Frederik agrees, relieved that Niklas is finally saying something.

But Niklas doesn't stop there. "He's a real go-getter, eh? Throws himself into all *sorts* of things."

"You shut your mouth!" I blurt.

Frederik raises his water glass and regards his son mildly. "What do you mean?"

"Well, that's just my impression."

"From what I was saying?"

"Yeah . . ." Niklas shrugs his shoulders, letting the word slowly dissolve to nothing.

Silence once more. Till suddenly Frederik looks horror-struck and gets to his feet so abruptly he knocks his chair over. He runs toward the front door. In this moment he must be healthy. Healthy enough to understand what the rest of us are thinking and feeling.

"Frederik! Frederik!" I shout. Followed by: "God damn it, Niklas! God damn it!"

Then I take off after Frederik. But he's gone.

I run through corridors, down stairways, back through other corridors. Around the grounds. Now he's going to die, I think. I shout, I look for him. Now he's finally going to do what he's talked about for so long.

He knows the area much better than I do, and he's disappeared without a trace. I run back to the apartment, and as soon as I'm in the door I yell, "Niklas, what were you thinking?"

"What was *I* thinking? What were *you* thinking? You think it's fun to hear that your mom's on her back screwing some white-haired man behind the hedge at the tennis club?"

I half fall onto the couch. My voice grows weak. "Did someone say that?"

"Of course they said it! Everyone's been gossiping about it! But you're totally off in your own world!"

"Yes, but . . . yes, I probably haven't—"

"Now I don't have my mother anymore either!" Niklas's voice sounds as if it's coming through the wall of another room.

"You do have your mother. I haven't changed."

"You have, you've turned into someone else too! God damn it, behind the hedge at the tennis club! That's not my mother. It isn't! That's not who she is."

"Niklas, I promise you I'll always be—"

"You're gone! Dad'll be in prison soon! And our house is gone too!"

It's impossible to get through to him. "It's not certain that Dad'll go to jail."

"I'm not that stupid. Of course he's not going to win this case. I'm not an idiot! *Every*thing's gone!"

I get up from the couch and go over to him to give him a hug, though I know he hates them.

He pushes me away, but I approach him again, and again he pushes me away. Normally I respect the fact that he doesn't like me embracing him, but not today. When I try a third time, he doesn't push me away. We stand there quietly in the living room. I wrap both my arms around him, I press myself against him and lean my head in against his shoulder.

"I'm here, Niklas," I say. "I'm right here. That's one thing you can always count on. I will always be your mother."

The evening sun no longer reaches our apartment, but it glints off the windows of the next apartment block. Some of the neighbors are eating Saturday dinner on their patios, the clink of glasses and the sound of happy voices blending in with the background thrum of the freeway.

Somewhere out there is his father.

I raise my face from Niklas's shoulder. I have an urge to tousle his hair, but I don't.

"Do you want to come with me to look for Dad?" I ask. "I think you'd be a lot better at finding him than I would."

"Can't we let him come back by himself?" Then he thinks about it for a moment, and he says, "Yeah. I'd like to come with."

...

We head down toward the freeway first. Up onto the high embankment that's supposed to shield Farum Midtpunkt from the noise. I lead the way along a narrow path trampled down between high stalks of wild grass, among ripe seedpods and flowers. Now and then we have to duck to pass under a pine branch. There's so much undergrowth here; so many places Frederik could hide. I'm thinking about what Niklas has been through. The humiliation in front of his friends. How can I ever make it up to him?

We draw near to the long slender footbridge that crosses the freeway. It seems the most logical place to jump, but there's no sign of Frederik. Maybe he's not out here at all. Maybe he's over at one of his friends'.

I hear Niklas's voice behind me. "Why didn't you come down *here* that night?"

"What?"

"Why didn't you come down here, instead of staying home so that it was me who found you?"

I turn to him and look at his face, the warm yellow evening sun striking it from the side. I know right away what he's talking about, but it's too much for me to process all at once, and I can't help repeating myself. "What?"

"That time in the kitchen with the tequila and pills."

"But Niklas, there weren't any pills! I didn't take any!"

Silence.

"I didn't want to die. As long as you're still alive, I never want to die."

Silence.

"No matter what happens."

Silence.

"Who told you there were pills?"

"I don't know, people just said that. That's the rumor, anyway."

The first time I see his small, wrinkled, blue-red face as he's placed upon my belly; he has his friends over, in the yard at Station Road, all of them hopping with delight in the inflated kiddie pool; he runs in from the street, crying from a fall on his bike.

"I could never think of doing that," I say, grasping him by the shoulders as I look into his eyes. My skinny boy who's now taller than me. "Never. I could never ever think of doing that, Niklas."

And then I watch as it unfolds before me. For the first time since he was thirteen, he presses himself against me. He sobs the way he could when he was a small boy. He's shaking, and I am too. He hugs me, he hugs the woman who is his mom. For the first time in all too long. My Niklas. My son.

YOU DISAPPEAR

When Thorkild and Vibeke come by to pick up Frederik and everything he owns—a stuffed suitcase, four garbage bags of clothing, and three moving boxes, two of them with LPs—they're polite. They say they understand that it's not working anymore, and they make an effort to remain cordial.

But they don't want any help carrying the things down to the car. And when I notice that Frederik forgot the power cord for his laptop behind the desk and run down with it, Vibeke says thank you with theatrical surprise—as if for the entire course of our marriage, right up to this very moment, I've been thinking only of myself.

As soon as Frederik moves into his parents' basement, he's allowed to be online all he wants, and every day he sends me an e-mail. Lots of them describe his dogged efforts to land a job.

The tests all show that his concentration, empathy, and organizational ability are now above average, and when he declares that he's well, I no longer contradict him. He's been cold-calling scores of primary schools to hear if they could use a substitute, but of course no one wants him.

He runs the risk of never joining the workforce again, but then rescue arrives in the form of Khayyat, from the neighboring staircase here in Midtpunkt. Khayyat gets his cousin to hire Frederik on a trial basis in his small corner shop in Lyngby. Frederik throws himself into it, trying to prove how dependable he is, how he doesn't have the least trace of ludomania or brain damage anymore. Once he has a year at the shop on his résumé, he wants to apply for jobs in the school system again. Unless of course his case ends badly.

In some of his e-mails he's effusively affectionate, in others he's angry that I want a divorce, and in still others he just tries to understand what happened to us and the marriage we once thought would last the rest of our lives.

Dear Mia,

It's really <u>you</u> who disappeared this past year. Not me. You.

The Mia I married was warm and loving. She engaged other people; she wanted to be a teacher so she could help at-risk children. She was so full of empathy and thoughtfulness for her friends, her family, and her students.

But since my operation, you've come to regard all of us as if we're no more than neurochemistry—mere brains in which everything is rigidly determined beforehand.

Yet brains are flexible! What we experience, what we think and feel, what we read—all these things leave their traces on the brain, traces that can be as hard to alter as if we were born with them.

That's what happened to you. My brain's recovered, so that I am once more myself. But after all you've been through, how will you ever become your old self again?

Here in Lyngby, the leaves are falling down. I walk along the lanes and grieve for the warmhearted wife I watched disappear.

Much love,
Frederik

...

Bernard's car is so tidy; ours never looked like this. By itself it doesn't really matter, but every hour that he and I spend together, I notice these little differences that tell me we're doing absolutely the right thing.

Bernard is also much more daring when it comes to new music. We go to concerts by weird unknown bands, while for a long time Frederik's been content to play the same old LPs over and over again. It's the way Bernard breathes, without blowing loudly through his nose, the way he can actually tell the difference between my blouses. And in bed, the attentiveness and love of adventure that shine through every minute we're together are in full blossom. There's no question I've met the man I've dreamt of for as long as I can remember.

So who cares that Bernard didn't get this way until after his and Lærke's accident. I can no longer see that it makes any difference.

...

Though we both told our families that we want divorces, there's still a lot of juggling we need to do to keep their daily lives functioning, and so make the breakups as easy on them as possible.

Bernard's moved out of his lovely house in Brede, and his in-laws have moved in to take care of Lærke. That also lets them spend a lot of time with the twins, who've just begun gymnasium.

Yet it's only a temporary solution. Bernard will probably move back in with the boys soon, and Lærke will enter an institution nearby, where he says he'll visit her every day. He'll never stop seeing her. He just needs to have a life of his own.

But it caught Lærke completely off guard to hear that Bernard missed having an equal partner in his marriage. The doctor's prescribed her some sedatives, yet she still weeps and talks about him all day long at the handicapped center. Bernard's had long discussions with her doctor and nurses about how to make everything as good as possible for her, and they're full of advice, having encountered this situation hundreds of times before.

And then there are the kids. We knew that if we were ever going to have a good relationship with each other's offspring, we couldn't just barge into their lives the day after the breakups. So Bernard hasn't been over to our apartment yet, and I make sure I'm home every morning when Niklas gets up for school.

Meanwhile, in the middle of this earthquake that's turning everyone's life upside down, Bernard and I have been like teenagers: living on cheap food, cheap wine, sex, love, and endless gazing into each other's eyes. We savor each day in the small student apartment he's sublet in Nørrebro, Copenhagen's most bohemian neighborhood.

One afternoon, I'm sitting with Andrea in a café nearby and telling her how happy I am.

"I've found the man of my dreams!" I exclaim. "I could live like this forever."

We have an hour before Bernard meets me here to take me to the opera.

Andrea looks tired. As usual, she isn't wearing any makeup, and she's at least a month overdue for a haircut. She's been telling me how, earlier today, she drove Ian to his fifth appointment for some bronchial problems caused by his paralysis.

"I only wish everything could fall into place for you too," I say.

She quietly raises her coffee cup. "But everything *is* already in place for me. That is, if you mean living a good life."

"Yes, a good life." I don't finish my thought. She knows quite well that what I wish for her is *my* form of happiness—a new man.

She says, "Only in the old days did people think it was critically important for a woman to end up with one man instead of another. It's the sort of thing that you once would have read in the last chapter of a novel: *Ah, she finally chose the doctor instead of the aristocrat. Hurray*, you'd say, *a happy ending!* But now we know that that's not the key to a good life. It's a lie, an oppressive delusion."

"The key *isn't* whether you get one man instead of another? And that's something we know?"

"Yes, it's an antiquated way of thinking."

"Then what *is* the key?"

"Well, happiness can occur when the brain's level of dopamine and various other neurotransmitters rises. That happens when you have sex, win the lottery, get a new house, that sort of thing. But the levels fall back down a very short time later, and then you're no happier than before."

"So you're saying that if we just think ahead a bit, nothing in life would really matter."

"No, that's not at all what I'm saying. Because there exists another form of happiness—when the level of activity in your left frontal lobe exceeds that in your right. This form of happiness doesn't run dry. On the contrary, you can train it so that it keeps increasing your entire life."

"So how exactly do you obtain this form of happiness?"

"You get it by doing good deeds, meditating regularly, and dedicating your life to something meaningful. These are all things that neuroscientists have measured and verified."

"So you meditate and you're happy."

"That's what I do. And I help Ian, and I help my kids. And yes, I'm happy. That's what's so brilliant about atheism, I think: it points the way to a worldview that's infinitely richer and more beautiful than what you'll find in any religious book. And it points out the most ethical approach to boot."

And then I ask her something that perhaps I shouldn't. "So you think I'd be happier in the long run if I went back to Frederik?"

"That's not something I can really say, of course. Or . . . no. No, I'm not saying that. I'm saying that I think the difference isn't as big as you make it out to be. Not as big for *your* life, anyway."

...

I still wake at night from dreams where I'm in love with Frederik.

He and Niklas and I are on vacation in Greece. We're having coffee and cake in the broiling sun near some ancient Greek ruins. Frederik wants to tease me, so he sprints down the slope next to the café tables and chairs, knowing that I'll think it dangerous and won't like it. But then he starts running too fast and can't stop and he falls into a deep chasm at the bottom of the slope. I scream and wake up.

I'm always so unhappy when I wake from these dreams. Why the hell do I still love him when I'm asleep?

I turn on the light and get up. I want to go out and pee—and more than that, to stretch my legs and try to drive the dream from my body. I open the door to the hallway and there's Niklas, standing outside my room.

He's had his Kurt Cobain hair chopped off. He's just as handsome without it, and now he looks even more like a man.

"What's the matter?" I ask.

"You were talking."

"Did I scream?"

"Yeah."

"Sorry if I woke you. It was just a dream."

Of course he's been upset that his father and I are no longer together:

nonetheless, I'd say my relation to him has improved. Since our talk by the freeway, there have been days now and then when he lets me in on something he's been doing or thinking.

I suppose I'm still waking up as I tell him about the dream. As soon as I finish, he asks, "Do you think you might still love Dad?"

"Yes, definitely."

But I need to find the right balance—more openness between us, but not too much. I don't want to get him tangled up in all my layers of doubt.

Will I end up in a situation like last time if I go through with the divorce? There's something within me that I don't recognize. Last time I threw Frederik out I was happy, I wanted to paint, I wanted to meet another man. I had tons of plans. And then it all went south, and I've never understood why. Perhaps I simply can't live without him. Which is precisely what Frederik says.

And my fear of dying without him—in some solitary fit of madness in the night—feels an awful lot like love.

Niklas shouldn't be involved in any of this. He should hear nothing but what I'm convinced, 90 percent of the time anyway, is the truth.

I look him in the eye, the way he and I are able to now, my son and I, the two of us alone in the dark hallway.

"But I love Bernard even more," I say. "I had to do it, Niklas. I love Bernard in another way."

He stands still, listening, his short hair above me.

"I had to. I didn't have any choice."

...

It's the day before the trial is scheduled to begin. Frederik's fired Bernard, though I did what I could to dissuade him.

On the news, they're reporting an industrial fire at a factory fifty miles west of Copenhagen. Twelve workers died in the explosion that started it, and firemen have been called in from all the neighboring cities.

I have TV2 News turned up loud while I clean so I can follow the story. They're warning people within a three-mile radius against going outside because of the chemicals in the air. But the rest of us, they say, should go out and watch the sunset tonight. The vast quantity of soot particles in the atmosphere won't be visible to the eye, but they'll act like a filter, only letting through the sun's red rays. If the clouds dissipate, the evening sky will turn blood-red like it's never been seen in Denmark before.

Maybe I'll step out for a bit to see it, but with my new life I've gotten behind on math assignments in all my classes. Tonight's my last chance to correct them before the trial begins; starting tomorrow, I can't expect to be able to concentrate on anything other than the sentence that the panel of judges will hand down.

The phone rings. It's Frederik, and I assume he's worried about tomorrow too. But no. Some way or another, he's heard about Bernard's brain injury, and that's the only thing he wants to talk about.

After a short while I have to interrupt him.

"Frederik, I'm happy to talk about your case if you want. I'm terribly anxious too. We all are. But you're going to have to stop criticizing Bernard and running him down. I don't want to hear it!"

"But he's been soaking in an artificial bath of hormones that's turned him into a teddy bear."

"Frederik, if you don't change the subject, I'm going to have to hang up."

"Do you really want a love robot like that instead of a real man?"

"Bernard's the man I've dreamt about for a very long time. Now let's talk about something else."

"Surely you have to admit that—"

I hang up the phone.

...

It's early evening, and I'm actually making good headway on the assignments when there comes a knock on the door. Niklas is down by the marina with Emilie and some friends, so I think it might be him and he's forgotten his keys.

But it's Frederik.

"I don't want to discuss it anymore," I say right away.

"We won't. I understand that."

"So what's up then? What do you want?"

"To show you something."

He doesn't look angry. He looks gentle, radiant, kind. Like he's in a good mood, yet at the same time miles from the manic high spirits of his illness.

"What sort of something?" I ask.

"Something outside."

"You mean the sunset? I can see that by myself. I heard about it on the news."

"Just come with me. It'll be a surprise."

"First I want to know what it is you'd like to show me."

"Mia, trust me. It's something nice. You won't regret it."

I think about Niklas; his father and I ought to try and cultivate a good relationship with each other. And I think of the trial tomorrow. It'll have a major impact on all of our lives, Frederik's most of all; he must be terrified. So I put on my jacket.

He gets four cushions out of the large closet in what used to be his room. We're going somewhere outside, apparently. That must be it—the sunset from some special place he's found.

We don't say much as he leads the way through Farum Midtpunkt. The sky is already amazing, and there's still half an hour before the sun goes down. A peculiar violet shade, not only in the west but also above us and to the east. He seems tense, but cheerful as well. I don't think there's any reason for me to be nervous.

"Any new developments in your case?" I ask.

He doesn't reply, just smiles mysteriously.

We head down toward the train station.

"Have you gotten a job at a school?"

"No, I haven't. But it'll be great at the corner shop too," he says. As if in another week he won't in all likelihood be sitting in jail.

From the station he takes me down Station Road.

"Are we going home? Frederik, what are you trying to do?"

Once more I grow uneasy. Is he sick again? Is he aware of what he's doing?

But then I see our house. I haven't been here since we moved. There are new curtains and the hedge is higher; I would have trimmed it. The garbage cans and the wicker enclosure around them have been moved, and it actually looks pretty nice; that's something we could have done too.

They've painted the door, and through the windows I can see one of those new origami lamps in the living room.

Frederik walks up to the gate and opens it.

"Frederik, it's theirs now. We can't just walk in there."

"I met Jens at The Square," he says. "He said that the new owners are on holiday for two weeks."

And then he strolls into the yard, as if nothing's happened.

"I'm really not sure that . . ."

But somehow he gets me to join him anyway.

My flowers and bushes have grown like mad during the past three months. I planted the trumpetweed last year and have never seen it like this. Everything's a little wilder than when it was mine. By next year it might be unmanageable, but right now—with the phlox and the asters blooming, the weigela fading, and night about to fall—the hint of neglect only makes the yard seem that much more fertile and lush.

"Come," he says. He takes my hand and leads me around to the backyard. I follow gladly.

When we turn the corner and see the sky, we can hardly move. Never have I seen the like: red flames tower up from the horizon and have driven the violet back. Toward the west there are no clouds, so that the sinking sun is colossal, bright and blazing crimson. And above us the clouds are lit from below, by all the red. The beauty is paralyzing. And I see from Frederik, who's standing still, that he can appreciate beauty again.

Our hanging sofa hangs where it always has. The grass is overgrown, though perhaps that's just because the owners are on vacation. Frederik places the cushions on the sofa and sits down.

"Come."

I seat myself at his side. The way we often sat during the good years.

Above us there's a maze of grey and white folds, splashed with red. There lies the sense of smell, and there visual processing. There lies muscular control of the speech organs, and there short-term memory.

The soot from the burning factory and its dead workers has filtered out so much of the sun's rays that we can gaze directly into its disk. The immense red sun. The unnatural sun. We can stare at it in silence: the beauty, this place, our life together. Here we sat once, and this was our world. We left the neighbor's party because it felt better to be just the two of us alone. We made love, we set the crooked row of tiles in the bathroom upstairs. We argued about Niklas's camera, and we shouted with joy when he showed us his tennis medal.

The hanging sofa rocks beneath us and that in itself is enough to make me smile.

Who shall I hold now as we gaze at our son? Who shall I smile at because we have made him? Who shall look at old vacation pictures with me? Or should those pictures just be thrown out? Should everything? And who should break into the yard with me and sit in this hanging sofa?

Finally, Frederik speaks. "Mia, I'm a real man. I pass gas under the covers and sometimes I talk too loud; sometimes I run my mouth off at the wrong time, or I forget to ask how you're doing. And there were those times, years ago, with Dorte and Gitte. I know all that. And yet I still believe that you and I are the ones who belong together. That it's you and I who are each other's mate, and the love of each other's life. Aren't we?"

I want to ask him not to start in on all this again, but I hesitate a moment, and he must be able to see that.

He rises from the sofa and goes down on one knee in the grass, looking up at me.

I want to get up. "No, Frederik, I—"

"Won't you please remain seated?"

"No!"

He rests a hand on my knee and I stay where I am, despite myself.

His voice is deep and a trace husky. "I know we're already married, so I can't propose to you."

"Frederik, I'm with Bernard now. He's my partner."

But he keeps going anyway. "Mia, over the course of the past year you've become someone else. Everything you've been through, along with all you've read about the brain, have made you a changed person—more changed than I am right now. The old Mia's disappeared. So I beg you: won't you please try to be warm again? Won't you please let me back in your good graces?"

The hanging sofa sways beneath me. I say, "When you wrote me, you said all the reading about brain damage had made me cold."

"But that doesn't really matter. I love you. You're the one I belong with."

"But why do you want to have me back then?"

"Because we do belong together! Because it's the two of us, you and me! I implore you: won't you please let yourself see that we're well matched? In our own way? That you and I belong together?"

I sigh deeply. Several times.

"Mia?"

"Yes?"

"Mia, will you stay with me?"

The sky has never been lovelier. The clouds spill across it like blood flung against a white wall.

But it's growing cold here. I'm getting the shivers as darkness pools under the trees and bushes that once were ours. Fall is beginning to take hold, and soon it'll be one year ago that we were on holiday in Majorca.

"I'm sorry, Frederik. I can't."

ACKNOWLEDGMENTS

Thanks to the staff and patients of the Department of Neurology at Glostrup Hospital, especially Hysse Forchhammer, chief neuropsychologist; Allan Andersen, chief attending physician and department head; and Jens Feilberg, neurologist.

To the many others who've taught me about brain injuries, especially Anders Gade, associate professor, Institute of Psychology, Copenhagen University; Louise Brückner Wiwe, neuropsychologist; Julie Lindegaard, founder, hjerneskadet.dk; Susan Søgaard, project manager, Center for Rehabilitation of Brain Injury; Kåre Fugleholm, attending physician, Department of Neurosurgery, Rigshospitalet; Britta Skovgaard; Svend-Erik Andreasen, director, Danish Brain Injury Association; and Jakob Ravn, physician.

To my discussion partners in the field of neurophilosophy, especially Lone Frank, neurobiologist and author; Kasper Lippert-Rasmussen, professor, Department of Political Science and Government, Aarhus University; Adina Roskies, associate professor, Department of Philosophy, Dartmouth College; and Patricia Churchland, professor, University of California, San Diego.

Also to Dorte Sestoft, head, Clinic of Forensic Psychiatry; Peter Kramp, former head, Clinic of Forensic Psychiatry; Knud Meden, defense lawyer; Niels Pontoppidan, former president, Supreme

Court of Denmark; Benedicte Ejlers, Center for Ludomania; Jeanette Melchior, senior deputy judge, Probate Court; Benny Rastemand, accountant; and Margit Kibsgaard, former head, Department of Adult Disabilities, Municipality of Furesø.

And from the field of primary education to Hans Kristensen, headmaster, Kildegård Private School; Per Toni Hansen, headmaster, Kvikmarkens Private School; Annette Parlo, teacher, Kildegård Private School; Helene Bundgaard, teacher, Nivå Central Elementary School; Sanne Rud, teacher, Trørød Elementary School; and Irene Jacobsen, teacher, Stavnsholt Elementary School.

To friends, colleagues, and others who have inspired the writing of this book, and who read and discussed the manuscript: Naja Marie Aidt, Trine Andersen, Ida Auken, Christina Englund, Sulaima Hind, Misha Hoekstra, Kirsten Jungersen, Dorte Klokker, Poul Lange, Karen Lumholt, Hanne Meden, Daniel Meyer, Channe Nussbaum, Simon Pasternak, Martin Tromp Permin, Johannes Riis, Bent Meier Sørensen, Christoffer Lumholt Stahlschmidt, Nan A. Talese, and Charlotte Weitze.

And most of all (of course) to Mette.

ALSO BY

CHRISTIAN JUNGERSEN

THE EXCEPTION

Four women work together for a small nonprofit in
Copenhagen that disseminates information on genocide.
When two of them receive death threats, they immediate-
ly believe that they are being stalked by Mirko Zigic, a
Serbian torturer and war criminal, whom they have recent-
ly profiled in their articles.

As the tensions mount among the women, their suspicions turn away from Zigic and toward each other. The
threats increase and soon the office becomes a battlefield
in which each of the women's move is suspect. Their obsession turns into a witch hunt as they resort to bullying and
victimization.

Fiction/Thriller

ANCHOR BOOKS
Available wherever books are sold.
www.anchorbooks.com